Praise for *The Moonlight Gardening Club* by Rosie Hannigan

'Sweet and heartwarming'
Marian Keyes

'The word "uplifting" was invented for this tender and poignant story. I adored all the characters and the warm, loving community of fascinating people who come together in support of each other. It's a beautifully written debut'
Judy Leigh

'What a delight . . . a gorgeous, emotional read with characters to hold your heart'
Liz Fenwick

'Full of warmth and heart, *The Moonlight Gardening Club* is an absolute delight. Ruby and Frankie are characters to really care for and will inspire you to grab your wellies and get out into the garden! Rosie Hannigan is an exciting new voice in Irish fiction. I look forward to reading more from her!'
Hazel Gaynor

'A beautiful, warm book with relatable characters and plenty of surprises'
Rachael English

Rosie Hannigan is the pen name of Amy Gaffney, who hails from Kildare and is a graduate of UCD's Creative Writing MA. In 2021 she was shortlisted for the Penguin Michael Joseph Christmas Love Story Competition. Her poetry is published in *Poetry Ireland Review* Issue 125, and the *Irish Times Hennessy New Irish Writing*. Amy's short story 'Mother May I' was shortlisted for the Irish Book Awards in 2019, in the Short Story of the Year category. She has mentored at University of Limerick's Winter Writing School and has been a panel member at various discussions there, and also hosted the Reading Corner at the Murder One Crime Writing Festival in Dublin in 2019.

Rosie Hannigan

THE SUNRISE SWIMMING SOCIETY

avon.

Published by AVON
A division of HarperCollins*Publishers* Ltd
1 London Bridge Street
London SE1 9GF

www.harpercollins.co.uk

HarperCollins*Publishers*
Macken House,
39/40 Mayor Street Upper,
Dublin 1
D01 C9W8
Ireland

First published by HarperCollins*Publishers* Ltd 2024
1

A catalogue record for this book is available from the British Library.

ISBN 978-0-00-859914-0

This novel is entirely a work of fiction.
The names, characters and incidents portrayed in it are
the work of the author's imagination. Any resemblance to
actual persons, living or dead, events or localities is
entirely coincidental.

Set in Sabon LT Std by Palimpsest Book Production Limited, Falkirk,
Stirlingshire

Printed and bound in the UK using 100% Renewable Electricity
by CPI Group (UK) Ltd

MIX
Paper | Supporting
responsible forestry
FSC™ C007454

This book contains FSC™ certified paper and other controlled
sources to ensure responsible forest management.

For more information visit: www.harpercollins.co.uk/green

For my children,
Mallory, Ellen and David.
Ye are my sunshine.

1

1st September 2003

Rosemary adjusted her sun hat and assessed the shape of her yew hedge. She'd already cut back her fruit bushes and was gasping for a cup of tea. Looking over to the far side of the garden, she wondered if Paddy would make his famous tea, but he was knee-deep in the perennial border dividing the overgrown achillea. It was a job she wasn't keen on doing so she didn't disturb him. She'd have to make the tea herself. There was heat in the early September sunshine that had only intensified as the day had progressed. Typical of them to have a heat wave just as the kids went back to school. Lauren, her granddaughter, had her first day of secondary school that morning. She'd promised to call in, but so far, the evening had been quiet and uneventful.

A chattering came from the lake at the end of her garden and Rosemary turned to see who was making the noise. Three girls in school uniforms were standing by Lough Caragh. Rosemary smiled. There was Lauren now, and it looked as if she'd made some new friends. She looked tiny in her new uniform. Her blazer was huge, and her skirt almost reached her ankles. Lauren would do well in secondary school, Rosemary knew. She'd a good head on her shoulders and was good at her studies. Her proud gaze moved on from Lauren to the striking tall girl beside her.

Heather Moore looked uncomfortable in a blazer that was clearly too small for her. Her hair was messily braided down her back. Rosemary's lips tightened at the sight. Cash and Pippa Moore, her neighbours, had sent their daughter to St Ita's in second-hand clothes, which was fine; she had nothing against that. Half of her own wardrobe had been thrifted, but the least they could have done was to make sure the clothes fit the girl. A new pair of shoes wouldn't have gone astray either. Rosemary resisted the urge to take the shears to the hedge again, just as every day she resisted the urge to tell Cash and Pippa to take better care of their children.

They'd only moved in a little over a year ago, but since then Rosemary had seen enough. Too often had young Heather sat at her kitchen table demolishing a sandwich as if she hadn't eaten in days. Often she'd send Heather home with a sandwich for her little sister, and had found posies of wildflowers left on her back doorstep as a thank you. It set her teeth on edge the way Heather had to take care of herself and her sister.

The only one of the three girls who looked in any way properly dressed was Niamh Kennedy, the only daughter of Colm and Mary Kennedy and the most cared for child in all of Lough Caragh. Niamh's blonde hair shone in the

2

sunshine as she began to remove her shoes. Rosemary frowned. What on earth were they up to? Dropping her shears onto the lawn she called to Paddy that she'd be back in a minute and made her way towards the stile at the end of the garden. She'd be at the lakeshore in minutes and would find out what kind of messing the girls were up to.

*

Heather raised her eyes from her scuffed school shoes. Rubbing the toe of her shoe against the back of her other leg to wipe the dust off, she sighed. Her new friends, Lauren and most especially Niamh, looked so polished. She glanced back at where she'd left her old bicycle leaning against the hedge at the end of the ragged and overgrown laneway that led from the road down to the lake. Her new school bag, the one new back-to-school thing she'd gotten, sat in the long grass beside it, next to Lauren's and Niamh's. She could hardly believe it. Was she really now friends with Lauren Dooley and Niamh Kennedy? She'd gone to primary school with them, but had never spoken to them before.

Twisting her lips, Heather wondered what had made Niamh talk to her today of all days when she knew lots of girls at their new school. Almost every girl from their primary school had enrolled in Saint Ita's, except for the few who'd gone to private boarding schools. There was no chance of a boarding school for Heather, much and all as she'd wished for it. St Ita's was as far as she'd go, unless she won the lottery, and the chances of that happening at thirteen were slim to none.

3

Niamh flicked her shiny hair from her shoulders. 'Right, let's get started. No time like the present.'

Heather's eyes skimmed over Niamh's spick-and-span appearance. Niamh's golden tan couldn't hide her peach cheeks, and the navy wool jumper only served to make her blue eyes sparkle. When she spoke, she revealed the whitest teeth Heather had ever seen. Running her tongue over her teeth, Heather wished she'd made more of an effort that morning, but her mother had stayed in bed, and Heather had had to finish making her lunch before she left. She brushed down her skirt, knowing her brown hair and freckles looked grubby and uninteresting next to the golden girl of Lough Caragh.

'It's going to be cold, isn't it?' Niamh said, staring out at the lake. 'You'd know, Heather. I've seen you swimming here all summer.'

Heather grimaced. A painful red flashed across her face. She knew what they all said about her family. Everyone in Lough Caragh village called the Moore family a mad bunch of hippies and said that they spent their days running around the mountains and skinny-dipping in the lake. Heather was sure that none of her family had actually swum in the lake naked, but that didn't matter to the people of Lough Caragh who were very pass-remarkable about those who didn't fit the traditional mould of what a family should be.

'I come down some days,' Heather said evenly as she watched Niamh taking off her shoes. She really hadn't believed Niamh and Lauren were serious about swimming in the lake after school. 'But it's not too cold. It's worse at the beginning. Once you move you warm up grand.'

'If you say so,' Niamh said. She pulled her new school jumper over her head. 'Aren't you going to undress?'

Heather gripped her skirt. 'We should maybe do this tomorrow, bring our swimsuits.'

'What's wrong with our underwear?' Niamh glanced up. 'Surely you've swum in the lake without a swimsuit.'

Heather shook her head. 'No. I haven't.'

Niamh looked at her. 'Right, okay.'

'No, I really haven't.' Heather gripped her skirt tighter. 'I would never . . .'

'I'm okay with waiting for tomorrow,' Lauren piped up. Her small face was as white as the swans out on the lake.

'We're doing this for you,' Niamh said, standing up. Her fingers paused from unbuttoning her shirt.

'I know but . . .' Lauren gasped. 'Hi, Granny.'

Heather turned and looked behind them. Rosemary was standing there, her greying hair tied in a low ponytail beneath her wide-brimmed hat. Her hands were on her hips and her long summer dress billowed around her.

'What on earth are you girls getting up to?' She looked from one girl to the next. 'Niamh Kennedy, it looks as if you're getting undressed.'

Heather watched as Niamh shrugged at Rosemary. She wasn't one bit afraid.

'I am, or I was,' Niamh said. 'We're going for a swim.'

'Going for a swim?' Rosemary's eyebrows rose. 'Lauren – do you want to run that one by me seeing as I know you can't swim a stroke.'

*

5

Lauren looked at Niamh, then Heather, then finally at the stern face of her grandmother.

This was not good. How could she explain the whole day to her grandmother? How could she tell her that St Ita's was at least three times the size of her primary school, and how the squealing from the other students had made her stomach queasy? With a deep breath she started her tale, hoping that her grandmother would understand.

She'd been so terrified standing at the bottom of the steps of St Ita's that morning. A river of girls had piled up the steps and flowed through the main door, noisily laughing and already forming friend groups.

Lauren had walked straight through the double doors and had gone to the back of the wide hallway that smelt like Fairy Liquid and wax. There she'd leaned against the bank of lockers that filled the wall, taking in the noticeboards on the left wall, all bare except for some carefully pinned-up posters of the Desiderata, the Serenity Prayer and a laminated price list for the tuck shop. The opposite wall housed a long glass and oak cabinet, dust-free and proudly lit. Within the pristine cabinet were trophies and team photos. St Ita's was known for its debating team – they were the undefeated champions – its camogie team, as well as its volleyball team. They were the ones to beat and rarely lost. The girls in the photos looked like winners. Tall, strong and confident, each one looked straight into the camera lens as if to challenge any viewer.

Lauren had caught sight of her reflection in the glass. She'd felt tiny compared to them. Her pulse throbbed in her neck. *What if it was true? That the girls were as rough and scary as Yvonne had said?* She'd widened her smile as her old friends passed her by, trying hard to shake the nerves from her body as not one of them stopped to include her. Her head struggled to understand what was happening, and she'd been glad when Niamh had walked towards her, although surprised to see Heather Moore with her.

She knew Niamh from primary school, but she'd never met Heather before. She knew of the Moores. Everyone did, but Heather looked too fit and healthy to belong to the Moore family. Yvonne always said that Heather was the opposite of a changeling. The rest of her family were all as light and willowy as fairies, while Heather looked like she could play on the Irish women's rugby team. But in fairness, compared to the rest of her family, Heather had seemed normal enough – she didn't smell of that weird incense that her mother smelled of, and she'd definitely made an effort to tidy herself up.

'This is Heather,' Niamh had said as easily as reciting her alphabet. 'We met outside just now. We don't get why they're all squealing like seals at a water park.' She nodded towards Lauren's old friends who were giggling and messing about. Lauren scratched her wrist.

'Yeah, you'd swear they were at a concert, or something.' Lauren turned her back on her old friends. She'd be a hot topic of conversation once they saw her with Heather and Niamh, but she didn't care – it was nice to have someone to talk to.

'So, do you know what class you're in?' Niamh had completely ignored the tittering girls behind Lauren. 'I'm in 1M.'

'Me too,' Heather said.

'Same.' Lauren had nodded. 'I'm taking Spanish, Business and Home Ec.'

'Spanish and Business for me, too,' Niamh said. 'You?' She looked at Heather.

'Yeah. Spanish,' Heather confirmed. 'Business and Art as well.'

'Great.' Niamh had beamed. 'We're all in Business and Spanish. We might as well hang around each other today so.' She'd rolled her eyes as a tall, thin nun hurried towards them.

'Girls, girls, what are you doing out here in the hall? You should be in assembly with everyone else. Hurry up now.' The nun had flapped her arms at them, then turned her attention to the gaggle of girls clustered around a plinth where a statue of St Ita stood grasping her crook and holding a small church.

'Come on.' Niamh had linked arms with Heather. She looked at Lauren. 'Are you coming with us?'

Lauren had tilted her head and watched Heather and Niamh go into the gym where the assembly was being held. She'd nothing to lose by hanging out with Niamh; after all, Niamh lived in The Old Rectory, a grand old country house on the outskirts of Lough Caragh village; but why should she bother with Heather Moore? Still, she'd pondered as she looked around the almost empty main hall, there wasn't anyone else she was mad about hanging out with. She walked into the gym. Her old friend group were leaning against the radiator under the window. They'd blanked her as she stood just on the sideline. She'd turned away from them as they threw her a glance and giggled. Lauren narrowed her eyes. Her stomach tightened.

She'd raised her chin and made her way towards Heather and Niamh.

And that had been that. They'd spent the day meandering from class to class and getting lost in the corridors. She'd been exhausted by the end of the school day and had sat down the back of the class, tuning out as their year tutor droned on about lockers and detentions. It was only when the year head mentioned something about kayaking and swimming as part of their school tour in May next year that she'd listened intently.

In their seats down the back of the class, Heather and Niamh had whispered excitedly about the tour.

'How much do you think it'll cost?' Heather had whispered to Lauren before she'd looked at her closely. 'Hey, are you okay?'

Lauren had shifted in her chair. She pleated her skirt with one hand, the other tucked a strand of hair behind her ear. Her head had felt tight, and her throat too. There was no way she could get away with not telling them, just as there was no way her parents would allow her to stay home on the day of a school tour. Her mother had always been adamant that she take every opportunity she could, always telling her that life was long and miserable enough when you grew up, childhood was the only time you got to have fun. There was no reason to imagine she'd change her tune now.

Niamh had looked at her intently too. Lauren stopped pleating her skirt.

'I, eh, I can't swim,' she'd said quietly.

Niamh's worried face morphed into a wide grin. 'Is that it? Jesus, I thought you'd gotten your period of something.'

9

'What do you mean, is that it?' Lauren had puzzled. 'I can't swim. Everyone will find out.'

'No, they won't,' Heather whispered.

Lauren had stared at her. What was she talking about? Heather could swim like a fish; she'd seen her in the lake all summer long. She darted a glance at Niamh, who she knew had learned how to swim properly under the instruction of an Olympian over at Glenrua Swimming Pool.

'I'll teach you.' Heather glanced at Niamh, her eyebrows raised. 'We?'

'*We* will.' Niamh nodded at Heather. She turned to Lauren. 'And you won't get finer teachers than us. We'll have you swimming by Christmas.'

'Are you two crazy?' Lauren had looked from one girl to the other. 'And where do you suggest you teach me how to swim? I can't go to the pool – they'll see . . .'

'We'll go to the lake,' Heather had said. 'In the mornings – before anyone is up and about. No one will see us.'

Lauren's eyes widened. 'Early?'

'Around six in the morning, right?' Niamh had looked at Heather.

'Yeah, that's a good time,' Heather had said. 'Trust us, you'll be the mermaid of Lough Caragh before you know it.'

'The mermaid of Lough Caragh,' Lauren squeaked. She'd laughed nervously and scratched her arm. She'd never swum in the lake. Never. The girls didn't know what they were letting themselves in for. Still – she looked from Niamh's smiling face to Heather's steady one – the mermaid of Lough Caragh had a nice ring to it. It couldn't hurt to try.

'We start after school.' Heather had nodded firmly.

'No time like the present,' Niamh had said, giving her the thumbs up.

And that's how she'd wound up standing on the shore of Lough Caragh with two new friends who were ready to strip down to their underwear and teach her how to swim.

*

Niamh listened to Lauren tell Rosemary about their day. It sounded mad, now that she heard it from someone else, but she was glad to hear that Lauren had been as terrified as she'd been. She hadn't looked that scared. Niamh watched Rosemary's face soften. The older woman smiled and Niamh felt a weight lift from her shoulders as Rosemary hugged Lauren.

'I'm sorry your day has been so stressful,' Rosemary said. 'But I'm glad you three seem to have found each other. It's very kind of you two to offer to teach Lauren to swim, but I think it's a little dangerous for you three to be out in the lake on your own.'

'But she needs to learn how to swim,' Niamh blurted.

'I know,' Rosemary said. 'So, I'm going to be here with you girls, and I'll help you.' She glanced at Niamh's stockinged feet. 'I don't think it's a good idea to swim in your underwear though.'

Niamh blushed. She hadn't really thought it through. 'Maybe we'll come down tomorrow in our suits.'

'Well, I have some spare costumes in the house. If you're not too proud, you girls can change and we'll have our first lesson, as you'd planned,' Rosemary suggested.

Niamh looked at Lauren. 'You up for it?'

Lauren nodded. 'I think so, thanks, Granny.'

'You're welcome, love.' Rosemary nodded at her house. 'Come on, let's get changed.'

*

Rosemary led the girls up to the house and sent them to the top floor to search for the swimsuits she'd bought for Heather but hadn't had the chance to give her. She'd bought them in the summer sale and, knowing how proud Heather was, had removed the tags.

'You've adopted more then?' Paddy's voice called over from where he was firming the soil around newly transplanted perennials.

Rosemary laughed. 'You won't believe it, but I'm going to teach Lauren how to swim.'

Paddy pushed back his hat. 'That's great, Rose. Do you want me to help?'

'I'm okay, and I imagine they'll be a little self-conscious at first, so maybe leave it for today.' Rosemary smiled as the girls' laughter drifted down from the open windows of the top floor of Mill House. 'Isn't that lovely? It's nice to have youngsters around the house again.'

'It is,' Paddy said, looking fondly at his wife. 'It makes me feel both young and old.'

'Well, I'm going to feel so old when I'm down by the lake with them in my swimming costume,' Rosemary said, taking her sun hat off.

'Would you go away out of that,' Paddy said. He pulled her close and kissed the top of her head. 'You're perfect.

12

Always have been and always will be. I love seeing you in your costume.'

'You're some smooth talker, Paddy Dwyer.' Rosemary laughed delightedly. 'Right, enough of this flattery. I'd best get a move on and get changed.'

As if on cue, the three girls tumbled from the back door, giggling and talking nineteen to the dozen. Rosemary was glad to see the swimsuits fit them all nicely, and they'd had the sense to grab some towels too. Lauren was looking a little peaky, but that was to be expected. Rosemary wondered for the millionth time why her daughter hadn't taught Lauren to swim when they had such a fantastic resource on their doorstep. She let the thought pass as Niamh slipped her a price tag.

'You missed one,' Niamh whispered. 'I saw them in town but didn't let on to the girls.'

Rosemary slipped the price tag into her pocket and patted Niamh on the arm. Then she hurriedly got changed.

*

Forty minutes later they'd succeeded in teaching Lauren how to float and Rosemary, wanting to leave the lesson on a high note, decided to call it a day just as Paddy arrived at the shore with an impromptu picnic. Sipping from her bottle of lemonade she watched the three girls and thought of her own group of friends. They'd helped her through thick and thin. Some of the most magical and her roughest moments had been safely navigated purely because of their support and love. Lauren, Heather and Niamh already looked like the best of friends. The way

13

they were chatting and listening to each other warmed Rosemary's heart. There was something special between them, and that, Rosemary knew, was the best thing in the world.

Deep in her heart Rosemary hoped they'd stay friends forever.

2

Niamh turned her car off the main road and onto a narrow lane with grass growing along the middle of it. Near the end of the lane her headlights caught the back of an old stag as it bounded towards the woods, where it stopped and turned to watch her. Parking her car close to the hedgerow, Niamh peered out of the car window. In the shadows of the trees his brown back shone brightly. Counting five points on each of his antlers, Niamh held her breath. It was rare to see such a fine deer, and it was as if he knew he was special. He held his great head high, his eyes watching her every move.

Niamh shivered. She'd often seen smaller deer here, but never an elusive stag. Her luck must be changing. Seeing a stag was meant to bring about a renewal, and Lord knows, she could do with something in her life changing for the better. The stag blinked slowly at her before he smoothly rambled into the depths of the wood, and Niamh breathed out.

She glanced at the dashboard clock. It was half eight, but she didn't need the clock to tell her she wasn't late. She hadn't missed the solstice sunrise; the sky above was still navy, with hints of deep peach and lavender hinting at a new day, and hopefully a new phase in her life. She waited for the clock to tick one minute closer to sunrise. Then she reached over and grabbed her tote and coat from the passenger footwell. Hopping out of the car she looked around. Everything was so peaceful. The lake glimmered softly in the distance and the bracken and grasses from the hedgerow were still in the morning air. A brightening sky in the east made her glad she'd come, especially as she'd found it hard to get up that morning. With renewed vigour Niamh made her way down the lane towards the lake.

Lough Caragh was wide and nestled comfortably in the lush valley like a new-born babe wholly content and safe in its mother's loving arms. Mist rose from the still water, shrouding the reflection of the sky. Niamh pulled the sharp, cold air deep into her lungs. Her feet crunched on the shingle as she made her way to the sandy beach that she knew so well. Once there, she shucked off her coat, shuffled out of her trainers and swiftly stepped out of her clothes until she stood in her swimsuit, the one she'd bought for the sun holiday that hadn't materialised last year. In the misty morning, its bright tropical colours stood out like rosehips in the dark hedgerows.

The cold air prickled her skin, and she rubbed her arms briskly. Evan always said she was mad, coming down here almost every solstice to swim in the lake. She countered his comments with her own, saying he was just as insane going out in hail, rain, sleet or snow to coach the under sixteens football team. At least her insanity was a twice-a-year thing, sometimes four if she remembered the spring and autumnal equinoxes; his was week in, week out.

And, she'd told him, the definition of insanity was doing the same thing over and over and expecting things to change. The team hadn't won a match in ages, and it wasn't likely that they would anytime soon, whereas she went to the lake at solstice for different reasons. She went for the release it gave her, the hope it brought, and the feeling of being renewed. Despite what he said, it wasn't the same as expecting a football team to suddenly win every game in their league and magically move up the table. *It was a different kind of hope.* She tiptoed towards the shoreline. *It was more personal. It was beyond words.*

Tying her long blonde hair up into a high ponytail, she scrunched her toes into the freezing sand, and wished she hadn't forgotten her swim shoes. Her phone beeped from the cosy space in the bottom of her tote bag where she'd tucked it away. Sunrise was here. It was the moment she'd been waiting for.

Stepping into the cold water, Niamh held her breath. It wasn't any colder than she remembered, but all the same, the water felt sharp against her legs. As the water reached her knees, the sun rose over the mountains before her, and the lake began to shimmer. Teeth chattering, Niamh blew out her breath and ploughed forward until the water was waist-high. Gasping at the cold, she dipped her whole body into the water right up to her shoulders and pushed forward, not caring that her ponytail was dragging in the water behind her.

17

Her breath billowed and her body slowly warmed as her arms came up and over her head. Ignoring the other swimming strokes from her childhood lessons, she continued to front crawl until she felt she was out far enough. She flipped onto her back and floated in the water as rays of sunlight rippled across the lake and shone on the mountains, making the bronze bracken appear to glow. The mist rose around her, and she stared up at the sky. A half-moon was still visible, low on the west horizon, and the mountains were turning from blue to warm mauves and soft greens.

Floating in the lake, Niamh felt the tension in her shoulders ease. The lake was a place of sanctuary for her. Staring up at the sky as it moved from night to day, she wondered when exactly her life had become so difficult, and why she didn't have the energy to figure it all out. If it wasn't one thing it was the other, and where she and Evan used to be a united front, now it seemed that they were drifting apart.

Getting pregnant and running away to get married at eighteen, and then living in the same house as her parents had never been easy at the best of times. Having another baby before she was twenty-one, and a third right before her twenty-fourth birthday, another surprise pregnancy, had made her feel that they'd never get back to themselves, ever. They used to be so good together. They were the teenage romance that had survived everything life had thrown at them. If anything, they should be even better and acting like a couple again – the kids were fourteen, twelve and almost ten now, and they weren't getting up in the middle of the night these days or dealing with chicken pox.

On paper they looked fine, but she missed the silly romantic things Evan used to do. Once upon a time he'd warm her side of the bed by hopping in while she was in the bathroom, or he'd send her texts on his breaks, silly jokes and photos of the bad homework he was correcting. To anyone else they might seem innocuous, but to her they were invisible threads of connection that kept them tightly sewn together. Lately she felt they were rather threadbare.

As she turned over and swam back to the lakeshore, Niamh acknowledged that she was going to have to be the one to pull them back together. Evan seemed to be woefully unaware of how far apart they'd drifted.

Emerging from the lake, Niamh hurried to her bag and pulled out her changing robe and set to drying herself beneath it before peeling off her swimsuit. There was no one around. There was no chance anyone would see her stretch marks and cellulite. She slipped her jumper dress down over her shivering body and pulled on her leggings, forgoing her underwear. Going commando until she got home wasn't going to thrill anyone. A quick shower and change when she got home, and she'd be good for the day.

*

The village of Lough Caragh was just waking up. The wide main street glittered with frost as shop owners swept their steps or switched on their Christmas lights. Every premises was painted a different bright colour. Saffron, lavender, royal blue, sunflower yellow. It was a colourful canvas that drew tourists in all summer long, even sometimes during the winter. The wide main street had a small square at one end where a huge Christmas tree stood, and a number of cute and just as colourful laneways filled with galleries, chocolate shops, craft shops and eateries wound away from it. It was very different now to the village Niamh had grown up in, and she was glad for it.

Driving past the first shop she caught sight of Sheila Monaghan directing Shirley Goodman on how to open the shop shutters, as if Shirley had never opened the shutters on her ladies' boutique. For as long as Niamh could remember, Sheila's shop, Champs-Élysées, had stood proudly on the main street. Shirley diligently opened the shutters and began wiping dust from the window. In the rear-view mirror, Niamh watched as Sheila's curls, washed and set every Friday evening in Knot Just Hair, bobbed and wobbled as she strode into her shop looking more like a hardy farmer's wife than the owner of the kind of boutique mothers of the bride from counties all around flocked to.

Spying the pretty pink and cream façade of Bake Me Home, Niamh decided to treat herself. Rosemary had said they had to nourish themselves after a solstice swim, and nourishment extended to her mental state too. Right now, her mental state demanded a fresh, warm chocolate croissant, maybe even two.

Niamh loved the cute bakery. Inside was painted pink and cream to complement the exterior, and a high counter with some stools snuggled in the bay window where you could sit with a hot drink and watch the world go by.

Not much was going by in Lough Caragh village at that particular moment, but something caught Niamh's eye.

Across the road, standing outside Billy's Newsagent and General Store, was a woman in dark glasses who seemed familiar. Taking a step away from the counter, Niamh squinted and peered at the woman. This tall woman's dark hair was cut into a long, shiny bob and was tucked smoothly behind one ear. Her outfit was refined: her ankle-length black skirt skimmed her kitten-heel boots; the sleeves on her spotless black knitted top were pushed up to her elbows, revealing a chunky watch and a tan. A classic Dior Saddle bag was tucked under her arm.

Niamh gasped. She pulled out her phone and went straight to Instagram and typed *Holiday Like Heather* into the search bar, though she already knew in her bones that it was Heather standing across the street. The first post on Heather's page confirmed it, with a photo of Heather standing outside the clock tower that stood in the middle of the village square. She'd simply captioned the photo: *Home for the holidays.*

Niamh ran a hand through her hair, her fingers catching in the tangles left over from her swim, and shuffled back to the counter. Tapping the counter with her phone, she willed Meg to hurry up so she could pay. What if Heather walked over and came in? Smoothing down her knitted dress, Niamh looked down at her breasts and wished she'd taken one minute to put her bra on.

Meg, wiping her hands on her apron, came from the back kitchens, a warm smile on her face. There was a dash of flour on her forehead and her greying blonde hair was scooped up into a loose bun on the top of her head.

Niamh turned away from the window. If Meg wasn't in the mood for a chat, she'd be able to slip from the shop and into her car without Heather noticing her.

'Niamh, it's lovely to see you.' Meg's gentle voice was earnest and happy. 'Are you all set for Christmas?'

'I've still a few things to do. I'm heading into Dublin tomorrow to pick up the last few bits.' Niamh's leg shook as she watched Meg slowly take a compostable cup from the top of the coffee machine.

'Your usual?' Meg asked over her shoulder.

'Yes, please,' Niamh said, half turning to look out the window again. Meg leaned forward over the counter and followed Niamh's glance.

'Is that Heather Moore across the way? It is! Sure that's great. She must be home for the holidays.'

Niamh grimaced. There wasn't much love lost between Heather and her mother as far as she could remember. But, then again, she hadn't spoken to Heather in almost fifteen years now. Actually, it would be fifteen years this June. A lot of water had passed under the bridge since then, but Niamh was in no hurry to say hey to Heather.

Scrunching shut the brown paper bag that held the two warm chocolate croissants that Meg had given her, Niamh leaned against the counter and held her phone to the payment terminal. Then, clutching her latte and her croissants, she hurried to the door. Lowering her head, she scurried to her car and slipped in quickly, confident that Heather hadn't noticed her. She reached for her seat belt. Glancing up she saw Lauren standing outside the bakery.

Niamh slid down in her seat. Lauren seemed too

occupied with watching Heather get into a gleaming black car to notice her. Lauren, she noted with a sigh of relief, looked normal – well, normal-ish. Her hair, still a gorgeous conker colour, was loosely clasped in a claw clip. Her blue jeans, ankle boots and blazer over her fitted Aran jumper looked cosy. Staying still, Niamh waited until Lauren had gone into the bakery before she started her car.

Driving home through the village she wondered what the hell was going on, what on earth had brought both Lauren and Heather back to Lough Caragh at the same time. Her head told her to calm down, a phrase she hated hearing. It was Christmas and surely that was why her estranged friends were home, but her heart told her otherwise. Tamping down her unease, Niamh parked in her driveway and groaned. She snatched up her croissants and latte and wondered how she could possibly avoid both women.

*

Gripping the strap of her handbag tightly, Lauren's shoulders dropped as she watched Niamh drive away. She'd almost not recognised her. Gone was the groomed and impeccable Niamh she remembered. This Niamh looked tired. She looked like a real mother, one who was busy with her children, always on call and in need of a good night's sleep. Lauren's mother, Debbie, had kept her up to date with Niamh's life, delighting in sharing the news every time Niamh had had a baby. Lauren's stomach tightened. *Oh, to be so lucky.* But still, Niamh had always been polished. If anyone had the ability to make motherhood look good, it was Niamh. Clearly that wasn't the case, Lauren thought a little unkindly. All the same, it made it easier for Lauren, since her friend didn't have her life together either.

Mind you, Heather looked as if she'd stepped from a catwalk. Whatever she was doing she was a head and shoulders above her family. As far as she knew Heather lived in London full-time. *What was she doing back here in the Wicklow Mountains?* Lauren opened the bakery door.

The sweet smell of freshly baked pastries made her mouth water. She needed something to settle her stomach after the drinks she'd had last night in Dublin with some of the other teachers. They'd gone out with her even though school holidays weren't until Friday. Her doctor had told her to take time off and take care of herself. What she needed was a complete reset. Shane had agreed with the doctor, much to Lauren's annoyance. Couldn't they see that she just needed to get on top of things, get organised and ahead of the game – then she'd be fine?

But to please him she'd left her Dublin home, taken the time off work the doctor had advised. It coincided with the revelation that her grandmother had left Mill House to her. This would be her first time to come back to it, and she felt somewhat ill knowing that it now belonged to her. It was a stark reminder of how she'd always wanted a house just like Mill House. She remembered telling Rosemary how much she loved the place and now she'd gone and left it to her without even a hint that she ever would. It was a lovely gesture, but Lauren worried her family were upset. Even though they'd

24

told her they were fine, she wanted to be sure. She'd talk to them about it again, if she could work up the nerve.

Putting the notion of that talk to the back of her mind, she selected a box of mixed pastries, adding two gingerbread men for her niece and nephew as the young girl behind the counter rang up the till. Then she set off up the street towards the small housing estate at the upper end of the village where her parents lived, dragging her suitcase behind her and swinging the box of pastries as she went. She hadn't been home since the summer, and it was lovely to be back.

Lough Caragh village was as bright as always. Even in the depths of winter it was like something from a Disney movie, and so different from the Dublin suburb Lauren lived in. Smiling, she noticed that Enda's Bookshop was open. Coloured Christmas lights lit up the window of the purple shop. A winter woodland scene filled the window, making it feel like an enchanted forest. An old chipped carousel horse was surrounded by fairies and elves, some suspended on clear thread so they appeared to be flying; books were stacked on the pretend forest floor. Catching the opening hours sign, Lauren made a mental note to pop in and pick up some books for her niece and nephew.

A few minutes later she was walking up the short path to her childhood home. The small, terraced house was looking well. It had been freshly painted and the windows shone. Her mother's old but much-loved fake Christmas tree was in its usual place, centre of the window, and a holly wreath tied with a red ribbon hung on the door. The house seemed smaller than she remembered. When she was a kid the three-bedroomed terraced house had seemed huge. After letting herself in, she stood in the hallway. The narrow stairwell was on her right, and she remembered that she used to think how high and steep it was. Now it just looked narrow. How did her parents get any furniture up there? For all its neat compactness, the house felt like home. It still had the same smell it always had, of Shake 'n' Vac and lemon drizzle cake, the one and only cake her mother could make without ruining.

Leaving her case at the bottom of the stairs Lauren called out a hello.

A muffled hello came from the living room. Lauren pushed open the door. Her mother was rooting under the sofa cushions. There was a wonky pile of old newspapers on the coffee table, the Christmas cactus her mother cherished woefully in danger of demise by newspaper landslide.

'Found it!' Debbie called from the depths of the sofa. 'Look at this.' She pulled out a tatty newspaper supplement from much earlier that year, opening it to a two-page spread on holidays. She spread it on top of the wonky newspaper pile.

'Ah, Mam, will you give me a minute? I'm only in the door,' Lauren grumbled. She slipped the box of pastries into the kitchen, then stood in the doorway between the kitchen and living room. The fire was lit, and the room was bedecked with tinsel and holly.

'That Moore girl has gone on to do great things. Have you seen her?' Debbie continued. 'High-flying and living the life. I never imagined I'd see the likes of it. Look at this – not one holiday that ordinary people could afford.'

Lauren leaned over the magazine. She'd seen this article

before, in January in a UK magazine about booking holidays early. Heather's recycled article was filled with enthusiastic praise for six glorious holiday resorts. The accompanying photographs all showed Heather wearing what Lauren knew from Heather's Instagram page were now her signature Chloé shades. Lauren skimmed the paragraphs, searching for any hint of the old Heather, but found only strong confident phrases and, to her teacher's eye, some hyperbole and cliché.

A clattering at the letterbox made her look up just as Yvonne blustered in then, with her twins, Mattie and Maisie. Debbie shoved the papers aside and clucked around her grandchildren, showing them their presents wrapped under the Christmas tree and asking them if they were behaving themselves. Yvonne pulled Lauren into the kitchen, away from the cosy fire and excited twins.

'You look like you could do with a cuppa,' she said, smiling as the opening chords of *Frozen* came from the sitting room accompanied by her children's off-key singing. 'Mattie particularly likes this opening. I swear he wakes up singing it.'

Lauren rubbed her face. 'Yeah, or something stronger.'

Yvonne glanced up at her. 'That bad? I'm sorry. Mam doesn't have anything in. She's hoping he'll stay off it this time.'

'Da's back on the wagon?' Lauren took the mug from Yvonne. '*Will* he stay off it this time?'

Leaning back against the sink, Yvonne nodded. 'He's a good few months off it now, but this time of year is challenging. Friday's the last day of work before the factory shuts down for the week. Graham said the lads are talking about a piss-up and he's doing his best to keep Dad out of it.'

'Fingers crossed.' Lauren wrapped her hands around her mug and tried to quell the hope that rose inside her every time her father gave up drinking. A few months was the longest time he'd ever been off it. Lauren allowed the bubble of hope to rise; maybe this time he'd manage to stay dry forever.

She sat down at the small dining table that was up against the wall. The salt and pepper set her mother had owned for as long as Lauren could remember sat in the middle of the table. It had been a wedding gift from Rosemary, who'd lived nearby in Mill House until she'd decided to travel around the world a few years ago, much to the surprise of her family. She'd then settled in Sydney, Australia, and had planned on staying there for another year or so before maybe moving on to New Zealand near her friend Maura's place, but she'd passed away just over a month ago.

Lauren squashed down the sadness that threatened to overtake her. What state might Mill House be in? It had been empty for quite some time since the last tenants had left. Now seemed as good a time as any to find out how Yvonne was feeling about Mill House being left to her. They were alone and Yvonne seemed happy to see her. Clearing her throat she said, 'Do you want to come up to Mill House with me? See what kind of shape it's in.'

'I will if I have time,' Yvonne said. She sat at the opposite end of the table. 'I haven't been there since Granny left on her travels. I'm not sure I want to see it yet.'

Lauren pressed her hands against the hot sides of the mug, ignoring the sting of the heat.

'I know, it's too weird, isn't it?' Lauren said. She glanced up at Yvonne to see how she'd react. 'I didn't think she would leave it to me. Do you think everyone's okay with it?' Lauren peered into her tea as if she could read the future in it.

'I think so,' Yvonne said. 'Thomas emailed me after he found out. He's no plans to come home from New York and doesn't want anything to do with it. Says it was always going to be yours; we all knew it. Rosemary and you had a special bond and he's right. Mam has no interest in it at all. It's too near the lake, and too far from the village for her liking, she said.'

'And what about you?' Lauren kept her eyes firmly on her tea.

Yvonne sighed. 'Graham did suggest that we ask for a share, but Laure, I feel that would be the wrong thing to do. Rosemary wanted you to have it. How could I contest that? I'm happy for you, to be honest. I've enough – our new house is everything we've ever wanted. I'd hate to jinx our luck by being greedy sods.'

'Thanks, Vonnie.' Lauren breathed out. 'I'm so relieved you said that. I was so worried . . .'

'Don't be worried,' Yvonne said. 'No one is bothered, I promise you . . . Oh God, what is that they're singing now?'

The singing in the sitting room grew louder. Lauren looked at Yvonne, who was shaking her head. They both snorted as their mother's thin soprano joined in with the twins as someone turned up the sound on the television.

'I think Mam is as bad as the kids,' Lauren said.

'Worse!' Yvonne laughed. 'It's great really – they love

coming over to Mam's. I didn't think I'd ever move away from Lough Caragh though. Mad how things go, isn't it?'

'I remember you giving me stick when we left.' Lauren raised her eyebrows with a slight smile. 'You told me I'd regret it. Now I'm back.'

Yvonne reddened. 'I was a big eejit back then. I couldn't see that the world was only as scary as you let it be. You were right to move closer to your job. Speaking of your job, are they all right with you taking time off?'

Lauren took a sip of her tea before speaking. 'They are, in fairness. They've been nothing but nice about it.'

'Even that miserable cow, what's-her-name . . . Muriel or Moonface?' Yvonne leaned forward.

'Well, aside from Marjorie, yes. She's . . .' Lauren shook her head as if to shake the thought of Marjorie from her mind. She gritted her teeth. 'She's just the biggest pain in the hoop! The woman has zero compassion and not one ounce of empathy. How she's teaching Social, Personal and Health Education is beyond me.'

'Those poor kids,' Yvonne murmured.

'Unreal!' Lauren carried on. She lowered her voice and looked down into her tea again. 'She even had the nerve to ask me how I was feeling seeing as this week was the week the baby should've come – and told me to take a break from trying because that's how her friend got pregnant. As if we haven't . . .' Pushing her mug away Lauren turned to look out across the kitchen to the back window. Her mother's back garden was completely at odds with the wild, scraggy Wicklow Mountains. It was tidy and bare of the pots that scattered the patio during the summer. Trimmed box hedging stood dark against the back wall, over which Lauren could just make out the purple shadow of the Great Sugar Loaf in the distance. The tall mountain peak was dusted with snow and reminded her of the time she and Shane had attempted to hike it. She scratched her arm. Shane . . .

'What a wagon,' Yvonne said, pulling Lauren back to their conversation.

'If you counted up all the wagons that went out west in America you wouldn't have enough wagons to credit her with,' Lauren grumbled, much to Yvonne's delight. 'No one in the staffroom likes her. She's a weapon!'

'Let it all out.' Yvonne laughed.

Lauren stopped mid-rant. 'Oh God, Vonnie, you've no idea how good that felt. I don't go on about it to Shane – he just doesn't get it – but then again, he's not listening to her jibes and passive aggression on a daily basis.'

'And when will we be graced with Shane's presence?' Yvonne picked up her mug and took a sip.

'He's coming down Saturday for Christmas,' Lauren said, avoiding her sister's direct gaze. Yvonne would know there was something up if she saw her eyes. She always could tell when Lauren wasn't quite telling the full story. Shrugging one shoulder she continued, hoping Yvonne wouldn't ask any more questions. 'I'm thinking we'll stay at Mill House for the holidays. See how we feel about it.'

'Without a Christmas tree?' Yvonne raised her eyebrows. 'Who are you and what have you done with my sister?'

'Hahaha,' Lauren said. 'I'm not feeling very Christmassy right now. It's been a tough year and I really could do with some quiet time. Maybe get a few walks around the lake in.'

'Well, if you are feeling in need of a little Christmas spirit make sure to come up to us. The kids will be delighted to see you.' Yvonne picked up their empty mugs and brought them to the sink. 'Do you think we can convince Mam to get a dishwasher in the January sales?'

'No, but we're going to try, aren't we?' Lauren smiled. She watched her sister rinse and dry the mugs and return them to the press. Yvonne had a heart of gold, she really did, but she'd never gone through what Lauren had. Lauren followed her sister into the living room. The last thing she wanted this Christmas was to spend time surrounded by Yvonne and her gorgeous children – they only reminded her of everything she could never have.

No, what she needed was to go to the lake, to take in the air and listen to the water lap against the rocks and stones. Being by the lake had always made her feel better. Rosemary had always said so, and she'd always been right. Lauren sighed. She felt like she was both part of the bigger picture and yet so very small when she was at the lake, and it was a good feeling. A feeling of belonging and hope, and what better day than today to go there – it was solstice after all.

3

Heather sat in the back seat of the hired car that was taking her to the golf resort where she was staying for the next twenty-four hours, a short business trip to fill space on her blog, *Holiday Like Heather*, and Instagram pages, both of which had been very quiet of late. She'd been slow to take up any offers these last couple of months and had offered older but slightly updated articles to publications whenever she could. She couldn't put her finger on why she wasn't excited about travelling anymore. Everywhere she went, people were the same. They cried over the same things – deaths, new babies – and laughed over the same jokes or happy moments. There was nothing new to learn these days. It was all a little soulless lately, especially the places where she'd been: literally in enclosed spaces and discouraged from going outside the compound where your every whim was catered to.

She shivered thinking of how she'd been all over the world and yet couldn't say what struck her the most. It felt like the worst payout for a job that she'd once thought was magical. Struck by her own ignorance, she glanced out the car window as the car slowed to take the corner right outside her home place.

She'd known they'd drive by it, but nothing could've prepared her for the rush of embarrassment that ambushed her. Her face flamed painfully red as she went by. She couldn't imagine bringing Simon here. He knew about her childhood, but knowing was different from seeing it. The last thing Heather wanted was for him to see the state of the place.

The shabby camper van was still shoved in the corner of the overgrown front garden. The stone wall that marked the boundary was crumbling in places. The bits that remained standing were covered in bright, almost childish paintings of bees, flowers and butterflies. A hand-painted sign hung from the rusty five-barred gate. The words, in red on a white background, said, *Save Our Planet*. Sinking lower into her seat, Heather turned her head away as the car silently passed. *Normal people don't live like that.* Normal people opened windows, drew back their curtains, mowed lawns and didn't accumulate other people's cast-offs. They made sure their kids ate a balanced diet and went on family holidays. They went out of their way to put their children first, to give them a childhood filled with joy, and didn't depend on them to do things that parents should do. Things like make sure there was food in the house, that clothes were cleaned, and that parent–teacher meetings were attended.

A shiver of distaste ran down Heather's back, quickly followed by a sense of guilt. These people were her family. Her heart sank. No doubt nothing would have changed, but she'd find that all out tomorrow when she went home.

34

Her mother had asked for her help to sell the place. Heather pursed her lips. Of course, it had fallen on her to have to help her mother. It always had. Shoving the thought of tomorrow's task away, Heather sat up to get a better view as the car swung into the wide gates of the golf club.

This was more like it. Vintage-style lampposts were festooned with lights all along the avenue, and dotted here and there were bronze, life-size deer statues. A huge fully lit Christmas tree stood proudly out front of the hotel, bringing a little magic to the otherwise austere building.

'Can you pull over?' Heather said to the driver. She tried to take a photo, but the shot wasn't good. Huffing, she got out of the car, telling the driver that she'd meet him at the hotel entrance.

'This is my job,' she explained to him. 'I'm a travel blogger. One of my selling points is that I catch my very first glimpse of a place, so my reaction is genuine.'

The driver nodded, uninterested in her explanation. Heather watched the car pull away and shook her head. Some people just didn't get it, like Simon, sometimes. He didn't understand why she took photos of absolutely everything, videoed herself walking along beaches or in clubs. He didn't have to. His job was more secure than hers; he didn't need to hustle the way she did. It would be nice to have the kind of security his job gave him, be nice to wake up and just go to work, nine to five, come home and be able to switch off, but being self-employed didn't work like that. Sometimes it irked, feeling like she didn't have a real home base, not having time off, being on duty twenty-four-seven. It was one of the things they'd been arguing about recently.

Heather pulled her cashmere hat from her oversized leather bag and slipped it on, relishing the cosiness of the soft wool. She dipped her hand back into her bag and took out a selfie stick. Within a minute she was walking along the avenue, recording the smooth rolling golf greens, absent of golfers, and the mountains beyond. The sun came out as she came closer to the hotel, gilding the white Georgian façade and making the place look warm and inviting. It was exactly the shot she needed.

Heather closed her phone and strode up to her driver. She tipped him generously after he removed her luggage from the boot. She nodded at the porter who'd silently appeared to take her bags, it was time to put her best foot forward – she'd better get to work and introduce herself to the concierge. The hotel offered a lot of facilities. There was a lot of ground to cover, and she wanted to make the most of every inch of it.

*

It was after three when Heather shut her laptop. She leaned back in the comfortable chair at the desk in the sitting room. Her room was outstanding. Clearly the hotel wanted her to be impressed as they'd given her a junior suite. There was a separate bedroom and living room, both with large flat-screen televisions, and superb internet connectivity which she'd not expected as the resort was situated low in the mountains. The icing on the cake was the balcony that ran the entire length of the suite, with views over the golf course and out towards the mountains.

Heather swivelled her chair back and forth. Simon

had seen her messages but hadn't replied to any of them. Her hand hovered over her phone. He should be able to take a call now. He'd mentioned that he was in meetings until lunch but would be at his desk after that. Would he even answer? Or would he let her go to voicemail, where he sounded so in charge and organised. The decision to call him, or not, was taken from her as her screen flashed into life, displaying Simon's name and a love heart beside it.

'Hi,' Heather said softly. 'I was just about to call you.'

'Hi yourself.' Simon's deep voice sent shivers down Heather's back. She wished he'd been able to come with her. 'What are you up to?'

'Nothing,' Heather said. 'Just finished creating content and on the phone to you.'

'I looked it up. It looks lovely,' Simon said. 'Have you tried the spa yet?'

'That's the plan for tomorrow.' Heather sighed. 'I've dinner booked in for half eight. The menu looks great. I think you'd enjoy it. They've a lot of fish on.'

'Maybe,' Simon said quietly. 'Listen, Heather, I'm sorry for arguing.'

Heather stopped swivelling the chair. She picked up a pen and ran it through her fingers as if it was a mini baton.

'I'm sorry too,' she said, her voice husky. 'I didn't mean to say those things to you. You know that don't you?'

A deep sigh came down the line, followed by a long silence. Heather's heart pounded.

'Look, Heather,' Simon said eventually. 'I know you don't mean it, but you keep saying the same things. You keep apologising and I keep wondering when you'll blow up next.'

'Si.' Heather leaned forward. 'Simon . . .'

'Heather, I need to say this to you: it's not right, what you're doing.'

'What do you mean – what I'm doing?'

'Pushing me away.'

Heather put her elbows on the desk and rested her forehead on her hand. She closed her eyes. She could picture the creases of worry on his forehead, the downturn of his lovely mouth. He'd be pacing; he always paced when he was worried or had to say something harsh. It wasn't fair that he pulled on her heartstrings this way.

'I can't go back to that conversation,' she said. 'I'm not pushing you away. It's not fair to say that.' She felt her jaw tighten.

'Listen to yourself,' Simon said. 'Heddie, you shut down conversations like this all the time. I'm serious. Every time I come to you to talk about this, you clam up. We need to talk, better. Communicate better. I want more, Heddie, I want you in my life – for the rest of my life, but I can't go on like this.'

'Are you issuing me an ultimatum?' Heather's eyes popped wide open. 'Emotionally blackmailing me into saying yes?'

'No! Heddie. For crying out loud. Don't you know me at all?'

'Sounds like it to me.' Heather tapped the pen on the desk. 'Listen, Simon, I can't have this conversation now.'

'When is going to be the right time for this conversation? You're already spending Christmas in Ireland and won't be back till after the New Year.' Simon's voice was low. He was met with silence. Eventually he sighed. 'Fine. Let me know when you're back in London.'

He hung up before Heather could say anything else.

'Gah!' Heather put the phone face down on the desk and got up. Outside, on the balcony, the cold air was a balm to her hot face. How dare he just hang up like that? She was right all along. He didn't have what it took to be in a relationship with her. She'd been right to not give him an answer – he shouldn't have asked in the first place. He didn't mean it anyway; she knew that deep in her heart. He hadn't meant to ask; he'd been carried away by the Parisian skyline and the romance of the Eiffel Tower. That was all. There was no substance to it, so there was no loss in his hanging up, not really, she reasoned.

The sun was setting in a clear sky. The moon hung low in the east. It was a heavy half-moon, bright and watchful, as her mother would say, a time to reflect on things. Shaking her head, Heather turned away from the moon and went inside. How was it that no matter how hard she tried to zone it out, her mother's sayings and voice still wafted into her thoughts as subtly as dandelion seeds blowing over a fence on a summer breeze and settling in a carefully tended garden.

Yanking the balcony door shut, she pulled the curtains over, overlapping them to make sure that there were no gaps that might allow the outside in. She could unpack. Her suitcase was open on the bed. Her dress for dinner needed ironing – that would keep her occupied for a bit.

Dress ironed and laid neatly across the bed, accessories laid out carefully so as not to crease it, Heather took a photo and dashed off a caption before posting it to her Instagram feed. Simon loved that dress, and she hoped he'd see it and feel bad. Somehow ironing it and posting the photo didn't make her feel any better. The suite, with all its cosy little extras, was still a hotel room, and it was beginning to feel smaller and smaller with each passing minute.

The sun had dipped below the horizon, and the sky was a dusty lavender grey. The air was decidedly cold, but the outdoors beckoned. Dinner wasn't for another four hours. She needed to do something, anything. She couldn't stay in the room any longer. Within minutes she was wrapped up warm in her long coat and cashmere hat and scarf. She grabbed up her phone and room key and flung them into her bag before she hurried downstairs where the concierge was chatting to a couple. The bar to her left was busy, filled with Christmas revellers, and piped Christmas carols. Heather turned away and hurried to the main door. A brisk walk would help settle her.

Before she knew it, Heather was striding along the narrow country road that led back into Lough Caragh village. The hedgerows were dark, and they rustled as the air grew colder. The day had grown quiet; not even a bird twittered from the bare branches of the surrounding trees. After fifteen minutes she paused. Not one car had passed her. It was as if time had stood still, but then again, not many people came along this road unless they were heading to the golf course. A few more steps and she'd be outside her home.

Inching forward, Heather went up onto her tiptoes, craned her neck and looked over the hedge. The attic room she had called her own was in darkness, but the kitchen was ablaze with light. She could just make out her mother, in her trademark long tunic and leggings, warming her backside before the stove. Shrinking behind the hedge, Heather pulled her scarf close around her neck. Coming back stirred up memories, but it also brought back the guilt she'd been trying to ignore for years now. Chewing on her top lip she remembered the last time she'd been home.

It had been a sunny Monday morning when she'd gotten up at the crack of dawn to wait for the taxi that was taking her to the airport. The whole house had been quiet, and no one had gotten up to say goodbye or good luck to her. She'd wanted to slam the front door behind her, but she hadn't. Instead, she'd silently left. That hadn't even been the hardest part, she acknowledged. The hardest part had been driving past Rosemary's house and seeing Rosemary standing in the garden waving at her. Heather pinched the bridge of her nose. She'd never said a proper goodbye to Rosemary, and it hurt like hell.

Standing on the side of the dark country road, practically in the ditch, Heather stuffed her hands deep into her coat pockets. Then lowering her head she scurried past, praying that her mother wouldn't spot her, a dark shadow in a dark landscape. The turn-off to the lake was only a few yards away from the house, and with a sigh of relief that she hadn't been spotted, she hurried along it.

Lough Caragh was quiet and steady. After a minute or two, Heather got her bearings. Nothing much had changed, except that the tree they'd sat under to avoid getting sunburnt as teenagers had grown taller and was surrounded by brambles. Heather walked to the lake edge and kicked a stone, watching it skitter into the water. The lake's surface was still and calm, and the clouds from earlier had long gone, leaving the stars bright and dazzling above her. It would have been wonderful to have been there as the sun had set, especially today of all days.

Heather wandered slowly along the stony beach. Solstice. Her hippie mother had always celebrated solstice – all of them – but it was summer and winter solstice that were magical to Heather.

'I don't need to believe in it,' she said to no one as she took her phone out and took a photo of the moonlit lake. 'Not anymore. The magic doesn't exist here anyway. It's long gone.'

Looking up, she saw the half-moon had a soft halo around it, promising a frosty night, and she tucked her hat down onto her head more firmly. She strolled further down the stony beach until it gave way to a well-worn earth pathway. Ignoring the signs that said *Private Land*, Heather strode along the pathway towards the stile in the dry-stone wall that marked the boundary of Mill House. Clambering over the stile, her breath billowing out into the night, Heather felt a huge weight lift from her shoulders.

Rosemary was gone, but there was still something of her presence in her garden. Someone, maybe a tenant, had taken good care of the place, although Willow, Heather's sister, had mentioned in an email that it was now empty. The soft gurgle of the stream that ran from the top of the property right down to the lake made the skin on the back of her neck and scalp tingle. It sounded a little bigger than it had been and every bit as glorious. Following the stream, Heather stopped every now and then to look around the long sloped and terraced garden.

Rosemary had truly loved this place, and to Heather it had always felt like what a home should feel like. No matter what time of day it was, if you called in at Mill House you were welcome. A mug of tea, or coffee, or something stronger – depending on the look on your face – was pressed into your hands almost immediately. The best seat by the fire was always offered, and the kitchen table always had an extra place set. There were many days Heather wouldn't have gotten through if it wasn't for Rosemary. Heather looked up the hill at Mill House, it was strange that she'd never met Lauren until that first day at secondary school. She'd known Lauren was Rosemary's granddaughter, but she'd avoided Lauren, nervous of how she'd be if she knew how much good Rosemary was doing for her. There was just something there telling her that Lauren wouldn't take too kindly to Heather knowing her grandmother as well as she did. When they finally became friends, Rosemary hadn't given her away.

Heather wiped away a tear. She made her way up the garden terraces towards Mill House. It was mad to think that here she was now, avoiding Lauren and Niamh again, although for very different reasons. Still, she'd nothing to prove to either one of them. She'd nothing to say to them either. Life had moved on and there was no need to revisit old memories. Nothing was going to change what happened that night, and she'd made a good life for herself without them in it. No, she was better off without them. Better off free.

The last garden terrace was bordered by a greying, lichen-covered wooden fence with a creaking gate in the middle of it. Pushing it open, Heather turned and looked down on the lake. From her vantage point she could see the pier where, almost every day, right from their first day of secondary school until just after their final exams, she'd gone swimming with Lauren and Niamh and, most times, Rosemary. They'd leave their towels hanging on the lowest branch of a hawthorn tree, stumble down the pebbly beach to the sandy lakeshore, and for half an hour at the break of day, they felt like they owned the whole world. No one else came down to the lake at that hour, and no one ever knew about their sunrise swims. Afterwards they'd troop up the path to Rosemary's where they'd dry off in the back kitchen and hungrily eat the porridge she'd ready for them.

Those were the days. Heather's gaze drifted to the right, towards the tiny sandy cove where they used to sit around a fire on summer nights, toasting marshmallows and talking about their dreams. She shook her head. She wasn't going to get emotional about it – what good would that do? Heather eased her grip on the gate latch and turned to face the house just as a light came on in the kitchen.

Jumping, she quickly pressed back into the shadow of the old apple tree and hoped that whoever was in the house didn't spot her. It wouldn't look good, a famous blogger found snooping around someone's house. Peeking out from the knobbly, bare branches, Heather squinted at the house as another light flicked on. She spotted Lauren hunkering down in front of the old stove. Quickly, and as quiet as the moon, Heather slipped from the garden and made her way back to the stile. Stopping, she glanced back up at Mill House. Smoke rose from the chimney, and the house looked as inviting as ever, but there was no way she'd go back while Lauren was in it.

4

22nd December 2023

The kids were barely out the door for school the next morning when Niamh's phone beeped. It was probably Edel, checking to see if she was still on for heading into town later to pick up the last few Christmas bits and pieces. With a grin, Niamh pulled her phone from her jeans' back pocket. Covid had kept her stuck at home for the last few Christmases, so she couldn't wait to potter from shop to shop in the dusk while coloured lights twinkled overhead. Edel had mentioned popping into the hotel for a cocktail or two, and Niamh could almost taste the Cosmopolitan she was going to have later. She nudged the door on the washing machine shut with her knee and stopped smiling as the phone screen showed that the text had come from her fourteen-year-old daughter, Ava.

One line, not even a hello: *Dad said you have to collect me after school.* Niamh snorted. It was typical of Evan to land the school pick-up on her without an explanation. It wasn't as if he couldn't make it to the school on time

– he taught Business in the same school, for crying out loud. Niamh texted Ava back telling her to put her phone away and that she'd be there to collect her. An overflowing basket of wet laundry sat at her feet. Stooping, she hiked the basket to her hip and pulled the utility room door firmly shut behind her to keep the draught from the back door out of the kitchen.

Niamh stomped upstairs to the empty bedroom they used as a storeroom. She'd set up three clothes horses in an attempt to stay on top of the never-ending washing and drying that inevitably came with having three active children. It was with bad grace that she flung vests, leggings, socks and pyjamas onto the clothes horse, for once not caring that they'd need ironing afterwards because of the creases.

Blast Evan. Now she'd have to dash from picking up Sophie and Katie at their primary school at twelve and then into Avonmor to pick up Ava for half twelve. Traipsing back downstairs with the next load of washing, tears prickled the back of Niamh's eyes. Evan had promised he'd come home today instead of heading out to the pub with the other teachers at lunch. It was the last day of school before the Christmas holidays, and he knew she'd made plans with Edel, which now she'd have to cancel. Niamh sat on the bottom step of the stairs and looked around the wide square hall. The place was a mess. Her girls were involved in everything: Scouts, swimming, camogie, rugby, dancing, stage school, and behind the front door had become the dumping ground for the previous night's activity. How had she let things become so bad? Ignoring the laundry, Niamh set to picking up abandoned hats and gloves and dropping them into the baskets she'd allocated to each child. She straightened up the trainers and wellies under the long bench beneath the coat rack. Her mother would be appalled.

When Niamh was a girl, this very hallway had always been spotless, with a fresh vase of flowers on the half-moon table and all outdoor paraphernalia tidied away in the small closet that was now a WC. Her mother had always had the house ready to receive callers at any time, and she'd been house-proud right up to her very last moment. Niamh rubbed her eyes remembering that day four years ago when she'd found her mother lying on the hall rug, the vase upturned, and water spilling into the carpet. Daffodils had been scattered around her feet. Sudden cardiac death they said. She wouldn't have felt a thing. She'd never forget the silly but kindly meant remarks made by the doctor that day: hadn't she lived a good and happy life, and hadn't she had Niamh and her grandchildren around her? She always said they made life worth living.

Niamh added visiting her parents' graves that week to her mental to-do list. Her father had joined her mother just over a year ago, and since then she'd felt a surprising sense of freedom as well as loneliness. Her father had run the house, even from the nursing home where he'd spent his last couple of months, leaving behind instructions for Niamh to get on with bringing back the small but successful B&B business that her mother had run from their home. For as long as Niamh could recall, they'd let out three rooms that had once been stables and sheds, and occasionally, upon recommendation, rooms in the house to older married couples who met her mother's high standards.

It seemed impossible right now when it felt as if she couldn't even manage a home, let alone even consider taking in guests. All the same, lately it was all she could think about. At night when she couldn't sleep she found herself considering her father's dying wish that she revive the B&B. It wasn't the worst idea; it was just that she'd need to convince Evan that it would be a *good* idea.

She recalled the last time she'd visited her father in the nursing home. Her heart contracted thinking of how frail he'd looked as he struggled to sit up straight in his chair by the window, the one he insisted on getting into every day because he didn't believe in 'lying in bed all day like a common scoundrel'.

'Get Bopper Quinlan to straighten out the rooms in the yard,' he'd wheezed. 'He won't do you wrong, and he owes me a favour.'

'Bopper,' she'd said and nodded at her father. 'I'll keep that in mind, Dad, but his son has taken over from him. Rory . . .'

'Ah yes, Rory. He's a grand fella,' he'd said. 'He straightened out the business good and proper when all Bopper did was hand me plastic bags stuffed with invoices and bank receipts. Bloody impossible to run a decent set of accounts for anyone working like that. You get him to take a look for you.'

'I will.' Niamh had thought of Rory Quinlan. They'd hung out together for a while when they were teenagers. He had been handsome with dark hair and sharp grey eyes – he still was handsome she'd admitted to herself –

49

there was a time when she'd almost dated him, but she'd wound up dating Evan and then . . . then she'd gotten pregnant and the rest was history. Rory had never settled down though, and sometimes she wondered why. Her father had shivered and she'd forgotten about Rory while she'd tucked the blanket around her father's knees. 'Will you try some more dinner, Dad?'

'No, I won't.' He'd been adamant, and she couldn't blame him. Dinner that day had been Irish stew and it'd looked weak and flavourless, but at the same time, he could do with putting on some weight.

'I'm doing a ham over the weekend,' she'd said. 'Do you want me to bring you in a bit?'

'That would be lovely.' His craggy face had creased into a smile. 'Are you cooking the cabbage in the bacon water like your mother used to?'

'Yes,' Niamh had lied. She hadn't been going to, but if it made him happy, she would.

'Lovely.' He'd patted her hand. 'I'll look forward to that.'

'I'll be in on Saturday,' she'd told him as she'd kissed him goodbye.

'Don't forget to contact Rory now, won't you? Promise me.'

'I promise.' As an only child Niamh felt obliged to reassure him. She'd squeezed his hand and left him looking out the window at the deepening dusk. If she'd known that was the last time she had with him she'd have stayed longer, but he'd seemed fine at the time. When the nurse rang to tell her he'd gone, she'd been relieved to hear that he'd gone to bed in good form and had passed away in

50

his sleep. It gave Niamh huge comfort to know that neither of her parents had suffered, and she knew that she was extremely lucky.

Yet knowing they'd passed gently wasn't making missing them any easier. There were days when she missed them so much it felt as if someone had reached into her chest and was grasping her heart so hard that it was difficult to breathe.

In her now somewhat tidier hall Niamh groaned. She took out her phone to text Edel. Her fingers hovered over the keys, unwilling to break their plans. A thud on the front door made her jump and she slid the phone back into her pocket, then opened the door just as a stunned coal tit took flight.

Niamh peered out the front door into the grey December day. The drive was flanked by old beech trees, which was beautiful in the spring when the place was filled with daffodils and crocuses. Now, in the midst of winter, the drive merely looked cold and bleak. Niamh knew everyone loved The Old Rectory. It was indeed beautiful, with its steep gables, fancy fascia and pretty bay windows. It was set on a little under ten acres of gardens and fields, but over the last few years it had been more than slightly neglected.

Evan was too busy to do any maintenance and anyway, he wasn't that way inclined. He was happier out in the community, training kids up at the pitch three times a week and giving private tutoring on two other evenings. When he did come home, he was too tired to fix the little things, which meant that they'd rapidly become bigger things. The gutter over the west end of the house was in desperate need of repairing, but so far, he'd only made the usual half-mumbled promises to sort it. Niamh closed the front door and leaned against it.

Her view into the house from the front door didn't inspire her to move. From where she stood, she could see into the sitting room on her right, where the fireplace was scattered with ashes, and someone, probably nine-year-old Katie, had knocked over a lamp and not bothered to set it right. The kitchen, she knew, was filled with clutter – bills, school flyers, Christmas cards and breakfast things. Casting an eye around the hallway, Niamh weighed up her options: straighten up the sitting room or blitz the kitchen. Neither appealed to her, and with sudden clarity, she realised she didn't want to be in the house at all. Grabbing her coat and handbag, she dashed out the front door. If she was going to have to cancel this evening with Edel, then she'd get out now and have some time to herself without feeling any guilt. Feck the housework – it would be there when she got back. It always was.

She started her car, then pulled out her phone and waited for it to connect to the car's hands-free system. As she pulled out onto the road, she called Edel, who answered after a few rings. 'Howya!'

'Grand. Actually shite.' Niamh put the car in gear. 'Evan has messed up this evening on me and I'm calling to cancel.'

'Listen, don't be worrying about that at all.' Edel's calm voice reassured Niamh. 'Martin has literally just told me that he's going to have to work late, so I was about to call you to let you down.'

'Ha!' Niamh snorted. 'Will we ever get a minute?'

'It's all go, isn't it?' Edel sounded tired. 'I'm told it'll get easier as the kids grow.'

'Yeah, I'm not buying that one. Remember when they told us we'd forget about childbirth?' Niamh said.

Edel's sharp intake of breath was clear over the phone. 'Ouch. There's a memory I wish I could bury. Hey, are you in the car?'

'I am,' Niamh said firmly. 'If I can't get out later, I'm getting out now – even if it's only up the village for a coffee.'

'You're dead right. I'll be up to you in a few. Meet you in Bake Me Home or Friends?'

'Friends.' Niamh parked her car on the main street outside the café. 'I'm here now. See ya soon.'

Hanging up, Niamh peered along the street. It was quiet for the last Friday before Christmas, but without a doubt the place would be buzzing with people once the kids were out of school. This was the calm before the storm. Everyone would be out getting their shopping and going out for a drink later. No doubt Heather would be out. Niamh could picture her swanning into The Coach House, head held high like it never had been when they were teens. She was probably dying to get in there and show everyone how successful she was now. It was for the best that she couldn't go out later, Niamh conceded. That way she wouldn't have to witness Heather's return, nor put on a smiling face for anyone who spoke to her about Heather, as they most likely would. No, she'd have a movie night with her girls instead.

Once inside the café, she ordered a latte and a chocolate croissant. Then she snaffled a window seat. Rory Quinlan's van slowed and reversed into the parking spot in front of Niamh's car. Niamh watched as he walked around the van and went into Enda's Bookshop. Leaning forward, she scrunched up her nose; she hadn't taken Rory for a book person. He seemed to be more of an outdoors person, always dressed casually in jeans and checked shirts, usually with comfy boots on, and a fleece jacket. Today he was in his workwear: black Snickers trousers with a multitude of pockets and a black fitted fleece bearing his company's logo. Heavy steel-toe work boots completed his look.

He came back out of Enda's with two full, heavy-looking bags. His bulky fleece didn't hide his trim but strong body, she thought as she admired him from the safety of the café. He looked great, she reflected as he climbed into his van, much healthier and fitter than she realised. Her heart beat fast as he looked directly at her as he pulled his seat belt on. He waved and she found her hand waving back as if it had a mind of its own. Closing her mouth, which had dropped open, she could almost hear her father say, 'Don't forget to contact Rory now, won't you? Promise me.'

It had been over a year now, and she still hadn't contacted Rory. She didn't think she'd broken her promise to her father. She preferred to think that she simply hadn't fulfilled it yet. Also, it was impossible to get Evan to sit down and go through any plans for the B&B renovations with her. He was so busy, and hadn't really listened when she tried to tell him the ideas that had been floating around in her head the last few months.

Pulling out her phone, Niamh opened her Pinterest app and found the board she'd created a while back. Images of cosy bedrooms, sleek en-suite bathrooms, tiny kitchenettes and colourful pottery appeared before her, firing her imagination even more. She'd taken a look at her yard late yesterday evening and even in the gloaming it didn't look that bad. Some hard grafting, *a bit of elbow grease* as her mother had always said, would go a long way towards making it look like somewhere people would want to stay for a night or two. Her father was right. She should be making her own money, just as her mother had done. The niggling thought that he was right had been growing since he'd said it to her last year. It's not that Evan wasn't generous with money. It was just that she felt incomplete in not earning and contributing to the house. Evan said she was crazy whenever she mentioned it.

'We made the decision that it was important for someone to be at home with the kids,' he'd reminded her the last time she'd brought up the idea that she might get a part-time job.

'I know we made that choice,' Niamh had replied. 'But that was when Ava was born – fourteen years ago, Ev. I agree, but now they're in school I *need* something to do.'

His only response had been to look around the kitchen at the mess and clutter. Niamh hadn't bothered to continue the conversation. She hadn't wanted to feel any more rubbish than she already felt. What she really wanted to say was that they were lucky. They'd no mortgage thanks to her parents, they'd minimal bills and although they could afford her to be at home, it was slowly but surely driving her demented. Being at home wasn't where she'd imagined she'd be at this age. While he'd always known

55

he was going to be a teacher, she'd dreamt of being a flight attendant and wandering around cities taking in all the sights and delights of faraway places. She knew she was cherishing a childish dream, but it had been *her* dream, and it had been taken away from her the moment she'd discovered she was pregnant with Ava. Evan had achieved his dream. He'd never understand her loss.

Picking at her croissant, Niamh pushed away that last discussion about her working outside the home. A flash of red grabbed her attention, and she watched Edel come up the street in a gorgeous red coat, her blonde hair in a curled bob. Edel waved and came inside.

'Bloody cold out there.' Edel slipped her coat from her shoulders revealing smart black jeans, ankle boots and a simple black knitted jumper with a gold star emblazoned on it.

'You scrub up well,' Niamh said. She brushed pastry crumbs from her lap and wished she'd changed outfit. Her blue jeans and oversized sweater were cosy, but she felt dated sitting next to Edel.

'Thanks.' Edel briefly struck a pose. 'Just something I threw on. Only kidding, they were the only things not in the bloody laundry basket. I've no choice but to look this cute.'

'You've no idea how I needed to hear that.' Niamh laughed. 'Go get a coffee and come back here. I've something I want to share with you.'

Smiling widely, Niamh looked down at her phone and reopened her Pinterest app. It was time she took control of a few aspects of her own life, and telling Edel about her idea would be a start. Just because Evan wasn't supportive of the B&B renovations didn't mean she shouldn't do something about it. Who knew what might happen, she thought as Edel sat down opposite her. It wouldn't be easy, that was for sure, but it was a helluva a lot better than waiting around for something to happen.

5

It was after eleven in the morning when Lauren woke up on the sofa at Mill House. She hadn't meant to fall asleep there, and now her back was sore and her head even more so. The bottle of wine she'd found in Rosemary's kitchen was empty, the *thank you* tag that had been attached to it was on the coffee table, and the fire in the stove was still glowing. What time had she eventually nodded off at? A text message from Yvonne made her sit up.

Do you fancy coming to bingo tonight? It's the last one before Christmas and they add a bonus prize? Please say yes! Mam is beside me demanding that I guilt you into going.

Lauren laughed. Bingo. Her sister was really scraping the bottom of the barrel now, but it could be fun. She never won but the thrill was always there. She texted Yvonne back.

Meet you at the door at 7.

Yvonne texted back immediately.

Whoop! Mam is doing a jig here. You've just made an old woman very happy. It's going to be great craic – can't wait to see how Old Moll gets on reading the numbers this year!

Smiling, Lauren pushed her hair back from her face and got up. The Christmas Bingo Bonanza was always packed, and usually a good night out with people heading to the pub afterwards. Raking together the embers in the stove, she piled in some kindling and watched as the fire took hold. Then she added a dusty log to the pile before sitting back on the footstool.

Mill House wasn't a real mill house. It had a small mill wheel on the stream that ran through the garden, but the house hadn't been built as a place of business. It had been built by a landowner and gifted to his spinster sister. Apparently, the landowner's wife had been jealous of the siblings' relationship and wanted her out of the house. Lauren didn't know how true that part was.

As the flames took hold of the log in the stove, Lauren held her head in her hands. What did Rosemary think she was going to do with a house this size? Three storeys high with two bedrooms and a tiny bathroom on each of the upper levels. The old stone house was built into the side of a hill and had a long garden that ran all the way down to the lake. Although the house was narrow from front to back, it felt spacious because of its high ceilings and large windows. Rosemary had only used the ground floor and the largest bedroom up on the first floor in her last few years living there. The second, slightly smaller bedroom had been turned into a dressing room. There Rosemary had stored her eclectic clothing, accessories and shoes with gusto, adding to it until she'd declared that she was going away to travel, that she needed to lighten her load and declutter.

It was there, on an August day in 2009, just days away from her Leaving Cert exam results, that Lauren had found Rosemary hugging a mound of clothes to her chest. Her eyes and cheeks had been wet, and she hadn't hidden her sorrow from Lauren at all.

'I can't give them up,' Rosemary had said. Sniffing, she'd hugged the clothes tighter. 'These glad rags mark so many occasions in my life.'

'You don't have to give them up,' Lauren had said. 'We'll pack them away for when you come back.'

'What if I don't come back?' Rosemary sniffed.

'You'll be back.' Lauren nudged her. 'You love the lake too much.'

'True.' Rosemary wiped her face. 'That's where Paddy is. Right, let's get started. I can deal with all of this when I'm home.'

Together they'd packed away the entire room up to one of the bedrooms on the top floor, which was then locked in anticipation of prospective tenants, and afterwards they'd sat out in the back garden with Sheila, Shirley and Mucker, raising glasses and laughter until even the stars were sleepy. Little did they know that Rosemary would never return to wear any of her beloved glad rags again. Now, sitting before the crackling fire, Lauren wasn't looking forward to sorting through them. She wished she'd paid more attention to what Rosemary had said about them, the occasions that were attached to each piece. It would make it easier if she could; it would feel as if Rosemary was there with her.

Lauren lifted her head from her hands and stretched them high above her head, grimacing as her back creaked and popped. The fire had taken hold properly, and the thick stone walls were keeping the heat in. The room was warming up nicely, but she desperately needed a cup of tea.

The kitchen was an icebox. Lauren shivered as she put water in the kettle before poking around in the presses. The previous tenants, an older couple who'd lived in the city all their lives and had rented the house for a year to see how they liked country living, had left the place spotless. They'd left the thank-you wine in the kitchen and the place ready to go for the next occupant, for which Lauren was grateful, although she would've welcomed a stray teabag and some sugar. Switching the kettle off, Lauren turned on the boiler and then rambled upstairs to use the bathroom, giggling at the old pink bathroom suite that was still in situ.

Rosemary had loved it. Pink had been her favourite colour. It cheered her up, she'd always said, all shades of it. The deep pink bathtub glowed as the sun shone through the frosted window. Niamh had loved this room too. Lauren's heart contracted. Niamh had looked lonely yesterday morning, standing there in front of the bakery on her own. She'd never been alone when they were teenagers. Back then, no matter where they went, people had flocked to Niamh as if she were a celebrity, and she'd been fun to be around. Yesterday she'd had a forlorn look of longing on her face as she'd watched Heather, as if she was missing her.

Lauren frowned. Was it possible Niamh missed her too? Maybe she should call on Niamh, see how life had treated her. Picking at a stray thread on her T-shirt Lauren tried to imagine what they'd say to each other after all this time. Fifteen years. It had gone by so quickly but there were moments where time had stood still, moments when she'd wished that Niamh was by her side, telling her, in her strong and confident manner, that everything would be okay. But after fifteen years it was hard to find the words to break the silence that had grown between them. After all, the road went both ways and Niamh could have made the effort to make contact too. Although, she was probably just super busy with her family. *Up to ninety* had always been one of her favourite sayings.

She was lucky to be busy, Lauren scratched her arm. *Family-busy.* It was exactly the kind of dishevelment she craved. She should have been cradling a new-born in her arms and wondering how they'd get through Christmas, but yet again all she was cradling were her shattered dreams of having a family. A full house. Noise, chaos and laughter. That's all she'd ever wanted. But the fifth miscarriage in almost as many years was crushing her hopes. It was more difficult to see her dream family as a reality. Once it had been sharp and clear; now it was fading around the edges like an old photograph. The feeling left her with the sensation of being uprooted and she didn't like it at all.

What she liked was the feeling that had started the

Christmas she'd gotten her first baby doll and pram, the feeling that one day she'd be a mother. It was the feeling she loved best and left her warm and planning family holidays and matching outfits for her imagined babies. That feeling had intensified when she'd discovered that Shane wanted the same thing she did. She'd never realised that boys wanted families and pets and all that kind of thing. Her family had been so traditional it was almost a joke, and even though she wanted a family she'd also been determined to earn her own money, unlike her mother.

Shane, ever supportive, had cheered her on all the way through college. They'd been happy in the knowledge that they were setting themselves up in the right way. Their children wouldn't want for anything. Well, that was the dream. But now the uprooted feeling was swamping her. Some days all she had was an overwhelming sense that she was freefalling into nothing. There wasn't anything she could grasp on to, no directions on where to go, or even on how she should feel anymore. Her counsellor told her it was normal to feel that way, but that didn't ring true to Lauren. Normal was having a family. This feeling was anything but normal. She'd rather push the pain away than feel it time and time again.

Until she'd been made to take time off work she'd been the most exemplary teacher, volunteering for everything and anything rather than go home to an empty house. Now she was on sick leave all she did was watch Netflix and sleep. It suited her perfectly. She'd rather feel nothing than feel out of control and be in agony, and she'd be better off alone than seeing Shane's concern for her every day.

Shane hadn't texted her, she realised as she ran her fingers through her hair in a vain attempt to detangle it. Sitting on the edge of the bath, Lauren closed her eyes. Her face warmed in embarrassment thinking of last Saturday night and the conversation they'd had when she'd told him she wanted to go to Mill House on her own.

He'd been shocked when she'd suggested it and upset when she'd said that maybe they should take some time apart. It had been half past ten, late enough, when she'd brought it up. He'd asked her to pause the programme they were watching and had turned to face her, his brow furrowed and his jaw tight. She'd sat back against the arm of the sofa with a sickening stomach, and watched a flurry of emotions cross his face. They'd sat in silence, the television stuck on an entirely inappropriate sex scene that made Lauren's cheeks flush. She'd longed to press play, not only to get past the scene, but so that they could maybe pretend her request was fine, and that he wasn't as hurt as she could see he was.

The silence had grown. She'd wished he'd say something, anything. He used to call her at lunchtime just to chat, to hear her voice, and they'd talk about nothing at all and everything at once. Her heart had sunk when she'd realised he was so upset that he wasn't capable of saying anything. His left hand, on the armrest, had been clenched into a ball, his wedding ring gleaming in the blue television light as he squeezed his hand tightly. He'd cleared his throat.

'Do you think that's a good idea?'

She'd paused before speaking. 'I do. You've a lot of work on, and I've a lot of thinking to do.'

'Thinking?' He hadn't looked at her as her mind whirred.

'Yeah,' she'd said softly. 'There's a lot to think about.'

He'd quietly sat on his end of the sofa.

'Is that okay?' Lauren had picked up the remote control, eager to move on and sorry she'd even started the conversation.

'I suppose.' He'd kept his eyes on the screen, but his leg gave him away. He always shook it when he wasn't happy with something.

'Okay, that's that decided.' Her voice had grown quieter.

He'd looked at her long and hard for a minute before tiredly shaking his head. 'I'm going to bed,' he'd said so quietly she almost didn't hear him. He'd turned away from her so she couldn't see his face, couldn't tell how he was feeling anymore.

Lauren had stared at his back as he'd left the room, her mouth shut tightly. He'd sounded so tired and confused, and she'd known that he was tired and confused about her. About them. The penny had dropped in that moment: *she should talk to him,* honestly and openly. But how? Lately she'd been struggling to find anything to say at all, while simultaneously knowing that what she should say was everything that was in her heart. But that was impossible. She barely acknowledged her own heart; how could she share it with him? The next morning he'd been kind to her and told her that he loved her, no matter what, and her heart had broken a little to think that even after all the awkwardness and unspoken words, he still wanted the best for her. It was just hard to believe that these days, especially when it was her body that wasn't capable of giving them everything they'd both longed for.

She got up from the edge of the bath now, then trudged downstairs and into the sitting room. The fire was cracking away merrily, but she added a few more logs anyway. Then she shoved the empty wine bottle into her bag. She'd drop it into the bottle bank on her way home. With her coat tightly wrapped around her, she let herself out of the back door of Mill House, deciding to take the lake walk. The road was just as quick, but it was boring, and you wouldn't know who you'd bump into. The last thing she wanted to do was to pretend to be merry and on form for Christmas.

Niamh and her family came back to her mind as she wandered down the garden towards the lake. Niamh was probably more on top of things than she looked yesterday. She'd always been organised and full of beans when they were teenagers. Niamh had been the one who'd arrange their lifts to town to buy the latest trends. She'd always known exactly where to go and who was cool. She'd been the one who thought of fun things to do and was always talking about the places she'd go and how she'd get there. She was probably fine. There was no need to try to talk to her, not when Lauren was far from fine.

Lauren hurried down the garden towards the stile. Once over the stile, she navigated the overgrown path, each step bringing her closer to the lake. Drawing a breath in deep through her nose, Lauren felt a headache begin at the backs of her eyes. She paused at the *Private Land* signs, catching sight of someone on the shingle beach that she was heading to. Someone familiar, looking out across the lake with their hands in their pockets.

Lauren began to hurry, stumbling over the grassland until she was standing on the shingle beach, willing them to turn around.

'Hi,' she called softly.

Shane turned around. Lauren's breath caught in her throat. It had only been a day since they'd been together, but it felt like it had been years. She slipped her hands into her pockets and watched him do the same thing.

'I knew I'd find you here.' He took a step towards her. 'I'm sorry. I'm intruding but . . . Laure, please say this is okay. I couldn't stay away.'

'It's okay,' Lauren said. 'Shane, I'm so sorry.' Her hands tingled, making her want to hold his hand. She wished she could walk up to him and hold him, but she couldn't move.

'I know. Me too.' His dark blue eyes were on hers. 'Laure, I . . .' He looked down at his feet, kicked up a stone and sighed heavily.

Lauren couldn't take her eyes from him. Here he was, looking as gorgeous as the day she'd first seen him, standing before her telling her that he couldn't stay away from her. Her heart pounded in her chest. He'd make a wonderful dad. He deserved better than her. He deserved someone who could give him the family they'd always wanted. If anything, she should let him go and have that chance. Swallowing the bile that rose in her throat, she nudged the stones with the toe of her boot, unconsciously mirroring his actions.

'What about work?'

'I told them I needed to take today off,' he said. He nodded at Mill House. 'How's it looking?'

'It's in good shape. Clean. Warm. No Christmas tree though,' Lauren ventured.

'That's okay with me,' Shane said. He looked down at the stones he was still scooching around. 'I think I'd manage without a Christmas tree this year.' He looked up and gave Lauren a half-smile. 'Am I allowed to come over there and give you a hug?'

Pressing her lips together to stop her tears from falling, Lauren nodded and tried to smile back.

'Yes,' she said hoarsely. The lump in her throat almost strangled her.

Taking a step towards him, Lauren tried to quell the urge to blurt out that she loved him. It wouldn't be fair to him, not when she'd practically decided that she should let him go. But he was smiling at her in a way that made her shiver. His eyes were warm on hers, and he was wearing the jeans she'd always complimented him on, and the green checked shirt that made his blue eyes sparkle. He knew she loved that shirt. He was bound to be wearing the aftershave that she loved too. He'd always spritzed some on even though he'd recently grown a beard. She took another step towards him, just as he began to walk to her. His stride was long and determined, as if he was sure of where he was going.

Within seconds he was in front of her, inches from touching. In the chill of the morning they stood, toe to toe, their breath mixing together as the lake lapped gently against the shore. Lauren looked up into his face, noting that the furrow between his eyes had deepened. There was a pallor in his cheeks that she knew came from sleepless nights. His lips parted but he stayed quiet. Then, as if they'd been apart for decades, he reached for her, pulling her to him with a groan that came from deep inside him. Lauren gasped and threw her arms around him tightly. He felt strong and warm beneath her embrace, yet soft and vulnerable. She could feel his pulse race as she laid her head on his chest. He leaned down and into her, holding her even more tightly.

'God,' he mumbled into her neck. 'I needed this; I needed you.'

Nodding mutely, Lauren groaned. Her body responded to him by pressing closer to him, and she groaned again. He ran his hands down her back.

'I'm so glad it's just us two tonight,' he whispered.

She wriggled from his hug.

'What?' Shane frowned. 'Did I do something wrong?'

'No.' Lauren scrunched her face up. 'It's just that I've promised Mam and Vonnie that I'd go to bingo tonight . . .'

'Bingo,' Shane spluttered. 'Are you kidding me?'

'It's the Christmas Bonanza.'

Shane laughed. 'They're still doing that?'

Lauren chuckled as he ran his hands through his hair, leaving it standing on end. 'But I'd rather be with you.'

'I'll make it worth your while,' Shane said, his voice low.

'Is that so?' Lauren asked, glancing at him through her lashes. 'Just let me text Vonnie that I can't go.'

Shane took her hand. 'You won't be sorry – I promise.'

6

The spa had been heavenly. Heather was the only person in the relaxation suite, and it was exactly the place she wanted to be. Later she'd be home, at her mother's house, and that irritated her no end. If she'd been concentrating and not distracted by Simon and Paris she would have been able to slip in and out of Lough Caragh without anyone noticing. She cursed her hurried email to Willow, her sister, earlier that month revealing her trip to the luxurious resort, but it was done now and she'd given in to Willow. There was nothing she could do – she'd never let her sister down and this wasn't going to be the first time.

Trying not to think of later, she lay back on a soft day bed, weak as a kitten after a hot stone massage that she hadn't known she'd needed. Her bed was tucked away in the corner of the room, where she could see everyone who came in. She roused herself, and strolled to the drinks station to make a cup of ginger tea. After overindulging at dinner last night, she needed to settle her stomach.

She'd gone the whole hog and had all the courses on

70

offer starting with luscious pan-roasted scallops with Clonakilty black pudding, followed by duck in a rich red cabbage purée. She'd even devoured a whole portion of a delectable praline slice complete with a dollop of cardamom ice cream and seasonal berries. It had been one of the best meals she'd had in a long time, and she'd taken a pic of every course, which would have annoyed Simon. He never understood her need to be constantly on the move, whether that was travelling around the world or hopping from one social media platform to another.

Laughingly, he'd once said that she was peripatetic. It had felt like a compliment back then, but now she wondered if it had been. Lately it felt that her desire to work and travel was her downfall, in his eyes at least. He couldn't understand why she was such a nomad.

The first time he'd said that to her she'd been catapulted back to her childhood, and her parents constantly moving house until just before her eleventh birthday. After moving house seven times already, her parents had decided to put down some roots and had bought the rundown house by the lake. Simon's observation that she was always on the go had shaken her. She wasn't like her parents. No. She was quite the opposite, she reminded herself. Her job took her places but that was simply geography. The rest of her life was stable and managed. Yes, she worked on the road a lot, but she had her tiny but elegant apartment in Redhill to come home to, and it had cost a pretty penny, so work had to be a priority. Not to mention that it was everything her parents' home wasn't.

Set on the grounds of Royal Earlswood Park, her apartment was solid, old, and close enough to Gatwick

Airport for those last-minute travel plans she always seemed to have. It had history, and a weightiness, that Heather loved. Most importantly, her apartment was not a halfway house like her own childhood home had been with people coming and going according to her father's whims and fancies. One of the things that had made her feel so small and insignificant all through her childhood was never knowing who was going to be in the house, how long they'd stay, and for how long Cash, her father, would be enamoured with them. How her mother had put up with his "free love" was beyond her.

Looking back now, she tried to laugh off the names the villagers had for her home, but it wasn't easy, especially when the one that had stuck, Hippie Haven, was as true as it looked. Hippie Haven, home to everyone who ticked Cash's ideal of living free, and plenty of those who didn't but who he wanted to sleep with, had never felt safe or sound. How could it? There were always strangers around, and her mother had never once said enough was enough. In fact, the more people that had come and gone, the more withdrawn and spaced out she'd seemed. Heather shook her head. She didn't want to remember those days, but the memories flooded in regardless.

It hadn't been easy growing up in a tiny village like Lough Caragh. Everyone knew everyone else, and no one was different. They all went to mass every holy day; Friday evening was the day everyone did their big weekly shop, and the men all went for a pint afterwards while the women got the kids to bed. Every spring they got the village ready for the tourists in between shearing the sheep; come summer they'd be flat out with hikers and the like, then the autumn was all about the harvest and bringing the turf in. Winter brought evening classes in the primary school and dances in the town hall.

No one in Lough Caragh could believe anyone would buy Dinny Mac's ramshackle place, so it was no wonder her family was the talk of the village even before they'd arrived. The general consensus was you'd have to be mad – Dinny Mac's was a mess. Then they'd nodded, glad they'd been proven right, when they'd seen Cash and his long dreads and loose trousers flapping around his legs, and Pippa with her long floaty dresses and hair down to her waist.

Cash had clashed with the farmers more than once. He'd argued over how they were ruining the land with their farming methods, and he'd laughed when they told him to live in the real world. Pippa, who believed what Cash had told her about formal education, had begrudgingly sent her two girls to the local primary school but only after a long and loud discussion with the principal at the school gates about how schools were killing children's creativity. It had been mortifying standing there in front of everyone and had marked Heather out as different from day one.

She'd tried to explain all of that to Simon, but he'd grown up in London and was used to seeing and hearing people from all walks of life. He was far more tolerant than she was, she realised, yet he still wanted a 'normal' life and for her to stop gadding around the world as much.

Heather felt her shoulders tighten. She'd wished for a normal life, like the one Niamh or Lauren had. What she'd had was watching her mother grow depressed as her father had, almost in rebellion to the villagers, become practically a caricature of what a hippie was. He was the most selfish man she'd ever come across. She was sure she'd hear all about it when she called in the next day. She'd promised her younger sister, Willow, that she'd stop in home for a few days, but she was already regretting it. Willow had alluded to the fact that something had happened between Pippa and Cash, but had refused to elaborate. All Heather knew was that her mother was set to sell the house and that she needed some help with it. Heather gritted her teeth. She'd find out later what help exactly was needed when she got . . . home.

Leaning against the tea station in the relaxation room, Heather dropped the used teabag into the small bin set aside solely for that purpose. That's exactly how she liked it – a place for everything and everything in its place. Order and consistent work allowed her to live the life she had, and she'd no intentions of changing that. These days she was only responsible for herself, and it felt good. Although, she thought as she slipped her phone from her robe pocket and took a few photos of the room, her job was starting to feel tedious.

At the start, all those years ago, it had been fun, but Covid had grounded her quite literally. She'd been surprised at how quickly she'd adapted to being at home, a homebird was not something she'd ever have called herself. But as the lockdowns had lengthened, she'd found herself enjoying the stillness and steadiness of being in the one place for a prolonged period. The only place she'd half wanted to return to was the lake, yet at the time that hadn't been possible. Now she was home, and the urge to be by the lake was growing. But first, work.

With a deep sigh, and even though phones were strictly forbidden in the spa, she put her best game face on and made a short video about the experience she'd had that morning. Looking back at the video she felt a weight in her stomach. She should be an actress; no one would be able to tell she was growing tired of her job. Then she put her phone into her pocket.

Back on her day bed, with a soft blanket over her knees, Heather sipped her tea and glanced up as the door whooshed open and two women, wrapped in luxurious robes, sauntered in, whispering softly. They glanced in Heather's direction before selecting their own day beds. One looked very like Edel, Heather thought as she lay back, her hands around the warm mug of tea, but surely Edel had moved on? She'd always been full of plans to get going and see the world, just as Niamh had.

Niamh. Heather shifted position, almost spilling her tea over the gorgeous blanket she was beginning to covet. Niamh . . . No one had ever expected Niamh to be the one to get pregnant and elope the summer they'd finished secondary school. Out of the three of them – Heather, Niamh and Lauren – Niamh was the one everyone assumed would succeed. Lauren was the one who was supposed to stay at home, have all the babies and live happily ever after, while no one had any plans for Heather at all.

Shivering, despite the blanket, Heather scrunched her toes up in her hotel slippers. The women next to her were talking softly, but as she'd turned away from them, their voices had risen slightly, and Heather's ears pricked up as their conversation turned towards her old friend Lauren.

'Lauren Dooley? Seriously?' Heather heard one of the women say. She wished she could turn around and place a face to each voice.

'I saw lights on in Rosemary's last night, then I bumped into Yvonne when I was on the way here. She said that Rosemary gave the house to Lauren.'

'Jammy git,' the other woman said. 'I wish someone would leave a house to me.'

Heather tuned out. Lauren Dooley wasn't a part of her life anymore. What did it matter how many houses she inherited? Fumbling with the blanket, Heather got up and left the relaxation room. There was no point lounging around when she had a job to do.

On the way to her suite her stomach tightened and for a moment she considered leaving – calling a car and escaping back to her home in London – but she knew she couldn't. Her mother needed her help, and, as Willow had gently pointed out to her, she'd been literally absent from her family for the best part of fifteen years, and it was time to come home, to see how things were now. As if she knew Heather was thinking of her, Willow's face appeared on Heather's phone as she closed the door to her suite.

Heather answered the FaceTime call and took in her younger sister. Her dark blonde pixie cut still suited her sweet sunny face, Heather thought as she smiled at her sister on the screen. Willow still looked just as she had when she'd left Lough Caragh and was still as warm and kind. She was wearing her veterinary scrubs, which reminded Heather of the animal shelter where she volunteered as often as she could, which wasn't as often as she liked.

Travelling the way she did made it hard for her to commit to anything, but the shelter was always glad to see her. It was hard for them to get staff at the best of times. She made a mental note to call them to see how her favourite animals were doing, especially the little family of goats that had decided she was their best friend. Returning to Willow's chatter, Heather relished listening to her sister's soft voice, then made her promise to come up to see her before she left for London again.

'I'll do my best – you know that,' Willow said. 'But January is always a busy time here – people giving puppies and kittens for Christmas don't think very practically and we're going to be inundated with appointments.'

'Fine, I'll take that excuse,' Heather said. 'But if you don't come down to Lough Caragh then you'll have to come to London.' She grimaced.

'You make it sound like a terrible place.' Willow frowned.

'I'm just tired of it.' Heather blinked in sudden realisation of a truth she hadn't even dared consider before. 'I might need a change of scene.'

'Get back travelling,' Willow suggested. 'Or come down to me, in Kerry.'

'Yeah, that might do the trick,' Heather said. There was a heavy feeling in her stomach that made her feel dizzy. Travelling and London. Once they'd held magic for her; now their sparkle had dimmed and their magic had been revealed to be all smoke and mirrors. She shook her shoulders back.

'Let me show you this suite they've put me up in,' she said. 'It's huge.'

77

Willow's hazel eyes widened as Heather gave her a tour of the suite before curling up on the sofa.

'How're you getting on with Mam?' Willow asked eventually, after all other chat had been caught up on.

'I'm not,' Heather said. 'I haven't been down to her yet. I'm going shortly – I'll be at Pippa's in an hour or so. I could do with your help.'

'I can't help her,' Willow said. 'This is more in your area of expertise. Give it a week – give her a chance to tell you her ideas.'

'Since when have any of Pippa's madcap ideas ever worked?' Heather rolled her eyes. She briefly wondered what on earth Willow was talking about. Pippa was selling the house . . . that wasn't an area Heather had any expertise in whatsoever.

Willow shrugged and tucked a short strand of hair behind her ear. There was a time when Heather had worried that her little sister hated her for leaving her like she did, but she'd never referred to it at all, preferring to keep her up to date with their parents' antics and her own education. Heather was proud of Willow. She'd managed to get into university and was now a veterinary nurse in a hospital in Kerry and loving every minute of it, with absolutely no help at all from her parents.

Willow interrupted her trip down memory lane. 'I've a feeling you're going to be pleasantly surprised. Give her a chance. For me.'

'Fine. For you.'

*

Half an hour later, after she'd finished chatting with Willow, Heather swiftly packed her bags, sad that her stay in the golf resort was over so soon, before slicking back her dark bob into a low bun. She was dressed in an oversized cashmere sweater and leggings. All black, she thought, as she pushed her feet into her trainers. Funereal, even though it was the season to be jolly. Shaking her melancholic moment away, Heather made her way down to reception where the concierge ordered a car for her while simultaneously, and with the least amount of subtlety, questioned her about her stay and what she'd say about the resort.

Ignoring his probing questions, Heather wheeled her luggage to the car, and threw a wave in his direction. She settled back in the warm leather seat and clenched her jaw. What was the driver going to say when she instructed him to stop outside Hippie Haven? Maybe it would be better to ask him to drop her in the village and she could walk back to the house? As the car approached the house Heather's leg muscles tensed. She leaned forward, eyes trained on the front windscreen for the first view of the place.

'You can let me out here,' she said. Her hands gripped tightly together on her lap. She flexed her fingers to try to relax them. 'I'll grab my bag; there's no need for you to get out.'

She was out of the car and opening the boot before the driver could even nod. Closing the boot with a thud, she waved as the car pulled away, then she turned and saw her mother, Pippa, standing in the front doorway.

Pippa was as willowy and straight as she'd always been.

Her strawberry blonde hair hung in a long, loose plait down her back, and her youthful face was free from makeup. Pippa didn't need makeup, Heather thought as she grasped the handle of her case, she was blessed with elegant yet strong features. Pippa's eyes were a vibrant navy-blue, her cheeks delicately pink and her eyebrows bushy and arched. The kind of eyebrows people spent a fortune on in the beautician's.

Her mother didn't move and neither did Heather. She looked at Pippa, who was looking back at her, and was half on and half off the front doorstep as if she couldn't decide on going towards her daughter or not. A slight throbbing in Heather's temples registered and in a flash it was as if she was a teenager again, looking at her mother with frustration and dismay, wishing she'd take some control of anything, wishing she'd behave like a mother should. Not for the first time Heather compared her mother to Niamh's mother. The longing for someone to fuss around her caught her off guard. If she was to wait for her mother to make the first move she'd be waiting forever. Taking a step, Heather pushed open the rusty gate.

'I thought you'd changed your mind,' Pippa finally called as Heather dragged her case over the mossy footpath. She stepped down and walked towards Heather, her hand reaching for the case. Heather stalled, her grip tightening on the handle. Pippa nodded, almost imperceptibly. Her eyes roamed her daughter's face until Heather felt her cheeks flush.

'I'm here,' Heather said, keeping the fact that she had almost changed her mind to herself. Feeling guilty for making the moment awkward, she half-smiled. 'Any chance of a cuppa?'

'Of course.' Pippa turned, her long skirt swishing around her legs and boots. 'I have chamomile, peppermint, oh any herbal tea you'd like. And normal tea too, of course.'

Heather pursed her lips, then followed Pippa into the house, expecting the dark, dreary and grubby hallway she once knew. It was quite the opposite, and it took her a minute to take it all in.

The hallway was painted in a warm white. It used to be purple and filled with junk her parents had picked up from various markets. It was distinctly tidy now, with a proper coat rack and a basket holding hats and scarves by the door. Heather followed Pippa into the kitchen. The kitchen had been given an overhaul too. The once-tangerine walls were now a soft pink, and the kitchen units were white and shining. The counter was a little cluttered, but nothing like it used to be. Heather bit the inside of her cheek to keep in the words she desperately wanted to blurt out. Instead, she slid onto a well-scrubbed pine kitchen chair and leaned her elbows on the matching table. There was no sign of Cash, which was to be expected, but all the same she looked around again then glanced out the window.

'It must have taken a million coats of paint to hide the orange in here,' she said, turning back as Pippa filled an old whistling kettle and set it on the small wood-burning stove at one end of the kitchen.

'You can say it.' Pippa focused her navy-blue eyes on Heather, making her squirm. 'It's very different from what you remember.'

'That's not what I was thinking,' Heather blustered. 'I was just thinking it must've taken a lot of work, and money.' Neither of which her parents were renowned for, but she didn't say that part out loud. 'And yes, I suppose it is very different from what I remember.'

'I got the paint on sale at the farm shop, and Bopper's son, Rory, painted it for me. He's done quite a bit of work around the place.' Pippa set two pottery mugs on the table.

'It's nice,' Heather said. She noticed that the place was spotless. It clashed entirely with the outside of the house. It was hard to believe that Cash had been on board with these changes. Again she wondered where he was.

'I'm only getting started,' Pippa said as she poured tea into their mugs. 'It took me a month to clear out this room, but I feel much lighter now. I didn't realise I was holding on to so much stuff, and that the stuff I was hoarding was imbued with memories. Not all good. It's going to take me a year to get through the entire house.'

'A year to . . . ? Hold on – I thought you were planning on selling up.' Heather frowned.

'I was.' Pippa stirred honey into her tea. 'But I changed my mind.'

'What does Cash think?' Heather scratched the table with her fingernail. She'd long referred to her parents by their first names.

'I couldn't care less what that man thinks.' Pippa put her mug down. 'He upped and headed off one day, with a group of youngsters. A "see ya" and he was gone, out the door like a hare from a trap.'

'Hold up, he's gone? Gone where? When did he go?' Heather frowned.

Pippa tightly folded her arms across her stomach. Her face stilled and she looked every day of her fifty-nine years. Heather's chest tightened as she waited for her mother to speak.

'It was around this time last year,' Pippa started. 'Let me explain.'

'Pippa, a whole year – and you never mentioned it to me.'

'I didn't know how to say that Cash had upped and fecked off with a band of bloody hairy wasters. I barely could get my own head around it.' Pippa sounded hurt.

Heather glanced at Pippa's pale face. She'd been crazy about Cash. She must've been devastated. With a heavy heart Heather twisted her hands in her lap. It was worse that Pippa hadn't told her, that she'd kept that heartbreak to herself for a year. She must've felt that she didn't care about her. Heather's ears grew hot. It wasn't that she didn't care, it was more that she needed not to, yet here she was, sitting before her mother and feeling guilty for not being able to help her. She took a breath and mentally folded her guilt away. Maybe Pippa had had some help. 'What about Willow? Does she know?'

'She says I'm better off without him, that we all are.' Pippa spoke softly. 'Look, I kept thinking he'd be back any minute, but there was no word from him. He stopped answering my texts and wouldn't pick up the phone. I thought he was dead, for a while. I even considered calling the guards and hospitals. Then he called and said he wouldn't be back. He's shacked up with some young one and she's pregnant, and he won't leave her side.'

'What?' Heather felt as if the room was spinning. Her

83

father, her sixty-two-year-old father, was about to have another child with some young one? He'd left her mother, the woman he'd claimed was The Love of His Life, The One, The Only Woman Who Understood Him. She shook her head. He'd always said that it was Pippa's free spirit that kept him feeling loved and grounded.

'I know.' Pippa sighed. 'The worst thing is I can't be mad at him. Our whole lives are built on the concept of freedom and choice.'

'But what about respect and trust?' Heather leaned forward.

'It's *all* about respect and trust,' Pippa said, twisting her fingers. 'That's the point. I just didn't expect it to be such a difficult thing to follow through with. I mean, there have been other instances, but they were fleeting. This time I know in my gut that it's different.'

'I'm sorry.' Heather sat back. Her heart squeezed tight in the face of her mother's clear anguish. 'How are you coping?'

Pippa laughed briefly and waved her hand. 'Can't you tell? I'm clearing it all out. All the stuff he left behind. Six months after he'd gone it occurred to me that all this stuff, all the colours, the bloody camper van in the garden – it all belonged to him. I'd started my business and needed some space to work, and all this was in my way, and it was like an epiphany.'

'I'm struggling here.' Heather shook her head. 'Cash is gone, I'm going to have a half-sibling, and you – you've started a business? I'm so confused, Pippa.'

'I wish you'd call me Mam like you used to.' Pippa picked a piece of fluff from her skirt and flicked it away.

'Anyhow, it's been a crazy year. I blame the lockdowns for the madness, I do. Psychologically, people are scarred, only they don't know it yet.'

'But a *business*? What is it?' Heather asked.

'I make beauty balms and body powders.' Pippa's eyes sparkled. 'Natural cream deodorants . . . soap. I'm hoping to expand the range over the next few years – you know, I could grow a larger selection of herbs and flowers. Maybe even have some animals . . .'

'That's why everything is painted so natural.' Heather looked around again and noticed a desk area built into an alcove beside the wood-burning stove.

'That's my office,' Pippa said. The strain in her voice lifted. 'I've even created my own website.'

'I'm . . . this is brilliant.' Heather beamed at her mother. 'More power to you.'

'I knew you'd understand.' Pippa leaned forward, her eyes shining. 'Running your own business too. This is why I need you here. You're able for change and I need someone to keep me on track.'

Heather's heart sank. The last thing she wanted to do was to be her mother's keeper; she'd done enough of that as a child.

'Pippa, I don't know . . .'

'Look, it'll only be for a while. I promise. You can work from here, can't you?' Pippa twisted the end of her plait with her fingers. 'I could do with some company. It's been a lonely time.'

'How long?' Heather pressed the tips of her fingers into her thighs beneath the table.

'A month, tops,' Pippa said.

Crossing her legs, Heather looked at Pippa closely. There was a spark in her mother that she'd not really seen before. She had lit up when she'd spoken about her business. Heather mulled things over. She could stay. She had contacts she could work with in Ireland, and January was typically quiet. It was the time she spent planning the rest of the year. She didn't normally head out travelling until February when she hit the slopes.

'One month,' Heather said. 'I'll give you one month.'

7

21st December 2005

Lauren rubbed her eyes and sat up in bed. The lurid red digits on her alarm clock said it was six o'clock, but it was so dark that she felt as if it was much earlier. Straining her ears, she listened out for any signs that someone else was awake. The last thing she wanted was for her parents to discover what she was up to. They wouldn't be happy to discover their fifteen-year-old daughter sneaking out to go swim in a lake to celebrate the winter solstice. There hadn't been a summer swim because Grandad Paddy had passed away, and Rosemary hadn't been herself since they'd scattered his ashes around the lake at summer solstice.

Lauren missed her grandfather, and Rosemary had taken so long to smile again, so when she'd suggested this swim Lauren had said yes immediately. Anything to cheer Rosemary up. All the same, it wasn't easy to get out of the house. The last couple of months her mother had taken to getting up at all hours of the night. She said she was too hot, couldn't sleep, and was as moody as hell. Niamh said it was menopause, that her own mother had been just as forgetful as well as anxious, and that she had at least ten years of motherly mayhem ahead of her.

Holding her breath, Lauren kept listening. The house was silent, not a breath stirred. She slipped from her bed and dressed quickly, pulling on her school tracksuit bottoms and hoodie over her swimsuit, then shoving her feet into her school trainers. She reached under her mattress and pulled out her torch. Then, kneeling on her bed, she pulled back the curtains and flashed the light three times across the green towards Shane's house. An answering three flashes made her heart soar. He was up, thank goodness.

The night before he'd been adamant about walking her down to the lake this morning. They'd been watching *Miss Congeniality* and were snuggled up on the sofa in his house, the only place where they ever managed to be alone.

'It's Lough Caragh,' Lauren had told him. 'Nothing ever happens here.'

'That's not the point.' He'd been very serious. 'It could be the one time it happens.'

'You're such a city boy.' She'd snuggled into him. He got a lot of stick from the other lads for being gentle and kind.

'I won't bother ye at all; I just don't want you walking there alone,' he'd said as he walked her back across the green after the film. 'I'll be at the gate when you're ready.'

She'd gone to bed earlier than usual, and now, when she saw how dark it was, was relieved he'd said he'd walk her down. Last year she'd stayed in Niamh's house as they'd been to a basketball match the day before, and there was never any issue with Niamh getting out of her house. Her bedroom was down the opposite end of the house to her parents' bedroom, and her mother used earplugs because, as Niamh said, her father snored like a train. Not only that, but Niamh's bedroom window looked out over a small flat-roof woodshed that was built onto the side of the house. Niamh had been coming and going as she pleased since they'd started in St Ita's.

Lauren had been terrified climbing out the sash window, and then lowering herself over the roof edge to reach down to stand on the garden wall had nearly made her cry. It had been awfully cold that night, she recalled. They'd been frozen even before they'd gotten halfway down to the lake. They'd met up with Heather on the way and she'd brought a bit of brandy, which they'd all had a swig of to try to warm up. But this year it was quite balmy for December, and Heather was staying at Niamh's. She'd meet the girls down by the lake instead of on the lane.

Quietly unlatching the back door, Lauren slipped out and scurried through the dark alley to the front of her house where Shane was waiting. He took her backpack from her as she fell in stride beside him.

'This is important then?' he whispered as they made their way out of the housing estate.

'Yeah,' she whispered back. 'Thanks for walking me down.'

'You're welcome. I don't get it. It's dark. I thought sunrise was the important part.' He took her hand in his.

'It's supposed to be a sunrise swim, but sunrise isn't

until after half eight.' She spoke a little more loudly now they were walking the country road out of the village. 'Since Rosemary is doing it, we said we'd do it too.'

'You'll be freezing.' Shane slowed down as they reached the top of the lane that led to the lake. He pulled her in for a kiss.

'In fairness, it is far nicer in the summer, but don't worry, I'll be grand,' Lauren said as they parted. 'Rosemary is bringing a flask and blankets. We're going to light a small fire too. We'll probably only be in the lake for a few minutes.'

'That's mad. Why bother then?' Shane wrinkled his nose.

'It's symbolic.' Lauren pushed him playfully. 'We're washing away negativity and – stop laughing! You're so bold!'

'I still don't get it, but it doesn't matter. All that matters is that you get it.' Shane playfully pushed her back. 'Go on, I can see a light down there. You're holding them up from freezing their asses off.'

Lauren stuck her tongue out at him. 'See ya later, after school.'

'Love ya.'

'Love you too.'

She hurried down towards the lake, her torch shining on the stony lane and the hedges glossy with holly and ivy. She could hear Niamh giggling and Heather instructing her to be more careful near the fire. Rounding the bend she saw them, their smiling faces glowing in the firelight. Beyond them the lake sparkled as if someone had sprinkled it with glitter. The mountains rose in a dark mass away from it, reaching for the sky where the moon was almost full, but not quite. It was huge and she felt as if she could reach out and touch it. She lowered her eyes and made her way over to the girls who were now looking out at the silvery lake as if hypnotised.

'What's up, BFFs?' She dropped her bag beside the long old tree trunk Heather had dragged closer to the small fire.

Niamh smiled. 'We thought you'd never get here.'

Lauren sat down beside Heather and held her hands to the fire that was slowly taking hold. 'What did you guys get up to last night?'

Heather rolled her eyes good-naturedly. 'This one kept me up till all hours because she was instant messaging some lads. I'll probably fall asleep in exams today.'

'You won't.' Lauren pulled her hat closer around her ears. She grinned at Niamh. 'Who were you messaging?'

'Some lad who goes to Belvedere.' Niamh giggled.

'Belvedere?' Lauren raised her eyebrows. 'Well, that's class!'

'Or so he says.' Heather looked up. 'You can't believe everything people say online.'

'You jealous?' Niamh winked.

'Not a bit.' Heather winked back. 'You can have all the lads, the whole bloody lot of them. They're all good for nothing.'

'Except for Shane.' Lauren nodded adamantly.

'Shane *is* perfect.' Niamh sat down on a rock on the other side of the fire. 'You're lucky you got to him before I did!'

Lauren laughed. Niamh was always going on about how kind Shane was, but Lauren knew he wasn't Niamh's type, even if she did tease her about how lucky she was all the time. Everyone knew how flirty Niamh was, and anyway, she meant well. Not to mention how she always called out the other lads when they teased Shane for being "under Lauren's thumb", telling them that they could learn a thing or two from him on how to treat a lady.

Niamh looked around. 'Rosemary's late.'

'I'm here.' Rosemary, puffing and panting, came across the stones from the direction of her house. Her grey bob swung around her smiling face, now pink from her walk to the lake. Her small frame was engulfed by a heavy-looking rucksack. Lauren jumped up, delighted to see her grandmother. She took the bundle of blankets and towels from her and dropped them behind the log. Niamh helped Rosemary take the rucksack off. 'What's in this? It weighs a tonne.'

'A couple of flasks, and some food for after. It's important to warm up fast.' Rosemary rooted around in the rucksack. 'And these: swimming shoes. I got ye all a pair from Lidl during the summer but forgot to give them to ye. Get them on and we'll get in for a dip before it gets too late and Mucker Madigan is out looking for his donkey and gets an eyeful of our gorgeous derrières.'

*

Heather pulled the tag off her new swimming shoes, a huge grin on her face. Mucker was hitting sixty, as fit as a fiddle with a shock of white hair. He reminded Heather of Donald Sutherland and had been making what Rosemary called 'overtures' towards Rosemary for the last few months. He was a fine man for an old fella, and maybe it would do Rosemary good to have some company. Paddy, her beloved husband, had passed on just over six months ago, but there was no chance of Rosemary giving Mucker the time of day.

'There's nothing wrong with Mucker,' Heather said. 'Sure, he'd take the gloom off a dark day for you.'

'Don't you start with that nonsense,' Rosemary grumbled good-naturedly. She sat down beside Heather to put her swimming shoes on. 'That man isn't worth the hassle. He's too used to getting his own way, and I am too. We'd murder each other.'

'You wouldn't.' Heather nudged Rosemary. Lowering her voice she asked, 'Don't you ever get lonely?'

Rosemary nudged her back. 'I do, but I've got you girls, and I've been helping out down at the parish centre doing teas and coffees for the meetings there.' She gave a small chuckle. 'Mucker's been coming in the last few weeks – he even attended an AA meeting just so he could get a cup of tea off me afterwards. The big thick.'

'No way!' Heather guffawed. 'You have to be nice to him now.'

'I do not.' Rosemary raised her chin. 'He's not called Mucker for no reason. And no, I will not explain that one to you. You're too young. Anyway, I like being by myself, and I can talk to Paddy when I want and that's all I need. I don't need to be changing for some man who's not going to change for me.'

Heather looked away to hide the tears that had come to her eyes. It must be wonderful to have loved and have been loved like that. For all his declarations of love and devotion to Pippa, Heather could count on one hand the number of times she'd heard her father actually say the words *I love you* to Pippa – and she sincerely doubted he'd meant them. It always came after he'd inveigled money out of her or convinced her to sell something that meant something to her.

Heather flexed her feet in her new footwear, then stood up. 'Rosemary, these are great. I can't feel the stones at all.'

'It's nothing.' Rosemary tugged at her swimsuit. 'Right, are ye ready for this? It's going to be cold so take your time going in. I don't want any heart attacks.'

Rosemary walked down to the water's edge. A warm rush of love for Rosemary washed over Heather. It was just like Rosemary to think of them like that.

Heather slipped out of her clothes. It wasn't as cold as she was expecting. Met Éireann had been saying that December had been warmer than normal, and her mother was telling everyone and anyone who'd listen that it was climate change and that it wasn't a good thing. Sometimes Heather wished she'd just shut up for a bit. It was so embarrassing having her go on about climate change all the time. Standing beside Rosemary she looked back at her friends. They didn't know how lucky they were to have normal parents, even if they had fights and arguments, it was better than feeling like you didn't matter at all.

*

Niamh added a small log to the fire. She'd taken a half bag of logs from the woodshed when they'd left her house that morning, knowing that there'd be hardly any decent firewood at the lake. Her mother would notice. She always noticed things like that. She'd everything budgeted, right down to when they'd light the last fire of the spring. She'd drive them all nuts speculating how they were missing logs, had she miscounted, had Niamh not been more careful when bringing in the firewood, was Mucker's son, Lorcan, who ran the fuel yard, tricking them by leaving them short?

Niamh would have to make up some lie about giving some to a traveller or something. Her mother always gave something to the travellers when they called. Niamh poked the fire with a stick and threw on another log. Satisfied that the fire wouldn't burn out while they swam, she got up and ran down to the lakeside.

'I'm so excited for this,' she said, rubbing her arms. 'I feel like this is something the sisters in *Practical Magic* would do!'

'Oh my God! Don't you go all hippie on me!' Heather laughed. 'I've more than I can handle with my parents.'

Niamh quickly plaited her blonde ponytail and twisted it into a knot feeling slightly chastised. Heather's family were a little weird she conceded as she hesitantly walked into the water, but at the same time it was their weirdness that meant Heather could do what she wanted – she could be whoever she wanted to be without anyone saying it wasn't good enough and that she should try living in the real world because normal people did normal things and traditions existed for a reason.

Only the night before her father had argued with her that it was natural for a woman to be at home surrounded by children. It was alright for his Mary to run the B&B,

he'd said, because she could do it from home, and it wasn't as bad as minding some other woman's children as some of the other women in the village did. At the end of the day, it was the man's role to provide for his family and Niamh had better choose the right kind of man when the time came to settle down – and the right place to start was at university. She'd find a young man with the right attitude in the right area of studies, he'd said: law, medicine, or even business, but definitely not the arts. Niamh looked up at the moon. She was so tired of having to do all the right things, which was why she'd started doing some wrong things, one of which was swimming in a chilly lake on a pagan festival.

And it was the right place to be, Niamh thought as the cold water reached her knees. She breathed out and stepped further into the water. She held her breath and shivered. At least her feet were okay, thanks to Rosemary. Once out in the lake, the water lapping over her shoulders, she began to relax. Rosemary was further out, with Heather by her side. They were both strong swimmers and looked as if they were thoroughly enjoying themselves. Lauren swam noisily up to her.

'It's cold,' she puffed. A cloud of mist formed in front of her. 'You look happy though.'

'I am happy!' Niamh laughed. 'I love this. I'm freezing my ass off and my mother would have me exorcised if she knew what I was doing but I don't care!'

'I hear ya,' Lauren said. 'My mother would kill me if she knew I was in the lake, at any time of the year.'

'Honestly, mothers!' Niamh said. 'Can I talk to you about something?'

'Of course,' Lauren's brows furrowed. 'Is everything all right?'

'Yeah, it's just – well . . . Is Heather all right? We had a laugh last night, but she was a bit quiet.'

'Well, she's going through a rough time right now,' Lauren said.

'A rough time?' Niamh said, feeling a little confused. Why hadn't Heather said something to her?

'It's her dad,' Lauren said quietly. 'He's seeing one of the women who's staying in the caravan beside her house.'

'Sure, but isn't he always dipping his wick in something? That's not news.'

Lauren lowered her voice. 'How would you feel if your dad was shagging someone else and everyone knew about it?'

'I'd hate it. You're right – I'm sorry. I just wish she'd talk to me about it.' Niamh glanced sadly at Heather.

'She barely talks to me about these things,' Lauren said. 'So don't feel bad. I think she relies on you for fun and doesn't want to change that.'

'Well, if it's fun she's after . . .' Niamh splashed Lauren. 'It's fun she shall have!'

'Feck off!' Lauren swam away with a huge splash.

Niamh watched her flounder out to where the other two were swimming before whooping and following her. She swam confidently up to the group and threw her arms around Heather. Rosemary smiled warmly.

'I don't know about you, but I'm freezing,' Rosemary said. 'I'm ready to set my intentions and get a hot cup of tea into me before I get hypothermia!'

Rosemary turned to the expanse of the lake and

whispered something, then she held her nose and went under the water. Popping back up she gasped and laughed.

'That's me done. Your turn,' she said to Heather.

*

Heather sucked in her bottom lip for a moment.

This is when it all changes, she thought, thinking of how her mother had changed once she'd realised Cash had shacked up with the young one in the camper van. She could see her mother's sadness in everything she did these days. In how she had at first tried to be better than Cash's newest love interest right down to yesterday when she'd stayed in bed all day, not even bothering to take Willow to school. Her cheeks flamed as she remembered overhearing someone in Billy's newsagents talking about Cash, laughing at how he got away with his infidelity over and over. With gritted teeth she set her intention. 'This is when I change my life. My family won't hold me back – I'm not like them and everyone will soon see that. I'm not a freak and I'm not ever going to give anyone power over me. From now on I do everything for me.'

Although it felt a little selfish, she held her breath and dipped down into the water. The cold washed over her head. When she emerged, she felt calm and in control.

*

'Well,' Niamh said aloud. 'I intend on having the best year of my life: I'm going to attract everything good and everyone gorgeous to me and party like it's 1999!'

98

Heather laughed through chattering teeth. 'I think you need to be more specific.'

'Okay, well then, Rory Quinlan is going to fall for me,' Niamh said. She called out over the lake. 'And he's going to have competition because he won't be the only one. I'll be turning them down in droves.'

Niamh dunked herself in the lake, but instead of thinking of Rory Quinlan and his flashing eyes, found herself wishing that Heather would be okay. With a warm heart Niamh also wished that she'd be able to be a better friend to Heather. Surfacing, she reached for Heather and squeezed her shoulder.

*

Lauren's eyes shone as she gazed across the lake. 'I'm going to pass all my exams and get a job this summer, and my parents will allow me to go on holiday with Shane and his family.' Holding her nose, she tightly screwed up her eyes and dipped down into the water just enough to say she was submerged. Spluttering, she came back to the top and wiped her face.

'Okay, intention is done and I'm frozen. Can we get out now?'

*

Back on the shore, wrapped warmly in towels and blankets, their feet close to the fire, the girls sipped on the hot chocolate Rosemary had brought them. She watched them fondly as they teased each other, and wondered what she would be doing without the three girls in her life. They'd brought her such joy and kept her company more than they realised. She missed Paddy with every fibre of her being. It was as if all her *joie de vivre* had gone with him. She knew it sounded mad but right up until the moment he'd passed she'd felt like a teenager, like anything was possible.

This year had been horrendous, and lonely. It wasn't easy being a widow so young. She'd felt every minute of her fifty-nine years the day he'd passed away. Oh, how she hated that phrase. Passed away. It was the most appalling way to describe how he'd left her bereft and alone, that she was now a shell of the person she'd once been, that he only now existed in her memory and she'd never again get to see him do all those lovely little things – like the way he made tea using loose leaves and how he'd always say it was the best tea she'd ever tasted. These days she just used teabags, and he'd hate that.

He'd been a part of her life for as long as she could remember. Their mothers had been friends and her earliest memory was of him coming up the lane with a jam jar of frog spawn and soaked from head to toe, his gappy smile huge and his blond hair plastered to his head. His mother, an almighty patient woman, had just shaken her head at her child's sopping clothes and whooshed him into the back kitchen of her house where she'd stripped him down completely. Rosemary remembered seeing his pale backside flash by as he'd streaked up the stairs with a flaming red face.

Drawn back to the girls chattering about what was going on in the village, she looked at each bright, open face. Heather, with her watchful eyes and her grit and determination; she'd go places. Rosemary prayed that she'd open her heart along the way – she was so black and white about things in a world that was made of many colours.

Niamh, now that little minx had a heart of gold beneath her blasé exterior and would do anything for you. It was a shame, young Niamh was as clever as a Russian chess master, but sometimes she was afraid of what the future would bring. Niamh had confided in her that all her father seemed interested in was when she'd find a 'solid young man and settle down a little' when all she wanted to do was to leave Lough Caragh and take off into the world, but she didn't know how she'd get away. Rosemary sent up a little solstice wish that Niamh would be all right.

As for Lauren – Rosemary knew she shouldn't have any favourites, but of all her grandchildren Lauren was certainly the one she preferred. She reminded her of what it was like to be young and in love, and there was absolutely no doubt that she would marry Shane. They were the most settled and happy young couple Rosemary had ever seen, and they seemed unfazed whenever someone said that their youth and lack of life experience was against them. Rosemary knew they'd be just fine. They were as steady as she and Paddy had been, and there was not a thing wrong with that as far as she was concerned.

The girls were talking about Mucker now, and how he'd tried to convince the Tidy Town Committee that Roundup was the perfect way to control the weeds that sprang up on the bridge into town, but he'd been challenged by Pippa and now there was a bit of a commotion between those who agreed with Mucker and those who could see Pippa's point of view. Laughing, Rosemary was glad she had the girls to keep her up to date with what was going on. They didn't know how lucky they were to have each other the way they did.

It had been a long time since Rosemary had been a girl, down here swimming with her friends. Maura had moved to New Zealand after her son had gone over and started a life and family there. Frances had passed away from cancer when she was only twenty-seven. Rosemary sipped her drink. It had been horrible seeing her suffer. She made sure to check her breasts regularly; in fact, she ought to teach the girls how to check theirs. Stella, the one friend she'd thought would have had the happiest life of all, had left after a horrible marriage breakdown. She was always asking Rosemary to visit her in her new apartment in Dublin. Maybe this year she would. She missed her friend.

'Did you know that Lough Caragh means the lake of beloved friendship?' Rosemary said suddenly. 'I used to come here with my friends all the time.'

'Lake of beloved friendship,' Lauren said slowly. 'That's really nice.'

'It is,' Rosemary said. 'You three are very lucky to have each other. Always remember that.'

8

1st January 2024

Groaning, Niamh rolled over and stretched out her arm. She picked up her phone and felt the beginnings of a headache at the backs of her eyes. Payback for drinking three cocktails and half a bottle of Prosecco last night. She wasn't eighteen anymore; that was for sure. In a glorious fit of romance Evan had booked a New Year's dinner at The Coach House, completely taking her by surprise.

How times change, she'd thought last night as she'd excitedly slipped into her LBD. These days it was a turn-on that he'd booked not only dinner but the babysitter too, and she'd been delighted. A frisson of joy had run down her back as she'd slipped into her heels and slicked on some red lipstick, just because she knew he'd like it. She smiled thinking of how he'd made the effort for her too. He'd bought new jeans, which he'd modelled for her, making her laugh as he'd pranced around the bedroom, before pulling on the shirt she loved best. He wasn't as

103

trim as he'd been when they'd first met, but after three kids neither was she. His sandy hair had lightened over the years, and was as abundant as ever. His hazel-green eyes had sparked at her as she'd twirled for him, almost falling over in her heels.

In the end it had been a lovely night. The food had been great and Evan, in his roundabout way, had said sorry for being so busy with training and work. Then he'd told her she was beautiful and that was it. Niamh groaned again. She'd fallen for his charm, as always, and they'd ended up staying in the lounge until three, much to her babysitter's delight as Evan had drunkenly handed her a hundred euro before she left.

Blinking rapidly, she stared at the screen. It was after midday, and the bed beside her was empty. The house was silent too.

Sitting up she pushed her hair back out of her face. He'd mentioned taking the girls to his parents' house today, and she was grateful he'd left her asleep. It was rare to have such a lie-in. Flopping back onto the hot pillow, she sighed. It was lovely to have the whole bed to herself and the house quiet. She shifted onto her side, then rolled onto her back again. Staring up at the ceiling she sucked in a deep lungful of stale air. Her bones ached. She needed to get up.

She flung back the duvet and hauled herself out of the bed remembering Evan pinching her bum as they'd walked into the lounge from the restaurant last night. She'd felt like a million dollars. She'd even spied Rory Quinlan at the bar and had bought him a drink and extracted an easy promise from him that he'd call over today to discuss her renovation plans. They'd known each other since forever but still, Evan hadn't been impressed.

'For God's sake, Niamh, let the man alone, will ya.' He'd taken his pint and moved away as Niamh had continued to chatter. She'd said goodnight to Rory and left him alone and joined her husband by the fireplace where a log fire blazed.

'Sorry.' She'd kissed his cheek. 'I'm just so excited.'

'We haven't even made a final decision,' Evan had said. 'You're making all these B&B plans and I'm still not sure about it.'

'I didn't mean to.' She'd dropped her hand from his arm. 'I was just asking for some advice, not going ahead . . .'

'Right,' Evan had said.

Niamh had swallowed. Looking down at her toes, in their new glittery heels, the ones Evan had said were sexy when she'd shown them to him on her phone, she'd felt a weight descend.

Evan's eyes had flashed in Rory's direction.

Niamh had reddened. He'd never been a fan of Rory.

Evan had breathed out then and taken her hand. 'Listen, let's not talk about it tonight. I just want to enjoy a night out with *my* beautiful wife.'

Niamh had nodded, half glad of the change of subject, but also slightly put out. They never had a moment to talk properly about her plans, and it was starting to get to her. It was as if he didn't want her to take it on at all. Rory's deep laugh had resounded across the room. A welcome intrusion to her thoughts on why Evan was evading all conversation surrounding the B&B renovations. When Evan wasn't looking, she'd turned to look at Rory. His head had tilted back revealing pale skin and the lightest stubble on his throat. He ran a tanned hand through his dark hair, and she'd sucked in her bottom lip. It was a shame, but she'd better tell him not to bother calling. Although she'd been raging inside; everyone knew Rory's work was top class, and he was booked well in advance. She'd been hoping to have the building work underway by summer. Now it wouldn't happen at all most likely.

'I'll cancel Rory so,' she'd said, turning back to her husband. 'But, Ev, promise me we will at least talk properly about it all.'

Evan had smiled. His smile always made her weak, and he knew it. He'd reached around her and pulled her close to him where they stood.

'Promise,' he'd said with a growl. 'Just not tonight.'

Leaning against him, Niamh ran her hand up his chest. He may have changed a little in the fourteen years they'd been married, but at that moment she had been reminded of how he'd managed to charm her in the first place all those years ago. It was the way he'd looked at her that had gotten her pregnant, and he was looking at her just like that. She'd blushed thinking of that time, then she'd gently pushed him away. Another baby was definitely not on the cards.

Now, in her bedroom, she opened the curtains and squinted at the wintry sunshine. Frost was on the ground in the shadows; there were no clouds and the sky was bright blue. The clanging chimes of the doorbell made her wince. Catching sight of herself in the mirror she pulled on her dressing gown and prayed it wasn't anyone important before hurrying downstairs to open the door.

Rory Quinlan, freshly shaven, smelling like a real-life Armani advertisement and looking like he'd been in bed at nine last night, not out singing in the pub when she'd left, stood on the front step. Niamh groaned inwardly.

'Rory!' Niamh pulled her dressing gown tightly around her neck. 'What are you doing here?'

'You made me promise to turn up – remember?' Rory leaned against the doorframe and laughed that deep laugh she remembered from the night before. He'd had the same magnetic charisma when they were teenagers, she recalled. Somehow, she felt she'd lost hers.

'I didn't tell you *not* to come.' Niamh rubbed her hands over her face, feeling gritty mascara on her fingertips. Slowly she lowered her hands. 'Evan asked me to cancel you today but . . .'

Rory raised his eyebrows. He looked down and nodded before raising his eyes to hers. 'Is Evan around?'

'No, he's taken the kids to see his parents.' Niamh swallowed.

'I can keep a secret if you can.' Rory raised an eyebrow.

Niamh's mouth dropped open. She drew back and opened the front door wide, scrunching up her toes against the chill that washed in around her feet. Should she just go ahead and get some advice without Evan knowing? Where was the harm? Evan might talk about making plans, but he was always slow to take up any plans they'd ever tried to implement. They'd still be in the planning stage next Christmas if she didn't take the reins. He'd be annoyed with her, but when the whole thing was done, he'd probably say she was right. And of all the builders in the county, everyone knew Rory was the best. She looked at him. He was smiling at her as if they shared a secret. Niamh felt a pang in her stomach.

Evan *really* didn't like Rory. It stemmed from when they were younger and there'd been a bit of a spark between her and Rory. *Nothing had ever happened between them.* She suddenly wondered what would've happened if it had, then swiftly shook herself. *Nothing had happened. That was that, so Evan really didn't have anything to worry about.* And this whole B&B revival wasn't about Rory and her. It was about her gaining some independence and feeling like she was contributing to her family. Surely that meant more to Evan than some petty rivalry over fifteen years ago. Surely he'd understand that much at least. Her whole body seemed to beat loudly as she stepped back and opened the door wider.

'Okay, come in.' She watched as Rory strode in. He was taller than Evan, by maybe five inches, and broader. He stood in her hallway and looked around, taking in the tall ceiling and the plasterwork.

'Gorgeous,' he said appreciatively.

'Sorry, what?' Niamh's hand shot to her hair.

'The coving – it's real plaster work, handmade on site I'd say. It's gorgeous.'

'Oh. Well, the kitchen is through there, if you want to make yourself a cuppa. I'm going to run upstairs and get something warm on.'

He nodded and she watched him stride into the kitchen, praying that she'd moved the pile of laundry from the chair, the pile with her knickers on the very top, the big comfy ones that she'd taken to wearing lately and very far removed from the wispy ones that had resulted in her

108

last pregnancy. The last thing she needed was Rory Quinlan thinking she wore those kinds of knickers.

Back upstairs she tore her pyjamas off and pulled on her jeans, her Uggs and a decent jumper, squirted some perfume on and peered in the mirror. Panda eyes, but not too bad; she licked her fingertips and ran them beneath her eyes to take away the worst of her smudged makeup. At least it looked as if she'd kind of intentionally done it that way. Ruffling her hair, she hurried back downstairs.

Just once did she consider what Evan might say if he came home. It was an honest mistake, forgetting to tell Rory not to come over. It hadn't helped that Evan had plied her with the third passion-fruit martini, and she'd been only too delighted to take it from him.

When Niamh returned, Rory was in the kitchen, looking as if he belonged there. He'd made a pot of coffee. The toaster popped as she walked in.

'I guessed you might need it,' he said as he slid a plate of toast across the island unit towards her. Butter, marmalade and a clean knife were already out waiting for her. He poured two mugs of coffee as she sat down.

'You said something about converting the stables into guesthouses?' Rory looked warmly at her. Niamh found she was smiling at him, until she realised he was waiting for an answer. She quickly pulled a piece of paper out from under a pile of kids' books and spread it before him.

'Behold my rudimentary plans,' she said. 'These were already converted but they're in bad condition. I think they need gutting. These ones here – they're currently old stables.'

'Are you thinking of self-catering apartments?' Rory turned the sketch around to face him.

'I'm not sure,' Niamh said. 'That's why I wanted to talk to you. Why don't we go outside and take a look?'

Outside, in the fresh air, Niamh felt her headache disappear. Rory was enthusiastic about the spaces she showed him, which lifted her spirits.

'I can fit you in sometime in February . . .' He banged on walls, then pulled down some old plasterboard. 'Could have you sorted with three guest rooms by the summer. I've a big job starting at the end of June, but I can come back in September to do the rest.'

'You're saying all the right things,' Niamh said. She squinted at him. 'Is this the part where we talk about money?'

Rory nodded. 'Money. Look, I'll take that sketch you made, and if you've any other ideas you could send them on to me and I'll work on a quote for you.'

'I have a Pinterest board,' Niamh said. She scrunched up her nose. 'You probably think that's stupid – I see loads of tradesmen saying they hate Pinterest.'

'No, it's a great place for inspiration,' Rory said. 'The only advice I'll give you is to try to temper your expectations, be realistic about the space and budget you have. That way everyone will be happy at the end of the day.'

Niamh nodded. She shivered as a gust of wind sent a pile of beech leaves scuttling by them.

'You should go inside, where it's warm, to . . . recuperate,' Rory said, his eyes twinkling.

'The cheek of you – you were still there when I left.' Niamh wrapped her arms around her body. 'How come you're so fresh?'

110

'Non-alcoholic all the way,' he said. 'Rolling on seven years now.'

'I didn't know . . .' Niamh said.

'It was the best decision I've ever made. I was afraid I'd go down the same route as my old man, and in all honesty, I very nearly was.'

'You must think I'm a lush.' Niamh glanced at him.

'No, I don't.' Rory put his hands in his pockets. 'You were having fun, but you knew what you were doing. You always did.'

A warm feeling washed over Niamh. He'd been keeping an eye on her all night. She felt a buzz inside and had to work not to smile too widely.

'I'll let you go back inside. Snuggle down by the fire or something.' Rory smiled, the corners of his eyes creasing as he did.

'Sure,' Niamh said. 'And Rory, thanks.'

'No worries. I'll give you a call soon – and you can send me any pins you like on Pinterest – you'll find me under the company name.' He strode around the side of the house.

Niamh hurried inside and made her way straight through the kitchen to the living room, which for once was tidy. *God bless the babysitter.* She watched Rory climb into his van and drive away, her heart pounding. The clock on the mantel ticked loudly as she watched his van turn out of the drive. Was she imagining it, or had he been a little more friendly than usual? She'd have to be careful he didn't get the wrong impression, but it had been fun chatting with him. It was nice to be taken seriously and for her vision to be possible instead of impossible.

She'd hold off talking to Evan about it until after Rory gave in his quotation, she thought as she wandered around the room. She'd found that the best way to get Evan to agree to anything was to present the idea as completely as possible, that way he was less inclined to say no.

Back in the kitchen she rummaged in the cupboards looking for a sweet treat, but all she unearthed was a Christmas pudding dated 2016, which she promptly dumped in the bin. It was probably a good thing there was nothing nice in the press. Sugar would just make her hangover feel worse. A walk by the lake would help the fogginess that still remained in her head; maybe she'd go for a swim. As Rosemary said, the lake always made you feel better. She ran upstairs to slip into her swimsuit, then changed into some socks and trainers, before she grabbed her walking coat and her hat.

Striding down the driveway she inhaled deeply, drawing the sharp cold air into her lungs. The wind whipped her hair where it poked from beneath her hat, but she knew that it would be calmer by the lake. It always was. With a spring in her step she turned towards the road and the laneway to the lake.

9

'You're sure you're okay with me staying on here a little longer?' Lauren leaned in the window of Shane's van. He reached down and planted a kiss on her forehead.

'Yeah,' he said softly. 'You need to be here; I can see that. Just be safe, and don't forget to lock up at night.'

She rolled her eyes jokingly at him. It was a running joke between them that she always left the house unlocked just because he was hypervigilant about locking up. As she watched Shane drive away her heart thumped hard in her chest. He paused at the crossroads and flashed the hazard lights three times, their code for *I love you*. She kept waving until he drove on, knowing that he'd be looking at her in the rear-view mirror, and remembered the first time they met.

It had been the short Indian summer in September 2002, just after she'd turned twelve. She'd leaned out of her bedroom window to watch the family move in across the green, marvelling at their gorgeous leather sofa and their two dogs. Before that she'd been doing homework and half listening to the radio when the clattering had pulled her away from her history project. She'd probably have gotten an A in her project if Shane hadn't come out of the house, flicking his hair back from his face, all lanky and full of laughter.

Lauren's eyes had widened as she'd watched him throw a ball for the dogs, laughing as they'd tumbled over each other in their haste to get to the ball first. The dogs were adorable, but it was Shane's wide easy smile that had made her heart pound. Shaking her head she'd returned to her history project, rapidly scribbling down facts and dates about Queen Elizabeth and the Plantations while her true attention was laser-focused on her new neighbour. Fifteen minutes later, she slammed shut her hastily finished project and galloped downstairs and out the front door, only to come to a halt at the garden wall.

Their houses were opposite each other, separated by a grassy area where the kids played all summer long – football during the World Cup, tennis when Wimbledon was on, and relay racing when the Olympics came around. After seven o'clock it was generally taken over by the older kids. Teenagers would lounge on the benches that the committee had put in, and chat and mess around until someone called them home.

That day everyone was out. Mandy Delaney, in her fake Juicy Couture tracksuit she'd gotten down the market, had been leaning on the wall, pushing the dogs away while giggling at everything the new boy said. Lauren's lips had curled, but she'd stood in her garden and just watched as the new boy talked to Mandy.

'They seem like a nice family,' her mother had called

from behind her. 'I was talking to them earlier. They've moved from Kildare and Shane, their son, will be starting in your school shortly. Why don't you go over and say hello? Welcome them to the neighbourhood.'

Lauren had shaken her head and gone to the shop to get sausages for tea, wishing with every step that Mandy bloody Delaney would get knocked over by the dogs and fall into a pile of dog poo.

When she'd come back from the shop Mandy was gone, and for a moment Lauren had almost believed her wish had come true. But Mandy was holding court down the far end of the green, sitting on the back of a bench, loudly demanding attention from the group of girls who hung around her. Ducking her head, Lauren had hurried into her house. After depositing the sausages in the fridge, she took an ice lolly and dashed back outside hoping the new boy would reappear.

Mandy and her cohorts had been making their way back up the green, so Lauren had swiftly turned left and hurried through the alley that divided the terrace of houses towards the back of the buildings where she'd promptly run into the new boy. Her ice lolly had tumbled to the ground, the red and orange ice rolling in the dirt for a minute before one of the dogs began slurping it.

'I'm sorry!' He'd run his hands through his strawberry blond hair. 'I didn't mean . . . I didn't see you. I was chasing Beryl . . .'

Lauren had tried to ignore how hard her heart had beat, and how blue his eyes were and how earnest he was.

'It's okay,' she'd said. 'It's fine.'

'My dad always says that when a woman says it's fine,

115

it's definitely not fine.' Shane had smiled. 'I'm Shane. Let me buy you a new one?'

Lauren had nodded and they'd walked to the shop at the end of the road and once she'd found her tongue had talked the ears off of him.

That evening they'd both had to be called in home, and later, as she'd closed her bedroom curtains she caught sight of him in his room too – the same room as hers – the boxroom above the porch. He'd waved and she'd waved back. After that no one else ever came between them. Her mother often said that she knew that night that they'd marry. Never before had she had to call Lauren inside, never before had she seen such light in her daughter's eyes, she'd told everyone on their wedding day.

'They were made for each other,' Debbie had said to anyone who'd listen. 'It's like something from a movie, watching them two. They do my heart good.'

Now, as Shane drove away from Mill House, Lauren sighed. They might well be made for each other, and even though they were both trying hard to hold things together, they were drifting apart, like two leaves floating downstream but getting caught in different currents. They were going in the same direction, only one seemed to be forced towards the shore while the other was being carried far away. It was unsettling and made her feel sick most of the time, like she was a fraud. If only she could talk to him like she used to, tell him everything in her heart and soul, share the heartache she carried that their dreams had been dashed, and her fear that it was all her fault.

But she couldn't because maybe he already thought them, and maybe talking about them would make it worse and he'd leave. She was doing her best not to let him see she was thinking about them breaking up, but it was getting harder and harder. She scratched her hand and frowned. Living without him would be the worst thing of all. She couldn't live without him. She didn't know how to.

Going back into Mill House she decided she'd make a start clearing out the top floor and work downwards. She'd work solidly for the day, and make sure to get the first room done by nightfall. Then she might know what to do with the house. She closed the door, locked it thinking of Shane, and then put one foot on the first step of the stairs. She paused. Lord knows what she'd unearth up on the top floor. Rosemary had stored everything up there before she'd decided to declutter her life. Lauren tapped her fingers on the newel post. Rosemary's way of decluttering her life had been to go start a new one, which was fine and all, but it wasn't really decluttering, was it? It was more like storing up memories, and some memories were best left alone.

Lauren lingered on the step. She'd practically lived with Rosemary at one point, especially the summer she'd finished school, the summer she, Heather and Niamh had fought and never spoken again. Lauren tightened her grip on the newel post. Sometimes she really missed them – Heather and Niamh – and other times, times when she felt like a failure, she still hated them.

Letting go of the newel post Lauren took two steps further up the stairs, determined to get through the mess on the third floor, but all she could think about was what Rosemary would have done if she were here.

Rosemary would've told her to cop on to herself; there was plenty of time to sort out the upstairs. There were a million things Rosemary would've said to her, but the one phrase that came to her was that she needed to go outside.

*

'Get out, go on,' Rosemary had said to her once. It had been a damp and miserable Saturday and the misty rain had kept everyone indoors. Lauren was sixteen and moody. Shane had gone away with his family for the Halloween break and Lauren had done nothing but mope around. 'You're too young to be this maudlin. Get down to the lake, and don't come back here until that foul humour has been taken away by the fairies.'

Lauren had gone out into the rain; she'd no choice. Rosemary had pressed an umbrella and her waxed jacket into her hands and opened the back door for her.

'Go.' Rosemary had firmly shut the door behind her.

Lauren had stood there sulking for a few minutes, but the day had been too cold for that, so she'd shucked on the jacket, put up the umbrella and stalked down the wet garden as best she could without slipping. Once by the lake her mood had picked up, slightly. She'd skimmed stones for a while, then had wandered up the right side of the lake where most people didn't bother rambling. After a while she'd turned back and walked straight down the road to drag Heather out, and together they'd gone to call into Niamh's house.

Mrs Kennedy had made them come inside. Lauren could

still remember her shocked voice when she opened the door to find herself and Heather looking like bedraggled rats.

'Girls, what on earth are you doing out in this damp weather? You'll catch pneumonia. Come in, this instant. Go in beside the range. I'll get towels.' Mrs Kennedy had marched away, all business and lectures. Heather had blushed and wiped her wet face with her hands, while Lauren had rolled her eyes. Niamh's mam was worse than her own mam was. Everything had to be just so.

'She's such a pain,' she'd muttered to Heather as they steamed gently by the Aga. 'When I have kids, I'm not going all sergeant major on them.'

Heather had frowned. 'Mrs K isn't the worst, you know. At least she cares.'

'Cares?' Lauren had blustered. 'She's super controlling.'

'I don't know,' Heather had said. 'I like her. I think she's nice.'

Niamh had swanned in then, looking like Jessica Simpson in a silky cami, low-rise flared jeans and freshly highlighted hair. Heather's mouth had dropped open, while Lauren had looked her up and down.

'Jack is going to love this look,' Lauren had drawled.

'Jack who?' Niamh had flicked her hair over her shoulder. 'This is all for me . . . and whoever else appreciates it.'

'What's happened with Jack?' Heather had asked.

'He's boring,' Niamh had said. 'I've set my sights higher. This village can't hold me back. I want to see the bright lights of New York, eat baguettes in Paris, and I can't do either of those things with Farmer Jack moaning about lambing or the weather, can I? Not to mention all farmers only want a childbearing wife, and I'm not that kind of woman. Children just tie you down.'

'It's not the worst thing to want a family and a home,' Lauren had said.

'It's not *my* thing,' Niamh had joked. 'It's *your* thing. We all *know* that.'

*

Lauren remembered feeling shame wash over her. Although Niamh hadn't outright said anything bad about her desire to have a family, it had still felt like a dig. There was nothing wrong with wanting a family. She and Shane had spoken about it privately, knowing that other people thought they were too young to be capable of making plans for a shared future. It irritated her that everyone thought they didn't know what they wanted, when they did: they wanted each other, a nice, warm home, four kids, two dogs and a goldfish called Cleo. Shane wanted to be an electrician.

'Everyone needs an electrician,' he'd said once. 'People are nervous of messing around with electricity – and I'll be able to get nixers too. We'll have enough money, and you can stay home with the kids.'

She'd been so happy that night. Looking back now, she felt the heat of shame rise again, but this time it was tinged with anger. The cheek of Niamh that day. Well, she'd gotten her comeuppance when she got pregnant at eighteen. Then married. She'd been well and truly grounded, although, Lauren conceded, Niamh had still managed to have it all: three gorgeous daughters, a husband with a state job and who was involved with the community. She was living the dream.

Now, standing on the stairs, Lauren gritted her teeth until her jaw ached. She needed to get out, away from memories and loss. Twirling around she jumped down the two steps she'd taken. In the utility room she found Rosemary's crumpled waxed jacket and pulled it on and slammed the back door behind her. The air was sharp and the sky bright blue, making her squint as she powered down the garden towards the lake. She seemed to end up here a lot lately, she thought as she clambered over the stile, her hands cold on the frosty wood, but it felt like the right place to be.

Down by the lake she wrapped her arms around her body and stood staring out across the water. Somewhere nearby the chirp of a robin made her look up, and every now and then the plop of a fish jumping sent ripples towards the shore. Everything seemed so clear and calm. Stones crunching behind her made her turn around. Her breath caught in her throat as she did. There was no mistaking who it was. Despite her elegant outfit and her precisely cut hair, Heather was still Heather. She stood at the edge of the beach, hands deep in the pockets of her dark wool coat, her eyebrows drawn together reminiscent of how she'd looked on their first day at secondary school. Lauren felt the same flitters of anxiety in her stomach as she had back then, and although her head told her to turn away, her heart told her to say something.

'Hi,' Lauren said, her voice husky from the cold. She scratched her arm and tried a small smile.

'Hey.' Heather nodded at her. 'I wasn't expecting to . . . I didn't think anyone would be here.'

'Yeah,' Lauren said.

Heather looked down at her feet.

'You look great,' Lauren said while pulling her scarf tighter around her neck.

Heather looked up. 'Thank you. You look good too.'

'It's been a long time . . .' Lauren's stomach turned over.

'Fifteen years I think.' Heather frowned again.

'Looks like you've done a lot in that time,' Lauren said. 'I've seen your Instagram and the kids in school tell me all about your TikToks – they all want to *Holiday Like Heather*.'

'You're a teacher?' Heather's eyebrows shot up. 'I didn't see that coming.'

'Why not?' Lauren sniffed. She had been sure Heather would've been a little friendlier.

'I thought you were planning on a different kind of life.' Heather's face turned red.

Lauren bit the inside of her cheek to stop from blurting everything out.

'My life hasn't gone quite to plan, like yours has,' she said. 'Not everyone gets what they want.'

'Laure, I didn't . . .' Heather raised her hands. 'Listen, I'm sorry. For whatever it is that has upset you, it wasn't my intention.'

Lauren swallowed. Hearing Heather call her Laure just like she used to shook her. It was as if they were back to normal, which they weren't, but it felt nice to hear her say it.

'No, I'm sorry. I didn't mean to snap at you.' She

122

shivered as a breeze blew her slightly forward. 'God, it's colder out than I thought.'

'It's bloody freezing,' Heather said. She blew out some air and it misted in front of her.

'It's a long way from Mauritius.' Lauren hazarded a smile. Heather returned it.

'Oh, now that was a holiday like no other.'

Lauren felt her shoulders relax. Heather's eyebrows lightened.

'Would you like a cup of tea?' Lauren said before she could stop herself.

Heather nodded. 'I would. I'd kill for a cup. Or coffee if you have it.'

'Come on, I'll make you the best coffee you've ever tasted.' Lauren led the way back to Mill House.

They turned away, neither one noticing Niamh watching them from the end of the lane, her face pale and stricken. She watched as they walked away and didn't move until they were gone.

10

Heather stood in the dining room. She could hear Lauren pottering in the kitchen. The soft thud of a cupboard door, the clang of glassware knocking together, and a running tap convinced her that Lauren was in her element. Heather chewed her lip. Why had she agreed to come for a cup of coffee? It certainly was interesting to see what kind of a person Lauren was now. She seemed to be the same, but no one was the same after fifteen years. Clearing her throat, she removed her scarf and then tucked it into her coat pocket. She looked around. Mill House was different than she remembered. Far less cluttered and very co-ordinated. There was still something quintessentially Rosemary about the place, but she couldn't put her finger on what it was. Lauren came in from the kitchen and caught her puzzled expression and nodded.

'I know – it feels like home yet doesn't,' she said as Heather untied her coat belt. 'The place was let out for a while when she went travelling, so all her stuff was packed away.'

'That's a good way to describe it.' Heather folded her coat

and laid it over the back of a dining room chair. She glanced warily at Lauren. 'I'd heard about her passing. I'm so sorry.'

'Thanks,' Lauren said quietly. 'Here's your coffee.'

Heather's shoulders shook as she took the mug from Lauren. She sat down as tears rolled down her face. This was not how she'd envisioned things going when she'd seen Lauren on the lakeshore.

A million thoughts had barrelled through her head: it had made sense to say hello, even if it was weird and uncomfortable – and that they'd go their separate ways afterwards and carry on living their lives as they had been. She hadn't expected to suddenly be on some kind of speaking terms with Lauren. She certainly had not seen herself sobbing all over the scrubbed pine table just as she used to when she was a teenager.

Lauren's hand on her shoulder made her jump. Scarlet-faced, she looked up. A packet of tissues was in front of her, and she tore them open, pulled out two and wiped her face. Slowly she raised her eyes to look at Lauren.

'Everything is horrible now she's gone,' Lauren said quietly as if they'd never stopped talking to each other.

Heather watched Lauren scratch her arm as she always used to do and wondered if she should reach out and take her hand for a moment, but she didn't.

'She was an amazing woman,' she said.

'She was.' Lauren half-smiled. 'Remember the year she caught you teaching me how to swim? She was horrified that her own daughter had never taught her children how to swim.'

'Your mam hated swimming though, didn't she?' Heather remembered Mrs Dooley's disgusted face the one and only time she'd taken her children to the swimming pool over in Glenrua. 'I remember her complaining to Mrs Doherty about how dirty and unhygienic it was.'

'Hates it with a passion,' Lauren said. 'The funny thing is, she's no clean freak. I don't know what made her hate it so much.'

'This must be hard for you.' Heather looked around the room. Dust mites danced in the sunlight, and the only sound came from the crackling logs in the stove in the sitting room where an empty bottle of wine stood on the coffee table.

Lauren ran her hand across the table as if to wipe the dust away. She pursed her mouth before speaking.

'It's not great, but it's also not too bad,' Lauren said. 'I'm not over her being gone, but Shane helps me talk it through – I'm still with Shane, by the way. Everyone thought we were just another one of those teenage romances and yet we're still together. We've really made a good go of things, you know – I mean, I've a great job and we've a good income. And now we've this.'

Heather nodded. She almost told Lauren about Simon, about how he'd been helping her come to terms with her unsettled childhood, how he'd been the first one to put a term on her trauma: *parentification*. Not one of her therapists had breathed that term and she'd been alarmed at how accurately it described her upbringing. She'd been a parent to her parents, taking on responsibilities that she never should have had to, that no child should have had to. The comprehension that it was a recognised trauma with real long-term effects had almost been as bad as reading about it.

She was sure Rosemary had known what was going on; after all, Rosemary had taken care of her more than her actual parents had. When she'd heard of her death, the first person she'd called had been Simon. He'd held her until she'd stopped crying and had sat with her even when she'd pushed him away. She hadn't told him much about Rosemary, but somehow he'd known that Rosemary had been everything to her. He really was a decent man, but it was difficult to lean on him, no matter what he said. It was good to have this space between them, good to have time to feel in control again. She quashed the knowledge that what she was doing was a trauma response as tears pricked the backs of her eyes, and her nose fizzed up. Blinking rapidly, she sniffed.

No. It wasn't the right time to tell Lauren about Simon, not when she wasn't sure how she was feeling about him. She was missing him more than she'd thought she would, and that left her in a muddle. How could she be independent and also in a relationship? And they were so different, it couldn't possibly work. The last thing she wanted was to become what Pippa had been – so devoted to her partner that she couldn't see how damaging it was to herself.

Lauren sniffed and sipped her coffee.

Heather looked at her old friend closely. There was a tiredness about Lauren that was strange, and a sadness too. Tell-tale circles under her eyes gave away Lauren's lack of sleep, and Heather could imagine her mother saying that Lauren's chapped lips were a sign of a mineral and vitamin deficiency. More iron, Vitamin B maybe, she thought as Lauren sipped her coffee, but why care about

Lauren now, when Lauren didn't seem to care about her? When they were teenagers, Lauren had tried, but failed, to hide her annoyance at how close Heather was to Rosemary.

Heather shivered. She remembered the countless nights when she'd sneaked up to Mill House. She remembered how she'd run to Rosemary while her parents, and whoever else was around, partied until the small hours. She'd slept on the third floor in Rosemary's warm and cosy cluttered spare room more times than she could remember. She'd told Lauren once, and Lauren had gone all weird, acting as if Heather was trying to muscle in on her life, and in a way that was exactly what she was doing. Shivering again she looked up and caught Lauren looking at her as if she could read her mind.

'Drink your coffee,' Lauren said, putting her mug down. 'Before it goes cold.'

Heather slid her cold hands around the mug and inhaled the rich, warm aroma. Sipping it, she felt the tension in her neck ease. It was close to the best coffee she'd ever had. Putting the mug down she looked at Lauren. Desperate to fill the silence, but equally desperate not to refer to the argument that had broken their friendship, she forced a smile on her face and shrugged.

'Tell me what you've been doing all these years.'

'Working, mostly,' Lauren said with a deep sigh. 'We bought a house not too far from Dublin. I teach in the city. Shane is on the go all the time with work. He's an electrician now, so it's nonstop. That's about it, really. No beautiful holidays or anything like that, you know. That's your thing. Free as a bird. What's brought you back home?'

Heather's grip on her mug tightened. Trust Lauren to stir something in that passive-aggressive way of hers. She'd basically told Heather nothing while still managing to get a dig in. Coffee or no coffee, she didn't need to sit here and listen to absolute rubbish talk.

'I'm back to give Pippa a hand,' she said tightly, determined to not tell Lauren anything. She pushed the coffee away while looking longingly at it. 'I didn't realise the time. I'd better go, or she'll think I've thrown myself in the lake.'

Lauren squinted at Heather. 'You haven't finished your coffee.'

'Yeah.' Heather looked at the mug. The memory of their argument came back to her, and she closed her eyes. No matter how she strived to forget, how hard she swallowed the words, she couldn't keep her mouth shut. She blurted, 'Have you been to see Niamh yet?'

'No.' Lauren looked away. 'You?'

'Of course not.' Heather reached for the mug as Lauren sat back down. 'I'm not in a hurry to.'

'That night . . .' Lauren began before trailing off. She pulled her cuffs down over her hands.

Heather felt as if someone had placed a sack of grain on her shoulders. Hunching over the table she took a deep breath and let it out slowly.

'Thinking about that night makes me feel sick,' Heather said. She scratched at the table with her thumb. 'I try not to think about it, to be honest.' She closed her mouth tightly. It was a bare-faced lie. All she did was think about that night and how it had ripped their friendship apart.

129

'Good for you.' Lauren sniffed. 'I wish I could forget it. Niamh said some really harsh things.'

'Well, look at her now.' Heather plastered a grim smile onto her face. 'So much for her jaunting around the world and becoming a model or whatever she said she wanted to be.'

'*You*. I think she wanted to be what *you* are right now,' Lauren said. 'She's exactly what I wanted to be. Surrounded by kids and living in the country.'

Heather stared at Lauren. 'And what does that make you?'

'I don't bloody know.' Lauren's face twisted. 'A failure?'

Heather sat back and looked at Lauren's puffy face. 'Lauren, that's really sad.'

'It's the truth.' Lauren averted her gaze.

'It's not a healthy way to think of yourself.' Heather's hands twitched to hold Lauren's hand. *So, there were no babies for Lauren*. Heather cleared her throat. 'Trust me.'

'I'm fine. I've come to terms with things.' She looked down at her lap. 'Some things you just have no control over. Others you do.'

'Yeah, maybe.' Heather nodded. 'Listen, Lauren. You have to stop comparing yourself to Niamh—'

'I do not compare myself to Niamh.' Lauren sat up. 'I'm far better off than Niamh Kennedy or whatever she's calling herself these days.'

Heather pressed her hands tightly against the sides of the mug. Her coffee had gone cold, but she sipped it anyway. The logs in the stove shifted and settled, sending a flurry of sparks up the chimney. Lauren was staring at the logs. Her hands had moved from her lap to her lower stomach. Heather swallowed the cold coffee, realising that Lauren was far from coming to terms with things, no matter what she'd said earlier.

'Lauren, I'm sorry,' she said eventually. She got up from the table and reached for her coat. 'Thanks for the coffee.'

Lauren watched Heather pull her coat on. 'You're welcome.'

Heather made her way through the main kitchen to the back kitchen. She stopped as she caught sight of Rosemary's old waxed jacket on the coat hooks behind the back door.

'I know.' Lauren leaned against the kitchen doorframe. 'It still smells like her too.'

Heather opened the back door. 'Take it easy,' she said as if Lauren was no one to her.

'I will. You too.'

Striding away, Heather stopped herself from looking back at Mill House although every cell in her body longed to turn around and stare up at the tiny window in the room where she'd spent so many nights. A sharp pain in the pit of her stomach warned her that Lauren wouldn't like it if she did. She'd been somewhat friendly, but not enough to change things. Maybe she regretted saying hello; maybe she wished that they'd just ignored one another. Her heart pounded in her ears as she hurried away, making sweat drip down her back.

Once back at the lake, Heather sat down on a weather-beaten log and stared out across the water. She squinted and watched two red kites soar over the lake. Lauren had issues, she thought as the red kites took off up over the hillside, big issues – and she didn't know how to help her. It wasn't nice to see someone who was clearly hurting, but what could she do? She'd never felt the same pull to have children that Lauren had always had.

With a grunt she hauled herself up from the log. Hitching her bag up onto her shoulder Heather glanced at her Apple watch. Two thousand and seventy-two steps so far. She needed to up the ante if she was going to hit her step count. Head down, she marched down the lane away from the lake, and turned towards the town. She may as well get the rest of her steps in and walk into the village, maybe pick up some coffee seeing as her mother had none.

She was slightly puffed by the time she got to Billy's store. She picked up a basket and rambled around looking for the coffee. Her mother still had a cafetière, so all she needed was some ground coffee, and surely Billy's had that in stock. With a sigh of relief, she spotted the familiar red and silver packaging of her favourite brand. Reaching down to pick up a packet she heard a familiar voice.

Niamh's voice carried from the front of the shop all the way to the back of the shop where Heather stood, coffee in hand. Peering over the shelves Heather had a full view.

Niamh was leaning against the till and, as always, had managed to captivate her audience. She spoke with such confidence and conviction that no one even thought to question what she said. Old Moll the cashier was all ears. She'd been behind the counter at Billy's for as long as Heather could remember.

Straightening up, Heather tilted her head and listened to Niamh loudly tell Old Moll that she, for one, was glad to see Mill House occupied again.

'Although I did hear that Lauren might turn it into one of those online B&B yokes,' Old Moll said as she totted up Niamh's basket.

Niamh widened her eyes.

Old Moll started filling the bag-for-life Niamh had handed to her.

'Have you heard about Hippie Haven?' Old Moll leaned forward.

Niamh nodded. 'Sure, of course I have.'

'I forgot you used to be great friends with Heather. She didn't really fit in there with her family at all, didn't she not? A completely different kettle of fish.'

Heather's mouth dropped open. With great restraint she didn't move, much as she wanted to.

'Have no doubt, she's as strange as the rest of them.' Niamh pulled out her bank card to pay. She leaned on the counter. 'Take it from me – I know the kind of stuff they got up to. Hippies? That doesn't even begin to cover it. The stories I could tell you – that place was constantly filled with weirdos and oddballs.'

Heather dropped the coffee and watched it fall from her hands as if in slow motion. Looking up she saw Niamh tap her bank card and take her bag of shopping and wave as she left. Picking up the packet of coffee Heather curbed her desire to run after Niamh and fling it hard at the back of her head. Instead, she held her head high and strode to the checkout and paid Old Moll, ignoring her open-mouthed stare.

11

It was just after four o'clock in the morning, and the sky was brightening. It looked like it was going to be a glorious day. Swathes of peach and pink reached into the blue night where the moon still hung low and bright. Dew lay heavy on the glass, glistening like hand-stitched gems on the most beautiful tapestry. Rosemary leaned out the bedroom window and breathed in, feeling the cool, still air lift the worry from her brow. Lately she'd been feeling more and more low. Sadness seemed to be sneaking into her home, through every gap in the woodwork, and every sliver of open window.

Maura had sent her a birthday card from New Zealand last month, and Stella had promised to visit in a few weeks, but it wasn't soon enough. There were only so many bingo nights and Zumba classes she could take. While the people at both were lovely, they couldn't fill the gap in her life. Strangely, she'd found Pippa to be the kindest and friendliest of all her village acquaintances. She

134

often strolled by and would stop to lean on the creaky gate and chat about anything and everything. Her latest thing, she'd told Rosemary during the week, was trying to make handmade soaps and lotions from organic flowers and honey, but Cash had laughed at her and told her that she was being ridiculous.

Rosemary wondered if there was a place for Pippa's handmade potions and lotions in the world right now. The balm she'd shown Rosemary was gorgeous, and over the past week she'd been using it and it had done more for her dry skin than any expensive moisturiser or elixir had in years. Maybe Pippa was on to something.

A rat-a-tat on her back door dragged Rosemary away from her musings, and she hurried to see who it was. A delighted smile spread across her tired face when she saw Niamh, Heather and Lauren beaming at her from the back step.

'Thought we'd give you a hand,' Heather said as she picked up the rucksack at Rosemary's feet. Niamh took the bundle of towels from the counter beside Rosemary, while Lauren held up a bag.

'Hot chocolate, coffee. Goodies. It's our turn to treat you,' Lauren trilled. 'Come on! The sun is almost up!'

'And we got you swim shoes this time.' Niamh dangled a pair of shoes in the air as Rosemary pulled the back door behind her.

The girls giggled and chatted on their way down to the lake while Rosemary looked around her. Her garden was overgrown and needed to be tended, but she was simply not able to get around it as easily as she used to. Slipping slightly on the damp flag path, she pressed her lips together and concentrated on keeping her balance. The last thing she wanted was for the girls to see she was off form. They relied on her so much, and she didn't want them to think she was getting frail, which she wasn't. It was just that things seemed to be darker these days and she couldn't pull herself out of the inertia that she woke up doused in every morning.

As the girls climbed the stile the word *depressed* briefly flittered through her mind, and she quickly scooched it away. *Depressed – that's something for teenagers, and young first-time mothers, not sixty-year-old women.* She clambered down the other side of the stile and hurried to catch up with the girls. *Depressed.* She shook her head. No, she wasn't going to think that way. It wouldn't serve her any favours, and anyway, it was just the weather. The winter had been long, and the spring had been lonely as the girls were all studying for their Junior Certificate exams. The exams were just about over. Niamh had her final exam in music later that morning, but she wasn't a bit nervous, she told Rosemary as they walked across the stony beach. Sure, she'd been taking piano lessons for years. Rosemary nodded. Niamh would be fine.

*

On the lakeshore the girls set up their things. Heather had a fire ready to light, and Niamh told Lauren to drag a log closer to the fire.

'It's not as warm as you think,' Niamh called to Lauren, who was rolling her eyes. 'You'll thank me when you get out.'

'Whatever,' Lauren replied, but she pulled the log closer anyway and then sat down with a humph. 'Did you hear back from school about Transition Year yet?'

Transition Year. Niamh frowned. Was it really all it was cracked up to be? A year without any exams or pressure from the school. Well, they'd to arrange their own work experience blocks but not much else. Was it worth wasting a whole year for? Sure, there were trips and outings planned, even a week-long trip to the Aran Islands, and the only thing about that was that she'd be away from her parents. If she didn't do it, she could go ahead with applying for cabin crew with Etihad a year earlier. If she did, what did she stand to gain?

Niamh sat beside Lauren. 'I'm not sure if I want to do a Transition Year anymore. Maybe it would be better just to get on with school and be done with it.'

'I like school,' Heather said as she piled some dry logs to one side. 'I want to stay in school as long as I can. Transition Year will be great – no exam pressure, trips away, and the teachers are always much nicer. Not to mention work experience. I can't wait for that.'

'Meh,' Niamh said. 'My dad is at me to work in his office. Secretarial stuff – boring.'

Heather sat back and rested her elbows on her knees. 'Some of the girls from last year's class got paid when they did their work experience.'

'Pocket money.' Niamh pouted. 'That's what he told me.'

'At least you've got the chance to earn some money and get experience. It's really important, you know,' Heather said.

'I suppose.' Niamh wasn't interested in the conversation. It didn't matter, she thought as she pulled on her swim shoes. If she went straight into fifth year there'd be the chance to go to a debs ball too, as only fifth- and sixth-year students were allowed to attend. There was every possibility Rory would ask her – he'd dropped hints that he would if she was in fifth year.

Rory Quinlan was gorgeous; tall, tawny and brawny was how she'd described him to Lauren only yesterday. He was perfect, even if he was Bopper Quinlan's son.

She tucked her hair behind her ear and tried to think what it would be like to be on his arm at his debs, but found that all she could think about was jet-setting around the world as cabin crew. Her mind drifted. She'd heard that Emirates was the best airline to work for, but she'd have to wait until she was twenty-one to apply. In the meantime, she was considering applying to Etihad as she'd meet all their requirements by the time she'd finished school, as long as they didn't change them in the meantime. Then she'd be unstoppable. She'd see the whole world and could choose where to go, and even where she'd live. Her heart pounded as she imagined exploring cities around the world. She'd heard that there wasn't much time off and that the newbies got stuck with all the tough schedules, but she was prepared to suck it up if it meant she'd get out of Lough Caragh.

Still, she'd say yes to Rory if he asked her to the ball. Maybe that's what she'd manifest, she thought as Heather checked her watch for the third time.

'It's almost time,' Heather said. 'Are you ready?'

'Born ready,' Niamh said.

'Come on then, Miss Ever Ready, get your ass into the water.' Lauren stood up.

'Don't say that – Ever Ready!' Heather gasped. 'It makes her sound like she's – you know . . .'

'What?' Lauren asked as she scrunched across the stones. 'Oh! Oooooh. Okay.'

'Yup,' Heather said. 'The boys are bad enough about all that without us giving them more bloody nicknames to call us.'

*

Wading into the lake, Heather felt a shiver run down her spine that wasn't coming from the cool water. The latest name they'd given her was Granola: sweet to look at, but nutty when you took a bite. Niamh had laughed. She'd said it was clever, but Heather had cried when she was alone. If it wasn't horrible names then it was remarks on her clothes, on her house, on her family, and musing aloud on whether or not she was like her father. Heather gritted her teeth until her jaw hurt.

Her father was seeing a woman in the village; she knew that, but she didn't know who. It was strange because he'd usually go for one of the hippies who were floating around. Pippa didn't know yet. Heather had realised that the night before when Pippa had been singing while hanging out the washing. She only sang when she was happy, and she was only happy when he wasn't seeing anyone else. Heather closed her eyes briefly, then opened them and walked further into the lake, ignoring Niamh's squeals over how cold the water was. The water wasn't

139

cold at all; it felt soft and comforting, but trust Niamh to be all dramatic about it. Rosemary was to her left, quiet and calm as always.

'It's not as cold as you think,' Rosemary called back to the others. 'You'll get used to it – remember the winter swim?'

Heather glanced over her shoulder at her two best friends. Lauren was so much braver in the water than she'd been a year ago. It was almost unbelievable to think that three years ago she couldn't swim at all. She wouldn't even dip a toe in the water. Now she was down at the lake almost as often as Heather was. Niamh was the same as always, grumbling about her fake tan getting streaky from the water and in the middle of tying her hair into a bun on the top of her head. At her side, Rosemary was striking out for deeper water, and Heather pulled a deep lungful of air in and followed her.

*

Lauren watched as Heather and Rosemary swam out further and began to float. Sometimes it felt as if Heather was Rosemary's granddaughter. Lauren brushed a pesky fly away. Heather didn't have any grandparents, or at least that's what she'd told them. Still, it could be annoying sometimes, seeing Rosemary getting on so well with her. Lauren could hear Shane's voice in her head telling her not to worry about it. There was no doubt that Rosemary loved her, and, as he'd reminded her last night, Rosemary had a big, soft heart. She was simply being kind and what was the point in being jealous of kindness? That only made you look bad, and as Shane said, jealousy didn't help anyone at all. She'd be better off channelling that energy into something else. Maybe she should channel it into her solstice intention. Then she'd be free to be more at ease around Heather than she had been of late.

She smiled at Heather as they began treading water. It felt good to be about to wash away her gripes and grievances against her friend. After all, it wasn't Heather's fault that Rosemary was so kind, and Heather never asked for help. Yet, Lauren realised, she was so good at giving help and support without anyone realising it. She'd made a point of studying maths with Lauren for two weeks before their mock exams and had somehow managed to teach her how to memorise all the equations on the course. Then she'd organised study sessions in the library in the week before the real exams, which Lauren now realised were refresher courses for her. Tears welled in her eyes. The day of their maths exam hadn't been as terrifying as she'd expected it to be, and afterwards she couldn't wait to tell Heather that she was sure she'd passed. Heather had squeezed her shoulder and told her that she knew she could do it, and then they'd carried on with their day as normal.

Lauren brushed away the tears that blurred her vision. There was no point in thanking Heather, for she'd simply brush off any form of thanks, but she could certainly be a better friend and appreciate her kindness and forget about how close she was to Rosemary.

Maybe her actions would inspire Niamh to be more considerate too, although Niamh would need more blatant direction. She was prone to ignoring things that were right

141

in front of her face, like Evan McNamara for example. He was mad about her, but she acted as if she didn't even notice him when clearly she did. It was obvious in how she flicked her hair when he was around, and how she would grow quiet when he'd gone. Lauren frowned. Niamh was such a flirt.

Swimming out almost to where her grandmother and Heather were floating, Lauren caught the first glimpse of the sun as it rose over the mountain.

'Look!' She pointed. 'It's sunrise! Let's make our intentions.'

Grinning, she splashed Heather, then ducked as Heather returned the splash.

'Hey!' Lauren turned to wave Niamh over. 'Get over here and make your intention count, before it's too late.'

Niamh bobbed closer and Lauren reached for her hand. 'Go on, hold Heather's hand.'

Niamh reached for Heather and then turned to invite Rosemary in.

*

Smiling, Rosemary gripped Niamh's hand on one side and Lauren's on the other and for a moment everything seemed perfect. There was no wind, just the sound of birdsong and the hum of insects. The sun was warm although it was early, and the girls were smiling. If she'd been asked, she'd have said that Paddy was watching over them in that moment because it felt as if he was there, swimming strongly the laps he always did, then blowing her a kiss as she joined him. With a lighter heart she held her breath and ducked

142

under the water at the same time as the girls and set her intention: this year she'd get herself back together. Paddy would hate to see her shuffling about the house the way she was. This summer she'd do something out of the ordinary. That's it, she thought as she wiped the water from her face, something challenging. Paddy would be delighted with her.

*

Lauren blew water from her lips and laughed, loving the cool wash of the lake around her shoulders. Her intention set, she felt at ease. She'd be a better friend, and a kinder person, because what goes around comes around, she was sure.

*

Niamh ran her two hands over her wet head and blinked rapidly. Her intention hadn't quite been what she'd planned it to be. Instead of hatching a plan to catch Rory Quinlan's eye she'd found herself thinking about how good it was to be friends with Heather and Lauren, even if they sometimes drove her up the wall. Her intention became a wish to spend more time with them, and to convince her father and mother, somehow, that they were the very best friends anyone could have.

*

Squeezing water from her long hair, Heather shivered. Her intention was the same as always: to be treated differently

143

than her family was. She'd made so many changes, had refused the clothes her mother had picked up for her and instead wore Niamh's cast-offs. She'd made sure she looked modern and fresh and capable, but still she was treated with disdain in some instances, and a freaky curiosity in others. She was beginning to wonder if these intentions had any impact at all.

Back on the lakeshore, Heather towelled herself dry and sat on the log beside Rosemary while Lauren poured hot chocolate for everyone. The sun was a disc of gold in the bluest sky, with only the slightest wisp of cloud high up. The day was going to be a scorcher. The good weather had most people in good form, but all Heather saw was time stretching out in front of her until school started again and nothing to fill it in with. Lauren handed her a mug, perfectly made, and Heather felt a little sad. Lauren had managed to get a part-time job in Billy's for the summer; Niamh was going to work in her father's accountancy firm. Rosemary had just said she was going to make an effort to do something – something that was going to shake things up.

As the sun rose higher and they dried off, Heather tried her best to think positively, but she knew it was pointless. No one was going to hire a Moore, not even as a babysitter. She looked down at the last of her hot chocolate and decided that if work wasn't coming to her she'd have to make something happen – she'd have to create some work somehow. Just what that might be, she didn't know, but if she didn't try she'd be stuck – just like her mother was. With a smile, Heather rinsed her mug in the lake and set a new intention: to be her own boss, whatever way it came.

12

14th February 2024

Niamh, carrying popcorn bowls and sweets, paused in the hallway and listened to her daughters arguing over which movie to watch. Ava was rebelling against any kind of romance movie, while Katie was adamant that she wanted to watch all of the *Pitch Perfect* movies in order. It wasn't how she'd envisioned spending Valentine's Day, but Evan had gone back to train the senior team after dropping the girls home earlier from theirs. She was sure he'd be home soon to join them. Niamh sucked in a breath, then pushed open the sitting room door.

'Who wanted butter on their popcorn?' she trilled.

'Urgh, no.' From the chair that Evan usually sat in Ava pulled a face and tucked her feet up under her. 'Just plain for me.'

'Me!' Sophie hopped up from the couch where she'd been sitting under a fleecy blanket. 'I'll help you, Mammy.' Niamh smiled. In the firelight with her new bob swishing against her pink cheeks, Sophie looked more than ever like Evan. Her hair was more red than her sisters' blonde tresses, and her eyes had that green tint that he had too. She was the easiest of her three girls, and took after Evan's side of the family in many more ways than just looks. Sophie was always the first to lend a hand. The other two were less likely to ever offer a helping hand. Niamh sighed as Ava pouted and gave the peace sign to her iPhone camera.

'Thanks, Soph,' Niamh said.

'Ava, put the phone away.' Niamh handed her a full bowl of popcorn. She'd liberally scattered the bowl with M&Ms, Ava's favourites.

'Mam! Why'd you do that?' Ava wailed as she looked into the bowl. 'I'm on a diet.'

Niamh blinked. 'You're on a what?'

'Never mind,' Ava said. 'I'll eat around them.'

'A diet?' Katie, the youngest, called from her cosy perch on the end of the couch. Her mouth already full of sweets. 'What's a diet?'

'Never mind,' Niamh said, horrified at possibly having to explain what a diet was to her uncomplicated nine-year-old. Ava rolled her eyes and snapped her friends again.

'Phone, now.' Niamh held out her hand. 'It's movie night, and you know the rules.'

'I'll put it away.' Ava slipped the phone between her knee and the arm of the chair.

'Ava.' Niamh eyeballed her daughter.

Huffing, Ava handed over her phone, pulling a face as Niamh placed it on the mantelpiece.

Niamh looked at her daughter, who at fourteen was

146

far more glamorous than Niamh or any of her friends had ever been. How on earth had she let this happen? How had she let her daughter, who'd been the most adorable baby she'd ever seen, who'd wrapped everyone around her little finger, who'd been the most affectionate and gorgeous child to walk the earth, turn into this self-absorbed little madam. She was so tired of this constant barrage of battles and pleading and bargaining with her family. What kind of a parent was she – all she did was let her kids walk all over her.

Ignoring Ava's mood, Niamh squished in between Sophie and Katie on the couch and picked up the controls.

'I believe we said we'd watch this.' Niamh pressed play as Katie snuggled in closer to her. Within minutes they were all engrossed in *How to Lose a Guy in Ten Days*, even Ava. Niamh sank deeper into the cushions. She'd have loved to have been out, sipping a cocktail before a romantic candlelit dinner, but she wasn't, so she may as well just enjoy being at home with her kids. Sophie leaned against her.

'I love girls' nights,' she whispered. 'Thank you, Mammy.'

Niamh's heart melted. Sophie was so like Evan. She kissed Sophie's head. 'Me too.'

*

The movie had been over for a good half an hour and there was still no sign of Evan coming home. Niamh carried the empty bowls back to the kitchen, pausing in the hall to listen to her daughters singing along to Taylor Swift upstairs while they got ready for bed.

'Showers, the three of ye, straight away,' she called as the three girls began to sing a second song.

'Mam.' Ava rambled onto the landing with her tracksuit in her hands. 'Mam, I need this for tomorrow.'

'Ah, Ava, are you joking me?' Niamh stared up to her eldest daughter who was wrapped in two towels. 'What about Sophie? Does she need hers?'

'How would I know?' Ava flounced away, but not before she'd dropped her tracksuit over the banister. Niamh watched the offending articles drift to the floor. She gritted her teeth and went to the bottom of the stairs and called up to Sophie, but there was no answer.

'She's in the shower, Mammy,' Katie hollered down eventually. 'She's taking all the hot water.'

Niamh's heart sank. 'Bring me down Sophie's tracksuit, and yours too.' She waited as Katie hurled herself into Sophie's bedroom and came back in her underwear.

'Bomb's away!' Katie tossed the muddy clothes over the banister.

'Katie! No!' Niamh darted forward to catch the clothes, her mouth an O as a muddy tracksuit bottom slithered down the wall, marking the paint. With a groan Niamh picked up the clothes and traipsed to the utility room.

She selected the quickest wash cycle feeling as if she lived in the utility room. She cast a critical eye around. The room could do with an overhaul. She'd ask Rory if he'd have any advice for her about it. After all, she was going to be spending quite a bit more time there if her plan took off – no, not if, *when*. When it took off was the only way to think about it, otherwise she'd give in and then Evan would be able to say I told you so.

The front door clattered shut at the same time she closed the utility room door. Evan called a quiet hello as he walked into the kitchen.

'Any tea going?' he asked as he slid onto one of the high stools at the island unit. His eyes sparkled at Niamh. 'The pitch was like a quagmire. I told the committee last year it needed reseeding. They're miserable. Won't spend a penny. I'm going to join the committee. At least I'll be able to make a difference then.'

Niamh switched on the kettle and groaned.

'I don't think that's a good idea. We're busy enough as it is.' He'd no idea how busy she intended on being. She'd yet to break the news to him about the plans Rory had come up with for the renovation. Reaching into the cupboard over the fridge she took down a large bar of Cadbury's Caramel and pushed it and a mug of tea towards Evan.

'My favourite.' He picked up the bar.

'Happy Valentine's Day,' Niamh said.

'You're too good for me – you know that?' He looked contrite. 'I forgot it was Valentine's Day . . .'

Niamh said nothing. She picked up a cloth and wiped down the counter, then wiped it again.

Evan put his mug down. 'Niamh?'

Niamh dropped the cloth in the sink and began emptying the dishwasher.

'Niamh, I'm sorry . . . I forgot with all the mock exams going on . . .' Evan's face clouded over as Niamh continued to put the glasses she was holding back into the dishwasher. How to tell him about the plans she'd made with Rory?

'It doesn't matter. I'm not that bothered about Valentine's Day this year.' She avoided looking at him.

'This has to be more than Valentine's Day.' He watched her carefully. 'What's going on? The last time you went this quiet was when you found out you were expecting Katie. Are we . . . ?' He grinned. 'Is that why you don't want me to join the committee?'

'No.' Niamh's laugh came out like a bark. 'God, no.'

'Oh, right.'

Niamh's eyebrows lowered. 'You sound let down.'

'A baby would be nice,' he said.

'A baby, now? After all this time? Katie is almost ten and we're only getting back on our feet.' Niamh shook her head. 'Haven't we got enough children as it is?'

'I'd love a boy.' Evan broke off a square of chocolate and popped it in his mouth. 'You know that, Niamh. It's not a surprise.'

'I know.' Niamh leaned back against the cooker. 'I don't want more children, and you *know* that. The girls are becoming more independent. I'm finally able to consider doing something with my life.'

'What exactly are you going to do?' Evan looked at her.

Niamh pursed her lips. He had that hard look in his eyes that meant he was feeling hard done by and ready to stand up for himself. She stared back at him just as hard.

'It's always this way,' she said eventually. 'Always about what you want.'

'Don't start that again.' Evan sat up.

'Easy for you to say,' Niamh said. 'You got your degree and a job. I've been a mother since I was twenty, Evan, well eighteen if you count motherhood beginning at conception. It's not been easy.'

'Do you think I don't know that? It hasn't been a walk in the park for me either.' Evan leaned back on the stool.

'No, of course I know that, but I want to *do* something with my life that doesn't revolve around parenting and I've decided what it is.' Niamh picked up the tea towel and twisted it tightly.

'You've decided something without talking to me?' Evan stood up.

'You were about to join a committee that takes up a huge amount of time without asking me how I felt about it.' Niamh twisted the towel tighter. 'You mentioned it, but you weren't asking me.'

'What is it? And how will it impact our family?' Evan placed his hands on either side of his empty mug on the counter.

'Any impact will be positive.' Niamh glared at him. 'I'll be home the whole time. Don't you worry.'

'Are you going to tell me or what?' Evan snapped. 'There's no need to be so cryptic.'

'I'm not trying to be cryptic.' Niamh leaned on the island unit opposite him. 'I'm trying to tell you that I'm going ahead with my plan. I'm using the money Dad left me to turn over the three old B&B rooms and run them as holiday rentals.'

'I'm sorry. We spoke about that before, and it's ridiculous.' Evan laughed.

151

'It's not ridiculous. It's what Dad wanted me to do.' Niamh stared at Evan.

'It's preposterous,' he said. 'What will people think when they see you washing and catering to strangers? They'll say you've turned into your mother.'

'That's a horrible thing to say.' Niamh felt the prickle of tears in the backs of her eyes. 'My mother was a good woman, and at least she had something to do with her life. I'm just a skivvy to you and the girls. All I do is clean, wash clothes, ferry kids about the place – I may as well get paid and appreciated for it!'

'If you say so.' Evan's lip curled.

'I do.' Niamh gripped the counter tightly. 'I'm already working on it. Rory's coming in to start in a week or so. He's given me a quote and I can afford it so I'm doing it.'

'Rory? Rory Quinlan? After me asking you not to get him involved?' Evan raised his voice.

'Shush, the girls will hear you.' Niamh glared at him. 'Yes, Rory Quinlan. What's the problem with Rory Quinlan?'

'Oh, there's no problem with Rory Quinlan, except that everyone knows he had a crush on you.'

'That was years ago,' Niamh said shakily. 'You can't be upset with me because someone had a crush on me when we were teenagers? I have no control over that, and anyway, we're just friends – actually technically I'm employing him.'

Evan shook his head. 'Niamh, you haven't a clue. Men don't just forget their crushes.'

'It's of no consequence to me if he likes me or not,'

Niamh said. Her throat constricted. A flush ran up her neck as she thought of how open and enthusiastic Rory was about her plans.

'Whatever.' Evan waved his hand at her and walked out of the kitchen, leaving Niamh hot and flustered. She grabbed the tea towel and flung it across the room, then stormed over to pick it up. Balling it up in her hands she felt bile rise in her throat. How dare he cheapen what she was doing by reminding her that Rory had once fancied her. She gripped the tea towel, grateful that he'd never known about how much she'd really fancied Rory.

It had only been a crush. Rory had been on her radar when she was sixteen, but they'd never actually gotten together. She'd thought he'd ask her to his debs ball but it hadn't happened. They'd flirted, but it had never gone any further than that. Back then she used to believe that there was nothing wrong with flirting, that it meant nothing and was all a bit of craic. Everyone knew flirting was harmless.

The washing machine beeped loudly in the utility room, dragging Niamh back from her memories, and she hauled out the girls' tracksuits and shoved them into the dryer. She stood in the room and felt a ball of anger grow inside her. Frustrated, she rushed from the room and grabbed her handbag from the counter, and then she ran from the house, slamming the front door behind her. Niamh dashed for her car, then changed her mind. She took her jacket from the back seat, grabbed an umbrella and walked furiously until she reached Lough Caragh.

Standing on the shore in the dark, she thought about

New Year's Day and how she'd seen Heather and Lauren together at the lake.

Heather had looked so put together, so tidy and organised. She was everything Niamh had once aspired to be. Lauren's eyes and nose were pink as if she'd been crying, but they'd been talking and smiling. Niamh's heart had pounded so loud that her headache had almost disappeared, and she'd slipped back behind the hedgerow to watch them. Compared to them she felt like she was drowning in uselessness. The day-in and day-out routine of taking care of her family and nothing else terrified her.

Lauren and Heather had jobs and lives outside their homes. People knew them as Lauren the teacher and Heather the Instagram sensation. She was sure that people went to them for advice all the time: where to go on honeymoon or asking about how to get their teens to study more. No one came to her asking for advice on so much as how to boil a potato. She was just Niamh. Mother. Wife. It was hardly surprising then that they'd migrated towards each other.

She'd been surprised to see them standing right where she was now. Chatting as if that night had never happened, those awful things had never been said.

What had happened that night was a bit of a blur to her now – they'd all had quite a bit to drink – but if she tried hard, she could remember what was said. She'd honestly never believed that they'd never see each other again, but that's exactly what had happened. Heather had gone to Italy and begun her new life without looking back. Lauren had blanked her and hadn't come to Ava's christening. After that she'd assumed they weren't speaking

154

to each other either, so seeing them together on the lakeshore like that had been surprisingly painful. Maybe they'd stayed in touch all along.

Looking out across the lake where she stood now, she felt overwhelmingly sad. It was scary how easily she'd kept her project from Evan for the past six weeks or so, but after the row it seemed that not telling him anything had been the right decision. He had been as angry as she'd imagined he'd be. She stooped to pick up a stone before throwing it into the lake. The ripples spread out across the still surface quickly. In the back of her mind she knew no matter how much it had been fun meeting Rory and discussing the project behind Evan's back, that it was wrong. She groaned. How many times had she hidden the plans and cost projections? She'd even made her Pinterest board private and only shared it with Rory. She'd had Katie lie to Evan one day when Rory had turned up to tell her the good news that she didn't need planning permission for the three existing rooms as they already had planning granted.

As the lake waters lapped quietly against the pebbles, Niamh found she'd turned to face the walk towards Mill House. Straining her eyes in the darkness, she could just about make out Heather's mother's place too. They were so close to each other, the houses. Did that mean that they'd become close in person too?

It seemed that she was drifting apart from everyone in her life. She was afraid to tell her husband her dreams and desires, her children were running roughshod over her, and Edel had enough on her plate at the moment with her in-laws ill. And even though Edel was a good friend, their friendship wasn't what she'd had with Lauren and Heather.

A sharp pain stretched across her chest and, for a second, Niamh thought she was having a heart attack, but then she realised what it was: she was sad. Heartbroken and utterly alone.

13

Placing her breakfast dishes into the sink, Lauren caught sight of the calendar on the wall. It said it had been six weeks since her last period, and the tight, dull ache in her lower back told her that she wouldn't have long to wait for it to begin. Shane was coming down on Friday and they were going to celebrate a belated Valentine's Day at the weekend, but she was nervous about seeing him. It had been a long and lonely six weeks since he'd been down last for New Year. The old saying *absence makes the heart grow fonder* sprang to her mind but it was quickly followed up with the opposite saying *out of sight, out of mind*. Lauren moved away from her calendar. There was no way *out of sight out of mind* applied to her and Shane. It wasn't possible. They rang each other every night before bed, but another saying was ruling their time these days: *make hay while the sun shines*.

At least it's not *what's for you won't pass you by*, Lauren trudged past carefully labelled boxes stacked in the hallway on her way up to the third floor. It was what her mother said time and again until Lauren had learned to not tell her that they were still trying for a baby. Even now, her mother was still prone to just dropping those awful words into a conversation. It was an absolute head-melter.

Make hay while the sun shines . . . that's what they were trying to do right now. Shane's boss had gotten a big contract to do the electrical work on a huge site. Two hundred and fifty houses, and the bonus was that it was only down the road from their Dublin home. The contractor wanted the houses done in double time. It was a huge company, and they had the money behind them, the staff and the ability to get houses up and sold in record time, which was great in an economy where there was a desperate need for housing. It meant overtime, all the time, which was something Lauren knew they couldn't turn down. He'd broken the news to her before he'd gone back to Dublin after the New Year.

'It's for six months or so,' Shane had said. 'I'll be doing sixty- or seventy-hour weeks, but we can pay off the IVF loans, almost all of them. It'll give us a chance to get back on our feet.'

'You'll be shattered.' Lauren had taken his hands in hers. They'd been curled up on the sofa that they'd pulled close to the fire. 'We should just sell Mill House – that would pay off all our bills.'

'Is that what you want?' Shane had asked. Lauren had cringed. She was supposed to be clearing out Mill House with a view to them selling it, but she'd been dragging her heels over the clear-out. It should have been done and on the market already.

'What do you mean?'

'I know you always imagined us living here, with kids,' Shane had said softly. 'It's tough letting that dream go.'

'I have to let it go,' she'd said to the fire, unable to look in his eyes. 'It's never going to happen.'

'Maybe we can try one more time,' Shane had said. 'Don't sell Mill House yet. Maybe we don't pay off the loans completely and instead we give it one more round?'

Lauren had looked at him then. 'I don't know. Do you think it's worth it? The injections . . .'

'I know, but I'll be with you.' He'd squeezed her hand gently.

'But you won't be, you'll be working almost twenty-four-seven to do this. I think we've given it enough chances. I'm not sure it'll work, and then we're back at square one – owing a small fortune and you exhausted from work, me drained from the whole thing again.'

He'd gone quiet then, and she'd felt bad. Maybe he'd been secretly hoping she'd say yes.

Now, she opened the door to the second room on the third floor, the room that she'd helped Rosemary move all her clothes, shoes and accessories into before she'd left on her travels.

The room was warm and painted pale coral pink with lace-trimmed chintz curtains. The sun shone in through the window in the evenings, but the mornings left the room dim and a little forlorn. Lauren turned on the light and stood on the threshold. Even though Rosemary's things were all packed away in brown cardboard boxes, her familiar and calming scent of lavender hung in the air as if she'd just been in the room. The floorboards creaked as Lauren stepped into the room. She ran her fingertips

159

over the boxes, marvelling at how dusty everything was. Sneezing twice, she tried to figure out why it was taking her so long to clear out Mill House.

This was the room she'd always imagined her firstborn in. In her imagination she'd had a girl first, then a boy, and this room at the top of the house was where she'd imagined her eldest daughter would sleep. Two babies was enough. Shane had always dreamt of four but the last few years had tempered his dreams, which made Lauren anxious. No matter what he said to reassure her, he was changing his dreams of a large family because of her; she was sure of it. If she'd been able to carry a child to term then his dream would probably have come true – and she'd do anything to make that happen. Even have four children. She touched the warm cardboard boxes again. Was she still harbouring a secret desire to try again? Did she really want to go through another gruelling round of injections and scans and taking folic acid and all the recommended and more vitamins and supplements like the last time? She'd noticed that Shane was still taking the cocktail of supplements the clinic had advised. Vitamin D, omega 3, zinc and folic acid too. She'd been surprised to see them in his wash bag but hadn't said anything knowing that he'd be upset to know she'd found them.

Sitting down on a low dusty box marked with the word 'books', Lauren blew out hard.

'I mean, of all the men to marry,' she said aloud to the room as a bright patch of sunlight appeared on the old cream floral rug. The room felt warmer and she could imagine Rosemary sitting on the painted stool by the dressing table in the corner, listening with her whole heart. Lauren continued, 'I had to marry the most perfect one. And all I'm doing is breaking his heart.'

She stopped and listened, just in case Rosemary was there and sent a sign, but there was nothing, just the patch of sunlight brightening and dimming as the clouds whipped by outside.

'Breaking his heart,' she said again before getting up from the box and looking around. They'd done such a good job packing away Rosemary's things the first time that once she read the labels, she remembered exactly what was in each box. There was no real need to open them at all, but she wanted to, if only to feel closer to Rosemary.

Selecting carefully, Lauren peeled the Sellotape off a small box marked 'Sitting Room Shelves'. An array of bits and bobs were carefully wrapped in newspaper and old pillowcases. The first parcel she unwrapped was a carved walnut box. Lifting the lid, Lauren saw all of Rosemary's thimbles lying on the velvet interior. She'd collected them for years but never displayed them, but when her grandchildren were over, she'd take one out, hide it, and they'd play Hunt the Thimble for hours. Lauren remembered rainy days climbing over Rosemary's coal bucket, rooting behind the sofa where her knitting was stuffed, and poking in all the nooks and crannies trying to find the chosen thimble before Yvonne or Thomas found it. Smiling, she set the box aside.

The second unwrapping revealed an old jam jar filled with heart-shaped pebbles. What a thing to unearth on Valentine's Day of all days. Lauren's heart squeezed as

161

she rolled the cold jar in her hands listening to the clatter of the pebbles as they moved against each other.

Rosemary had always found heart-shaped pebbles down at the lake. She used to say that it was Grandad Paddy leaving them there for her. He'd always loved the lake. When she was nine he'd tried to teach her how to swim. It'd been such a hot day when she'd sat on the shore and watched him swim out to what seemed to her child's eye as the very centre of the lake. She'd panicked until he was back on the shore. He'd smiled as she'd run to him with his towel.

'You need to learn how to swim, *a leanabh*, then you won't be afraid,' he'd said.

'No, Grandad, Mammy says it's dirty.' She'd shaken her head. 'I'll catch worms in my belly. She said she'd redden me if I stuck one toe in the lake.'

Paddy had pressed his lips tightly together as he'd dried his hair while Rosemary had huffed.

'I'll never understand that child of ours,' Rosemary had said. 'Worms, in the lake. Is she gone in the head, Paddy?'

'Enough, Rose, less said.' Paddy had folded his towel and walked away. Then he'd stopped and exclaimed. He'd bent down to pick something up. Coming back to where Rosemary was sitting drying her toes, he handed her what he'd found.

'Would you look at that!' Rosemary had held up the stone. 'A heart-shaped pebble. I've never seen the likes. That must be a one in a million find. Paddy, love, do the lotto, would ya, before your luck runs out!'

'I will,' he'd said with a grin, and he did. They didn't win the lotto, but Lauren won three medals for Irish dancing at the *feis* that weekend and as she was known for having two left feet, her grandad teased her that it was the magic heart pebble that had helped her. She'd believed in its magical powers for years. She remembered fondly how she'd run up the road to her grandparents' house to touch the pebble for luck before every *feis*. Then she remembered how Shane had scoured the pebble shoreline trying to find her very own heart pebble, but he never did find one.

Back in the pink room, Lauren popped open the jam jar and tipped the pebbles out onto her lap. There were eighteen in total. A number of them had turned up after Paddy's passing. Lauren turned them over until she found that very first one that he'd found. Rosemary had written the date on it in her elegant script, blue biro bright on the grey pebble; in fact, she'd written the date on all but three of them. Instead, Rosemary had written each of the girls' names: *Lauren, Heather, Niamh*. Holding those pebbles in one hand, Lauren frowned. Quickly she dropped them back into the jar and gathered up the others. She put them in on top of the three already in the jar and closed the lid tightly.

She could remember the date that was supposed to be on each of those three stones as easily as she could remember the day and date she'd met Shane for the first time.

But this date didn't hold any kind of a warm memory. Sunday, 21st June 2009. The Sunday after she'd finished her final exams. It was to be a celebration, but their plans had all gone to the dogs.

Shutting her memories away as quickly as she'd shut

163

the jam jar, Lauren shoved the jar down into the box. There really was no need to sort through Rosemary's things. She put the walnut box of thimbles back in and pressed the Sellotape back into place. It wouldn't stick no matter how hard she pressed, and after a few minutes she gave up and sank down onto the dressing table stool.

'I can't get anything to stick,' she said aloud and closed her eyes. Her hands crept to her stomach, cradling where her babies should have grown. The dark thoughts she'd been having more and more of tumbled in on top of her. She tried to organise them so she'd be able to explain to Shane why he should leave her, why she had to let him go. It wasn't the first time she'd thought about it, but lately it had begun to make more sense. If she loved him so much, then she'd let him go. Balling her hands into fists, Lauren squeezed her hands so tightly that she was sure her nails would break her skin. Opening her eyes, she pulled the letter she'd been writing to Shane from her jeans pocket and read it slowly, each word a barb to her soul.

Shane,

I love you. Always remember that, because that is why I'm letting you go.

Go and find a woman who you can have babies with, and live happily ever after because you won't get that with me. I'm only capable of breaking your heart and turning your dreams into nightmares.

You say you love me, and that that's all that matters, but it isn't, is it? How can you love me

the same way as you did years ago when we
thought that a family and babies were a possibility,
no – not a possibility, a given.

We thought we could just ping out babies like
sparkles bursting from a firework. We should have
our family by now. God. I never once imagined
that we'd be told there was no reason why we
aren't conceiving. I always thought it'd be easy. If
I'd known back then I'd never have stayed with
you, and I'm sorry. I know that hurts to hear, but
you should have everything you've ever dreamed
of. I'm sorry. For all of it. I really am. I want your
dreams to come true—

With a groan she crumpled up the letter, then smoothed
it back out again. She could pinpoint the moment when
she'd come to this conclusion, that she had to let him go.
The feeling had come to her quite naturally one day last
September as they'd walked along the park near their
Dublin house. She'd noticed his eyes linger on new babies,
toddlers and even on the pregnant women they passed.
And they were everywhere: pregnant women and babies.
The sun had been golden that day, and they'd sat under
a tree, in silence, and let the world pass them by.

She'd realised how quiet they were, and how quiet their
life would be without children. Shane was an only child.
He'd told her about his longing for a busy, loud house;
his own had been subdued and serious. Just like they were
now. The idea that he should be able to have his dream
even if it meant losing him had come then. It was as if it
had filtered through the sun-kissed leaves and settled on

her lap like a butterfly on a daisy. Lately the feeling had been coming back time and again and each time it made more sense. She was going to have to tell him sooner rather than later. They weren't getting any younger and by the time they'd divorced he'd be running short on time to start a new relationship with someone who could give him the children he'd always dreamt about. Divorce. The very word made her heart hurt, but it was the right thing to do.

Lauren got up from the stool, folded the letter and slipped it into her jeans pocket again, and left the room, pulling the door tightly behind her. She knew that she was in a really dark place and there was no way out. Down in the kitchen she looked out of the window at the birds pecking in the grass. Lauren glanced at the clock. Midday. The day was dragging. She made a cup of tea and took it into the sitting room.

The sorting and clearing could wait. She scrolled past the romantic films on Netflix before settling on *Derry Girls*. Right now, she didn't want to think of anything. It was enough to just watch the programme and see what 'divilment' Erin and her friends were getting up to.

14

Heather, gripping her suitcase, stood in the living room of her London apartment. It was still bedecked in Christmas decorations. In the pale February evening light her Christmas tree leaned slightly to the left as if someone had stumbled into it. The timed white lights flickered on, making her flinch. She groaned realising that everyone in the apartments nearby would know she'd left her decorations up till mid-February. They'd all think she was a freak. It was probably why Jemima from number seventeen had waved at her as she'd trundled down the hallway. Jemima had left her Christmas tree up for a whole two years during the pandemic. She'd updated the residents' WhatsApp group regularly with her tree's seasonal changes and sent in uplifting quotes and poems. Heather had had to put the app on mute. Jemima reminded her too much of Pippa and she'd come to London to get away from all of that.

In her bedroom she unzipped her almost empty suitcase. She'd packed enough for a night or two as she'd come back to gather what she'd need for the next month or so.

She was staying in Ireland longer than she'd expected, and it wasn't the drag she'd thought it would be. Instead of champing at the bit to get back to work, she found herself fully engaged with Pippa's new business and, strangely, loving every minute of it. Her own business was limping along and all she could do was watch it while wondering why she didn't seem to care about it. Heather flopped onto her bed and lay back and ignored the questions of why she didn't care about her work. She stared at the ceiling instead, then she placed her hands on her ribs and tried to control her breathing just as her Pilates instructor had shown her. She remembered trying to do the same in January when Pippa had told her that her old room was ready for her.

Heather sighed, thinking back to January when she'd dragged her case down the hall towards the tiny and steep wooden staircase at the far end of Pippa's house. As she'd lugged her case up after her, she'd wondered what her mother meant by 'ready for her'.

She'd gasped when she'd opened the door; after all, it had been fifteen years since she'd last stepped foot inside it. When she'd left home her parents had been at the height of their open-door policy. Everyone and anyone who needed a bed was welcome to bunker down wherever they wanted, and she'd fully expected to find her room looking like a dishevelled, abandoned dormitory. Instead, it was warm and calm, just as the hallway and kitchen were. The walls were apricot and the curtains linen. The light even had a shade on it, and lamps stood on bedside tables on each side of a new bed. Her old bed had been a small, saggy affair. This one was a simple bed she recognised from IKEA. The duvet, pillows, linens, cushions and throws all looked new too. A yellow dressing gown hung from the back of the door, and slippers were under the end of the bed. A rose-scented candle on the windowsill made it feel like her home back in London where roses bloomed in the gardens near her apartment.

It had been an unsettling evening. She'd unpacked hesitantly, hanging her clothes in the new fitted wardrobes, feeling confused. Pippa had worked hard to have it ready for her, and had remembered she'd loved roses and that yellow was her favourite colour. Sitting on the bed she'd waited before going back downstairs, her head in her hands, wondering what this meant? For the first time in her life she felt as if her mother knew her, and had always known her. Heather hadn't realised she'd been crying until a tear dropped onto her knee.

When she'd gone back downstairs, she knew Pippa must've felt the million and one questions that she'd wanted to ask but didn't volunteer any information. Instead, she'd opened a bottle of wine and they'd sat by the stove and drank it while they waited for a pizza to come from Roberto's. They both were shamefully hungover the next day, but by then it had felt too late to ask about her room. She probably never would. Instead, they'd just got stuck into clearing out the large sitting room at the front of the house.

Now that had taken some work. Several times Heather had found items of clothing that didn't belong to her mother, and she'd swiftly shoved them into a black bag before her mother had spied them. No one needed any more reminding of the women who had come and gone, least of all Pippa. It had taken them the whole of January to clear that room out, and almost two weeks before they'd been done painting over the deep burgundy walls. Five coats of pale primrose paint were what it had taken to remove the sordid feel of the room. Afterwards they'd both stood in the room, dazed at how different it felt.

'Well,' Pippa had said from where she stood in the middle of the room. 'I never realised . . . I mean, this room is . . .'

'Huge.' Heather had opened the window to let the smell of paint out. 'The sofa is lost in here.'

'The sofa is going in a skip.' Pippa had kicked the sofa with a clogged foot. 'That sofa could probably walk out of here.' She'd shuddered. 'Like so many other things, it was your father's choice, not mine.' Pippa had walked out of the room before Heather could say anything, and although she hated her father as much as Pippa did, she really did wish Pippa would stop calling him 'your father' as if she was responsible for him or something. It made her feel grimy and uneasy.

Now, on her huge London bed, Heather rose up onto her elbows. She'd a few other tasks to complete before heading back to Lough Caragh, and she didn't relish doing any of them.

First, she needed to leave her key with her neighbour, Sally, the only one she could trust not to go poking about, which was fine and all, but Sally liked to talk and there was no time for that. Then Heather needed to pop into the animal shelter to let them know that she wasn't sure how long she'd be gone. She was dreading telling them. It wasn't going to help her heart to walk away from those

170

trusting little furry faces. She loved each and every animal there, particularly, and for no reason she could fathom, the family of goats who'd been abandoned outside the shelter in November.

They'd taken to her immediately and she to them, and now she knew an almost unnecessary amount about goats. They'd be glad to see her, she knew, but then she'd be gone for God knows how long and she wouldn't have a say in how they would be taken care of. Glen, the manager, had warned her that if the right candidate came along and only wanted two then he'd have to split them up even though every bit of advice from all the animal foundations was to keep them together. Her heart broke a little, wondering what was going to happen to them.

Then there was Simon. Simon with his brown skin, his warm cinnamon-coloured eyes, his bright smile and deep laugh. He made her skin feel all tingly just by catching her eye from the corner of the room, and he always followed through on all of his promises. Her breath caught under her ribs as she thought of the promises he'd kept and how often he'd kept them. He was the first man she'd ever felt satisfied by, and now she was addicted to him and his gentle love. But she'd said no, and there had been no mistaking the hurt and confusion in his eyes, and there was no way that she could take that back. Not to mention that she'd practically skedaddled off to her mother's house almost as soon as she'd said *no thanks*, and he knew how she felt about home – and then she'd stayed there for two whole months.

Okay, it wasn't an immediate skedaddle back to Lough Caragh. It was a few days after Paris. It was a coincidence, and unavoidable. It wasn't her fault. He knew she'd the five-star golf trip lined up, and he knew she'd be calling in to see Pippa. They'd talked about it. He'd helped her iron out so much of her past, which, she realised, was probably why he'd proposed in the first place. She got up from the bed and rubbed her eyes.

It wasn't as if she'd ignored him for the last two months, not exactly. They'd talked, and had FaceTime conversations. Some of the conversations had been stilted but there'd also been moments just like before he'd proposed, and things had felt normal. It was just now she'd have to see him face to face. In the flesh. That was the hard part; it always was. She knew she'd immediately want to loosen his tie, to undo that top button and kiss away his work from his mind, but this time she'd a feeling he wouldn't allow it. She couldn't blame him. Still, maybe things would be okay between them. She'd a few hours before she needed to catch the train into London to meet him after work. In the meantime, she'd be better off getting her act together and doing what she came home to do.

Forty-five minutes later her suitcase was filled with everything that she might need back in Lough Caragh. Her swimsuit lay on the bed beside her closed case. She debated packing it. It wasn't the one she used in her social media photos. It was a plain navy one-piece, made for swimming in the pool in the apartment complex, not lounging poolside drinking cocktails. Picking it up, she took a breath. The cool silky fabric reminded her of the last time she'd swum in Lough Caragh.

She'd gone down to the lake every morning in the months leading up to her Leaving Certificate exams, even on the days it had rained, thinking that she couldn't possibly get any wetter anyway. The year 2009 seemed like a dozen lifetimes ago. She pinched the swimsuit fabric between her fingers, remembering the amount of rain that had fallen that year. It was depressing, as if they all needed further depressing as the economy had crumbled. Yet somehow, no matter what the news or the weather, swimming in Lough Caragh had made her feel better. It had been a day like today the first time she'd ever swum across the lake.

That day, there had been another row with Cash over him leaving them short for grocery money. In a storm of anger, Heather had gone to the lake and made her way to the tiny jetty that some local boys had built but never used. She dropped her clothes on the silvered planks and dived in without hesitating, then had swum out as far as she'd ever gone. The lake was huge, and until that day she'd never been to the other side. A soft rain was falling, but she hadn't cared. She'd struck out and kept going until she had reached the opposite shore.

The shore was as stony as her own side was, but the sun had come out as she'd hauled herself from the water, shivering and panting. The air had been spicy with thunder, and under the sheerest layer of rain, the gorse was as dry as crackling and ready to go up in flames should the slightest spark hit it. It had felt smothering and hadn't helped soothe her gasping lungs. Even though the sun shone through the hazy air as the rain passed, it hadn't been warm enough to shake the chill from her. Standing on the far shore she'd wrapped her arms around her body and firmly clamped her mouth shut to stop the scream that threatened to free itself.

Blast them all. Idiots, the lot of them. There was no

escaping them, but there had to be. She hadn't worked this hard on herself to just be swamped down by Cash and his selfishness. Niamh had said something recently. Something about how cabin crew always insist you put your own oxygen mask on first before you help anyone else. Well, she was certainly about to do that, and then she was going to get the hell out of there. Only then would she be able to see clearly, and maybe she'd be able to help Willow too. She didn't know how, but she did know that she had to look out for herself first. With that in mind, she'd swum back and gone to work, grateful to her Transition Year head, Miss Tully, for helping her get a position in a travel agency. At least there she felt a step closer to getting away from them all.

Sitting on her bed in her spacious London apartment now, Heather's stomach tightened just as it had that day when she'd thought that she'd never get away from them, but she had gotten away and now she was going back. She groaned, the swimsuit still in her hands.

To pack, or not to pack? She dropped it back onto the bed. She'd no intentions of lake swimming, but maybe she should take it, just in case? Her phone reminder sounded: it was time for her to leave to meet Simon. Throwing a cursory glance at her reflection, she nodded and turned away. There was no point in getting too dressed up. The meeting wasn't going to be a fun one, and it would be a snub to arrive looking like a million dollars when she'd turned him down. Still, she couldn't stop herself from pulling a brush through her hair and spritzing his favourite perfume before she unplugged the lights and plunged the apartment into darkness.

For the whole train journey her heartbeat pounded low in her stomach. She'd been itching to message Simon all day but hadn't, expecting him to text her first, but he'd been uncharacteristically quiet, and his silence was making her throat ache. She had caught herself behaving as Pippa had when Cash had gone off with someone, and had to force her grip on her phone to loosen. Then the Tube was chock-a-block with people, but it kept her mind busy as it rattled underground. Emerging from the Tube at Liverpool Street, Heather took a breath and walked towards the square where the restaurant was. Everywhere was buzzing with people, all trim and tidy. Even though she knew she looked as polished as any of them, Heather felt as hick and grimy as if she'd walked in from Lough Caragh village wearing wellie boots and mud.

She turned down New Street, passing The Magpie on her left as she reached the archway into Devonshire Square.

Chattering and laughter rang out as Heather made herself slow down, not feeling as fearless as Niamh once said she was. The covered-in pedestrian space had pulled in a crowd eager to make the most of the cosy area on a chilly Valentine's Day evening. The warm yellow brick buildings and the glow from soft neon lights and patio heaters almost convinced Heather that she was looking forward to the evening, but not quite. She strained to see if he was there, craning her neck to look through the upbeat crowd. For a moment she worried that he hadn't come, but then she spied him on the mezzanine. He was at a table just outside a restaurant, looking down at his phone.

Swallowing hard, she tried to smile, but found her face

175

frozen as she watched him scroll through his phone. He looked amazing, but a little tired. His hair was longer too – she hadn't noticed that during their FaceTime calls. A woman nearby shrieked as a bouquet of flowers appeared before her and Heather was struck by the fact that it was Valentine's Day. How had they made the decision to meet today of all days, but if they hadn't then not meeting on such a day would have felt just as weird. Blinking back the tears that smarted at the back of her eyes, she pulled herself together and was smiling by the time she reached him.

'Hey,' she said as he stood to greet her. 'You look great.'

'Hi.' He leaned in to hug her, holding her slightly away from him in a way that made her feel as if she'd been relegated to friend or acquaintance.

'You're back for a while?' Simon said as they sat down.

'Till Saturday morning.' Heather picked up the drink menu and lowered her eyes to read the cocktails on offer.

Simon nodded. 'Any plans?'

'No,' Heather said. She read the cocktail list again. 'No plans.' She raised her eyes and found him looking softly at her.

'No plans? That's not like you.' He stopped fidgeting with his phone and looked at her.

'Not this time. Actually, I was considering going back tomorrow instead.'

'Oh.' Simon's face fell. 'There's nothing keeping you here, is that it?'

'Simon . . .' Heather reached for his hand, but he sat back and folded his hands on his lap. Heather spoke quietly. 'Simon, it's not that. It's not you—'

'Come on, Heddie,' Simon said. 'Don't say it's not you, it's me – it's insulting.'

'It's not meant to be insulting.' Heather's face flamed up on hearing his nickname for her. 'It's me being honest with you.'

'We both know that's not true.' Simon's eyes never left her face. 'Come on, Heather. Be fair.'

'I don't know what you want me to say,' Heather whispered. The crowded cocktail bar was loud, but he nodded, and she knew he'd heard her.

'I don't know what I want you to say either,' he said after a minute. 'I thought I wanted you to come in here and say Happy Valentine's Day, then kiss me, and then you'd tell me how much you missed me. That going back to Ireland was all a mistake, and you were coming home. To me.'

Sliding her hand back to her lap, Heather shivered. 'I do miss you.'

'I miss you.' Simon shook his head. 'Heather, I love you, but while you've been gone, I've had time to think about us.'

Heather gripped her hands tightly together under the table. This was it; this was the moment she'd been waiting for since the day they'd met. He was going to leave, just like her father had, and there was nothing she could, or would, do about it. She pressed her tongue to the roof of her mouth and clamped her mouth shut. Best to let him get on with it. Then she could go back to Ireland and get over it all. At least she had Pippa's new business to occupy her; she'd be able to forget him in no time.

Simon shifted in his chair and loosened his collar.

'Heddie, I don't want to lose you. I need you to be honest with me . . . You said no in Paris. Does that mean you don't want me in your life anymore?'

Heather's mouth dropped open. The clattering of people eating and drinking faded as a rush came to her head. He wasn't dumping her.

'I know I said no, but Si . . . why would you think that I don't want you?' Heather took in his bewildered face.

'Because I've no reason not to think it.' Simon kept his voice low. 'Listen, it's up to you now. I've tried everything I could think of to make you happy, and I've run out of ideas. Every time I try to get closer to you, you literally hop on a plane and all I get are a few messages to let me know you're alive . . . and working.'

'That's what I do; that's my job.' Heather sat forward. 'You can't hold that against me. Ever consider that your timing is off?'

'I know it's your job, Hed, and you know I'd never hold that against you.' Simon sat back with a long sigh. 'It seems that my timing is always off. I'm going to take a step back and let *you* figure us out. I need a break from doing all the chasing.'

'Chasing?' Heather's eyebrows rose. 'Did you just say you're chasing me?'

'Us. I'm chasing us,' Simon said. He stood up as a waitress wound her way through the crowd towards her. 'I'm sorry. I'm worn out, so I'm going to go now.'

'You're going to go? Like, leave?' Heather jumped up and caught his hand. His skin was warm and soft. Squeezing his hand, she felt her ribs tighten. 'Simon?'

'I'm not leaving us, just leaving here.' Simon looked

down at his feet. 'It probably wasn't the best idea to meet, not tonight, and not when I'm feeling this way.'

'Which way?' Heather grasped his hand tightly, suddenly terrified that he'd disappear on her.

Simon's jaw twitched as he twisted his lips together.

'Unwanted.' His eyes were bright when he finally looked at her. 'Heather, I love you, I want you, and I want you to want me too. But I can't make you want me, and it hurts that you don't. Let's just take this time out – it almost feels as if it's been handed to us – and see how we do apart for a while. When you're ready – if you're ready – to come back to me I'll be waiting for you.'

He leaned over and kissed her cheek and then was gone. Heather stood still, hardly drawing a breath. Her hands scrunched into balls at her sides until she forced them to unclench. She couldn't focus on which direction he'd gone, even if she'd wanted to. The waitress stood looking at her, a menu dangling uselessly from her hands. Shaking her head, Heather turned and hurried away.

15

20th June 2007

The heat was stifling in the travel agent's office where Heather worked part-time. The fan was doing nothing but moving hot air around, and Heather's feet were beginning to swell from sitting so long. It didn't help that her work uniform – a neat black skirt, a white blouse and a neck scarf – made her sweat profusely. Wiping her top lip, Heather glanced up from her desk. There was no one waiting, for once.

She sat back and patted her hair, which was neatly tied up in a high bun. Niamh teased her incessantly about the bun, telling her it made her look like a ballerina crossed with a hockey player. It didn't matter what Niamh said; Heather picked up her wastepaper basket and took it to the shredder. Niamh hadn't been the one to organise a cheap sun holiday for the three of them. They were flying out tomorrow morning and would be in Mallorca in no time where they'd meet up with Rosemary and her friend Stella who had been there a week already. That was the only way their parents had agreed to let them go. Everyone else in their class was going off places to celebrate their graduation from Transition Year – some of their classmates were leaving school early and going into hairdressing or training to be beauticians and nail technicians, but the majority of them would return to school in September to carry on their second-level education.

TY, as they called it, had been a great year. The year had flown by, and they'd done so much. She'd learned how to kayak in the Liffey, trained by some ex-Army men who'd been easy on the eye but strict and disciplined. It had been brilliant but the best thing to come out of it was this job.

Miss Tully, the head of the Transition Year project, had anticipated that Heather would have trouble gaining her work experience placement. She'd intervened and the next thing Heather knew was that she had a job in Glenrua, in a travel agency of all places. At first Heather didn't know what she'd learn there and spent most of her time emptying bins and running to the shop for milk and teabags, but over time she'd proven to be an asset. She was friendly and a great listener and helped people looking through the holiday brochures while they waited for one of the agents to be free. By the time the people were seen, Heather had helped them narrow down their choices by making sure most of their requirements were met. It was something she never imagined she'd enjoy, and a place where she finally felt accepted for her own merits. Without the job she'd never have booked a holiday with her two best friends.

Alcúdia – she couldn't wait. The brochure promised

sandy beaches, nightclubs and an old town with a weekly market too. She'd packed her brand-new suitcase, Primark's finest, since last week and had been on tenterhooks until her passport had finally arrived only the day before.

'This time tomorrow . . .' she said to Claire, the owner, who had come in from the back office and was fanning her face with a Sandals Resort brochure. 'It'll be sun, sand and s . . .'

'Sunscreen, please say sunscreen,' Claire said. 'You're too young for the other thing.'

'I'm sixteen,' Heather said.

'Under the age of consent.' Claire wagged her finger at her.

'I've no intention of getting it on with anyone. I'm happy to wait.' Heather grimaced. There was no doubt Niamh's antennae would be up, but she'd no sense. Boys their age were only interested in fooling around, and even if they weren't, there was no guarantee they'd be decent or kind. At the very least they'd be messers; at the best they'd be like Lauren's boyfriend, Shane, and both prospects were just too much for her to think about. Her sights were on being as independent as she could, and boys would only get in her way. There'd be time enough for men – not boys, she thought as Claire sat at her desk.

'Good,' Claire said. 'That's the right attitude. Now come here, I've had a phone call from . . .' she checked her notepad '. . . Sheila Monaghan. She said she'll only deal with you. Apparently half of Lough Caragh has gone on holidays on your recommendations and everyone has had the best time.'

'Sheila Monaghan?' Heather grinned. 'Wow. I've reached the heights of it now.'

'She'll be in shortly, but she left me this list of what she's after.' Claire handed over a page filled with notes.

'Ouch,' Heather said, taking the page. 'She's not asking for much, is she?'

'Nothing short of seven stars would suit her, by the sounds of it.' Claire stood up and stretched. 'I hope she's not too much hassle. Let me know what she's after when you're ready and I'll make the bookings.'

'Thanks, Claire.' Heather read down through Sheila's list, then grabbed a bunch of brochures and began narrowing down destinations that might suit Sheila. In no time at all she'd a shortlist of twelve. She normally had fewer, but this was Sheila Monaghan, and heaven knew what would please her.

Half an hour later, Sheila swanned in the door of the travel agency looking chic in a lime-green dress suit. The heat didn't seem to bother her at all. She patted her neatly coiffed hair as she sank into the chair as elegantly as any royal lady would.

'You look lovely, Sheila, eh I mean Mrs Monaghan,' Heather said.

'Thank you, Heather – that's kind of you to say.' Sheila patted her hair. Her pink lipstick had smudged on her top teeth, but Heather didn't know how to tell her. Surreptitiously running her tongue along her own teeth, she pulled a few brochures from her drawer and began listening as Sheila spoke.

'Rosemary said you sorted out her accommodation, so I took her advice and came to you,' Sheila said. 'I like the heat, so I'm not concerned about places being too hot. I'd prefer air conditioning as standard in the rooms. Close to a beach but also a private pool. I don't want a flight that requires me to rise from my bed at an ungodly hour – a day flight if you don't mind.'

It took an hour for Sheila Monaghan to settle on a five-star hotel in Portugal, and another ten minutes for Claire to make the booking. Sheila breezed out as easily as she'd breezed in. Heather leaned back in her chair and breathed out.

'She's something else,' Claire said as Sheila, in her lime dress suit, bounced down the road in the June sunshine. 'Look at her, she's full of energy. I hope I'm like that when I'm older. Why don't you head off now. Go home and get ready for Mallorca.'

'Seriously?' Heather grinned.

'Seriously. And Heather, you've a real knack for this. If you're interested, I could put you forward for training next year.' Claire leaned back and looked at Heather closely.

'Training – to be an agent? Here?' Heather stood still. Becoming a travel agent hadn't even crossed her mind, but it would be a start, wouldn't it?

'Yes,' Claire said. 'Listen, go on your holiday and think it over. No rush, and no pressure.'

'Thank you,' Heather said. Already she could imagine making her own money, and the commission was bound to be great – she was great at the job already. She'd be able to move out and get her own place. Smiling, she turned to Claire. 'Thanks, I will.'

'Go on! Have a lovely time and wear sunscreen,' Claire said as Heather picked up her bag. 'See ya in a week.'

*

Niamh sat on her bedroom floor surrounded by bikinis, sundresses and sandals. Her empty suitcase lay beside her. Lauren sat at her dressing table.

'It's hopeless,' Niamh said. Shrugging she shook her head. 'I'll never be ready on time.'

'Don't be ridiculous,' Lauren said. 'Just pick some clothes out and pack them. It's not like you're going to be waltzing down a catwalk so who cares.'

'Meanie.' Niamh frowned. Then she raised her eyebrows and tried to smooth the lines that were developing between them by massaging them with her fingertips.

'Niamh, we've been here hours and you won't make any decisions,' Lauren said. 'I want to see Shane. I'm going to miss him when we're gone.'

Niamh dropped her hands into her lap. 'I'm sorry, okay. It's just, well, I want to look nice.'

'You always look nice,' Lauren said. She knelt down beside Niamh. 'Come on, you know that. Look, let's start with evenings – we have seven evenings so pick seven outfits for that and we'll go from there.'

Seven complete night-time outfits later, they'd moved on to bikinis and daywear.

'Just pack it all,' Lauren sat back on her heels. 'I can't take this anymore.'

'I can't take it all – there's a weight allowance, and I

have to pack my toiletries yet,' Niamh said, holding up two almost identical bikini tops.

'That one.' Lauren pointed to the one in Niamh's right hand. 'And this, and this. Don't argue, just put it in the case. You won't wear the half of this anyway.'

'Fine,' Niamh muttered. She put the items Lauren had selected in the case and quelled her worry. What if she met the boy of her dreams on this holiday? What if she didn't and came home with tan lines and Rory Quinlan saw? What if she bumped into a famous person and they invited her onto their yacht?

Mrs Kennedy popped her head around the door. Seeing the girls still sitting in the middle of a pile of clothes she pushed the door open more. The smile on her face slowly disappeared as she scanned the room.

'What's going on here?' She placed her hands on her hips. 'Niamh, you should have packed hours ago.'

'I know, it's just hard.' Niamh's shoulders slumped.

'I think we're on top of it now, Mrs Kennedy,' Lauren said, standing up as Niamh's mother stepped further into the room. 'Just toiletries left – that shouldn't take long.'

Mrs Kennedy tried to peer past Lauren. 'Well, I'm putting the kettle on. I expect you both downstairs in ten minutes.'

'Thank you, Mrs Kennedy.' Lauren picked up a toiletry bag and put a bottle of sun cream into it. 'Ten minutes.'

From her place kneeling by her suitcase on the floor, Niamh breathed out.

'Thanks,' she said, getting up. 'If she'd seen the bottoms to that bikini, she'd have taken my passport away.'

'I know.' Lauren grinned. 'I'm the bestest friend you

ever had. Come on. You've enough clothes packed – let's get this done and get some tea. I'm parched.'

Down in the kitchen, Mrs Kennedy laid out a plate of homemade scones and a pot of tea. Niamh groaned thinking of the bikinis she'd just packed.

'Eat up.' Niamh's mother interrupted her thoughts. She sat at the chair to the right of the head of the table. 'Remind me again, what time is your flight tomorrow?'

'Seven,' Lauren said around a mouthful of scone. 'Shane's dad is picking us up at four. We have to be there three hours in advance.'

Mrs Kennedy took a long look at Niamh. 'This is the first I've heard of it. Thank you, Lauren.'

'No problem,' Lauren said. Finishing her tea, Lauren got up. 'I'd best be off. I need to do a few last-minute things myself. Thanks for the tea, Mrs Kennedy. It was delicious.'

Niamh watched her mother walk Lauren to the front door. It wasn't that she'd been purposefully hiding holiday information from her mother, it was just she didn't think she needed to know every detail.

'Well, Niamh, I can't believe you didn't tell me that piece of information.' Her mother stood at the end of the table. 'I shouldn't have to drag it from your friends.'

Niamh looked away. 'It's just a holiday. And we're going with Rosemary. It's not like we're all heading off to Ibiza like the rest of them are.'

'That's neither here nor there,' Mrs Kennedy said. 'Niamh, you're sixteen years old. As your parent I'm responsible for you. I worry about you *all* the time.'

'Ah, Mam,' Niamh said. 'You don't need to worry about me. I'm grand.'

'Niamh.' Mrs Kennedy picked up the teapot. 'That's not fair. Your father and I are doing our best. You're our only child, of course we're going to worry about you. You're the most precious thing in the world to me.'

'Sorry, Mam.' Niamh pressed her fingertip down on a crumb. 'I know. I didn't mean it that way.'

'I'm sorry too,' Mrs Kennedy said. 'I know you didn't. You're growing up, and it's hard for me to see. I'm the world's biggest worrywart, that's all. You're going to have the best fun on your holiday. I remember when I went away with my friends, mind you, we were in our twenties not our teens. Rome, for a whole week. It was spectacular. We'd such fun, and the style – oh the style was amazing. I could've sat all day outside a trattoria and watched the style and done nothing else.'

'Rome? For a week? You never told me that before.' Niamh looked at her mother. She was turning fifty-six in September and was much older than any of her friends' mothers. Wearing a smart pair of trousers, belted, with a crisp linen shirt, turned up at the collar, her mother looked calm and organised. Niamh sighed inwardly. She couldn't begin to imagine her mother on holiday with a bunch of girlfriends at all.

'It was so hot,' her mother said dreamily. 'Of course, no one wore sunscreen back then. Leslie got terribly burnt and had to stay in for a day or two, but nothing could keep her in at night. There was a bar down the street where we spent a few evenings. The barman was very good to us.'

Niamh watched her mother's eyes grow misty. What on earth had she gotten up to in Italy? Grinning, Niamh pressed another crumb with her fingertip. She'd a feeling her mother knew exactly what kind of holiday she was after.

'Those were the days,' Niamh said. 'I'm looking forward to making some great memories.'

Her mother blinked and looked at her. She raised her eyebrows. 'Safe memories.'

'Always, Mam. I promise.' Niamh got up. 'Let me clear up for you.'

'You're a good girl, Niamh, I know that.' Mrs Kennedy put down the teapot. 'You'll make someone a lovely wife one day, just don't make it too soon, okay? Have fun, but please be safe.'

The hairs on Niamh's arms prickled. Her mother sounded uncharacteristically sad. While loading the dishwasher, Niamh pondered over what she knew of her mother's life.

Her parents had met each other at an ABBA concert in Dublin in 1979, and for some reason her mother, a huge ABBA fan, had fallen for her father who'd only gone to the concert at the last minute because his cousin had been sick. Maybe it was his steadiness that had attracted her to him, Niamh pondered. He'd a good job, and this house. They'd married the following year, and she knew, from previous snippets of conversations, that one of the reasons her mother accepted his proposal was that she was afraid of getting older and never getting married. She had been thirty then, and Niamh hadn't arrived until she was forty when they'd all but given up on the idea of having children. They'd named her Niamh because it meant *bright and radiant*, and *princess of the golden hair*. All her life she'd been treated as such. It was only in the past couple of years that her father had become stricter and more insistent on her behaving herself. It was hard being an only child. If only they'd had more then she wouldn't have to carry the burden of all their dreams and expectations.

Although, she thought as she wiped the counter, her father didn't really expect that much from her at all beyond being a good girl, which meant not hanging around the streets, and not seeing boys. He'd die if he knew what she really got up to, she acknowledged as she put the milk in the fridge, but she couldn't align her dreams with his. There was no way she was going to get married and have children any time before she was thirty, for sure. Her life didn't have to be the same as theirs. She had the world to see, boys to adore her, places to go, and it all started this summer.

No. Niamh marched back upstairs. She was not going to be all prim and proper and wifey material just because her father was fearful she'd have trouble starting a family as her mother had. Nope, not a chance. She'd take a leaf out of her mother's book and enjoy her freedom before settling down when she was good and ready. With renewed enthusiasm, Niamh picked up the shortest dress rejected by Lauren earlier and stuffed it into her case. This holiday was going to be fun.

*

Lauren plodded up the hill towards her house, sweating but eager to see Shane as soon as she could. She'd the

190

whole evening to be with him. Her case was packed, filled with the new clothes and sandals she'd bought in Primark. Her mother had bought her a proper beach towel too, and she felt glamorous. Shane was waiting for her, sitting on the wall of his house. He jumped down and ran towards her as she came around the corner.

'Hi.' She wrapped her arms around him as he planted a kiss on her lips.

'I was wondering if Niamh had accidentally packed you into her case.' He slung his arm around her shoulders. She slipped her arm around his waist. They walked towards the green between their houses and sat on the bench.

'I'd never fit in a case.' Lauren laughed. 'Although, Niamh's case is quite big.'

'You're so tiny you'd fit in a backpack,' Shane said.

Lauren elbowed him. 'I'm not that short!'

'You are.' Shane nudged her back.

They sat in silence for a few minutes, holding hands and watching nothing in particular until Shane spoke.

'You're going to have the best time.'

'I'm going to miss you.' Lauren squeezed his hand. 'I wish you were coming too.'

'Then it wouldn't be a girls' holiday.' He squeezed her hand back.

'Fair point. Doesn't mean I don't want you with me though.'

'I know, but we can text each other.' He pulled her into his arms and rested his chin on her head.

'I need to top up my phone credit,' Lauren said. 'Don't let me forget. They say it's expensive . . .'

'Let's just text in the morning and last thing at night

then,' Shane said. 'Just try to have fun. Don't worry about me, about us. We're good.'

'I'll try.' Lauren snuggled in closer to him. She took a deep breath, inhaling his scent and holding it in for a minute.

'You'll be with Niamh, so there'll be lots of fun, and Heather so you know you'll always get home safe,' Shane said. 'It's just a holiday – seven days, Laure. You need it. You've been working in Billy's and helping out the Tidy Towns Committee.'

'I sound like a right old biddy.' Lauren laughed. 'I'd better shake that persona off.'

'Yeah,' he snorted. 'You'd better.'

Lauren hugged him. He was right. While she was slightly concerned that Niamh would want to go clubbing every night, she knew that Heather would keep them on track. It was sometimes far too easy to just go along with Niamh. Having Heather would make it easier to stand up for herself if she needed to.

'Let's go get an ice cream, and phone credit,' Shane said.

Standing up, Lauren felt a twinge in her back. Her period. It was late and she was anxious.

'Give me two minutes. I need to use the loo.' Lauren dashed into her house, flew up the stairs and into the bathroom.

It wasn't her period. There was nothing at all. Sitting on the toilet Lauren stared at the back of the bathroom door and prayed that her period would arrive soon.

'Even on holiday,' she whispered as she washed her hands. 'Please.'

Then she hurried back down to Shane knowing that

he'd no idea what was really bothering her and, not knowing how to tell him, she slipped her hand into his.

'Let's go.'

They meandered through the long grass on the green, sidestepping footballs and lost tennis balls. The whole time Shane chatted away, and Lauren held his hand tightly. She chose the same ice cream as his; it was easier not to have to think or make choices. Then she followed him back outside and unwrapped her ice cream in silence.

'Hey,' he said, watching her closely. 'Stop worrying. It'll be grand.'

For a moment she thought he knew, that he, too, had been counting the days on the calendar, that he'd been staring at the ceiling in the middle of the night listening to cars pass by. That he'd sat in mass and prayed that everything would be all right, promised that it wouldn't happen again, silently apologised for breaking the rules . . . but then he smiled at her, and she realised he was talking about the holiday again.

'Dad said you can pop your case in his taxi later on, save you dragging it around the house and waking everyone up.' Shane flicked his ice cream stick into the bin. He always finished his food fast.

'Thanks, that's a good idea,' Lauren said. She looked at her half-eaten ice cream. It was beginning to drip, and her stomach churned. She held it out to Shane. 'Do you want this? I'm not really in the mood for ice cream today.'

'You know me – I never say no to ice cream.' He finished it off in record time and she wondered where he put all the food he ate. Then she remembered that was exactly what his mother always said, and a shiver ran down her back. Maybe one day she'd be thinking that very same thing about . . .

She forced the thought from her mind. They'd talked about being together, forever. When they watched telly, they chatted about what kind of house they'd like, what they'd do with the garden and how many kids they'd have. It had been fun then, but now it was terrifying. She found her hands cradling her stomach and wrenched them away. Having a huge belly filled with a baby, then having to give birth – all that mess – the pain. She'd overheard her mother and her friends talking but when they'd noticed her listening, they'd all said it was worth it, and you soon forgot how bad it was, which sounded like a cop-out. It was a lot to take in, yet she still wanted a family, just not now. Not when she was sixteen, and she was full sure that Shane, if he knew, would feel the same.

She walked alongside Shane towards the square, wishing she could tell him. But it wasn't right to tell him now, not when she was going away for a week – he'd have no one to talk to. It wasn't like they could just walk into the pharmacy and pick up a test and find out. Everyone in the village knew everyone else. They'd be in trouble in no time. No, they'd have to take a trip to Dublin when she got home from Mallorca – that's what they'd do. Until then she'd just have to keep quiet and try not to tell the girls.

They stopped outside her garden gate and kissed. Breaking away from her, Shane gazed at her. He put his hand in his pocket and tipped his brow against hers.

'It's not a pebble,' he said. 'But I just wanted to give this to you: my heart.'

He took her hand and suddenly she was holding a tiny heart button.

'Don't laugh,' he said. 'It was the best I could do.'

'It's perfect,' Lauren said. 'I'll treasure it always.'

She held the tiny heart button in her hand tightly as he walked across the green to his house, her eyes trained on his back until he'd gone inside.

*

Rosemary checked the bedroom again. Three single beds pristinely made up, fresh towels laid out, and the balcony window was wide open. The furniture was all pine, the walls were white, and the terracotta tiles warm where the sun shone on them. There was one big dressing table and she knew the girls would love it. She ambled downstairs and into the kitchen where her friend Stella was putting slices of lemon in two glasses.

'They're good girls,' Rosemary said as Stella passed her a plate of melon. 'You'll love them. I know you will.'

'I'll take your word for it.' Stella picked up the glasses of gin and tonic she'd prepared and followed Rosemary out onto the small patio. They sat on the white plastic patio furniture. 'They're going to love this, judging by what you've told me about them.' She gestured to their private garden, complete with a small swimming pool. A tiny gate in the back wall led directly onto the beach.

'The upgrade was worth it,' Rosemary said. 'You only live once.'

'That's true.' Stella raised her glass. 'Cheers! I have to

say, it's been nice to have you to myself for the past week. I've missed you.'

'I've missed you too. I'm so glad we're doing this.' Rosemary clinked her glass against her friend's one. 'What time is Eileen arriving?'

'She should be here around eight. She's flying in from Morocco.' Stella picked up a piece of melon. 'You'll like her. She's a real livewire. I honestly can say that I wouldn't be here if it wasn't for her.'

'What?' Rosemary sat up. 'What do you mean?'

'Oh, not that way,' Stella said with a wave. 'I mean, I'd be stuck at home. Eileen travels solo all the time, and she was there when you rang to ask me if I'd come with you. She wouldn't allow me to say no!'

'Well, I'm glad she was there then,' Rosemary said, leaning back in her chair. 'Where has she travelled to?'

'You name it and she's been there,' Stella said. 'Even Egypt.'

'I'd love to go to Egypt,' Rosemary said. 'Wouldn't it be amazing to see the pyramids?'

'Not before I see Newgrange though,' Stella said. 'They're older than the pyramids. Did you know that?'

'I did, but I've never thought of going,' Rosemary said. 'But we should go. What do you think? Will we make a plan to go soon?'

Stella nodded decisively. 'My inner Eileen says yes!'

Rosemary laughed. 'Good woman yourself. Let's make a plan.'

'That would be great – I'd really like that,' Stella said.

'So you know that tomorrow is solstice . . .' Rosemary

took a sip '. . . well, I promised the girls that I'd go down to the sea with them in the morning for our solstice swim.'

'Solstice swim?' Stella asked.

'Each solstice we go to the lake and take a dip at sunrise; well, we try. Sometimes it's a little too cold in the winter, but we have managed every sunrise swim for the solstice for the past few years,' Rosemary explained. 'We decided that, seeing as we're here by the sea, why not continue the tradition. We, er, we dip ourselves in the water completely to wash away anything negative and set good intentions for the rest of the year. Sounds a bit mad, but it's really helped the girls. And me.'

'Would it be all right if Eileen and I joined you?' Stella sat up. 'I think it sounds lovely. I could do with something washing the negativity away from me right now. Henry has been a bit of pest lately. He's whingeing over stuff that was settled during the divorce and I'm losing the will to battle him.'

'Absolutely join us,' Rosemary said. 'Let's wash that man right out into the sea!'

'Without a paddle!' Stella whooped and then covered her mouth. 'Oh, that was awful. I shouldn't say such things.'

'Yes, you should.' Rosemary nodded at her. 'It's only a joke, and anyway, he deserves it!'

Stella started laughing again, and Rosemary grinned.

'It does me good seeing you happy again, Stell. I was so worried about you for so long.'

Stella grew serious. 'I can see that, now. Back then I couldn't see anything. I thought that was what marriage was, you know, that it was supposed to be difficult. My parents, well, their marriage was anything but easy. They were always at odds with each other.' She looked directly at Rosemary. 'I know you tried to talk to me a number of times. I'm sorry I didn't listen.'

'It's not your fault.' Rosemary reached for her friend's hand. 'You were only doing what you thought was the best thing at the time. I suppose it can't have been easy seeing me and Paddy the way we were either.'

Stella cleared her throat. 'Well, no, but at the time I had this notion that you two simply needed to grow up. That you couldn't stay in honeymoon mode forever, but you proved me wrong. You must miss him so much.'

Rosemary looked down. Her hand shook as Stella held it tightly. 'I do. I miss him more and more every day. All this nonsense about time making things easier, it's not true. I'm falling apart, to be honest, Stell. I don't know how to live anymore. Some days I don't want to.'

Stella squeezed Rosemary's hand. 'Rose, are you serious? Don't say that.'

'I wouldn't do anything, I swear,' Rosemary said quickly. 'But the thought is there, sometimes. More times than I'd like it to be. But I'm okay. I've got the girls and they keep me going.'

'Oh, Rose. I didn't know. I wish you'd called me sooner.' Stella sniffed. 'I'm sorry. I've been so wrapped up . . . I've been a bad friend.'

'God, no, you haven't.' Rosemary wiped her eyes. 'The best thing has been knowing you're free from that weird little man, and that you're getting through every day too. You've no idea how much it's helped me just knowing that you're getting up every day and living a brand-new life. It's so brave.'

'Christ. It's not brave. I'm always afraid,' Stella said. 'Some days I just want to crawl into bed and not ever leave it. But as Emer always says when they call me from the States: *Just keep swimming, Nanny.* I try to keep swimming just for her.'

'That's hard,' Rosemary said quietly. 'You must miss them too.'

'I do, but what can I do about it?'

The two friends sat in silence. Each lost in their own thoughts, until a particularly loud seagull squawked them out of their reverie.

'Look at us, two mopey fools.' Rosemary fixed her hair. 'We've got the sea in front of us, and friends arriving any minute. We are lucky, aren't we?'

'We are.' Stella nodded. 'Tell me, what time are we doing this solstice swim?'

'Brace yourself,' Rosemary said, glad to have moved on from their emotional talk. 'Sunrise is at twenty past six, so we'll be up and out at six.'

'Six? Okay, that I can do.' Stella smiled. 'Once an early riser, always an early riser.'

*

At six the next morning everyone gathered on the patio, shivering and yawning. Niamh pulled her towel tighter around her.

'I thought it'd be warmer,' she muttered.

'It'll warm up when the sun comes up,' Rosemary said.

'Will the sea be cold?' Lauren piped up.

'It'll be freezing,' Eileen said. 'But we're hot stuff so we'll warm it up for everyone else.'

Stella stifled a giggle.

'Well, we are!' Eileen said. 'Aren't we?' She nudged Niamh, who grinned.

Heather took a step towards the tiny gate and clenched her fists. Releasing them she looked back at the others. 'Come on then, what are we waiting for!'

'That's the spirit!' Eileen laughed.

Heather was through the gate in a shot. Her feet flashed on the cool sand as she ran to the water's edge, flinging her towel to one side as she ran. Laughing, the others ran after her, dropping their towels too.

The water was cold, colder than the lake, but it was refreshing, and stinging.

*

Heather dove under and relished the power of the waves. As the sun rose she set her intention. *This is the year it's all going to happen for me, and not before time either. Thank you.*

*

Lauren went out as far as she felt safe, then ducked quickly under the water. Spluttering and spitting salt water as she surfaced, she turned to the sun and begged for everything to be like it used to be. She gazed at the sun. *I'm not able for this, help me.*

*

Niamh floated on her back and stared at the sky and wished for the life her mother never had. *Maybe that's asking too much, but I don't know what else to do.*

*

Rosemary bobbed up and down beside Stella – Eileen having plonked herself down in the shallow waters. With her eyes tightly closed, she found her mind drifting instead of focusing on her intention. She imagined Paddy beside her, swimming those strong strokes he always did. He'd have loved Mallorca. She wished they'd come here when he was alive. "Better late than never", she could almost hear him say. Smiling, she dipped her head under the foaming waves. *You're right, Paddy, better late than never – it's time to start living again.*

16

Niamh drained her mug of tea, feeling like a bad mother for enjoying the peace and quiet now that everyone had gone to school. Evan was barely talking to her since last week. She'd almost found it amusing, but it was childish, and it hurt. He'd never been this angry before, and he'd never shut himself away from her like this either. Normally he'd be the first to apologise, usually with flowers. But this time it was different, and she couldn't really blame him. Niamh put her mug into the dishwasher. His ego was hurt – that was all. He'd get over it soon enough. He'd have to. The kids had noticed the tension and she knew he'd hate them to be upset. She'd have to talk to him later. They had to iron things out, especially as Rory was starting work today, and there was no way she was backing down now.

A clattering in the yard sent her hurrying to the window. Outside in the frosty air, Rory was unloading a skip from the back of a huge lorry. Dashing outside, Niamh couldn't help smiling. It was good to see someone enthusiastic about her dream.

'Morning!' Rory waved from the far side of the yard. 'Mind yourself there. Those things swing a bit.'

Niamh watched as the huge battered yellow skip was slowly lowered to the ground. It landed with a dull thud, and she shivered as a gust of wind blew her hair into her eyes. Swiping her face, she walked over to Rory, who was waving the lorry driver off.

'I can't believe we're getting started.' She stood beside him.

He smiled down at her, bright and fresh as always. 'It's going to be brilliant. I've a few more ideas I wanted to show you – finishing touches, nothing crazy but they'll make a huge difference.'

'And what will it cost me?' Niamh laughed. 'I'm all about the money these days.'

Rory shrugged. 'A cuppa every now and then should just about cover it, I'd say.'

'A cup of tea?' Niamh raised her eyebrows. 'Come on now, there's no such thing as a free lunch, even I know that.'

'Ah but you make the best tea.' He pulled out his phone. 'Look at these.'

Niamh leaned over his arm as he showed her the ideas he'd come up with. He was right, they were great and would elevate the rooms from ordinary to boutique. She yawned as he put his phone away.

'Sorry, I'm just tired,' she apologised.

'Not sleeping?' Rory seemed genuinely concerned.

Niamh shrugged. 'I fall asleep, but I wake up around three and it's a couple of hours before I nod off again.'

203

'Do you know what's good to help you fall asleep?' Rory leaned back on the skip.

Niamh's stomach spun as if she was on the waltzers. She looked at him and tried not to think of how Evan liked to help her sleep, which had nothing to do with sleeping at all, but always conked her out afterwards. There'd been none of those kinds of shenanigans since their row.

'What?' she said to Rory a little breathlessly. 'Tell me.'

'Get up,' he said with a twinkle in his eyes. 'Go into a different room and read a book.'

'Hah,' Niamh said. 'I don't think that's going to work.'

Rory raised his hands. His eyes were warm on hers. 'I've one other option that might help you when you can't sleep – you know, if reading a book doesn't work, but I'll leave that to your imagination.'

Niamh tilted her head. A thousand thoughts ran through her mind but the one that was the loudest was the one she couldn't say aloud: he was flirting with her! With difficulty she looked away from him. His relaxed posture and inviting smile were very easy to look at, but this chat was inappropriate. And it was proving Evan's point that Rory still had the hots for her.

'Okay.' Niamh pointed to the back door. 'I'm going back inside. It's freezing out here. Give me a shout if you want a cuppa later.'

'I will, thanks.' Rory saluted her as if nothing had passed between them. 'And just a heads up: there'll be a few of my lads here later, three of them. They're good lads, but I'll tell them to mind their p's and q's. They can be a bit . . . well, like young lads.'

'Like young lads,' Niamh said at the same time. She blushed. 'Thanks, Rory. I appreciate that.'

She went inside and straight to her phone where it was charging on the counter. It would be wise to tell Evan that Rory was here. But her head pounded as she held her phone in her hand, even imagining his response was making her blood pressure rise. It wasn't just Rory that was annoying him. He was really put out about the reinvigoration of her mother's B&B. It was as if he was challenged by her gaining some independence, which was ridiculous. *It hadn't always been like that.* She put the phone down on the counter. He used to be delighted to see her achieve anything, even if it was something as simple as making a cake for the first time.

Now, in their kitchen, with the sound of the skip being filled outside, she strove to remember what it was like when she and Evan had first gotten together.

It had been so strange, she remembered. She'd known him for years, but it had only been since her eighteenth birthday that she'd decided that he was worthy of more than the odd flirtatious banter. She and her then boyfriend shared a late November birthday, something that she'd felt meant they were made for one another. Unfortunately, he'd never subscribed to the same notion as he'd literally been caught with his pants down and Mandy Delaney's legs wrapped around his waist.

Niamh had been devastated. It had been her first and only teenage heartbreak. Looking back now she could see that it was her ego that had been bruised, not her heart. Yet it had been a good thing; it had brought her and Evan together. He'd comforted her, had taken her to the cinema to take her mind off things, had even walked her to school every day for a month. Everyone had started talking about them, saying they were a couple, and by that Christmas she'd convinced herself that maybe they were. But once bitten, twice shy, she'd kept things friendly between them, but the odd time she'd hold his hand, and sometimes she'd talk to him just as she'd talk to Heather and Lauren.

Nevertheless, she found him more attractive as time passed. It was she who asked him if they were going steady, and when he kissed her that first time she'd wondered if she'd made a mistake in not asking him sooner. The night of their school graduation – that was when it had gotten serious. That was the night she'd realised that she loved him, and the night that changed their lives. They'd be fifteen years married this summer. Fifteen years. It felt like three lifetimes ago. He always said he'd never regretted it, she thought as she stacked the dishwasher, but lately it seemed as if he did.

There was a knock on the window, and Rory's warm face appeared. He held his hands in the shape of the letter T and she pointed to the back door. He disappeared from sight, only to come in the back door and straight into her kitchen. There was something in how he moved so elegantly around her space that made the hair on her arms stand up. His ease and calmness made her bones feel warm. Again she wondered what would have happened if she hadn't said yes to Evan when he'd proposed. Would Rory have stepped in? With shaking hands she picked up the kettle.

'Tea – is that what you're after?' She filled the kettle with her back to Rory, hoping he wouldn't see how her hands shook.

'If that's what you're offering,' he said in a low tone.

'It is,' she said, her heart beating ever so slightly faster.

'And maybe something sweet?' He raised an eyebrow.

'I might have something,' she said and hurried to the fridge. The cool air calmed her red cheeks, and she stared inside at the shelves of yogurts and cheese before grabbing Evan's Caramel bar. 'I'm afraid this is all I have . . .'

'My favourite,' he said, looking right at her as she handed him the chocolate. He snapped off a square and offered it to her. 'Fancy a nibble?'

This is bonkers, she shook her head. *Is he really doing this? To me – in my own house? Or am I reading into things after what Evan said the other night?*

She looked at him sitting at the island unit. He looked very much at home, but she shouldn't think like that. Trying to clear her mind she went back to what they had in common: the refurbishment. 'I wanted to say thanks for being so encouraging about the rooms. It's been nice to have someone to go through everything with.'

'You're welcome,' he said. 'Don't you talk to Evan about it?'

'Not really, no. He's not happy about it,' Niamh said, surprising herself. She hadn't meant to give Evan away.

Rory gave a small laugh. 'Why not? It's a great idea, and you've wonderful vision.'

Niamh fell for the compliment easily. 'It *is* a great idea, thank you.'

'Is it your vision he doesn't like, or does he still not like me?' Rory suddenly said.

His comment took Niamh by surprise. 'Not like you?'

'He's never liked me,' Rory said. 'It's not a secret. He made it clear to me years ago.'

207

'Oh my God.' Niamh gripped the counter. 'What are you talking about?'

'Didn't you know?' Rory frowned. 'He warned me not to ask you to my debs. I wish I'd told him where to go, because I've always regretted not asking you. Who knows what might have happened between us.'

'Rory,' Niamh said, a little too loudly. Clearing her throat, she started again. 'Rory. You can't say these things to me, not now.'

'I'm sorry.' His mouth turned down. 'I'm not trying to stir anything. I thought you knew. Maybe you thought the same.'

'I didn't know.' Niamh shook her head. 'Rory . . . look, I don't know what you're saying to me here, but I think it's bordering on inappropriate, and it needs to stop. Now.' She looked around the room as if wondering where to run. *What was he talking about? He wished he'd ignored Evan? He wondered if anything would have happened between them?* Her heart pounded loudly in her ears so that all she could hear was a ringing sound.

'I'll leave.' Rory stood up. 'I'm sorry, Niamh. I thought . . .'

Niamh watched him leave, her hands shaking as the back door closed gently behind him. She heard him talking to the lads in the yard and for a split second thought he was going to pack up and not do the job at all. That would ruin her plans completely. Grabbing her bag and jacket from the kitchen table she raced out the front door.

She walked straight to the lake, only stopping when she got to the place where Evan had proposed. It was overgrown now; the wet grass was thick and already halfway up her calves. The memory of that day made her stop walking.

She'd gone to Evan and asked him to come for a walk with her. They'd gone to the lake. She hadn't been able to think of anywhere else to go. He'd listened to her as she'd stammered over the words.

'Are you sure?' he'd asked.

'Of course, I'm sure.' She'd looked at him in horror. 'Do you think I'd say this if I wasn't?'

'Christ.' He'd paced up and down, his hands in his hair before standing and staring out at the lake. 'What will you do?'

'What will *I* do?' Niamh had gaped at him.

'Is it even . . .'

'Don't finish that sentence,' she'd cried. 'You know it is.'

'I'm sorry.' Evan had blanched. 'It's just . . .'

'It's just what? The typical thing lads say? I thought more of you. I see how it is now.'

'What do you mean, you see how it is?'

'You're the same as the rest of them: selfish and immature . . . and only out for yourself.'

'I'm not.' He'd grabbed her hand. She'd tried to shake him off, but he wouldn't let her go.

'Evan, stop. I'll manage on my own,' she'd whispered. *We*, she'd thought, *it's we now, me and this baby*. Wiping away her tears with her sleeve she'd walked away, but he'd run in front of her.

'Niamh. Stop. You don't have to manage on your own.' He'd got down on one knee. 'Marry me.'

'Jesus, will you get up!' she'd hissed. 'What if someone sees you?'

'Who'd see us down here? Anyway, I don't care if anyone sees me,' he'd said. 'Stop ruining this.'

'Evan.' She'd allowed him to hold her hand. 'You don't have to do this.' The knee of his jeans had been getting wet. She'd seen the dampness rising. He'd kept looking at her with his green and hazel flecked eyes.

'I do. Just say yes. We'll run off and get married and come back and tell everyone and it'll be the most romantic thing in the world.'

She'd said yes. Of course she had. Now, walking on to the sandy part of the shoreline, she wondered what would have happened if she'd said no. She sat on a log and crossed her arms tightly across her chest and tried to slow her breathing.

Rory . . . he still fancied her. Niamh held herself even more tightly. She felt desirable, for the first time in a long time, and it made her head spin. Shaking her hands out in front of her, she tried to take some breaths and calm her nerves. She felt as if she'd cheated on Evan, but nothing had happened.

Nothing, she tried to convince herself, she'd done nothing. There was no need to think beyond what hadn't happened because thinking about what might have happened was sort of inviting it to happen, wasn't it? Her phone pinged and she reluctantly broke from her thoughts to read a message from Ava's school: *Your daughter has been marked absent in her first class. Please confirm her absence from school on your school app.*

Niamh grasped the phone tightly. Ava had gone to school that morning with Evan, as she did every morning. How on earth did Evan not realise she wasn't in school?

Why hadn't the school contacted him? He worked there for crying out loud? God Almighty, why was it always the mother who had to deal with everything? Almost dropping her phone, she angrily sent a text to Evan to double-check if Ava was in school; maybe there'd been some misunderstanding. She'd been marked absent incorrectly or something.

She stared out at the lake, then turned away. Then she saw Lauren striding towards the lake, in her swimsuit, a towel draped over her shoulders. Niamh sat down again and watched Lauren. What on earth was she doing?

17

Lauren woke at her normal time of six o'clock, as if she needed to get ready for a full day of teaching. Lying there, she groaned. Shane had gone home last night, and already Mill House felt hollow without him. Lauren stared up at the cracks in the ceiling. The weekend had been strange, they'd pottered around Mill House and gone for walks, but she felt that something was missing. It wasn't Shane, she knew. He'd been happy to see her. It was definitely her. She'd held herself back from him, and she was sure he'd noticed. She followed the longest crack in the ceiling until it disappeared, then she hauled herself up, stretched and went downstairs.

On the coffee table was the photo album they'd looked through last night. Blurry faces smiled up at her. She couldn't take her eyes from the open pages. The first photo was of Rosemary. She looked so young, standing as if she was in a beauty pageant. Rosemary was kitted out in a short dress that ended just above her knee with modest elbow-length sleeves and a turned-up collar. She was immaculately coiffed. Lauren instinctively touched her own ratty hair, which had been swiftly tied up in a bun yesterday evening.

Plucking the photo from the photo corners, Lauren turned it around. In pencil was the date: *21st June 1966*. Rosemary had just turned twenty. She had her whole life ahead of her and yet within a year she'd married and had her first baby, Debbie, Lauren's mother, named for Debbie Reynolds. Within three years she'd had another baby.

The next photo was of Sheila outside her newly opened boutique. The date said 21st June 1970. Rosemary had told Lauren how she'd helped Sheila paint the interior while Paddy had installed clothing rails. Afterwards Sheila had called into Mill House with a bottle of gin to say thanks and they'd sat out in the garden chatting, laughing, drinking gin and tonics. It had been the start of what became a regular thing: Rosemary's friends would come over and they'd stay out late chatting and giggling as the day turned to night. Stella used to be there too, Lauren suddenly remembered, and Maura.

Poor Maura. She was so kind and had volunteered to make the arrangements to have Rosemary cremated as Rosemary had wished. She'd said it would be easier for them all, and she would bring Rosemary's ashes home with her when she came back to Ireland in the summer. Lauren rubbed her eyes with her fingertips and held hard to the memories of Rosemary and her friends out in the garden. They'd play cards sometimes, and other times all the ladies would go for a swim in the lake before they settled down at the garden table.

Rosemary was always the first in, Sheila second, Stella was always more reluctant but would go in after some persuasion. Lauren would sometimes wade in the shallows, but she was ever mindful of Debbie's admonitions and never went in deeper than her knees. Afterwards they'd all traipse up to Mill House for tea and snacks. Her mouth watered thinking of the home-baked ham sandwiches Rosemary would cut when the ladies popped in.

Lauren used to love the nights she'd stay in Mill House when she was allowed to stay up with the ladies. They'd sit and chatter and laugh, and nothing was wildly inappropriate, but it felt sometimes like it was, particularly when the ladies started talking about their favourite movie stars, or possibly passing comment on Mucker and his antics. It was there Lauren had her first glass of wine, although she'd had to swear that she wouldn't tell her mother.

Lauren flipped over the page and glanced at more photographs: Rosemary and Paddy and their three grandchildren having a picnic down by the lake; Rosemary in the lake waving at the camera. Then she came across a photo of Rosemary and all the ladies together.

They were sitting around the old wooden outdoor table, laughing. The table was laden with glasses and food. Sheila was clutching a handful of cards; Rosemary held a cigarette aloft. Lauren had forgotten her grandmother used to smoke before giving it up for good. Not one of them was looking at the camera. They were so engrossed in each other it made Lauren's heart ache. She'd had that with Heather and Lauren once, that easy laughter, the crazy jokes, the sharing and kindness. And now it was gone. Rosemary had never learned what had happened between them. Lauren had never told her. It was too hard to talk about, back then, and after a while Rosemary had stopped asking about the girls. Yet the question always hung in the air, Lauren felt, and the sadness, but there was nothing she could do about it now.

Rosemary would never know how truly horrible Heather and Niamh were, and maybe that was a good thing. She'd passed away thinking they were good people, and that was just fine.

Lauren snapped the photo album shut. Her head was pounding. Before Shane had arrived on Friday she hadn't been out of the house in almost a week. Every night she fell asleep thinking that tomorrow she'd get some air, take a walk by the lake, get some shopping in instead of ordering from Roberto's, but every morning she felt prematurely exhausted simply thinking of the length of the day ahead of her. Meeting people and smiling seemed like monumental tasks. She'd been like this when her period had finally arrived the first time she'd thought she was pregnant. There was no one she could tell, not at sixteen; no one to discuss how relieved she was or also how guilty she felt. Guilt over having unprotected sex, at being unmarried, at possibly being pregnant, for not telling Shane. He'd thought she was sad after her holiday in Mallorca, but in reality, she'd simply not been able to figure out a way to tell him how terrified she'd been.

For three months she'd prayed for her period to come. When it did it came with excruciating pain, which she'd welcomed as her punishment for having sex outside of marriage. She'd lied to Shane when he'd asked her what was wrong. She'd blamed working extra hours in Billy's and said that she needed to study more as she was falling

215

behind. He'd never once questioned her, which had made her feel worse, but after a while he'd asked her if she was depressed. If she was, she should get help, he'd begged her. He'd even go with her if she wanted. That was when she'd told him about their pregnancy scare. He'd turned so white she'd thought he'd faint, but he didn't.

After that they'd been more than careful, and slowly she'd come back to herself as they leaned into each other even more.

But she couldn't keep leaning into him anymore. It wasn't fair to have him worry about her again.

So, she'd lied to Shane over the weekend, said she was doing fine when he called, said that she went for a walk every day, just as she'd lied to her sister and told her she was just busy clearing out the place, and that she'd pop over to see her new house soon. She'd lied to her mother and said that she'd call down to see her, then she'd lied about having a tummy bug on the day she was supposed to go. It was easy to lie to them, but it didn't make her feel any better.

'Who am I really lying to?' she muttered as she pulled back the curtains in the kitchen.

The sun glinted on the lake below, catching her eye. It looked so calm and beautiful, and inviting. Lauren could imagine Rosemary, towel over her arm, swim shoes on, and her trusty flask tucked into her carryall, calling her to *come on, it'll do you the world of good!*

Shaking her head, Lauren tried to ignore Rosemary's voice in her head. But something inside her couldn't. Rosemary had always known what was best. Maybe it was time to listen to her, even if it was just her memory she was listening to. Before she could change her mind she hurried upstairs and pulled out her old swimsuit, one that she'd last worn a few years ago before Rosemary had gone travelling, from where she'd left it then in the top drawer of the dressing table. Shimmying into it, Lauren sucked in her stomach, then let it out. Surveying herself in the mirror she was satisfied to see that it fit her fine, and anyway, no one went swimming in the lake anymore. The kids all went into Glenrua to the pool as their parents felt it was cleaner, although what could possibly be cleaner than a mountain lake fed by freshwater streams?

After pulling on a hoodie and an old pair of tracksuit bottoms, she clattered downstairs, stopping only to grab a towel from the bathroom, and her bag from where it hung on the newel post. Then she texted Shane that she was going for a swim in the lake, thinking that she may as well tell him something that wasn't a lie. He rang immediately and she sat on the stairs to take the call.

'Hey, good morning.' She tried to sound bright, but her voice croaked.

'You sound rough.' He laughed, then his voice deepened. 'Are you okay? You sound like you've been crying.'

'I'm fine.' She closed her eyes remembering that he never believed it when she said she was fine. 'I was looking through the photo album again, and it got to me. You know how I am.'

'Are you sure that's it?' Shane asked.

Lauren could sense him leaning forward as he spoke. It's what he did when he was worried about her.

'Of course – why would I say it was if it wasn't?' She got up, then grabbed her towel from the bottom of the stairs.

'Laure, I know you,' he said quietly.

'It was just the photos. Nothing else.'

'Okay, I believe you. Hey, listen, I've good news,' he said. 'We're ahead of ourselves on the site. There's nothing for us to do here so Matt is giving us a few days off, so I'm coming back down tonight.'

Lauren paused at the open kitchen door. She leaned against it and steadied her breath and tried to inject something like excitement into her voice, but the letter that she'd still to finish played on her mind. It was stashed in her handbag where she'd tucked it away in a fit of despair one afternoon, still unable to imagine how she'd give it to him. 'Oh, that's great.'

'You don't sound too happy about it,' he said.

'Sorry.' She lifted her tone. 'I am happy – of course I am.'

'Okay,' he said carefully.

Lauren glanced back into the hall. 'What time will I see you?'

'Around seven. I just need to tidy up a bit back at the yard,' he said. 'I was thinking I could bring a takeaway. Your favourite?'

'That'd be so good.' Lauren's stomach growled.

'I can't wait to be back with you. It's not the same without you here; everything is too quiet.' She could hear the sadness in his voice.

'And tidy, I bet.' She tried to laugh, but he didn't join her. 'This is good for us, Shane. We've never lived apart . . .'

'It doesn't feel good,' Shane said. 'It feels like . . . it feels like everything is disintegrating. I don't like anything without you around. It all feels wrong. Don't you think so?'

'I suppose,' Lauren said. She poked at a sliver of thick eggshell paint that was lifting from the doorframe.

'Aren't you lonely?' he asked quietly. 'I'm so lonely.'

'I am,' Lauren said quietly.

'A few more hours,' he said. 'And I'll be there with you, with your favourite dinner and a bunch of daffodils.'

'I can't wait.' Lauren picked the paint sliver off the frame and left a blemish in the paintwork.

'See you soon. I love you.' He waited for her to say it too before hanging up.

Lauren held the piece of paint in her palm and looked at it. Then she blew it from her hand and watched it flitter away. It landed on the floor at her feet, right in the centre of the old saddle board. She nudged it with her toe.

All she could think of was that bloody letter . . . She paced up and down the kitchen. What was she to do with it now? She'd hide it away until she was ready. And anyhow, it might be nice to have some more time with him before she let him go. It would be the right thing to do.

The sun beamed in through the grimy window and she lifted her chin. She'd go to the lake and wash off all the tiredness. The water would wake her up well and good. It didn't matter that she couldn't remember the last time she'd gone swimming, or that she could only find an old dusty pair of swim shoes in the back kitchen.

Shaking the dust off the shoes, she pulled the back door shut behind her and made her way to the lake, eager to feel energised and able. Then she'd be capable of making inroads into the cleaning and maybe even head into the village to pick up some fresh food. The air was crisp and for a minute she considered going back for her jacket, but then hurried on. She'd warm up in no time, if she moved a bit.

Puffing, she climbed the stile and pounded through the bright new ferns and damp grass towards the shoreline. She wasn't as fit as she'd thought she was. She was sweating already, and she wasn't even walking as quickly as usual. Wiping her hand over her face, she kept her eyes on the water so that she wouldn't change her mind. A quick dip, she promised as she realised it was going to be freezing. Just a quick dip – it'd only take a minute.

Leaving her clothes in a bundle on the grass, she pulled on the dusty swim shoes and walked to the water's edge.

18

Pippa handed Heather a mug of tea and sat beside her on their new sofa, which was the only piece of furniture in the sitting room.

'Thanks.' Heather stifled a yawn.

'Couldn't you sleep?' Pippa asked. Her smooth forehead creased.

Wrapping her hands around the mug Heather sat back and stared out the window at the crisp morning. She'd forgotten that Pippa had always liked to rise with the sun. Concentrating on not spilling her tea, Heather folded her legs beneath her. How could she tell her mother that she'd the biggest sense of having made a huge mistake? Ever since she'd gotten back from London a few days ago, she'd done nothing but make a heap of mistakes. She'd ruined a pot of balm her mother had been making by simply not reading the recipe correctly, and she'd almost knocked over a tin of paint in Willow's old bedroom.

Her head was spinning, and she found she was easily distracted. Instead of being able to focus on her work methodically as she normally did, she kept checking her phone, scrolling through all sorts of nonsense. Since she'd first come back to Ireland in January, she'd felt less inclined to make arrangements and travel. Everything felt like a burden, and she'd ignored most of her usual routines, and instead of feeling obligated to help as she usually felt, she was *choosing* to help Pippa before anything else. She tried to tell herself that the sooner Pippa was up and running and making some money the sooner she'd be able to go back to London and live her life without any guilt, but she knew deep down she was kidding herself. She was in no hurry to get back to London at all.

All their hard work on Pippa's business was paying off though. Pippa had chosen a clean and simple brand design, her website was concise yet warm, and the new recycled packaging they'd sourced was of an even better standard than they'd hoped. Then there was the great news that they'd three new retailers this week and a number of enquiries requesting more information. She'd never have guessed that there'd be such a demand for products like the ones Pippa was making. She looked over at Pippa and caught her looking at emails.

'You shouldn't be doing that,' she said. 'You need to keep boundaries in place – you are entitled to your own time. Don't let the business eat into it.'

'Is that how you got so good?' Pippa put her phone down.

'No.' Heather wrinkled her nose. 'I was on duty the whole time. Trust me, it's exhausting. You'll get burnt out if you don't take care of yourself.'

'Did you get burnt out?' Pippa turned to face her daughter. Her face flushed pink.

Heather nodded. 'Yeah, but when you're a travel blogger you're not allowed to say you're tired – everyone thinks you're living the dream, but they forget it's all work.'

'I mean, is that what happened here – at home – between us? Did you growing up so fast burn you out and make you leave?' Pippa looked down into her mug, her voice gritty.

Heather sat up. A prickle of sweat in her armpits made her shift position. Was her mother really talking about this now?

'I . . . well, I haven't really thought too much about it.' Heather fell silent. Her mind whirred over her past conversations with Simon, about how she'd been forced to grow up and how it had affected her relationship with her mother. Twisting her lips, Heather thought of all the times she'd had to be the mother of the house. Her breath quickened and shallowed. The rage she'd suppressed back then began to bubble just under her skin, but she knew it was just a physical reaction to those memories. It wasn't a reaction to what was happening right now. Then, as if someone had removed a blindfold from her eyes, she knew that her rage was never directed at Pippa. It was at Cash. He'd never been there for her; he'd never even tried to be a parent. Heather looked at Pippa, whose gaze was still lowered to her mug of tea. Cash had never even tried to be a partner either.

The silence stretched between them.

Pippa finally spoke. 'Sometimes I think I was more burnt out when I was with your father, you know? It was a full-time job being the kind of person he expected me to be. I was always second-guessing myself, and always putting off what I wanted to do.'

223

'Why didn't you just do what you wanted to do?' Heather asked.

'I think about this a lot, and I don't know the full answer yet,' Pippa whispered. She wiped a tear from her cheek. 'I was so caught up in him that I convinced myself I was who he told me I was. Not that he told me so directly, you know. It was more subtle than that. I think I learned to watch him carefully from early in the relationship, and I could gauge what mood he was in, how he'd react. I didn't know how lacking in personality I was. I didn't see that I wasn't being a person at all – and least of all a mother to you and Willow.'

Heather sat up. 'What do you mean?'

'You left, and I was so angry – for such a long time. It forced me to do things that I hadn't been doing – the things *you'd* been doing.' Pippa tapped the arm of the chair and scrunched her eyes shut for a moment. 'It was only when Willow left that I realised how bad a mother I was.'

'You weren't always bad,' Heather whispered, afraid of Pippa's confession. 'Remember when we lived in Kerry – you used to bring us swimming on Derrynane Beach and then afterwards we'd always have a bubble bath before a story by the fire . . .'

Pippa nodded. Tears rolled down her face. 'I loved living there. We'd such good times in that house – it's probably why Willow has gone back to Kerry.'

'Probably,' Heather said softly. 'Pippa . . . it's okay. We're all grown up now.'

'It's not really okay though, is it?' Pippa sniffed. 'I had no backbone, and I should have. Moving here was a mistake. I was depressed for years, but now he's gone I think I'll be okay.'

A huge lump in Heather's throat prevented her from speaking. She'd never had such an honest conversation with her mother before.

'I'm sorry.' Pippa leaned over and took Heather's hand. 'I should have put you first – not him. I wish I'd understood that I could've stood up for myself and the life I wanted sooner. They say you learn from children, and I should've learned from you.' She cleared her throat as if she didn't want to say any more on the subject. 'The first time I got it was when Sheila stopped me in the street to say how amazing you were. She'd just come home from a holiday – the one you'd helped her with. She said it was above and beyond her expectations and it was all down to you.'

'I never knew that happened,' Heather said softly. In all the years of therapy she'd never even once considered that her mother would apologise. She'd always assumed that she'd go through her whole life without any kind of closure, or apology. If anything, she'd envisioned that it would be down to her to bring up the topic of her childhood – not Pippa. Now she didn't know what to say to her mother. All she knew was that this moment was something she was unprepared for. She looked at Pippa with new eyes and blinked back tears. She didn't want to talk about it anymore – she wanted time to think over what had just happened.

'In all my wildest dreams,' Pippa continued, 'I never imagined Sheila saying such things to me. Never. It made me stop and think. Anyway, things began to change after that day, but not soon enough.'

Hoping to change the conversation, Heather looked down into her almost empty mug of tea. 'My tea is cold.'

Pippa looked at her daughter and Heather felt that she was looking right into her, that Pippa could tell how uncomfortable she was. Pippa squeezed her hand, then got up from the sofa. 'I'm making a new hair oil today – using rosemary – so I really should get cracking.'

'Rosemary?' Heather immediately pictured Rosemary on the lakeshore, her long bobbed grey hair untidily pulled back in a low ponytail, a huge smile on her face, the kind that made crinkles on the side of her eyes. She could almost hear her soft voice urging them to come swim.

'God, I miss her so much,' she said softly.

'Rosemary? Me, too,' Pippa said. 'She was good to me, you know. After you left, she'd always talk to me. She missed you too.'

'You were friends with Rosemary?' Heather stared at her mother and tried to imagine the conversations they might have had.

'Oh yes, for years.' Pippa went into the kitchen. Heather followed her, eager to hear more. 'We talked at the gate, at first, then we'd sit out in the garden. She showed me her herbs and I remembered how much I loved gardens. She was the first person I told, besides Cash that is, about my business idea.'

'For real?' Heather shook her head.

Pippa picked up a tea towel and began drying last night's supper dishes. 'For real. It was the nicest time of my life, you know. We'd all sit in the garden and talk. She missed Paddy so much and it made me realise that I

wasn't in as great a relationship as I'd thought I was. Anyway, it was nice to be included for a change.'

Heather sighed. 'Rosemary had a knack for bringing the best out of people, I think.'

Pippa nodded. 'I've sometimes wondered if I should call the others and invite them down for a drink in the garden, but . . . this garden is still too wild and well, it wouldn't be the same without Rosemary.'

They both looked out of the kitchen window into the wilderness of their back garden. Pippa's shoulders dropped and she turned away. Heather kept looking.

'We'll get to it,' she said, suddenly wanting to do something good for her mother. The feeling was strange but warm and it made her feel lighter. 'I promise. We'll get another skip, and we'll clear the garden a little at a time.'

Pippa smiled. 'Don't worry, I have Rory Quinlan lined up to clear it for me. Then, this summer I'll be able to grow my own herbs. Chamomile for comfort, dill for good spirits and of course, rosemary for remembrance.'

'That sounds good,' Heather said. 'As soon as the weather picks up, we'll get started.'

'So, you're staying on?' Her mother tilted her head at her. 'What's brought this on?'

'Like you, I'm still looking for that answer.' Heather shrugged. 'I'll let you know when I figure it out.'

'We're awful maudlin this morning,' Pippa said suddenly. Decisively, she threw the tea towel onto the counter. 'Come on. I remember when you used to go to the lake with Rosemary every morning. After you left I went with her for a bit. She said it made her feel better, like she could

227

do anything. She always told me that if I was ever in doubt that I should go to the lake and either get in, or just sit there and absorb nature. I, *we*, could do with taking a bit of Rosemary's advice right now.'

Heather shook her head. She'd always thought her mother hadn't known about her swims. It was funny, it seemed Rosemary had been far more of a hippie than her mother had ever been. How had she not seen it? Looking out beyond the wild garden, just over the brambles and gorse at the end, she could, if she stood on her tiptoes, make out the lake. The sky was blue, and the morning was yellow and bright. She should go down to the lake. What had she to lose?

Minutes later she was following her mother along the overgrown path through their garden and down to the rusted five-bar gate she'd discovered as a teenager. The grass was too high to open the rusted gate, so they climbed over and carried on. Heather's worries felt lighter as they went. Her feet, finding the familiar path with ease, trod lightly along the narrow fern-lined path. The warm woody smells and soft sounds of the Wicklow countryside made her heart light. Nearby a robin chirruped a warning that they were near, and a rustling made her look up.

A stag stood feet away from them. Both women stopped moving. Pippa stepped backwards, her hand reaching for Heather's as the stag raised his huge head and turned to look towards the lake. Heather held Pippa's hand gently. Her mother's hand was warm, soft and a lot smaller than she remembered – it was a strange and comforting feeling. The stag then turned and rested his gaze on them, his soft brown eyes blinking as he watched them. With the slightest rustle of the ferns and old bracken, he then walked away as if unbothered by them.

'That was amazing,' Heather whispered.

'In all my years here, that's never happened.' Pippa's eyes sparkled. 'Did you see how big he was?'

'He was massive,' Heather said. They began to walk on.

Heather watched her mother move ahead, pulling brambles back and stepping around nettles and briars. She'd never given her much of a chance, she realised as her mother's apology forced itself into her consciousness. Pippa had been a different person when Heather had been a teenager and longing for her mother to pay attention to her and Willow. She'd been selfish and immature, Heather remembered, choosing to spend her time and energy on things Cash said were important. Not once had she or Cash gone to parent–teacher meetings or awards nights. Whenever Heather had called them out for their lazy parenting, Cash would laugh and tell her that she was learning life skills. She could hear his mocking voice telling her and Willow that they needed to learn how to be independent.

Heather snorted as she followed Pippa down the grassy pathway. Cash's laziness meant that she'd had to shoulder the responsibility of taking care of her little sister, of walking her to school, making sure she had food and clean clothes every day. She'd been the mother and father Willow had needed, but there'd been no one there to be a parent to her. Heather chewed her bottom lip as she glanced in the woods for the stag.

Simon had once told her that she needed to lighten up.

Not long after that she'd opened up to him about her need to be in control. No one else was going to look out for her, or Willow, so she always had to. He'd been so upset when she'd told him about her parents. That was the first time anyone had ever told her that what she'd gone through was wrong. He'd said the word: parentification, and after he'd explained it she'd felt sick to her stomach. She'd realised he was right: everything she did and had done since she was a teenager was in rebellion to her parents' lifestyle. Which she felt was a normal reaction but it left her hyper-responsible and unable to relax, even on all the holidays she'd taken over the years for her business. She rubbed her hand over her hair. What a mess it all was. Her business had always been about being free and enjoying the world and life, and yet it was built on the strictest self-imposed rules.

It was hard to forgive and forget her parents' lack of care, but Pippa was different now. She was no longer the flustered and somewhat hyper person who waved away her children while she painted a wall in the house or hosted yet another party. She seemed to be a calmer and more centred woman now, one who had made friends in the village and who was aware of her faults and her mistakes. Her mother had blossomed in her father's absence, she realised, and maybe Simon would blossom in hers. Her heart caught in her throat: was she to Simon what her father had been to her mother? Had she been too controlling and wrapped up in herself to really see him?

Pippa looked back and smiled at her, and Heather dragged a smile shakily from what felt like the bottom of her soul. It was the truth. She was every bit as bad as her father had been – constantly running away from everything and only content when things were going his way, according to his haphazard plan or mad notion. The only difference was she was organised; she was more conscious of her moves. It didn't make an ounce of difference when you really looked at it, it was all the same. She had been wrong, and Simon had finally called her out; and now, as he'd said, the ball was in her court, but she didn't know the game, and she was certain she'd broken all the rules already.

Stumbling after her mother, she wondered how Pippa had managed to come out of such a poisonous relationship so balanced. How was she so serene, or was she? Maybe she was just getting by day to day. It was entirely possible that her mother was struggling; in fact, if she read between the lines of what Willow had told her, and looked more deeply at her mother, she'd have seen it sooner. Pippa was only beginning to find herself, Heather realised, and she was in the privileged position of being able not only to witness it, but also to help her. Heather felt the crunch of gravel under her feet, and she looked up, surprised to find that they'd reached the lakeshore.

The lake lapped gently against the stones, and as Heather scanned the hills and mountains surrounding them, she became aware of some laughter and shouting. Turning her head, she caught sight of two groups of youths far out on the lake. One group of four were in a small rowboat; three others were on a rough raft of some sort.

'Oh, I didn't think there'd be people down here so early,' Pippa said. 'They're a little rowdy.'

As she spoke, Heather squinted at the youths.

raft. The girl had gone so pale and quiet that Heather feared she was losing consciousness. For a moment she considered trying to hoist Ava onto the raft, but the two lads weren't capable of helping her; they were shaking like leaves and were clinging on to each other while not taking their eyes off of Ava. Heather struggled to look behind her, praying someone was able to help her. Her stomach sank as she realised there was no one in the water. They were alone, and Ava's grip on her arm was loosening.

Heather only realised she was crying when her face felt warm. She gritted her teeth and grasped Ava harder even though her arms felt like jelly and her legs were cold and aching. The water lapped over the back of her head, splashing loudly in her ears. She shook her head, trying to shake her wet hair from her eyes. A droning sound carried across the water to her, getting louder with each passing second. Blinking against the stinging water that ran into her eyes, she threw a quick glance behind her. A small white boat skimmed the lake, quite a distance away from her. Heather's heart beat loudly in her ears. The boat seemed to be heading for them. With renewed strength Heather hoisted Ava up again so that her chin was out of the water, all the while keeping the boat in her sights.

The engine cut out as the boat approached the raft, sending waves cascading over Ava and Heather. Ava cried out, and Heather breathed out, happy to hear the girl make some sound.

Mucker Madigan and a much younger and stronger man were in the boat. With chattering teeth, Heather realised it was Rory Quinlan with Mucker, Niamh's old crush. He was saying something to her, but she couldn't make out what it was until she felt Ava being pulled from her arms.

'It's okay, we have her,' Rory called out. 'You can let go. You're safe.'

It was hard to let Ava go. Heather's arms were stiff and cramping as she watched the two men haul Ava into their boat. Never in her life had Heather been so relieved to see Mucker and Rory.

'Give me your hand.' Rory reached out to her, but Heather shook her head. There was little room left in the boat, just enough for the two boys on the raft who were openly crying now.

'The boys,' Heather called out. 'Get the boys.'

She swam away from the boat and moved to the other side of the raft, hoping she was helping to steady it as the boys clumsily clambered into the boat beside Ava and the men. The engine noisily kicked in and Heather breathed out as the boat turned towards the old jetty. Only then did she begin swimming back to shore.

19

Niamh sank to her knees as the men hauled Ava onto their boat. Her ears began ringing and she had to hold her hand over her mouth to keep herself from screaming again. One of the guards knelt beside her and asked her if she was all right. Nodding, she kept her eyes on her daughter, willing her to be okay. Her phone rang and she stared at Evan's name on the screen for a second before answering.

'Where are you?' She felt as if she'd swallowed too much air. Her head spun. 'I need you. Here – at the lake – Evan. It's Ava . . .'

'Ava? The lake . . . Niamh? What? Oh God, Niamh is she . . . ?' Evan stuttered.

Niamh could hear the catch in his voice. Ava was his favourite. It was something she found strange – that a parent could have a favourite child. Maybe it was because he had siblings – she didn't know how else to explain it.

'No, Ev, no. She's alive. I can see her now.' She tried to calm him, realising he'd imagined the worst-case scenario. 'They have her in a boat now. She's okay, I think. Hurry.'

She hung up as the boat came alongside the old wooden jetty. Shakily standing up, she pushed her phone into her pocket and began to run towards the jetty, passing Heather as she staggered from the lake. Blood ran down Heather's arm, and somewhere deep in her mind Niamh registered her old friend, but her heart was pounding so hard that she couldn't do anything but keep moving towards her daughter who was now lying on the stony beach being attended to by Rory. Rory who only half an hour ago had been dangerously flirting with her in her warm kitchen. Niamh shook her head and crashed down onto her knees beside Ava. She looked at Rory for a second, tried to speak to him but found her voice had deserted her. With a cry she threw her arms around Ava, and didn't look at Rory again.

*

Heather had never felt as weak in all her life. One of the guards had picked up her towel and had wrapped it around her shoulders before leading her towards a log where she sat and tried to breathe normally. It was no good. There was no way she could stop the shaking that had set in, and her teeth chattered together so hard she feared she'd break them. Pippa ran towards her and threw her arms around her. She rubbed her arms and legs frantically and then pulled her in close to try to warm her up.

'Oh my God, Heather,' Pippa kept saying over and over again. 'Are you all right? We need to get you warmed up. You're shaking . . .'

Over her mother's shoulder Heather watched as Rory

20

21st June 2008

The lake was grey, reflecting the cloudy sky above it. It was twenty past four, almost sunrise, and the forecast was for a cool day with the likelihood of drizzle. Not much chance of the sun shining down on the girls as they gathered for their swim. There hadn't been the usual heatwave at the beginning of the month when all the Leaving Cert students began their exams.

'This is it,' Heather said as they stripped down to their swimming gear. She shivered in the light breeze and stared up at the moon as it lay low in the sky to the west, skimming in and out of the clouds that wreathed the mountains. 'The last summer before we have to grow up for real.'

'What are you talking about?' Niamh looked up from pulling on her swim shoes.

'This time next year we'll be finished our final exams,' Heather said. 'And then we'll have to get jobs.'

'We have jobs.' Niamh stuck her tongue out.

'*Proper* jobs.' Heather stuck her tongue out back at Niamh. 'Not just working in your father's office.'

'I'm going to apply to be cabin crew,' Niamh said. 'He's going to have to hire someone to do the work I did these last two years.'

'My dad says the airlines won't be around next year,' Lauren spoke up. 'He says we're heading into a recession, that it's going to be bad.'

'No, we're not.' Niamh waved her hand at Lauren. 'Don't be ridiculous. That's just scaremongering.'

Lauren sat down beside Niamh. 'It's not ridiculous.'

'Nope, it won't happen.' Niamh stood up. 'Everyone always thinks this way when things are looking up – someone always says the good times won't last. Well, they'll last as long as you believe in them – it's the doom and gloom brigade that bring it all down. The thing is, if they keep saying it then it'll happen. So, we need to act like it won't.'

'Your logic is flawed,' Heather deadpanned.

'Whatever, Miss Top of Business Class Three Years in a Row.' Niamh pouted. 'Of course, you'd know. Now when will you be advising the government?'

'Listen to yourself.' Heather laughed. 'You talk as if you know what's going on when you haven't the first clue. It's not all *if you build it, they will come* you know.'

'Urgh, can't you ever just stop being such a misery guts.' Niamh adjusted the straps on her swimsuit. 'Live in the moment.'

With a flounce she spun and walked to the lake's edge where Rosemary stood with her friends, Stella and Eileen.

Heather shook her hair back from her face and gathered

it up into a ponytail. She'd very nearly not bothered coming down for the solstice swim. But Rosemary was looking forward to it. Stella and Eileen were visiting Rosemary, and they'd said they'd come down too. They'd been such good friends to Rosemary over the last year, she thought as she tightened her ponytail. Rosemary had told her how they'd checked in on her since Mallorca, and how happy she was to have them in her life.

Somehow it was impossible to imagine that she, Lauren and Niamh would be as close when they got older. Lauren was spending all her time with Shane. All she talked about was houses and kids' names and how many dogs she and Shane wanted. It was all pie in the sky as far as Heather was concerned, and one thing was for sure: it wasn't a good idea to be so dependent on each other. At some stage it would all go wrong. Just look at her parents – they were so messed up. Her father was such a hypocrite, always making new rules about who could do what – or who, she thought as Lauren put her phone away. She'd probably been texting Shane. Heather twisted her lips. In a way it was sweet, but they were so serious about each other it made her uncomfortable. Sooner or later, it would all go wrong; it always did.

Niamh turned around, posed, and flashed them a smile.

'Pfft. It'd be nice to live in *her* world,' Heather snorted.

*

Lauren nodded. Money was tight at home, and her father was always going on about the impending gloom and doom. She'd a funny feeling in the bottom of her stomach that he was right.

'Mark my words,' Tom had said only the night before, his forefinger jabbing the tablecloth. 'It's all going to go up like an atomic bomb. No one will know what's hit them. We have to be careful.'

'We're always careful.' Yvonne had passed the water jug to Lauren. Yvonne had twisted her engagement ring around her finger. Lauren knew she was afraid that he was right – that the factory would close. Then what would they do? Tom had managed to get Yvonne's fiancé, Graham, a job there and if the factory shut down then they'd be in big trouble. There'd be no big family wedding, let alone a mortgage for a first home.

'It's all right for you,' Yvonne had said. 'You're almost done paying your mortgage. We haven't even applied for one yet.'

'Don't get one.' Tom had pointed his fork at her. 'These banks and their 110 per cent mortgages and their tracker rates. I'm telling you now, it's all going to go up in smoke.'

'Ah, Da, stop. Will ya?' young Thomas had groaned. 'Can we not just have one dinner without talking about it?'

Tom had banged his fist down on the table then, almost knocking over his bottle of beer. 'I'll talk about what I want at my own table. I've earned that right. What have you earned?'

Young Thomas had rolled his eyes before going back to eating his sausages and beans. Lauren had tried to catch his eye, but he'd kept them firmly on his plate until he'd cleared it.

Now, standing on the lakeshore as the sun struggled to rise in the east, Lauren sighed. If this was the last summer before they all had to grow up then she was going to enjoy it. She swung her arms to warm up and hoped the weather would pick up. To think that this very day last year they'd been jumping in the warm clear waters of the Balearic Sea, making intentions and getting tanned. What she'd give to go back there and feel the sun on her skin and to enjoy a cool glass of sangria. Well, she wasn't in Mallorca, she was in Lough Caragh, and nothing was going to change that.

'Ahoy there!' a voice called out. Lauren turned around. Her face broke into a grin as she watched Sheila prance across the cold sand waving a yellow towel in the air. Shirley Goodman and Old Moll, both in their swimsuits, followed at a slower pace.

Sheila disrobed in a flourish, revealing a yellow swimsuit with a red belt.

'We decided we'd join you,' Sheila trilled as she tiptoed to the edge. 'You made it sound glorious and I said to myself, Sheila you haven't been in the lake in years, decades – you should be ashamed of yourself.'

Rosemary beckoned Sheila to come in. 'I didn't think you'd make it, not after that last G&T last night in the garden.'

'I've barely slept,' Sheila called over to her. 'It looks cold.' She dipped a toe in.

'You'll be grand once you're in,' Eileen chimed from where she floated. 'It only froze my ass off for two minutes.'

Sheila waded in. 'My Lord, this is treacherously cold.'

'Come on, get in. Let a roar out of you if you have to

– you'll be grand afterwards.' Rosemary splashed her gently. 'You said you wanted to see what the fuss was about, so here it is.'

'It's quite lovely, actually.' Old Moll swam out past Sheila, leaving Sheila gaping after her.

'There's a ledge there now. It gets deeper after this spot,' Shirley said as she took the plunge and swam out towards Rosemary. 'This is lovely, Rose. I don't know why we stopped doing this.'

'Kids. Men.' Eileen chortled. 'That's why I stopped doing anything. There wasn't enough time in the day for me and what I wanted.'

'True,' Shirley said. 'Very true.'

*

Niamh watched the introductions happening between the older women. They all seemed so settled and yet so full of life. But they looked old, and she knew for a fact that Shirley was the same age as her own mother: fifty-seven. They'd been in school together. And Old Moll was older. In her seventies or something. There was no way she was going to allow herself to become that kind of older woman. The kind that looked older than they were. She was going to age like Raquel Welch or Jane Fonda. She'd keep her wrinkles at bay with Botox, she thought as she lowered her shoulders beneath the water and began to swim. In fact, she'd ask her parents for Botox for her birthday in November – it was never too early to start.

A volley of laughter broke into Niamh's beauty planning, and she turned back to see Sheila gasping and gripping onto her breasts as if they'd float away of their own accord.

'Oooooh!' Sheila cried out. 'My boobs, oh you never said it was so cold!'

'It's only because you have enormous knockers.' Eileen laughed.

'Just because you have two fried eggs!' Sheila called out.

'Not by choice,' Eileen said. She raised her hands to the sun that was peeking over the mountains. 'But I'm alive and kicking and loving every extra minute that I have.'

Sheila dropped her hands from her breasts. Her face softened.

'I'm so sorry.'

'Nothing to apologise for. You didn't know.' Eileen shrugged a shoulder. 'It's life, and I'm lucky to be here.'

Niamh moved away, her stomach leaden with shame and embarrassment. She'd only imagined that a life without a perfect body was because the person owning the body was lazy, or fashionably challenged – both of which, in her opinion, could be fixed with a bit of effort. She'd never ever thought of illness affecting the body. Or life. She shivered. That part of life was out of your control, she realised sadly, and crossed her fingers that it would never happen to her. Maybe that should be her intention today.

She looked out across the lake. It was shrouded in a light mist that was lifting as the sun weakly peeked over the mountaintop. But then again, what was the point in worrying in advance of something going wrong? The chances were that nothing would go wrong – at least not in the next year or so. Shaking the goosebumps off, Niamh let her mind wander. This year she'd turn eighteen, she'd get Botox and she'd set health intentions later, when she was hitting forty or something.

*

Rosemary gazed at her friends. It had been years since they'd all been in the lake together. Their laughter lifted her spirits and she allowed herself a moment to cherish it all. Sending a kiss up to Paddy, she turned around and made her intention, then set off back to shore where she wrapped her towel tightly around her shoulders before briskly rubbing herself dry. Niamh joined her within minutes and Rosemary watched the young woman with warm interest.

'You're out of sorts, Niamh. What's up?' Rosemary slipped her robe on.

'Nothing.' Niamh towelled dry her hair.

'Nothing and everything.' Rosemary nodded.

'Yeah. That's kind of it.' Niamh sat down and frowned. The old robe that she kept at Rosemary's house just for swimming was pulled tightly around her. It was beginning to look a little threadbare; there were threatening holes here and there.

'Try not to worry,' Rosemary said as Niamh's frown deepened. 'You're young. You have your whole life ahead of you. Things are only as difficult as you make them out to be.'

'That's what I keep telling myself,' Niamh said. 'But

everyone keeps talking about how hard it's going to be after school is finished, and then this bloody recession talk is melting my head.' She prodded a stone in the sand with her big toe.

'I wish I had something insightful to say,' Rosemary said. She pulled the flask out of their now upgraded picnic backpack. Her old rucksack had been retired at Christmas. 'All I can offer you is a place to talk and a cup of tea.'

'Thanks, Rosemary.' Niamh wrapped her hands around the mug Rosemary gave her. 'It's just that sometimes I wish I could get away from here, you know – head off into the great wide open and see the whole world. But they're nailing my feet down before I've even had a chance to do anything. Dad wants me to stay and become his secretary, and I can't find a way to tell him that I can't think of anything worse. He'd have me married off and tied to a kitchen sink if it meant keeping me in Lough Caragh, you know.'

'He loves you very much,' Rosemary said. 'They tried a long time to have you.'

'I know they did,' Niamh said. 'But they can't keep me forever.'

'You're right,' Rosemary said. 'The hardest part of being a parent is letting your children go.'

'I never want to be a mother,' Niamh said. 'The whole idea of it makes me feel sick. I suppose you think I'm a monster now.'

'No, I don't,' Rosemary said. 'But I have to be honest and tell you that I don't quite understand it either.'

'No one does.' Niamh sighed. 'It's okay, Rosemary. You don't have to pretend not to be shocked.'

Rosemary looked down into her tea. What would Paddy say? He always seemed to know the right thing to say when someone was in a dark place. She closed her eyes and tried to hear his voice, but it was Sheila's voice she heard. Rosemary's eyes popped open. Sheila had come out of the lake and was drying herself off with her gorgeous yellow towel.

'I understand,' Sheila said. 'My parents were mad to have me marry Mucker's brother, Paul. Remember that, Rose?'

Rosemary nodded. 'I do. He wasn't a bad catch.'

'Just not the right fish for me,' Sheila said. 'You'll be fine, young Niamh. Don't let your parents bog you down though. Let them have their dreams while you live your life.'

'But . . .' Niamh started. She bit her lip and looked away.

'What is it?' Sheila sat down beside her.

'Well, it's not that I don't want a relationship. I do. I just don't want kids. I want to be free at the same time.'

Sheila nodded. 'I did too. But you know, just because it didn't happen for me doesn't mean it won't happen for you – the world is changing, and you girls have so much more choice than we did.'

Rosemary handed Sheila a mug of tea. Niamh didn't look any more cheered up than when she'd sat down, but at least she knew she could talk to them about it. Yet something Niamh said niggled at her.

Wriggling into a more comfortable position on the log, Rosemary lowered her gaze to her feet. Feet that were twisted from the high heels she'd worn out dancing, calloused from her gardening boots, yet she painted her toenails every Saturday night without fail. Today they were a bright orange, reminding her of the fresh oranges she'd juiced each morning last year in Mallorca. Her feet itched to go back, she realised, but not only there. She scratched the bottom of her left foot with her right big toe. She wanted to go to lots of places. Japan, for a start. Paddy had always said he'd go to see the cherry blossoms if he'd half the chance, while she'd said she wanted to go somewhere where they had those white sandy beaches, crystal blue sea, and where the cocktails came in a coconut shell. They'd thought they'd lots of time. She remembered how they'd said they'd go for their joint sixtieth birthdays in 2006, but by then she was alone and in no humour to even consider taking a lone trip halfway around the world.

She was sixty-two now, well, almost sixty-three. Not old by any standards, but the longer she was alone the older she was beginning to feel. Maybe Niamh was onto something. Maybe travelling would be just the thing to make her feel more alive.

'Niamh, where would you start – if you were going travelling?' Rosemary looked up.

Niamh brushed some hair back from her face. 'I suppose it depends on my budget, which currently is hostels all the way.'

'Pretend you've no budget,' Rosemary urged.

'Now, that's silly,' Sheila interjected. 'There's always a budget. Don't be tormenting her with this no-budget nonsense.'

Rosemary pulled a face but nodded. 'All right, fair

enough. Say you have enough to go at least four stars then.'

'Now you're talking.' Niamh lit up. 'Paris. Italy. Australia. Just to start.'

'I like it.' Rosemary sat up.

Niamh grinned. 'Definitely Venice.'

Rosemary leaned forward, her face aglow. 'Yes! Venice would be the perfect place to start.'

'You sound like you're up to no good.' Sheila nudged Rosemary. 'What's going on?'

'Only good things.' Rosemary nudged her back. She sent another thank you up to Paddy.

*

One by one they all came back in, dried off and drank tea. Lauren sat on the log beside her two best friends. She pondered over what they'd said earlier, about growing up and recessions and jobs . . . Life went on, she knew, but she didn't always want it to. Some moments, moments like these at the lake with her two best friends, she wanted to hold in her heart forever. She never wanted them to end.

'I have a proposal,' she said suddenly. Her face grew pink. 'No matter where we are in the world, no matter what is happening, we should come back here to do this every year.'

'Every year?' Niamh frowned.

'Every year.' Lauren nodded. 'What do you think?'

'I like it,' Heather said slowly. 'Summer solstice, no matter what. I'll be here.'

255

'Fine, me too.' Niamh giggled. 'I can't leave you two alone . . .'

'Seriously, Niamh . . .' Lauren looked at her friend earnestly. 'I really mean it. I love you two.'

Niamh stopped giggling. 'I love you two, too. Of course, I'll be here.' She held her hand out, palm down. Lauren put her hand on top, and then Heather.

'I fecking love you guys,' Heather said as they promised to be there always for their solstice swim.

*

Rosemary watched the girls before sipping her tea. No one shared their intentions this time, and she was glad. She'd found that knowing others' intentions made her forget her own and concentrate on them instead. Which was not an inherently bad thing, she knew, but she was, and always had been, prone to putting other people first. Paddy said it was her most endearing and annoying trait.

She listened to the chatter, passed yesterday's scones out, and felt more at peace than she had in a long time. They all seemed content to huddle around the smoky fire that Heather had tried to start. It had long gone out. The wood was too damp for a fire to take hold. She didn't see Niamh smirk in Lauren's direction when Lauren spoke about Shane, nor did she catch Heather rolling her eyes as Niamh said something about the debs ball next year.

She was lost in plans and wondering if she dared to do it. Dare she go travelling, alone? It wasn't as if she was short of money; it was more that she was short of courage, but courage, Paddy had always said, was just taking the first step, then the next step. Draining her mug, she decided that she'd take the very first step by going to the travel agent's and asking for advice. One step at a time, that's all it takes.

21

19th February 2024

Niamh sat on the hard plastic chair in the corridor of the emergency department, her elbows on her knees, her hands clenched together. Ava had been admitted immediately and was now in for an X-ray. Evan was pacing up and down, stopping now and then to look out of the window. Niamh wished he'd take her hand – like he used to – or go get a coffee, anything other than the irritating walking back and forth that he was doing. He looked at her, his eyes red. While she'd gone in the ambulance with Ava, he'd driven behind them in their car. He must've been crying all the way. He rubbed his hands up and over his face and head, making his hair stand on end.

'I didn't think she'd do something like this,' Niamh said hoarsely. 'I thought we'd been better parents.'

'Better parents?' Evan looked at her squarely. 'We should've seen this coming a mile off.'

'I'm sorry?' Niamh looked up at him. His face was

grim; his lips were pressed tightly together. He stared at her for a minute before shaking his head.

'It's those kids she's been hanging around with,' he said. 'They're far too old for her.'

'What kids?' Niamh stood up. She racked her brains. She knew about Holly and Zach, and the others were all in Ava's sports teams and Scouts' group. They were great kids, and not ones to act the maggot.

'You'd know if you weren't so wrapped up in your project . . . and Rory Quinlan.'

Niamh's mouth dropped open. Did he know what had happened that morning? He couldn't. It didn't make sense.

She shook as the words tumbled from her mouth. 'That's right. It's my fault. Nothing to do with you at all, or the fact that you work in the same school your daughter goes to, and you didn't even know she wasn't there!'

'I was in class. Teaching. Working. How could I know?' Evan stood his ground. 'You, on the other hand, were probably too busy choosing paint samples with Rory Quinlan.'

Niamh lowered her voice as other waiting patients walked by them. Her face heated up, thinking of what had transpired between her and Rory that morning. 'That would be like me saying: look at you running off every day to teach other people's children and not our own.'

'It's not a real job, Niamh.' Evan shook his head. 'Can't you understand that? This notion of running a B&B – it's just something for you to do.'

Niamh sat back down. The plastic was cold beneath her thighs. She looked up at Evan sadly.

She tried to keep her voice from breaking. 'This is not just *something for me to do*, and if you see it that way, then we have some serious talking to do. Clearly our paths are not going in the same direction.'

'They haven't been for quite a long time now,' he said, resuming his pacing.

Niamh sat quietly looking at him as he paced. His shoes squeaked every time he turned. The beeps from machines around her grew louder and more chaotic. Niamh squinted as the yellow light above them flickered. Her lungs tightened and she gripped the chair seat hard as she tried to translate what exactly he was saying. She was used to Evan being dramatic over silly things. But this wasn't simply deciding what starter to have for Christmas dinner. It was bigger and more complex. It felt as if he'd been thinking about it for a while. It felt like the beginning of the end.

Struggling to take a breath, Niamh staggered from the chair and hurried along the corridor, her own shoes silent. She pressed her palm down hard on the button that allowed her back out into the emergency waiting area, and practically ran through the double set of doors to the ambulance bay. Leaning against the far wall, away from the smokers and the hospital patients who were wandering around in their dressing gowns and slippers in an effort to break the monotony of the ward, Niamh choked back tears. She looked down at the weeds at her feet, then up at the tired old building in front of her.

Ambulances seemed to arrive with injured people every ten minutes, then leave in a hurry to go to get more. She could see through the window that the waiting room had filled rapidly since she'd come outside. She pushed her hands down deep into her coat pockets. Evan hadn't come looking for her. He hadn't even texted her to see where she'd gone. She bet Rory would have, then immediately banished that thought. It was despicable, and not at all helpful.

'When did it get this bad?' she asked no one, then feeling bonkers she looked around to see if anyone had noticed. What on earth had happened to have her outside an emergency department talking to herself while her daughter was being assessed for drowning, not to mention that her husband was blaming her for it and for their marriage problems. Her phone beeped and she pulled it out quickly. Disappointed, she saw that it was only Edel texting to say that she'd collect Katie and Sophie from school for her, that she hoped Ava was okay, and to let her know if there was any news.

Quickly Niamh sent back a reply, grateful to her friend for being so thoughtful. Another ambulance pulled in and reversed into the bay. She watched as a frail, old woman, wrapped up in blue hospital blankets, was gently wheeled inside. The woman's plaintive voice carried back to her – she lived alone, she was saying to the smiling paramedic, and was worried about her houseplants. It made Niamh want to cry. Evan appeared in the doorway as the old woman was wheeled straight through the waiting room and into an assessment area. He looked tired, Niamh thought as they stared at each other across the ambulance bay. But then, these days so did she. Pushing away from the wall, she walked towards him and back into the emergency department.

*

Back at Mill House, Lauren stripped out of her swimming suit and pulled on her jeans, her warmest jumper, and her favourite socks. She couldn't stop shaking. She wished Shane was with her. It was hard to forget the look on Niamh's face as she'd climbed into the ambulance. She'd looked scared and lonely. Ignoring the thought, Lauren rolled up her sleeves. She turned on the tap at the kitchen sink and began to vigorously wash up the pile of delph that had accumulated over the weekend and tried not to think about anything – not Shane, not Niamh, not her daughter. Within an hour she'd cleaned the kitchen until it sparkled and was in the middle of hoovering the sitting room when there was a loud knock at the front door. Opening it she found Pippa Moore standing there.

'Lauren?' Pippa said. 'I don't know if you remember me – I'm Pippa. Heather's mother.'

'I remember you, Mrs Moore,' Lauren said. She peered over Pippa's shoulder but couldn't see anyone else nearby. 'What can I do for you?'

'I saw you at the lake earlier,' Pippa said, shaking her head. 'It's hard to believe what happened.'

Lauren nodded. 'It was horrible. Thank God Heather was there.'

'That's the thing,' Pippa said. 'She cut her arm on the raft, or at least that's what she thinks happened, and she didn't realise it until we got home. Anyway, it's deep and it needs to be looked after. She needs to get stitches.'

Lauren frowned. Didn't Pippa realise she was a teacher, not a nurse?

'I was wondering if you had a car,' Pippa continued. 'We need to go to the emergency department, according to our doctor. I've no car and don't want to be calling an ambulance for just a cut – it's not life-threatening – so I was hoping you could help us out.'

'I wish I could,' Lauren said. 'But I've not got a car either. I left it in Dublin – I wasn't supposed to be staying here this long, you see.'

'Thanks anyway. I'm sure you'd help if you could.' Pippa twisted her hands together.

Lauren watched as Pippa walked down the garden path, through the gate and down the hill towards her house. Then Lauren ran down the garden path, flung open the gate and called out.

'Mrs Moore! Hold on!' Lauren ran down the hill to where the slight woman had stopped in her tracks. 'Shane is coming later, in a few hours. I'll ask him to bring the car instead of the van. We could go then – if you can wait, that is?'

Pippa's face lit up like the lake did on solstice mornings. 'That's fantastic. Yes, we should be able to hold on. I've made Heather rest – you know what she's like, wanting to be up and about – but now she's lying down. Thank you.'

Lauren nodded as Pippa walked away.

Back in the kitchen, she called Shane. She could hear the clamour of the city in the background as she told him what had happened that morning. It faded as she listened, and all she heard was crunching footsteps as if he was moving somewhere less noisy.

'Talk to me, Laure. Are you all right?' he said.

'I'm fine,' Lauren said. 'Sure it had nothing to do with me.'

'They're your friends,' Shane said firmly. 'You must feel something?'

'I'm fine, honestly.' She listened to him sigh, sure that he didn't believe her.

'You know what my father says about when a woman says she's fine . . .' Shane half-heartedly attempted their old joke.

'Ha-ha,' she deadpanned. 'I mean it, though. I'm fine and I'll be extra-fine when we have this favour Pippa has asked over and done with.'

'I'll be there as soon as I can,' Shane said. Then more softly: 'I'm worried about you.'

'Don't be. See ya later.' Lauren hung up quickly. Her heart was in her mouth. How could she let him go when the thought of seeing him again made her whole body tingle? It was disconcerting. She'd have to get her head and heart together before he arrived later, or else she'd be in real trouble.

Putting her phone back in her pocket, she picked up the sheets she'd selected for their bed, then put them down again. She smoothed the warm brushed-cotton duvet cover with the palm of her hand. Shivers ran up her arm. Shane loved brushed-cotton sheets; he said it felt like coming home. She must've made the selection with that in the back of her mind, but what did that mean? Grabbing the sheets, she hurried back to the kitchen and put them back into the airing cupboard and pulled out crisp cotton ones. Then she shoved those back onto the shelf too.

It means that I'll always love him. She stared into the cupboard. Her breath caught in her chest. Swaying, she gripped the cupboard door handle to try to steady herself.

Then she took the brushed-cotton sheets out again and firmly closed the door. There was no point in being cruel, not before she'd told him to go, she rationalised. They may as well enjoy their time together while they had it.

Running up the stairs, she held the sheets tightly to her chest, breathing in the freshly washed scent, unaware that she was crying. Only when she'd smoothed the top sheet over the duvet did she wipe the tears from her face. She was longing for him to arrive, looking forward to his things being scattered around the place – he always hung his fleece on the back of the dining room chair. Which drove her mad, but the last few months had been lonely. She'd realised how many quirks she had – and they weren't all good.

She'd spent years harping on at him to move his fleece, or tidy his keys, but now she'd discovered that *she* had a terrible habit of leaving teabags in the sink. He'd never complained. She realised she'd never had to bleach the sink at home after the teabags had stained the so-called stainless-steel sink. She seemed to spend an inordinate amount of time bleaching the kitchen sink at Mill House.

The crunch of gravel made her get up and look out of the window. Shane had pulled into the garden and was taking a bag from the boot of the car. He was earlier than she'd expected. Lauren's stomach lurched the same way it had the very first time she'd laid eyes on him from her old bedroom window. She gazed down at him; he looked so good. His sandy hair needed a cut, but that was the way she liked it – it reminded her of the first summer they'd met, but he'd be dying to get it cut. He hated having to tidy it up every morning when it was just that little too long. She watched him for a minute, then ran down the stairs to open the front door.

He smiled at her, the smile she loved most in the world, the smile that was only for her.

'I know I'm early, but I didn't want you to be alone after this morning,' he said, walking towards her. 'But I couldn't get the Indian takeaway . . .'

'It doesn't matter,' Lauren said, glad she'd chosen the soft sheets for their bed. 'Hi.'

'Hi.' He dropped his bag at her feet and wrapped his arms around her, almost lifting her from the ground. Lauren allowed her arms to wrap around him, her body to lean into his. It was so different from how they'd been over the weekend, and somehow it felt perfect. It felt like home.

'You smell good,' he whispered into her hair. 'I've missed this.'

Lauren buried her face in his chest. Her fingers caressed the hair at the nape of his neck, and her heart pounded so fast that it made her ears hot and her head spin.

'Me too,' she said. 'More than you know.'

She leaned back and looked into his face. He was holding her steady, his blue eyes crinkled at the edges as he smiled wider, and her heart flipped. She needed him; she always would. Maybe he would be okay with them not having children, maybe they needed to have that conversation one more time – then she wouldn't have to break both of their hearts.

'Come on in,' she breathed out. 'It's chilly out here.'

'I'd love to,' he said. Then he pulled her in for a kiss, moulding her against him with firm hands. When he let her go, his eyes were dark and his breath quick. 'But we have to get Heather to the hospital. Best we go now before it gets too late. The last thing we want to do is to be stuck there all night.'

'Us?' Lauren groaned. 'Can't you go? I'll stay and get some food ready.'

'Lauren, Heather is *your* friend, not mine.' Shane looked at her as if she were crazy. 'Come on, we'll go together. It'd be weird of it was just me.'

'*Was* my friend. I keep telling you,' she grumbled. 'It's going to be awkward.'

'It'll be awkward for me if you don't come, so I'd rather we share the awkwardness, if you don't mind. Grab a coat.' Shane picked up his bag and dropped it just inside the door, then went back to the car.

Lauren watched him. A huge urge to pull a face at him washed over her, but she reached for her coat and handbag instead. As usual he was right, but it was incredibly annoying, she thought as she got into the car beside him.

*

Heather stood looking out of the sitting room window, frowning as a strange car pulled up at the still-to-be-painted arty wall outside of the house. She leaned forward and squinted. Someone was getting out of the car, and she could hear Pippa opening the front door. Her heart dropped to her stomach when she saw Lauren making her way up the path.

'Heather,' Pippa called. 'Lauren and Shane are here to take you to the emergency department.'

267

Heather opened the sitting room door and stared at Pippa.

'What the hell?' she hissed.

'Hurry up now,' Pippa said as if she didn't see Heather pulling a face at her. 'Here, take my jacket.' She slipped a jacket into Heather's hands.

'Won't you need this?' Heather said through gritted teeth to her mother.

'What would I need it for?' Pippa stared at her.

'For later, on the way home,' Heather said.

'I'm not going.' Pippa laughed. 'I'll pop a casserole on, and we can all have some later.'

Heather watched Pippa saunter into the kitchen as if she'd not a care in the world before turning to look at Lauren, who was standing on the doorstep as if she was a bold child caught playing *ring-a-bell-run*.

'Right,' she said. 'Let's get going.'

Lauren nodded, her lips pressed together. The pair walked in silence down the path and got into the car. Seeing the stiffness between them, Shane rolled his eyes and nodded hello to Heather before pulling out onto the road.

Heather snapped her seatbelt on and looked out the car window. The hedgerows flew by. Fields and forests loomed in the dusky evening as the sun began to set. She pulled out her phone and put the hospital into Google Maps. It was twenty minutes away.

She leaned against the window and closed her eyes. It was going to be a long twenty minutes, but she was damned if she was going to make the first move even though it felt rude not to say thanks for the lift. She

268

opened her eyes and caught Shane looking at her through the rear-view mirror.

'Is it sore?' he asked.

'A bit,' she said, conceding to speak to Shane. 'The doctor gave me painkillers, but I think it's wearing off a little.'

'Was it Doctor Reilly? He'd hand out pills like they were sweets.' Shane smiled at her through the mirror.

'Yeah.' Heather laughed. She flashed a glance at Lauren, who was looking out her window. 'He must be well past retirement though.'

'Without a doubt,' Shane agreed. 'Wasn't his daughter supposed to take his place?'

'You're right,' Heather said. 'I'd forgotten that. Carmel – I think that was her name.'

'Caroline?' Shane said. 'Carol? It definitely begins with a C.'

Heather frowned. 'I can't remember. No, hang on, wasn't it Catherine?'

'Celine,' Lauren said. 'Her name was Celine.'

Heather sat back. 'Thanks.'

They grew silent again. Heather twisted her fingers together in her lap.

'Thanks for the lift.' Her voice disappeared as Shane turned on the radio. It blared up, making everyone jump. Quickly he turned it down and grimaced in the mirror at Heather.

'Sorry about that,' he murmured as he turned the car into the hospital car park. After two laps of the car park and no sign of an empty space, he pulled over at the main door.

'Right, you two go on. I'll park on the road. Text me what's happening.' He nodded.

Lauren stared at him, but he ignored her. With a snap she unclipped her seatbelt, then grabbed her phone from her bag. She stood on the path with Heather and they watched Shane drive out of the car park.

'Right,' Lauren said briskly. 'Let's get inside.'

Heather shrugged but began walking fast towards the emergency department, her eyes down. Looking up, she stopped. Niamh was leaning on the wall just outside the doors, looking pale and tired. She looked up as the two women approached and began to cry.

22

Niamh stood away from the wall. She couldn't believe it. The girls had turned up for her. After all this time they'd come to help her.

'Hi,' she said, her voice cracking slightly.

'Hey,' Heather said. Her eyes were wary. Niamh felt a shiver of shame run down her spine. The last thing she'd said to Heather was that she was a jumped-up scruffy hippy who'd notions of a grand life that would never materialise. But it wasn't the worst thing she'd said that night. Not to mention Lauren, who'd given as good as she'd got. Niamh remembered clearly how she'd had called her a walking petri dish because of the way she let lads into her knickers. Shaking, Niamh pulled a well-used tissue from her sleeve and wiped her face until the tissue all but disintegrated. She balled the tissue up and shoved it into her pocket.

'Heather,' Niamh said. 'Thank you for saving Ava. I froze, I couldn't remember what I was supposed to do. I wanted to run in and then there you were – already in the water and then you had her and I don't know how to thank you enough.'

'Please, stop.' Heather shifted from foot to foot. 'Anyone would've done it.'

'How is she?' Lauren stepped forward. Her chin quivered as she looked at Niamh.

'She's doing okay.' Niamh shook her head. 'At least that's what they've told me. They're keeping her in for observation. Her oxygen levels are great, which I think is a good sign.'

Lauren nodded. 'That is good. She's going to be okay, Niamh. Try not to worry too much.'

'All I do these days is worry,' Niamh said. 'I go to sleep worried, and I wake up worried.'

Heather snorted, and Niamh felt her face heat up. Heather wouldn't understand, not with her jet-setting lifestyle to sun-kissed places. She didn't have a care in the world. Niamh swept her hair back from her face and stood tall.

'Well, thanks for checking in on me and Ava,' she said lightly. 'I appreciate it, really.'

'What?' Lauren frowned. 'Well, we're also here to have Heather checked out.'

Niamh looked at Heather with wide eyes. Inwardly she kicked herself. It hadn't occurred to her that Heather might need assistance too. 'Oh? What's wrong?'

'I cut my arm on a nail or something sticking out of the raft.' Heather shrugged. She watched as an ambulance reversed up to the hospital doors. 'I'd better get inside. It looks busy – we don't want to be here all night.'

Niamh watched as the two women went inside and then resumed her leaning against the wall, grateful that the smokers and vapers had moved on to the smoking shelter a couple of yards away. As the sky darkened, she wondered what Evan was doing. With a heavy heart she looked at the rising moon and wondered what it meant that she was kind of glad he wasn't with her, when there was once a time when all she craved was his company.

*

Heather marched up to the counter to check in. After answering a dozen questions, filling out forms and a quick assessment by the triage nurse she was told to sit in the waiting area to be called.

Lauren had selected a seat away from the drunk who was telling everyone how he'd walked a pole before falling into the gutter, yet she didn't think that adequately explained the huge cut under his eye. Lauren had however chosen the seat close to a deathly pale man in a white bloodstained coat and a butcher's hat. He was holding his leg tightly. Lauren looked a little peaky herself, Heather thought as she took the seat opposite Lauren.

'Are you all right?' Heather asked as Lauren averted her gaze from the man's bloody trouser leg for the third time in about as many minutes. 'You look a little green about the gills.'

Lauren nodded, and leaned away from the butcher. 'Do they think it'll be long before you're seen?'

'No one knows.' Heather sat back in her seat. 'Looks like yer man beside you might be in more need of a doctor than me.'

The butcher attempted a smile, but it came across as a grimace.

273

'What happened?' Heather nodded at his leg.

'Wiped the blade on my jeans, didn't I?' The man pulled a face. 'It went right through.' He lifted his hand and showed them the clean, but blood-soaked, cut in his jeans. 'I haven't looked, but the doc did and sent me here. What about you?'

'Something similar,' Heather said. 'Cut my arm. Doctor wants me to have it stitched and there was no one at the surgery to do it.'

'She saved a girl from drowning,' Lauren interjected.

A nurse, who was asking the drunk man to sit down, looked up.

'That was you?' She looked at Heather. 'You're a hero.'

'No, I'm not.' Heather shifted in her seat.

'Come on,' the nurse said. 'Follow me and we'll get that seen to.'

Mouthing *sorry* to the butcher, Heather got up as another man walked into the A&E. He was similarly dressed to the butcher she'd just talked to.

'Jimbo,' the seated butcher called over. 'What the?'

'Don't start,' Jimbo called back. 'Looks like you're not the only eejit.' He held up his hand, which was heavily bandaged. Then burst out laughing before groaning in pain.

Heather looked at Lauren, who shook her head and grinned.

'Honestly,' Heather whispered to Lauren as they followed the nurse. 'I'd be checking my dinner for fingers and toes if I bought my meat at their shop.'

*

Lauren stifled a giggle as they passed patients on trolleys and in wheelchairs. The emergency department was much quieter than the waiting room. There was no television showing evening cooking programmes, no drunk blurting random race tips, and no vending machine constantly whirring and chugging. The muted sounds of bleeping machines, whispers from relatives, and groans from patients filled the air alongside the quick steps and friendly talk from the medical staff who were back and forth picking up new charts before disappearing behind cubicle curtains. The nurse led them down a dim corridor and into a small room. A gurney rested against the wall, the curtains tied back, and a window was open allowing the cool evening air in.

Sitting down on one of the three chairs, Lauren looked at the wall of cupboards opposite her as the nurse took a look at Heather's arm.

'That's nasty,' the nurse said. 'I'll be back in a moment.'

Lauren looked at Heather, who'd gone pale.

'Are you okay?' She touched Heather's leg.

'Just a bit woozy,' Heather said. 'I didn't see it before and now I wish I hadn't.'

'Maybe put your head between your knees.' Lauren looked around for some water. 'Or lie on the floor.'

Heather leaned forward. Her breath was shallow. Lauren dashed to the door and looked out. Rosemary would have known exactly what to do, but she wasn't here. The nurse turned a corner with a young doctor. Lauren waved at them.

'She's feeling faint,' she said. 'I told her to lie down.'

The doctor and nurse hurried into the room where

275

Heather was now on the floor. Lauren slipped out and stood uncomfortably in the corridor as they tended to her old friend. Looking into the room she wondered what their friendship might have become had they not fought that night. Heather looked forlorn. She'd been fiery the night of their row, angry and explosive. Lauren leaned against the doorframe and recalled how she'd been shocked to hear the things that had come out of Heather's mouth. Most of it had been directed at Niamh, in fairness, but some of it had been aimed at her too, and it had struck home hard.

Although it was what she herself had said that had come true. She'd told Niamh she'd get herself into trouble, that she'd wind up married with kids and what use were her dreams then. Now that she thought about it, Niamh must've already been pregnant then, or suspected that she was. It must've been horrible to hear such a stark warning, knowing it was already too late. Lauren turned her back to the doctor as the nurse handed over a needle, probably for tetanus, but all the same the sight of it made her knees want to buckle. She'd seen enough needles during her IVF cycles.

Niamh came out of a curtained cubicle at the end of the corridor and, catching sight of Lauren, waved. Lauren glanced back at where Heather was now lying on the bed with her eyes closed tight, then moved towards Niamh to keep them out of Heather's view.

'I had to come out of there. Ava is fast asleep as if nothing happened, and the walls were pressing in on me. Do you think you'll be here much longer?' Niamh sounded tired.

'I'm not sure. Heather is being seen now, so I can't imagine we will be.'

'She's all right though – Heather?' Niamh's forehead creased.

'I think so,' Lauren said.

'Have ye, um,' Niamh started. She took a breath. 'Have you two been in touch long?'

'Not a bit.' Lauren looked at Niamh. 'Look, I just want to say how sorry I am, about Ava and today. You had such a fright. It must've been terrible.'

'I'm sorry too,' Niamh blurted. 'About today, and well, about everything. Life is so short and so messed up. I'm so tired the whole time and so alone. I think about you all the time. And Heather. I wish I could go back in time and change it all, every last bit of it.'

'Surely not everything.' Lauren stared at Niamh.

Niamh looked at her squarely. 'Sometimes yes, everything. I love my kids, please don't think that I don't, but it's so damn hard, all the time. Lately I can't stop thinking of how my life might've been if things had been different.'

Lauren felt ill. It was awful to hear Niamh speak as if she regretted her family, as if she'd change it all out in a heartbeat. Didn't she realise that she had the most precious thing on earth? Lauren often wondered if that first pregnancy scare at sixteen was the beginning of all her fertility problems, but she couldn't be sure. She'd never taken a test and had celebrated quietly when her period had finally arrived. Now she wondered if that had been her first miscarriage only she hadn't realised it.

But wanting to change things when you had the dream – that was difficult to understand.

'That's a dangerous way to think,' Lauren said eventually. 'Yet, I kind of get it. There isn't a day that goes by that I don't have similar thoughts. I wish that what happened to you had happened to me.'

'Lauren, you don't. You really don't.' Niamh grasped Lauren's arm. 'It was awful. Evan's parents didn't speak to us for almost a year. They only came to the christening because my father made them.'

'Niamh, you got pregnant, then ran away and got married. I'd be pretty annoyed if I was them.'

'What choice did we have?' Niamh slumped against the wall. 'Everyone was watching us, pointing the finger at me, sniggering wherever I went. It was all Evan's idea . . . *Run away with me to Rome*, he'd said. *It'll be fine, they'll be delighted for us.* They weren't delighted, not a bit.'

Looking at Niamh, at the dark circles under her eyes and how faded she seemed to be, Lauren wondered what it was that Niamh wasn't saying.

'How is Evan?' she asked.

'Oh, he's fine.' Niamh sighed. 'He's blaming me for this, and I'm blaming him. He thinks I'm checked out of the family at the moment.'

'Oh?' Lauren thought of Rory and how he'd looked at Niamh down at the lake.

'It's just the renovations are important to me,' Niamh continued as if Lauren knew what she was talking about. 'And money doesn't grow on trees, so I have to be on top of things. I'm lucky to have Rory to help me because I'm getting absolutely nothing from Evan.'

'Rory Quinlan?' Lauren raised her eyebrows. He'd

always liked Niamh. He'd never made it a secret, and she got why Evan wasn't happy. But was Niamh happy?

'Yeah, that's him. He's been a real rock these last few months.' Niamh shook her head. 'I'm sorry, I'm bombarding you with all my burdens and we haven't even had a chance to properly talk, to catch up and well, you know.'

'Don't worry. I'm sure it's the shock of today, and everything.' Lauren shrugged. 'I'm sure we'll get a chance at some stage – to talk – if you're up for it. There are a few things I'd like to apologise for.'

Niamh shifted against the wall. 'Listen, we were young and silly. Idealists. We all said stupid, mean things to each other. If anyone needs to apologise it's me. I said some horrible things . . .'

'Mammy,' Ava's voice came from the cubicle opposite Lauren. 'Mammy, where are you?'

'You'd better go in to her,' Lauren said, glad to be interrupted. A hospital corridor didn't feel like the right place for a conversation like this.

'I should.' Niamh turned to go, then turned back. 'Lauren, thank you, for listening and even talking to me. I know I wasn't fair to you either, back then.'

Lauren nodded. 'It's okay, go on. We'll talk soon.'

Watching Niamh go back to her daughter, Lauren tried desperately to swallow the lump in her throat. Whenever she'd imagined bumping into Niamh, she'd always imagined Niamh would've had something scathing to say, but she hadn't. Nothing had happened today as she'd expected. Actually, she mused as she leaned against the cold wall, nothing had happened in her life as she'd expected. The strange thing was that it seemed to be the same for Niamh.

Somewhere down the corridor the familiar jangle of the six o'clock news sounded, and Lauren sighed. It had been hours now. Rubbing her eyes, she wondered how Shane was doing out in the car. He hadn't been allowed to come into this section of the emergency department.

'I can go home now.'

Lauren jumped and looked up. Heather was standing nearby, looking ghastly. Her hair was straggly and her eyes pink.

'Come on, let's go.' Lauren nodded towards the cubicle in front of them. 'Niamh is in there, if you want to say anything to her.'

'No. I've nothing to say to her.' Heather's face hardened.

Lauren watched her walk down the corridor. She couldn't blame her, but after all this time surely Heather knew that what had happened between them had been silly teenage drama. They'd grown up since then, hadn't they? Lauren smiled at a passing nurse and scratched her arm. Sometimes it felt as if they were still eighteen. With a sigh she hurried to catch up with Heather.

*

Lauren hunkered in front of the stove in Mill House. She could burn the letter now, but Shane would be bound to notice. She cast a glance at his fleece on the back of the dining room chair. A smile flickered over her face at the familiarity of it, but it disappeared just as swiftly. Putting a match to the kindling in the grate she chewed her lower lip. He'd been extremely quiet the whole drive back from the hospital. He'd barely said goodnight to Heather when they'd dropped her off. And there was no mention of what they'd have for dinner now. Not even a cup of tea. Her mouth watered thinking of the Indian takeaway they were missing out on. As the flames took hold she heard Shane flop down on the sofa behind her and when she looked around his eyes were closed, his hand over his forehead. Scooching across the floor, Lauren began undoing his boots, but he jumped as if electrified the moment she touched him.

'Sorry,' she said quietly. 'I was just taking your boots off. You were asleep.'

'I'm grand,' he said, moving his feet away from her hands. 'I'll get some logs.'

Lauren frowned as he got up. 'Do you want tea?' she called to his back as he grabbed his fleece from the chair and strode through the kitchen to the back door.

'Tea would be nice, thanks,' he called back with the barest wave of his hand.

Lauren scalded the pot and waited for him to come back in. It wasn't like him to be so subdued. Maybe work was on his mind. She swirled the water in the teapot. Maybe he hadn't really been able to take a half-day. She peered out into the darkness again. He really was taking a long time. Putting the teapot down on the draining board, Lauren went to the back door and looked out.

'Shane?' She stepped out into the chilly night air.

Lauren wrapped her arms around herself and walked around the side of the house to where the log pile was stacked beneath a deep overhanging eave. Shane was there, leaning against the logs, his breath billowing in front of him as if he'd been running.

She hurried towards him. 'What's wrong?'

'Just looking up at the stars,' he said. 'I'd forgotten how many there were, and how bright they seem here.'

Lauren breathed out. 'I thought something had happened to you.'

'I'm okay,' he said quietly. He kept looking up at the night sky.

Lauren looked up. The stars above them twinkled. A satellite soundlessly skated past the countless sparkling stars. Lauren watched it until it disappeared. She lowered her gaze back to Shane, but he kept his eyes on the sky.

'Come back inside.' She touched his arm gently.

'I'm waiting for a shooting star,' he said. 'I want to make a wish.'

Lauren laughed softly. 'You'll be a long time waiting, I think.'

'You might be right,' he said. With the deepest breath she'd ever heard him take, he looked away from the starry heavens and bent forward to pick up the logs, then followed her back inside.

*

'Any chance of a cup of tea?' Heather called out as she let herself in the front door, relieved to be away from the quiet tension that was evident in the car. Something was off. Shane had been very quiet, and Lauren had filled the silence by chatting incessantly about the drunk and the two butchers in the waiting area. It had almost felt like old times, but really, things between them hadn't changed much. They hadn't touched on the subject of that night, and she was glad. She was too tired to even contemplate that kind of talk.

Pippa stuck her head out of the kitchen door. 'I was wondering how much longer you'd be. Are you on your own? I have a casserole in the oven – enough for everyone.'

'They went on.' Heather hung Pippa's jacket on the hook.

'Did you offer them tea?' Pippa asked.

'No, I didn't.' Heather winced as she moved her newly stitched arm. 'And before you start, I think there was something going on between them and that it wouldn't be fixed by a cup of tea.'

Pippa stood back and let Heather into the kitchen. 'In that case then, you go and sit down there by the stove and have a look at what's on my laptop. Let me know what you think. I'll make you tea – chamomile. It's good for healing.'

Heather sank into the rocking chair beside the stove, glad for the warmth. She groaned as she sat down. 'Tetanus shot.' She explained before continuing. 'Just normal tea, please. I'll take any other tea you give me tomorrow – but just normal tea for now.'

Pippa smiled. 'Fine, this once. Then you must let me take care of you.'

Heather picked up the laptop with her good hand. Her mother had pages open with recipes for new products. The last few pages were all for soaps and moisturisers. They looked ambitious and luxurious. Scanning the ingredients, Heather frowned.

'These look great,' she said as Pippa handed her a cup of tea. 'But they need goats' milk. Have you a supplier in mind?'

'I thought I'd just get some.' Pippa blew on her tea.

'Get some what?' Heather felt a bubble of panic rise in her stomach. What on earth was her mother planning now? There wasn't a dull moment – it was a wonder Cash hadn't had the sense to stay with her. His life would've been filled if only he'd let her be who she really was and hadn't dominated their life with his own selfish desires, because, as Heather was coming to realise, her mother was fun, and adventurous and *ambitious*.

'Goats,' Pippa said. Her eyes shone and she waved her arm to the window and the dark landscape beyond it. 'There's five acres of land out there. Once it's cleared off a bit, I can get some goats.'

Heather sat up. 'Goats are lovely, but they're not the kind of animals you just let off outside and fend for themselves. There's a huge level of care and money involved in keeping them.'

'I do know this,' Pippa said in a calmer voice. 'I've been talking to Willow about it. She's been sending me information – I'm well aware the level of work involved. I've been doing my homework, Heather. I'm enrolled in a goat-farming course, and it's not like I'm looking for a massive herd. Just a few to get me started – to see if I can do it. There are so many products for skin issues out there, and suppliers have been asking if I make any.'

Pippa took a sip of her tea before carrying on.

'Hal Goodman's father used to have goats, and he's been telling me how to mind them. I've been speaking with Rory Quinlan. He said he could have the land cleared by the end of May for me, and that he'd be ready to build a shed for them in June. He's busy until around then with Niamh's refurbishment.'

Heather put the laptop down, wondering when exactly Pippa had become friends with Rory Quinlan and Hal Goodman. Then she wondered what her father would have made of that. He'd have been jealous. He'd have made his jealously known too, although he'd frame it in a way that made Rory and Hal look like the odd ones, not him.

'You've got it worked out so,' Heather said.

'Well, not exactly,' Pippa said. 'I'm nervous about it. Hal thinks I'll be fine. He said they're easy to manage if you get them young.'

Heather sipped her tea. She'd never told Pippa about her little goat buddies back in the animal shelter in London. Glen had emailed her to let her know that they'd been successfully homed together in a smallholding only an hour away from her apartment. She could go see them any time she wanted – if she ever got back to London that was. But that seemed more unlikely as time passed, and her mother's new ideas weren't helping either. The urge to get back to her own business was floundering more and more, and she knew that she was actively ignoring it. It wasn't like she'd been ignoring emails or invitations. She'd simply put them off, explaining that she had things going on in her home life that needed her full attention right now. If they thought their hotel or glamp site was more serious than helping her mother set up her business and buy a few goats, then that was on them.

'What's so funny?' Pippa looked sideways at Heather.

'What?' Heather blinked.

'You're grinning, like a Cheshire cat.' Pippa started to smile too.

'Goats. I like it. I think we could manage a few goats,' Heather said.

Pippa got up and took Heather's cup. 'Let me get you a fresh sup.'

Heather leaned back in the rocking chair and closed her eyes. Tiredness washed over her. It had been a long day – one of the longest in a while. Her last thoughts before she drifted off to sleep was that she was actually enjoying being at home. Learning about Pippa and helping her was the most fun she'd had in a long time. London's streets of gold seemed gold-plated instead of solid. Maybe it was time to make a change.

She was snoring gently when Pippa came back with a fresh drop of tea and didn't see her mother's face soften as she gently laid a crocheted throw over her.

23

20th February 2024

It was after midnight when Evan texted Niamh to see how they were getting on. Sophie and Katie were sound asleep, he assured her, and he was going to bed himself. He'd talk to her in the morning. Niamh replied with *xxx* but received no reply. Worn out, she tried to get comfortable on the hard chair beside Ava's bed and not think about the day's events.

She woke up with a jolt at six thirty as a nurse checked on Ava.

'Is she okay?' Niamh sat up, struggling to wipe the sleep from her eyes.

'She's absolutely fine. I'd say you both will be going home in an hour or two. I'll get the doctor in as quickly as possible for you, so ye can be on your way.' The nurse put the chart back.

'That's a relief,' Niamh said. Tears sprang to her eyes. 'I'm so grateful . . .'

'It's okay,' the nurse said. 'Someone must be watching

287

over her – if it hadn't been for that woman it might have been an entirely different story.'

'I know,' Niamh said quietly. 'I don't know how I'll ever repay her.'

'She was in yesterday to get her shoulder looked at, but I can't give you any details about her,' the nurse said. 'You know what? I could contact her with your details if you'd like me to?'

'No, it's okay. I actually know her.' Niamh half-smiled. 'Thanks though.'

'Sure that's brilliant. You can send a bunch of flowers and a thank-you card so.' The nurse picked up her notes and left the cubicle.

'How do you know her, Mammy?' Ava croaked from her gurney.

Niamh laid a hand on her daughter's brow. Ava's temperature seemed normal.

'We went to school together,' Niamh said softly. 'Before you were born.'

'Well, duh,' Ava said.

Niamh scooted her chair closer to Ava. 'How're you feeling?'

'Tired.' Ava yawned. 'It's horrible in here. The smell . . .'

'I know.' Niamh squeezed Ava's hand. 'Hopefully the doctor will be around soon.'

'Mammy,' Ava said in a tiny voice. 'I'm so sorry. I didn't mean to – I just really wanted to hang out with Luke and they all said I wouldn't skip school so – I dunno – I just wanted to prove something to them. I bet my Taylor Swift tickets that I would do it and I couldn't lose them. I'd die if I did.'

Niamh was about to lecture her daughter when she stopped. Now was not the time, not by a long shot. Not when she'd recognised that daredevil carefree attitude in her eldest child as the same one she'd once possessed. Evan was right; she should have expected it. Ava *was* just like her.

'I know how you feel,' she said eventually. 'We'll talk later, at home with warm PJs and a cup of tea.'

Ava nodded, pale and tight-lipped.

'It's okay, Ava,' Niamh said. 'Well, it's not okay, but it's not *not* okay. But there's a way to talk about what happened and yes, it's not going to be pleasant for you, or for me and Daddy, but it won't be a fight. I promise you. And of course, you couldn't lose your Taylor Swift tickets, but you shouldn't have made that bet either.'

'Thanks, Mammy.' Ava squeezed her hand, grinned and tried her old trick. 'You're the best mammy in the world.'

Niamh laughed. 'You're a cheeky monkey.'

'I had to say it.' Ava giggled.

They were still laughing when a tired-looking doctor came in.

'That's what we like to see,' he said, raising his tired eyes from Ava's notes. 'I think you can go home, young Ava, but behave yourself. You were very lucky.'

'I promise.' Ava looked at him with starry eyes and Niamh inwardly tutted. Yup, her daughter was just like her.

*

An hour later they sat at the kitchen table, with a pot of tea and a packet of Jaffa Cakes. Niamh stirred her tea and glanced over the sheet of paper on the table with information on secondary drowning and the signs that she needed to watch out for over the next day or so.

Ava yawned and pushed her tea away. 'Can I go to bed?'

Niamh nodded. 'Yeah, of course. You're feeling okay? No pains in your chest?'

'No, Mammy. Nothing.' Ava stood up. 'Just tired.'

'Go on, brush your teeth.' Niamh watched her gangly daughter leave the room. She'd not realised how grown up Ava was becoming. How had that happened? Laying her head down on the table, Niamh nodded off, waking only when the front door closed with a bang. She heard Evan curse quietly.

'I didn't mean that,' he said, coming into the kitchen. He stood halfway between the door and the island. His face was drawn and his eyes bloodshot.

Niamh got up. 'I'll make some fresh tea.'

'No.' He rubbed a hand over his face. 'I'm not staying. I just came back to pick up some things.'

'Things?' Niamh turned to face him. Her mouth went dry as she noticed he was trying not to look at her. 'What do you mean – things? Stuff for school?'

'No. Other things.' Evan rubbed his hand on his jeans. 'Look, it's obvious there's something going on between you and Rory. I need some space to think about what's happening here.'

'I'm sorry but what?' Niamh's voice rose. 'How'd you figure that absolute pile of crap out?'

Evan sighed. 'Look, Niamh – it's no secret that you're not happy, is it? And lately, since *he's* been around, you've perked up – you're putting on perfume and makeup. For crying out loud, it's as clear as day.'

'That's absurd. And untrue,' Niamh blurted.

'Do you think I came down in the last shower of rain?' Evan put his hands on his hips.

'I'm not happy – that bit is true. But there's nothing going on between me and Rory.' Niamh's hands shook. She'd been that close. She'd imagined it and she'd been flattered but she hadn't done anything.

Evan looked directly into Niamh's eyes. 'How do you explain his being at the lake yesterday – with you.'

'I can't. I have no explanation because I didn't know he was there.' Niamh stared at Evan. 'By your logic I'm having an affair with Mucker too – he was there, and Heather who I haven't spoken to in over a decade, and Lauren. She was there at the lake as well. Oh, and Pippa Moore, because hey – in for a penny in for a pound.'

Evan tiredly rubbed a hand over his hair. 'It's always been this way, Niamh – you're a flirt. I've seen you in action since we were in our teens. Just ask Heather or Lauren . . .'

'Flirting isn't the same as having an affair.' Niamh's temples began to throb. 'And leaving because you only *think* I'm having an affair is pathetic.'

He stared at her. She drew herself tall and stared back, wishing she knew what was going on in his head. It felt almost unreal – this whole conversation – he couldn't be serious, could he? She hadn't actually done anything.

The kitchen clock ticked louder and louder, and the sound of a trailer beeping as it reversed into the yard irritated her no end. She once had looked forward to Rory arriving to work on the rooms; now she'd do anything to get rid of him.

'I don't want you to leave.' Niamh broke the silence, unable to bear it any longer. 'It'll upset the girls.'

'Is that it?' Evan squinted at her as she tried to hold her head up. 'Because it'll upset the girls?'

'Maybe it is.' Niamh felt her stomach flip as the words flew out of her mouth. 'Maybe that's all it is. I'm going to lie down. You do whatever you see fit, but if the girls are upset then that's on you. Not me. I'm *not* seeing Rory Quinlan. I won't take any blame for you causing a rift here.'

Shaking, she hurried from the kitchen and up the stairs to their room. Her fists clenched, she stood just inside the door and let the tears fall. What else could she do?

24

19th June 2009

Niamh held her tongue as her father said it again.

'Trinity College would be lucky to have you,' he said. 'How many points do you think it'll be this year? I'd say it'll be down on last year, taking the recession into account.'

She looked at him for a minute, wondering how to tell him that she'd no interest in university and had only applied because he'd stood over her as she'd filled out the application. She'd changed her courses behind his back to ones that would work in her favour as cabin crew, but he didn't know that, yet. Her father kept talking. None of it was new to her. When he wasn't talking about how many points she'd need to get into Trinity College Dublin – the only college he thought that mattered – he was pondering on which courses would be the most popular this year.

Niamh tuned out. Under the table she counted on her fingers, just as she had earlier during her Religion exam. Her period was two weeks late. She'd been late before, almost two weeks once. So maybe this was nothing.

Everyone said that the stress of the Leaving Certificate was massive, and everyone knew that stress caused periods to go crazy. That had to be the reason. It couldn't be anything else. Everyone knew you couldn't get pregnant your first time. Her period would probably start any minute now. As long as it didn't start tonight, she'd be fine. She was planning on going out and partying with the rest of the gang and crippling cramps weren't welcome.

Niamh stopped counting her fingers and picked up her fork. Every mouthful of perfectly mashed potato felt like she was swallowing a ball of cement. Her mother smiled at her, and she smiled back wishing her mother hadn't made bacon and cabbage smothered in parsley sauce, but there had been no stopping her. She'd insisted on making it, calling today a day to celebrate.

'I can't believe my little girl is finished school and heading off to college soon.' Her mother dabbed her mouth with her napkin. 'Can you, Colm? What will we do when the house is empty and rattling without her in it?'

'The house won't be empty. She'll commute to Dublin, Mary,' Colm said. 'There's no need for her to stay in digs.'

'Digs!' Mary laughed. 'No one calls them digs nowadays.'

Niamh felt as if she was floating up by the ceiling, looking down at her parents as they laughed over the odd expressions and words they used to say. Despite her father's misgivings about digs or whatever they called it these days, he was in flying form. Her mother too. It was rare to see them both so cheerful at the same time.

'Walking out,' her father said. 'That's what my mother used to say. You were walking out with someone.'

'Going steady – remember that one?' her mother said with a giggle. 'Are you walking out with anyone, Niamh?'

Niamh coughed. What on earth was going on?

'Eh, sort of.' She grabbed her glass and took a gulp. How was she to tell them that she'd been seeing Evan McNamara these last six months?

'Evan McNamara,' her father said with a stern expression. 'Don't think I don't know what's going on in the village.'

'Is that Francis and Margaret's young lad?' Her mother leaned forward. The crease between her eyes deepened. 'Colm, when did you find out about this?'

Niamh saw a deep flush of red rise on her mother's neck. Her mother wasn't a bit worried about Evan or Francis or Margaret McNamara, she knew for sure. She'd never rated them at all until this moment. What was bothering her was that she hadn't known. Niamh twisted her fork in her potatoes. Now her mother would feel embarrassed. How many times had they bumped into Mrs McNamara since she and Evan had started *going steady*? Loads was the answer, at least once a week for the past six months, and each time Mrs McNamara had been warm and friendly while Mary Kennedy had been more reserved. Niamh waited for her father to answer.

'What does it matter how long I've known?' Colm said.

'It matters.' Mary's face was as red as the strawberries that sat in the bowl on the sideboard waiting to be spooned over the pavlova.

'Well, not that long, if that makes you feel any better,' Colm huffed. 'A week.'

'A week. Well, that's fine.' Mary brushed a hand over

her newly set hair. She turned to Niamh. 'I hope he's treating you decently.'

Niamh nodded, then shovelled another forkful of mashed potato into her mouth.

*

After dessert, and cleaning up the kitchen, which she'd insisted on doing as a thank you for dinner, Niamh ran out the front door into the evening. She stooped to kiss her mother on the cheek as she weeded the rose bed, and waved to her father who was walking around wondering aloud about cutting the grass.

It had been a funny sort of a day. It had started off cool enough, and then at lunchtime as their last exam was done, it had rained. Now it was bright and warm, and she'd dressed to suit. In her lavender one-shoulder mini-dress she couldn't wait to kick up her platform heels with the girls at The Coach House.

'Will you be warm enough in that?' Mary called after her. 'It's a little . . .'

'It's the style, Mam,' Niamh called back. 'I'm fine. I've got my cardi.' She waved her waterfall cardigan at her mother.

'If you've any trouble up at The Coach House you let me know.' Colm stood with his hands on his hips. 'I've left a few pound behind the bar for you and the girls to have a celebration drink – you're all over eighteen, aren't you?'

'Thanks, Dad, and yes, all eighteen.' Niamh blew her father a kiss and trotted out the gate and headed towards the village. It looked like they'd start the night in The Coach House; free drink was free drink. Texting Heather and Lauren about their good luck, she wondered how much money her father had left behind the bar and did a little dance. Whatever it was, they'd make the most of it.

Well used to walking in heels, she strode down the country lane, breathing in the green, as she called the scent of the hedgerows, and enjoying the warmth as the sun attempted to make an appearance. A shout behind her made her turn around. Shane was running to catch up with her. He ruffled her hair and fell in stride with her.

'Stop it!' She swiped at him. He giggled and she side-eyed him. 'You're drunk!'

'I'm not,' he said and fake swayed. 'I've only had a few cans.'

'Give over,' Niamh said. 'Your eyes are spinning in your head. Lauren is going to kill you.'

'She'll be grand.' Shane linked arms with Niamh. 'You'll mind me and get me sorted before she sees me.'

'Sees the state of you, you mean.' Niamh laughed. 'What were you up to?'

'Nothing,' Shane said with wide eyes. 'Just down the lake with a few of the lads. Escaping my mam – you know how it is being an only child. I thought she'd never stop crying.'

Niamh rolled her eyes. 'Mine made bacon and cabbage for me. I had to eat it.'

'You've lined your stomach for the night ahead – wise move.'

'You'd better do a bit of lining your own stomach,'

Niamh said as they came into the village. 'Get a bag of chips or something into you. I'm heading into The Coach – there's a few quid behind the bar for me. Come in when you're ready.'

'You're a star – you know that.' Shane smiled down at her. 'If only all girls could be like you.'

'Like me?' Niamh felt a shiver of worry run down her spine. Had Evan told him about how far they'd gone? 'What do you mean like me?'

'Just cool about everything, you know. Easy-going.' Shane staggered and caught hold of her arm to keep himself steady.

'Oh,' Niamh said. She reached for him as he stumbled again. 'Yeah, I don't like to stick to plans too much.'

Shane nodded and Niamh realised he was still holding her by the arm. She stepped back. 'Go on, get a bag of chips. See you in a bit.'

He tried to ruffle her hair again, laughing as she ducked away from him. She watched him head into the chip shop before she went into the lounge at The Coach House.

Sliding into a banquette near the bar she touched her arm where he'd held onto her. Never before had he expressed a longing to be free. As far back as she could remember he and Lauren had always spoken about settling down together, having children and all that kind of thing. They'd even talked about getting engaged this Christmas and planning a wedding in a couple years' time. Was he possibly settling for a dream and a future that wasn't his? Maybe everything she'd heard Lauren and Shane talk about were just Lauren's dreams. Maybe Shane felt he had to share the same dream as Lauren.

Niamh rubbed her arm where he'd touched her, feeling claustrophobic thinking of that kind of life. She never could imagine living that way. Why would you want to, until you were older? The world was wide open now they'd finished their exams. Tonight was where the fun all began – and tomorrow she'd start packing for a holiday to Ibiza with some of the other girls from school. Heather had a job lined up and was starting more or less immediately, and Lauren refused to leave Shane. It was going to be wonderful. If only her period would arrive to calm her nerves, then she'd be better able to relax. Picking up a bar mat, Niamh tapped it against the table. She crossed her legs and pushed all notions of children and getting married at twenty or whatever out of her head. It was all nonsense and wouldn't happen – no one got married that young these days. Their parents surely wouldn't allow it.

She pulled visions of sandy beaches and jugs of sangria to her mind and imagined the sun on her skin and all the boys gawping at her in her bikini.

*

Heather rambled in and made a beeline for Niamh.

'Did you see the state of Shane?' she said as she slid into the seat. 'Lauren will go mental.'

'I know. I've never seen him this tipsy so early.' Niamh frowned. It felt as if Shane was rebelling and if he was, well, she couldn't blame him. His life was his life, and he could make his own mind up on anything and everything. It wouldn't do him, or Lauren, any harm to realise that.

She shrugged one shoulder as if she didn't care. 'But what about it – it's not like we'll ever sit the Leaving Cert again.'

'Hmmm, yeah – if he passes, but . . .' Heather sat back. 'It's just that he and Lauren are so . . .'

'Rigid?' Niamh said. 'I don't get why – they're too young to be set in their ways.'

'I was going to say devoted.' Heather crossed her arms over her chest. 'And it's really none of your business.'

'Pfft.' Niamh got up. 'Whatever. I'm going to the bar. What can I get you?'

'I'll have a Bacardi Breezer – orange. Thanks,' Heather said, looking down at her phone. 'Lauren's on her way so get her a Smirnoff Ice.'

'Did she check in with Shane before she decided that?' Niamh flicked her hair over her shoulder and flounced away.

*

Heather smoothed her skirt. Niamh was tetchy. You'd think she'd be buzzing now that their exams were over. Instead, she was on edge and rude, although that wasn't far from Niamh's usual carry-on. It was strange that she seemed to focus in on Lauren so blatantly. It was as if she was jealous or something. Niamh was never normally jealous of anyone, so it felt weird.

Niamh flirted with Ben the barman and Heather watched him laugh at her banter. She clinked the bottles together as she came back to the table. Taking a swig from the bottle Niamh passed to her, Heather went over everything again in her head, knowing already that she

300

was set to leave early on Monday morning. Nevertheless, it gave her great pride to be going over her checklist once again. Her passport was in her backpack, her suitcase was packed, a rainbow ribbon tied tightly around the handle, and her savings had added up to exactly what she'd budgeted. She'd planned a night in Florence, then a couple of nights in Rome, followed by a night in Naples before she flew to Venice where she was to meet her new boss, Samantha Wilson, at her palazzo in the heart of the city. From there she'd tour some of the finest palazzos and accommodations in Northern Italy in order to begin building her list of properties. She couldn't wait to get started.

Her old boss, Claire, had cried when Heather had said she was leaving, but she'd met Samantha at a conference and had been happy for Heather. Samantha's business was exactly what Heather was after. Her clients wanted luxury; they wanted somewhere chic and with a little nightlife. Heather was more than capable of sourcing those needs. She'd proved herself time and again in the travel agency. The clients she'd pulled in had loved the upgraded options she offered them, and as a result Claire's clientele had increased as word of mouth got around. However, it was inevitable that Heather would leave. The recession had hit the travel agency hard and it was only a matter of time before Claire would have had to let her go anyway.

'You're doing it again, aren't you?' Niamh winked at her. 'Mentally going over your plans.'

'I can't wait. Florence.' Heather gazed into the distance, a twinkle in her eye. 'Then Rome, then Naples and then—'

'Venice, I know. I'm not at all jealous.' Niamh clinked

her bottle against Heather's. 'I wish you were coming with us to Ibiza. Or that I was going to Venice.'

'Maybe next year we can meet up there. I can't believe it. I never thought I'd be doing this – well, I did, but I also didn't think I'd get here.' Heather grinned.

'It's great.' Niamh fidgeted with the shoulder of her dress, her brows knitted together momentarily before she gave a tight smile. 'We're all growing up and doing exactly what we said we would do.'

'For real,' Heather said.

Niamh took a swig from her bottle. 'You're lucky. There's no way I'd be allowed to run around Europe like you.'

Heather bristled. She wasn't going to be running around Europe like some brat with a trust fund. She was going to be working, hard, every single day. It wasn't going to be easy, but she was willing to put the long hours in. Typical of Niamh to see it as fun and games, and also typical of Niamh to say something in as off-putting a manner as possible. She didn't mean it, Heather knew, but when would she learn to filter what came out of her mouth?

'I'm a little nervous,' she admitted to Niamh. 'This is completely different to what I'm used to.'

'You'll be grand, sure look at you. No one would think you're one of the "mad hippie Moores".' Niamh air-quoted.

Heather sighed. 'For God's sake, Niamh.'

'Sorry, but you know what I mean. It's a compliment.' Niamh shrugged. 'You'll fit right in there on the *Rich*-iera and on *Costa del Muchos Dosh* and *Playa Rolling in Dough*.'

Heather laughed. 'Only you – you're a real pain in the left and right butt cheeks, you know that.'

'Yeah, but you love me.' Niamh laughed.

'And that is my biggest problem!' Heather raised her bottle.

'But at least we're doing something, right?' Niamh began, serious. 'Not like . . . Lauren.'

Heather frowned. 'Um, sorry?'

'Listen, hear me out.' Niamh leaned closer to Heather. 'Before they get here – what is this life she's planning? Like is she serious? Getting married and having kids young, trying to convince us all that she'll be living it up in her forties with grown-up children while we're all only getting started – you know that's just a dream, it's not practical.'

'Since when have you worried about practicalities,' Heather groaned. 'Look, Niamh, I don't know what your beef is with Lauren and her life goals, but I'm really not comfortable talking like this.'

'I know it sounds bitchy, but it's not. Promise,' Niamh said. 'I have some concerns, and yes, I do worry about the practical things in life. I'm not a complete moron you know.'

'I know. Sorry. But you know Lauren and Shane. They've been talking about this since they were kids. I think they're pretty happy and set with their decision,' Heather said. 'Who are we to judge? What we should be doing is supporting them.'

Niamh frowned. 'I've a bad feeling it's not going to go to plan.'

Heather looked at Niamh. It was rare for her to be so concerned about the future. For as long as she could remember, Niamh tended to think very much in the short term. This delve into the *what-ifs* and *imagine-ifs* of the future was very strange.

'What's going on?' Heather asked. 'You're not yourself. Are you okay?'

'I'm grand. Ah, finally!' Niamh waved her hand and called out to Lauren, who was standing just inside the door. Heather smiled. Lauren looked amazing. She'd gone all out, and it looked like she'd gotten the highlights in her hair just as she'd been talking about. She bounced over to them looking like a walking advertisement for an Irish cailín, all golden and auburn tresses and bright eyes. Her green top complimented her creamy skin and there was a smattering of freckles on her nose.

'I like the hairdo.' Heather patted the seat beside her. 'Knot Just Hair?'

Lauren picked up her Smirnoff Ice. 'Yup. I take it this is mine?'

Heather nodded. 'They did an amazing job. Show me the back.'

Lauren turned around and flipped her new layered hairdo back and forth. Heather sensed Niamh tense up next to her. She nudged Niamh.

'What do you think?'

'It's fab, very Sienna Miller in her boho phase.' Niamh blew a kiss.

Heather frowned. 'Isn't Sienna Miller always in a boho phase?'

'Whatever you say.' Niamh raised her eyebrows. 'It's gorge, Laure. Shane will absolutely love it.'

*

Lauren took another sip of her drink. Niamh wasn't being very nice, but sure what was new? She was probably feeling threatened by her new look, although neither of her friends seemed to have noticed that her denim shorts were the tiniest she'd ever worn, and her bra pushed her breasts up and out. She tugged at her ruffled top, then made herself stop fidgeting. Shane had said he liked this style. She just wished he'd hurry up and join them so she could see the look on his face when he laid eyes on her.

They were on their fifth drink and at the end of Niamh's bar money when he rambled in. Jumping up, Lauren hurried towards him. She almost did a twirl to show off her new look when he bumped into the back of a chair. Giggling, he apologised to the people at the table before turning back to Lauren. She stared at him, her heart in her mouth as she noticed his unfocused gaze.

'You're falling around the place.' She ushered him into a chair next to Niamh. 'No more drink for you.'

Shane waved his hand at her and made to stand up. 'I'm fine.'

Lauren looked from Niamh to Heather, her eyes beseeching them to help. Heather hopped up and took Shane by the arm.

'Sit down here for a minute,' she said. 'Tell me, where've you been until now?'

'Just out with the lads.' Shane grinned at her. 'You know, out with the lads.'

Heather nodded. 'Yeah, out with the lads. I get it.'

'I'm getting a drink now,' he slurred. 'What can I get you?'

'Nothing for me,' Heather said.

Lauren looked on in horror. She plonked down on the seat where Heather had been sitting and watched as her friend kept talking to her boyfriend. It was like watching her father come home after work and her mother trying to keep him from going back out again.

'You'll have a drink,' Shane mumbled. 'On me like. I'll get you a drink.'

Heather looked up at Lauren's pale face, then at Niamh, who was rolling her eyes.

'Niamh!' she said loudly. 'Niamh's getting the drinks. It's her round.'

Niamh's mouth dropped open and she glared at Heather. Lauren gripped the edge of the table and watched in silence as Niamh got up.

'Drinks it is so.' She made her way to the bar, looking back at Heather with raised eyebrows.

'See,' Heather said to Shane. 'She's getting drinks.'

Lauren turned to Niamh and mouthed '*just get him a Coke or something*'. Niamh gave her the thumbs up and turned back to the barman.

Shane settled back down and gazed at Lauren.

'You look different,' he said. 'Gorgeous.'

'Thanks,' Lauren murmured. She blinked back tears. The evening was ruined. They'd planned to go down to the lake later and light a fire, roast marshmallows and then afterwards . . . well, she shook her hair back. Later wasn't going to happen now, clearly. A wave of anger washed over her, and her fists clenched. This was bull. She watched as he rambled on to Heather about all sorts of nonsense. She didn't have to tolerate being made a fool of, and most of all, she refused to be just like her mother.

He could either sober up or get lost. She was about to say so when a pint landed on the table in front of Shane, and a fresh Smirnoff Ice was pressed into her hand.

'What the hell?' she glared up at Niamh. 'Why did you get him a pint?'

'Why not?' Niamh shrugged. 'It's one night, Lauren. Let him enjoy himself – for once.'

Lauren glared at Niamh. Her grip tightened around the cold bottle. 'What is that supposed to mean?'

'It means nothing, Lauren, other than exactly what I said,' Niamh said. 'Don't go making a drama out of this.'

'Am I hearing her correctly?' Lauren looked at Heather, who had managed to get a glass of 7-up for Shane and was trying to manoeuvre the pint out of his sight.

'You had to expect this, Laure – he's just like all the other boys,' Heather said.

'Unreal.' Lauren shook her head in disgust. 'You're unreal, the pair of ye, do you know that.'

'Stop going on.' Niamh pshawed. 'You know what I meant – just live a little will ya? Before you go off and repopulate Ireland to pre-famine levels.'

'Let it all out,' Lauren said shakily. 'Go on, I dare you.' She put her bottle down sharply on the table and braced herself. She'd a feeling she knew exactly what Niamh was talking about. She'd been nothing but sneery about everything she and Shane had planned for their future. Lately she'd never missed an opportunity to dismiss her dreams. She looked at Heather for backup but Heather grimaced at her before speaking.

'No offence – I mean this in the best of ways,' Heather

307

said. 'You two are quite co-dependent. It's not healthy. You need to be able to stand on your own two feet, Laure, and not be so wrapped up in him.'

Lauren gasped. 'I see where this is coming from. Maybe you could give that spiel to your mother, huh? Everyone knows she's a fool for Cash – just look at how she behaves every time he's got a new woman on the go. You're just jealous that me and Shane are doing fine.'

'I'm sorry, but what the hell?' Heather gaped at Lauren. 'What did I do to deserve that?'

'Oh where should I start? Maybe I should start with how you've managed to slither your way into *my* grandmother's house as if you're her grandchild . . .' Lauren shook as she stared at Heather, hardly believing she'd dared to say it. Taking a breath she continued. 'It's so weird. It's the kind of thing that happens over and over. What are you gaining by being friends with *my* grandmother, huh? Hoping to be left money in her will?!'

Heather gaped at Lauren, then shot a side glance at Niamh.

Niamh smirked. 'I'm saying nothing.'

'Pity you hadn't thought of that line before you opened your mouth five minutes ago, isn't it?' Heather spat. 'You're the one who started this.'

'Leave it alone,' Shane spoke up. His eyes focused on Niamh, much to Lauren's dismay. 'Niamh's grand. She's easy-going and you're all picking on her. If it wasn't for her sure I'd be pissed right now.'

'You *are* pissed.' Lauren glared at him.

He smiled at Niamh. 'Isn't that right, Niamh?'

'It is,' Niamh said. Her lips tweaked.

Lauren looked from one to the other, taking in Niamh's sneaky smile and Shane's dopey one. She jumped up.

'You've got to be kidding me. I'm not staying here to watch you two make eyes at one another. You're both disgusting pigs.'

'You're not seriously going?' Niamh sniggered. 'Over nothing.'

'Mind your own business,' Lauren snarled at Niamh. She turned back to Shane. 'Are you coming with me?'

'Leave him alone.' Niamh's lips curled up. 'You can't keep dictating his life to him.'

Lauren's eyes almost popped out of her head. 'Dictate his life to him?'

'You're always planning everything: kids, houses, even fecking dogs. How do you think that makes him feel?' Niamh said firmly. 'I'll tell you: trapped.'

'Niamh!' Heather blurted. 'Stop it. Now.'

Lauren looked at Heather. 'Do you think this too?'

Heather gave a tiny shrug. Then she said, 'No. Of course not.'

Feeling deflated and sick to her stomach, Lauren began to shake.

'You do. You think I'm trapping him into a life he doesn't want.'

'Look,' Niamh said in an even tone. 'It's like this: why would you want to settle down in the first place? It's not normal, and maybe it's because of your family life, you know – your dad's drinking – that you want to create some sense of order in your own life.'

Lauren gripped the back of the chair in front of her tightly. Her jaw ached from clenching it so hard. She leaned forward and hissed loudly, 'Well, Miss Know-It-All, at least I don't use my looks to get what I want all the time – and what exactly is it you want? Oh, wait – you want to fly around the world – like seriously, it's not a long-term vision, is it? You've no personality beyond *look at my ass in this skirt, boys*. Well let me tell you this – looks don't last. You'll get old like all of us and your looks will fade and what then? Nothing! Unless your stupid empty head gets you pregnant and then you'll end up married with children like us "not normal" people.'

Niamh paled and Lauren smirked. Good, she'd hit home on something.

Heather raised her hands between the two young women. 'Come on, stop this.'

'Stop what?' Lauren found her voice. 'Telling the truth? I think it's only just begun.'

'Lauren,' Heather said with a warning sound in her voice. 'Please, this isn't necessary.'

'Will ya cop on to yourself,' Lauren rounded on Heather. 'It absolutely is necessary. Do you want me to sit here and listen to her tell me that I dictate to Shane?

'You do,' Niamh blurted. 'And I know for a fact that he doesn't want to be tied down so young.'

'How would you know?' Heather got in before Lauren could even fathom what had been said.

'Because he told me,' Niamh said with a flourish. 'That's right – he told me that he wanted to be free – like me. Free and easy.'

'Easy. That's the key word here.' Lauren felt her heart race. 'Easy, Niamh. Freewheeling her way to every STI known to man.'

Niamh's face flamed up. Heather stared at Lauren. 'That was low.'

'Yeah, low, like her knickers every night of the week. She's nothing but a walking petri dish.' Lauren clenched her fists and instantly regretted saying those words. None of it was true but she'd said it now and there was no going back.

Niamh was on her feet in a heartbeat. 'The real Lauren has arrived. Finally. And look what a joy she is. Shane is going to have the *best life* with you – as long as he does exactly what he's told. Mark my words, Lauren – he won't be happy with you. He wants more from this life than a house full of screaming kids and a harpy for a wife.'

'Again – what would you know about kids and being a wife? Your own house is like a mortuary. Everything up there is so sterile and dead,' Lauren snapped back.

'Oh, I know.' Niamh smirked. 'He told me what he wants. Shame he didn't tell you.'

Lauren shoved the chair at the table. She looked at Shane for confirmation, for backup, but he'd fallen asleep sitting up. Her stomach lurched. His head lolled forward onto his chest. He was oblivious to everything. She spun around and made her way through the pub and out into the street.

Gulping in the humid air, she staggered over to the bench outside the pub. What the hell was Niamh on about? How could she say those things? They weren't true – they couldn't be. Shane had always shared his dreams with her and not once had he ever mentioned being 'free' or whatever that meant. More than that, there had been an underlying threat there. There had been some sense of possessiveness in Niamh's actions. How she'd aligned herself with Shane had been strange, but it was also familiar. It was exactly how Niamh behaved when she'd set her sights on a lad. Well, if she thought she'd get her claws into Shane then she'd another think coming. Lauren's hands balled into fists.

*

Heather took a drink. Shane was beginning to snore lightly. Niamh had gone to the ladies. Heather angrily peeled the sticker from her bottle. Niamh was probably checking her reflection to make sure that her real self wasn't showing. Mind you, Lauren had shown some true colours too. Until now she'd only guessed that Lauren was jealous of her friendship with Rosemary – but accusing her of befriending the older woman because she might gain something material from her wasn't fair. Didn't Lauren know her at all? That was the way Cash behaved, and she'd spent all her life trying to be as unlike him as possible.

Heather rubbed her wrist. Now every time she called to see Rosemary she'd have this cloud over her. What if Rosemary felt obliged to take care of her? What if she didn't really care for her at all? Heather took a long and deep swig from her bottle and replayed the argument in her mind. Niamh had been so hurtful. How could she have done that to Lauren? The things she'd said were . . . Heather paused. Were they true? Had Shane really said that he wanted to be free?

Niamh came back. She picked up her drink and took a long sip.

312

'Did he *really* say that to you?' Heather picked at the label on her bottle.

Niamh nodded. 'He did.'

'What made you say it tonight?' Heather asked. 'Could you not have kept it to yourself?'

'No.' Niamh's brow furrowed. 'She was annoying me, sitting there all smug and . . .'

'Happy, Niamh, she was happy.' Heather shook her head. 'You've no idea what you've done, have you?'

'I've given them something new to talk about.' Niamh laughed. 'Lord knows they need it.'

'You're so heartless.' Heather stared at Niamh as if she'd never seen her before.

'No. I'm honest. Listen – if he wants to be free then she should let him go. Let him live the life he wants.'

'And what's that?' Heather looked up.

'You know, free,' Niamh said. 'Don't act like you've no clue – look at your family. They live freer than anyone I know. They seem happy.'

'Don't bring my family into this.' Heather flushed. 'You've no idea what my life is like.'

'Come on, Heather. Don't you start now.' Niamh's blue eyes flashed. 'You have the best of it – you've the freedom to do exactly what you want and look at you – you're heading off into the world to explore and be exactly who you want to be. I'm telling you one thing – your parents did it the right way – they let you live your life, didn't force you to do anything. And now you can do exactly as you've always done—'

'Survived. That's what I've always done.' Heather spoke through gritted teeth.

313

'It's not survival.' Niamh flicked her hair back. 'Don't say you didn't relish the freedom you had as a kid.'

'I didn't,' Heather said. 'Why would I? I never knew what to expect when I got home – whether there'd be new people in the house. I had to scramble to get what I needed, Niamh, every single day. There were days when I wasn't sure if there was anything to eat because someone had mentioned how we should forage for our food and my father thought it was a good idea.'

'It couldn't have been that bad,' Niamh said.

'It *was* that bad.' Heather leaned forward. 'Do you know how many times I wished for your life? How many times I wished my mother would take me into town for new schoolbooks and uniforms – to pack my lunch like yours did? Countless times, Niamh. At least fifty times a day I looked at you and wished for your life.'

'That's not true.' Niamh twisted a strand of hair around her finger.

'It is.' Heather tapped her bottle against the table before placing it a little away from her. 'You haven't a clue. You don't know how lucky you are.'

'You think it's lucky to be monitored twenty-four-seven? To have to know where you want to be in five years' time – I barely know where I'll be in five minutes' time.'

'And you don't see how good that is?' Heather shook her head. 'I have to plan and scheme everything, every step. No one was there to care, to fight my corner for me. No one. You're a spoilt princess who doesn't appreciate anything she has. And it's all been handed to you by people who think so much of you that they can't see your flaws at all.'

'Shut up.' Niamh's face crumpled. For a split second it looked as if she was going to cry and Heather wondered if she'd been too harsh. Niamh, twisting the end of her hair, took a breath. Her face calmed and she shrugged. 'You know what, Heather? I don't care what you think, or what you do anymore. I'm done with this conversation.'

'Conveniently.' Heather glowered at her. 'Pity you couldn't have been done before you started it with Lauren. Now you've destroyed her.'

'I have not.' Niamh stood up. 'I'm out of here. I'm done with you. Completely.'

'Go on so – go home, where you'll have clean sheets and plenty of food in the press. Parents waiting up to make sure you're safely home and hot water to wash your expensive makeup off with.'

Niamh stuck her tongue out at Heather.

'Wow.' Heather burst out laughing. She began to clap her hands. 'Encore, Niamh. Do it again.'

'Get lost, you stupid muppet. I should've seen it before.' Niamh squinted at Heather and tapped her bottom lip. 'You're nothing but a jumped-up scruffy hippy who has notions of a grand life that will never materialise – when I think of all the things I gave you, and all the times you sat at my kitchen table eating my mother's food, I see it clearly now. You were just using me. I wouldn't put it past you to have filled your pockets with food. Yeah, and that designer dress I loaned you that I never got back – I bet you sold that. That's just the kind of person you are.'

'You're calling me a thief,' Heather said quietly. Two red dots appeared on her cheeks. 'Nothing you gave me was of any value to you. Everything was a cast-off. I never once stole from you.'

'Well, it's your word,' Niamh said. 'Who'd believe you – you're a Moore.'

Heather jumped to her feet. 'Take that back.'

'I will not.' Niamh edged around the table. She grabbed her bag and stormed through the lounge and out the door.

The barman looked over at Heather and Shane for a long minute. Then he jerked his head towards the door. Heather's face flamed as she realised he was kicking her out. She grabbed her bag as quickly as possible, casting an eye around to see if anyone had noticed. No one had, it seemed. Shane was still snoring as she took another look at Ben to make sure she'd got it right. He was glaring at her, hands on his hips. Heather looked down at Shane. She was damned if she was going to take care of him. With her chin held high she hurried out of The Coach House and into the street.

The streetlights came on just then, lighting up Niamh chatting to a group of lads down in the square. A ball of anger lodged in Heather's throat. It was quickly followed by shame as Niamh looked over at her and said something to the lads. They all laughed, and Heather shivered. She'd never have the control Niamh had. She plucked it out of thin air – and just like a cat, she'd always land on her feet.

Heather started walking home. There was no going back now. Things had been said and they couldn't be unsaid. She wasn't a thief, and she wasn't a scam artist trying to fool Rosemary into anything. She'd never taken anything from anyone that hadn't been offered to her. Yet just as Niamh had said, who'd believe her when she was just one of the Moores: that mad hippie family who went skinny-dipping in the lake? One thing was for sure, she was never getting back in that lake again. Not even this Sunday for their solstice swim.

Rosemary. A tear slid down Heather's cheek as she walked on. Rosemary would be upset, but she'd understand. She had Lauren, Heather thought. *The only person losing out here is me.*

*

Niamh looked at Heather's back as she walked up the hill. Good riddance. The bloody cheek of her. Pontificating to her about how good her life was and how she got everything she ever wanted. It wasn't like that in her house. Her parents were much older than her friends' parents were, and didn't see life the same way she did. They thought college was essential, but still wanted her to settle down and have a family. Sometimes she felt like she was living in another time where women had no rights at all. Her whole life was planned out for her.

Her hands slid down her stomach and she bit her lip. Her whole life might flip upside down if what she felt in her bones was true. She was pregnant. And eighteen. *I'm a statistic now,* she thought as Evan strolled up the hill to join the group. He slipped his arm around her shoulders. Niamh's stomach clenched. He had a right to know, she realised as they all began walking in the same direction Heather had taken.

'I can't wait to get you by the lake,' Evan whispered in her ear.

Niamh shivered and he slipped his jacket around her shoulders. She gripped it tightly and counted her steps instead of listening to what they were talking about. The last time she'd been at the lake with Evan they'd . . . Now she wanted nothing more ever to do with the place. Ever again.

*

Lauren stood in the shadows in the side alley across the road from The Coach House. She'd watched Heather standing outside the pub for a few minutes and had almost gone over to her. But why should she make the first move? It wasn't as if Heather had jumped to her defence in there. Heather had sat on the fence as usual, afraid to rock the boat and stand out. Lauren leaned against the cold wall and turned her attention to Niamh.

She watched Niamh flirting with the boys, and her stomach turned to lead. She'd always been flirty, and it had been fun to watch her hook and demolish a boy. Now it just looked awful. From her viewpoint in the shadows Lauren could tell that the boys were loving it, which she knew they would, but they were also more in control than she'd realised before. There were subtle glances shared amongst them, and nudges and laughing. Niamh wasn't as powerful as she thought she was. Lauren sniffed. Served her right – one day she'd wake up and realise she'd been made a fool of.

The group turned towards the hill and Lauren slipped further into the shadows as they passed by. She waited a few minutes until their voices grew quieter. As the town hall clock chimed eleven, she slipped across the road and found Shane where they'd left him. Dragging him to his feet, she half carried half pulled him out of the pub and to the bench. Sitting down she sighed heavily. He opened his eyes, goofily grinned at her and pulled her close to him. Laying her head on his chest she wondered if she had the strength to get him home, and if she had the strength to break up with him if he ever did that to her again.

25

21st June 2009

Rosemary waited on the lakeshore. It was almost sunrise and there was no sign of the girls. She felt the bubble of excitement that had been inside her deflate. After many long conversations with Stella and Sheila in the garden, and Maura over the phone, she'd finally made the decision to go travelling and was desperate to share her plans with the girls, knowing that they'd be only delighted for her. First stop was London, then Paris and of course Venice – all the romantic cities she'd wanted to go to with Paddy. Then she was planning on heading further afield to the places she'd never even imagined going, but because they were en route to Maura in New Zealand, they were now dream destinations. From Venice she was heading to Abu Dhabi.

Butterflies fluttered about her stomach. It was really pushing her comfort zone, but it would be good for her, and she was only staying there for four days so she'd manage. She'd managed worse; she thought of the holiday in Wexford where the caravan they'd squished everyone into had been lopsided and in a field of nettles.

After Abu Dhabi she planned on stopping briefly in Malaysia before the longest flight of the whole holiday, which would take her to Christchurch in New Zealand where she was meeting Maura. She was hoping to pick Heather's brains about her route home.

The sun began to rise, and Rosemary looked around one last time. There was still no sign of the girls. *Maybe they'd slept in.* She lingered at the shoreline, waiting just in case they came running and laughing down the lane, calling apologies and begging forgiveness. The lake glimmered as the summer solstice begun and Rosemary sadly took a step into the waters. This would be her last solstice swim in the lake for a long time. She was staying with Maura for at least six months, and then heading to Australia. Maura said she'd been dying to do some sightseeing there, so they'd make plans once she arrived in Christchurch.

The lake water was soft and gentle, caressing her body as she swam out towards the sun. Rosemary flipped over and floated for a while, wondering where she'd be in a year's time and what on earth had happened to the girls. *They were missing a wonderful morning.* The mist began to rise and the sun to glow. The lake was on fire from the soft light. It was as if it knew it wouldn't see her for a while. Rosemary swam back to shore and dried herself off quickly. Picking up her damp towel from where she'd dropped it, she was startled by a noise. Looking up she saw a stag in the copse nearby. He watched her momentarily with his warm brown eyes, chewing as if he was thinking over something to say.

Goosebumps prickled all over Rosemary. Her mother had always said that seeing a stag was a good omen – it was a message from a loved one in the next world. Maybe it was Paddy approving her plans. Her towel slipped from her hands. She picked it up again. Beneath it were three heart-shaped pebbles, almost next to each other. Rosemary touched her heart and looked around for the stag. He turned and strolled elegantly into the deeper woodland, and Rosemary, with a happy sigh, stooped to pick up the pebbles.

26

Lauren woke up early. Her hand stretched to touch Shane, but his side of the bed was cool to the touch. She rubbed her face. He'd stayed at Mill House every night since the accident on the lake, getting up at five every morning to get ready for work, and coming home at nine just to fall into bed, snoring almost before his head hit the pillow, but at least the job was easing up and the pressure was almost off. They'd painted the bedroom since then, and the cracks in the ceiling had been filled. She stared up at where they used to be, wondering why things between her and Shane weren't getting better. She'd been trying, but he'd withdrawn from her a little. Sometimes he was himself and other times he was more subdued. It had to be work, and the long commute. He'd a lot of responsibility these days now the site was almost finished up, but he seemed to enjoy their weekend hikes.

It was their new hobby, and the only time that she felt they were normal with each other, possibly even kinder or gentler with each other in a way that reminded her of their first few years together. Only now they never spoke of their future or any of the dreams they'd spent all their teenage years talking about. They only spoke of the past week, the hike, and what they'd have for dinner. It was very relaxing not to be always thinking about the future, she realised, as she heard him clatter about in the kitchen below. She hopped out of bed. She was feeling fitter than ever, a strange feeling, but she put it down to the hiking, drinking less wine, and the lack of stress.

But her sick leave was almost over, and she'd be back teaching in September, she thought as she pulled on her leggings, so she'd better put some measures in place that would support her. Maybe they could continue hiking – that might be the thing. Dashing down the stairs she sniffed the air. Shane had cooked a big breakfast, as he did every Saturday lately. She sat opposite him at the table and tucked into her scrambled eggs, not noticing he was quiet and not talking about the route they'd take that day.

*

They'd found the most beautiful place. Settled in the glittering granite rocks, surrounded by yellow gorse and purple heather, was a small pool. A mini-waterfall cascaded into it and at the edge another mini-waterfall tumbled out of it. They both stood and stared at the landscape before them. The sky was bright blue, with skeins of clouds so high up they were barely visible. The sunshine bathed everything in a golden glow; even the waist-high ferns looked bright and cheerful. The coconut scent of the gorse wrapped around them deliciously; the gurgling water sounded like music.

Shane laughed out loud and looked back at Lauren. He was smiling from ear to ear. She felt herself grinning back at his genuine happiness. They stood on a large flat granite rock and she felt as if they were the only people in the world.

'Look at this. It's amazing – I feel like we're the first people ever to find it,' he said.

Lauren stopped to catch her breath. 'Look at the colour of the water . . .'

'We should get in.' Shane was already tugging his T-shirt over his head. Lauren laughed, thinking he was joking. She stopped as she caught sight of his toned chest and shoulders, her breath catching in her throat. They hadn't seen each other naked in months. They'd been too tired to do anything intimate too, or at least that's how it seemed. Her mouth dropped open as she watched him shuck off his hiking boots. He looked up at her, entirely unselfconscious.

'Aren't you coming in?'

'Yes, yeah.' She gulped, letting her rucksack slide from her shoulders. He continued getting undressed until he was in his boxers. Lauren bit her lip and carried on undressing.

'It feels weird,' she said, keeping her eyes down. 'To be so naked in public.'

'We're not in public,' Shane said.

'We're in our underwear.' Lauren wrapped her arms around her middle, conscious of her belly.

'I've seen smaller bikinis on you,' Shane said with a laugh. 'To hell with it.' He started taking off his boxers.

'Are you serious?' Lauren let out a laugh.

'Deadly,' he said, standing there in all his glory. Lauren glanced down, then up again. She blushed as she watched him wade into the pool.

Lauren stood on the warm granite and watched him swim out to the middle.

'It's warm,' he called to her. 'Gorgeous.'

Lauren felt her cheeks get hotter. Was he talking about the pool or her? With a sudden urge to be with him, she tugged her bra off and stepped out of her knickers and hurried into the pool, gasping as the water washed around her. He was right: it was warm, and so clear. Different from the lake, she thought as she swam over to him.

'It's not deep,' he said as she reached him. 'You can probably reach the bottom.'

Lauren placed her feet on the bottom of the pool. She could just about reach it with her tippy toes. She threw her head back and gazed up at the blazing sky.

Raising her head she found Shane staring at her. His face was soft, his eyes full of wonder at her. Catching her hand, he pulled her to him until they were body to body in the water.

'You really are the most beautiful woman,' he said, his voice deep.

Lauren stared into his eyes, shivering as his arm tightened around her waist, pressing her whole body against his. She could feel him solid against her, but his eyes were watching her, waiting to see how she'd react. He was always this way, careful and considerate. Lauren couldn't tear her eyes from his. It seemed that he was holding his breath until he was sure she was okay, just as she was holding hers waiting for a sign that *he* was okay. How could she ever have thought of leaving him? They were meant for each other – children or no children. Without looking away from him, she touched his face, pressing her body even closer to his.

'Laure,' he said breathlessly. 'You sure?'

'I am,' she whispered.

A flurry of emotions washed over his face and then he kissed her, gently at first, then with more passion. Without bidding, she wrapped her legs around him and let herself go.

*

They dried themselves with their T-shirts, then lay on the rock eating their picnic. Shane had pulled on his boxers saying he had to protect the crown jewels, which made Lauren laugh, but she put her own underwear back on thinking it a wise move. The stillness of the air and the sound of the water was soothing. She thought of Rosemary.

'Rosemary would have loved to hear about this,' she said to Shane. 'She'd be amazed at me in the nip – that's for sure.'

Shane lay back on the warm rock. 'She'd be happy for you.'

Lauren nodded. 'She's coming home – well, Maura sent me an email last night. She's bringing Rosemary home in a week.' She was loath to say ashes. In her mind she could only imagine Rosemary as a smiling and slightly mischievous grandmother.

'Just in time for your solstice swim,' Shane said.

'I didn't think of that,' Lauren said as he lay back in the sun. 'It's perfect timing really, isn't it?'

Shane murmured a yes.

Lauren lay back and closed her eyes. She'd take Rosemary to the lake and scatter her there. It was where Paddy's spirit was, where they'd scattered his ashes, and it was what Rosemary would want more than anything in the world. She was sure of it, and no date could be more perfect than the summer solstice.

*

Later that evening, as the sun went down, Lauren sat on her bed and replied to Maura's email, telling her what she was thinking of doing. On a whim she typed: *Maybe you'd like to be at the lake with us, Maura. I think she'd be happy if you were.* Maura replied instantly, making Lauren double-check the time difference. She read Maura's email and felt a sense of peace wash over her. Maura was delighted to be asked. She'd even brave the lake, she said, just for Rosemary. Lauren got up to go tell Shane.

The door to the sitting room was ajar and she paused for a moment looking in at him. She smiled thinking of how wonderful their day had been. After their swim and picnic they'd hiked on and she'd come home feeling refreshed and hopeful. She would pull herself together, for his sake if nothing else. With him helping her she could get through anything. Maybe she'd talk to him, tell him the awful smothering thoughts she'd been having over the last year and how she hated them. She'd tell him she loved him and always would and that she believed they could

328

make it work. She knew he'd listen. He always had, but she'd forgotten that in the depression that surrounded her each time they'd failed to get pregnant. He needed to know she was sorry, that she would get help, and that she needed him. She smiled again. She might tell him now, as soon as she'd told him about Maura.

He was kneeling before the stove. He pulled something from his back pocket, and Lauren's heart stilled. Her stomach lurched as she recognised her letter – the one she'd never finished – the one she'd been looking for. She'd given up the search after a while, thinking that maybe it had gotten lost at the hospital that night. She couldn't remember bringing her bag in and had assumed she must have, just as she'd assumed that she'd lost it that night. Seeing it in Shane's hands made her want to throw up.

She watched as he held it for a minute. He opened it and her heart tightened. Holding her breath, she wanted to fly in and grab it from him, but it was too late now. With a heavy heart she watched him read it. Then he put it into the flames and watched it burn. Lauren started to cry, and he looked around. He was with her in a second, his arms holding her tight.

'I didn't mean it,' she whispered.

'I know.' He kissed the top of her head. 'I know.'

27

Niamh bundled up the bed linen from room one and rambled across the yard to the new laundry room Rory had recommended she include in her renovations.

He'd stayed away in the days following Ava's accident, as if he'd known he wasn't welcome. Eventually he'd called her, about a week after the row with Evan, to see how Ava was. He'd quietly told her how Mucker had called him because he'd seen the teenagers messing around and was worried something would happen. He was a member of the local volunteer group who were trained in mountain rescues, so he'd been the obvious choice. He hadn't been following her, he'd said grimly, but yes, he did like her, and yes, he'd been flirting with her, and yes, he'd been hoping for more than friendship but he realised he'd made a huge mistake.

He was sorry, he said. He'd gone too far. His deep voice had trailed off and Niamh had sat down on the bottom step of the stairs, gripping the phone tightly to her ear as he started apologising again. Listening to him apologise for upsetting her she knew that Rory Quinlan, no matter how handsome or amazing he was, wasn't the man for her. It had been easy to see him as better, at the start, but faraway fields always look greener and she realised she'd forgotten to pay as much attention to her own field. So had Evan. It wasn't anyone's fault, in particular, it was just that they'd been busy and time had flown by so that special moments had been lost in the daily monotony of living.

Rory was exciting – that much was true. He always had something to talk about, places he was going . . . and initially that had been attractive. Making herself pretty for him, finding time to listen to his ideas, never finding fault with him . . . well, it was a little wearying. Niamh was exhausted trying to be perfect for him when he was around. It had never, ever felt that way with Evan. He'd taken her faults and made it seem like they sparkled, even when she drove him mad. This past year had been the toughest one for them both, and she'd played a big role in that. How she wished she hadn't, how she wished she'd concentrated on her marriage more. The rooms might not be done, but at least she'd be happy.

With her head in her hands she'd tried to wind her conversation with Rory up by saying she needed to go but found herself apologising too.

'You're not the only guilty party,' she'd said.

'You didn't do anything,' he'd insisted. 'It was all me.'

'No, that's not true,' she'd told him. 'I enjoyed it, the flirting, the banter but . . .'

She'd thought of how she'd changed when he was around, the little things she'd done just for him that he'd never understand – the perfume, the makeup, the chatting, and the lies she'd told Evan. She'd even given him Evan's chocolate. It sounded silly but they were all little betrayals of her marriage and they ate her up all the time lately.

'I wish—' he'd started but she'd cut him off.

'No. No more wishes.' She'd sat up straight. 'You can't say things like that, Rory.'

'I'm sorry . . . does Evan know about any of this?'

'No, and I don't want him to know. He'd leave me if he did.' She'd almost been sick saying it. After their row he'd slept in the spare room for a few nights before coming back to their king-size bed. They'd slept like Egyptian mummies, all straight and careful, for the first week but she'd woken up one morning to find she'd snuggled into his chest and his arm was holding her close. It was a feeling she treasured, and she didn't want to lose it. 'And I don't want that, do you understand me, Rory?'

'I do.' He'd been quiet. 'Listen, I'll finish up the work on the yard and rooms in double time, and get out of your hair. If you still want the other two rooms done in the autumn . . . just call me. Okay?'

'We'll see. Thanks, Rory.' She'd hung up quickly, afraid of what else might get said.

Now, standing in the sunshine in the yard she smiled as her phone pinged. Bookings were flying in, and she could easily see the renovation costs being covered by the end of the summer. Ava came out into the yard in her PJs. Secondary school summer holidays were long. A whole three months – and, surprisingly, Ava had asked if she could earn some pocket money by helping out with the rooms.

'Morning, sleepyhead,' Niamh called. 'You missed breakfast duty.'

'Can I start work on Monday?' Ava said.

'Ava Rosemary McNamara, you are unreal!' Niamh shook her head. 'Not on your nelly. You signed up for today and I need the help. I've all the rooms ready for today's guests, but I need you to take over the laundry while I check emails.'

'Okay,' Ava sighed. 'I'll get dressed.'

'Good girl. And thanks,' Niamh called as Ava went back inside. She needed all the help she could get. Evan had apologised for saying she was seeing Rory, but things weren't the same between them. It was bittersweet. For once she was on top of things, she felt alive and purposeful, but her heart was sore most days. She knew it would take some time but most days she thought that maybe they'd never be okay again.

Niamh looked around the pretty backyard and tried to feel happy. The stone walls had been washed down. Old milk urns and stone planters were crammed with cottage flowers, all fragrantly in bloom. Behind the yard she could see the washing line full of white sheets cracking away in the breeze. They'd be dry in no time and smell like summer. As for her own home. She didn't know how she'd managed it, but the kitchen was as clean and tidy as it had been in her mother's day, and every room was gleaming. The kids had taken to this new sense of orderliness with gusto, and she realised that she'd never taken control of things before.

Upstairs in the spare room she switched on her laptop, but unable to concentrate she sat back and thought of Evan. He was still doing the little things she loved, like bringing her coffee in the morning, but somehow it felt

333

hollow. Staring at the screen all she could think was *I don't know how to fix us*.

'I give up,' she murmured as she opened her emails.

'Give up what?'

Niamh looked up. Evan leaned against the doorframe, watching her work.

'Trying to please everyone,' Niamh said steadily, unwilling to tell him what was really on her mind.

'You knew it'd be tough,' Evan said gently.

'Not the guests.' Niamh took a shaky breath. 'It's us. I'm beginning to give up trying to fix us. It feels impossible, and . . . I think that maybe you don't care about anything here anymore. And you should, Ev, because it's always about us at the end. But I'm tired. I'm worn out trying to pull this family together – I've been worn out since day one.'

'I know.' Evan's tired voice stopped her tirade. 'The past fifteen years haven't been what either one of us planned. I thought that if I carried on doing all the things that I wanted to do that I'd be fine. But I'm tired too.'

'Where do we go from here?' Niamh looked up at him sadly. 'Are we done?'

'I don't know,' he said. 'I hope not.'

Niamh swallowed the lump in her throat. A tear splashed onto the back of her hand.

'I was genuinely happy to marry you,' she said. 'You know that don't you?'

'Christ, Niamh,' Evan said huskily. 'For years I thought you hated being married. That I'd forced you into this . . .' He waved his hand around.

'No,' Niamh said. 'You didn't, but it did happen too

fast for us. I felt trapped. I didn't know how to be a parent, and you seemed so set on it that it scared me. Every day I felt as if I was failing somehow.'

'Me too,' he said, walking into the room. He sat on an old armchair that had been put there temporarily ten years ago. Leaning his elbows on his knees he shakily took a breath. 'I felt like I never measured up.'

Niamh sat back in her chair. 'We were just kids, Evan.'

'Yeah,' Evan said. 'We were.'

'I don't know what to do.' Niamh wiped her eyes with her sleeve.

Evan looked down at his feet. 'I wish . . .'

'What? What do you wish?' Niamh leaned towards him, eager to hear his wishes in a way that she'd never been when Rory had said the same words.

'That we could go back and take it slower. Have more fun together. Things might have been different then.'

'We could start now?' Niamh tried not to cry.

'I'm quitting Thursday night and Saturday morning training,' he said.

'You don't have to do that – don't give up everything.' Niamh felt tears roll down her face.

'I do.' Evan's voice deepened. 'I want us to be fine – more than fine. I want us to be in love again, like before.'

'Love?' Niamh's breath caught in her throat. 'Evan . . . I still love you. I never stopped.'

'You did,' he said. 'You stopped for a while, but I hope that maybe it was like pressing the pause button on us. We've had a lot to deal with over the last few years. Your mam passed away, your dad in the home, then Covid, well, it felt like I was drowning in responsibilities – I can only imagine how you felt. Then you kept talking about the B&B idea and I just didn't want to think about it. It was another mental load to carry so I stopped being involved with you and I'm sorry for that. I still love you, too.'

Niamh gasped. She never would have guessed that this was what he was feeling. She wanted to go to where he sat in the old armchair but he was already getting up.

'If it's okay, I'd like to help you with the rooms,' he said. He looked at her from under his eyelashes, reminding her of when they were eighteen. 'I won't charge you too much.'

'Ah here now, you're jumping the gun a bit,' Niamh said, swallowing down the sob that was choking her. 'Freaking me out completely.'

'I love it when you freak out,' he said.

Niamh felt a warm shiver wash down her body.

'Niamh?' Evan said.

'Yeah?' She looked up at him.

'I'm sorry about the whole Rory thing too.'

Niamh stood up even though her legs were weak. She watched a flush creep up his neck and she felt sick.

'No, don't say that – you don't need to be sorry.' She reached for him. He caught her hand as she laid it on his chest. 'I'm sorry for making you feel less than . . . loved.'

He looked down into her face, his own serious and still except for a twitch in his jaw as if he was trying not to say something. Niamh pressed her hand against his heart. It was beating like crazy. She gave him a small sad smile, hoping he'd forget about Rory.

'Let's not talk about him, ever.' His eyes searched her

face until she nodded mutely. 'Okay. I'm making a cuppa. Do you want one?'

Niamh held his hand as he kissed her gently on the forehead.

'I'd love one,' she said quietly. Then she gestured to the laptop. 'I'll be down in a minute. I want to reply to this email – it's from Maura. Remember her? She was a friend of Rosemary's. She's looking to book three rooms for a whole month.'

'A month?' Evan's eyebrows shot up.

'Yes.' Niamh sat at the makeshift desk and read the email again. 'She's bringing Rosemary home to Lough Caragh. She says she's taking her ashes to Lauren, who's going to scatter them at the lake.'

'That's nice of her,' Evan said.

'Poor Lauren.' Niamh let her hands drop from the keyboard. 'She's going to be devastated.'

'You should go talk to her,' Evan said.

'I don't know,' Niamh started. 'I was so mean.'

'That was fifteen years ago. We were all stupid and said and did mean things. And as we've just discussed – we were kids. Things have changed. We've all grown up.' Evan stood in the doorway. 'You should go talk to her. Try at least.'

'I'll think about it.' Niamh rubbed the back of her neck. 'Ev . . . thanks.'

'No problem. Right – tea.'

Niamh watched him leave. She stared at the doorway he'd passed through only seconds ago and sucked in a breath. Closing her eyes she replayed the whole conversation they'd just had and felt the knots in her shoulders loosen.

It would've taken a lot for him to come to her and say those things, she knew, and she was so grateful. With some luck, time and a lot more honesty, she hoped they'd fix their marriage. Opening her eyes she turned her attention to the email and replied to Maura, then block-booked the rooms for her as she requested. Then she read the rest of Maura's message, her heart pounding as she read the words.

Rosemary mentioned that you girls had a bit of a falling-out. She said she never got to the bottom of what happened – but it broke her heart that you three were at odds. She often mentioned she'd met you, or that Lauren had been up for a visit, and she'd send me snippets of what Heather was up to. Heather used to email her a lot. Rose said that she was inspired by her travels.

Anyway, that's neither here nor there. The reason I'm coming home is, as I've said above, to bring Rose back to the lake. It's what she wanted and missed more than anything in the world. She used to call me from her travels, send me postcards of the places she'd been, and the one thing she always said was that she needed to get home to Lough Caragh, to the place her beloved Paddy adored, and the place where she felt most at home.

Now, if you don't mind me saying so, you have to swallow your pride and get past whatever happened between you girls and be at the lake this solstice. That's when Lauren has decided is the best time for it. I know what you're thinking: you're afraid, what if it all goes wrong? Well, I don't care for any of that. I'm telling you now that Rose loved you and that you have to be there, whether you like it or not. It's what she'd have wanted, and you can't deny her that last wish, can you?

Niamh swallowed thickly. Had it been so terrible, really? She felt her face redden. She'd been such a horrible friend. So short-sighted and selfish. To think that Rosemary had been upset all these years. Niamh started to cry, huge heaving sobs. It didn't bear thinking about. It was horrible. *Maura was right.* She wiped her nose on her sleeve. There was no way she could deny Rosemary her last wish. If it killed her, she'd be there, on that lakeshore, to send Rosemary on her final journey to her beloved Paddy's arms, wherever that was.

28

Heather looked up from her keyboard. Her London apartment was stifling. Every window was wide open, the fan was going full throttle, but there was barely a breeze. Heather wiped the sweat from her upper lip. The air outside was crackling and hopefully they'd have the storm the forecast had predicted. Beneath the table she'd plunged her feet into a basin of cold water in an attempt to cool down. It was helping, marginally, but was a pain every time she had to get up to do something.

Stretching her arms above her head she tried to count the number of emails she'd to catch up on. Far too many. She opened her phone and looked at her Instagram page. Curling her lip she scrolled through her posts. Her old life of constant luxury and travelling looked fake to her now. What had she been trying to do? What was she selling? She frowned. None of it made her happy. Every place she'd been had been about work. The truth was that she couldn't recall anything good about any of the destinations on the screen. She'd never felt in the moment no matter how much the photos and the captions beneath them claimed she was. Closing the app, she wondered what was happening back in Wicklow.

Picking up her phone again she called Pippa, eager for any news. Rory had outdone himself and had cleared the fields in record time. He'd even listened to Pippa's pleas, and now at the end of the first acre stood two pretty pink and white shepherd's huts. They had delightful curved roofs and the windows had been finished to look like cottage windows. Pippa had sent blurry WhatsApp photos to Heather, who couldn't believe how adorable it all looked.

After a few rings her mother picked up.

'Hello? Heather?' Pippa sounded stressed. Heather could hear papers rustling and her mother cursed.

'What's going on?' Heather frowned.

'I'm looking for . . . oh, there it is, hang on a minute.'

The sound of the phone being dropped on the counter made Heather jump. She made out a male voice in the background and strained to recognise it. It wasn't her father – that was for sure. This man sounded more down to earth than Cash ever had.

'Hello?' Pippa's voice came down the line and Heather felt her shoulders relax as her mother sounded a little less panicked than before. 'I was looking for the money I'd left on the desk to pay the goat man.'

'What?' Heather sat up straight. 'They've arrived! Why didn't you tell me they were coming today?'

'I didn't know until an hour ago.' Pippa laughed. 'He called and said he was on the way, and it was all go after

341

that, double-checking the sheds and the fences. Heather – they're gorgeous! They've settled right in and are already coming over to me the minute they see me.'

'They must like you,' Heather said. She looked down at her soaking feet. 'I wish I was there.'

Heather moved her feet, making the water splash out onto the towel the basin stood on.

What's that noise? Are you at the pool?' Pippa asked.

'No.' Heather explained the cold-water foot-bath situation. 'It's so hot here.'

'Talking about water, you need to come home.' Pippa sounded serious.

'Why? What's wrong?' Heather frowned. She heard Pippa take a breath in.

'Okay, just agree to hear me out before you want to say no.'

'Just tell me.' Heather tapped the table with her pen.

'Sheila was over last night, and she told me that Maura O'Carroll is coming home from New Zealand,' Pippa said. 'We don't know Maura O'Carroll, but she was a great friend of Rosemary's. She moved to New Zealand the year before we moved here. Anyway, she's bringing Rosemary's ashes home with her.'

Heather put the pen down on the table and rubbed her temple. 'That's kind of her.'

'Isn't it? It's the kind of thing friends do,' Pippa said. 'I know how much Rosemary meant to you. She was there for you when I should have been.'

Heather sucked in her bottom lip and shook her head. She'd never imagined Pippa saying anything like this. Her mother continued softly.

'And for that I'm so sorry, Heather. All I can say is that I'll make it up to you.'

'It's okay,' Heather whispered. 'Thank you.'

'Sheila told me that Lauren and her family are planning on scattering Rosemary's ashes by the lake. I thought you should know in case you wanted to be here for it.'

'When?' Heather asked softly.

'June 21st,' Pippa said. 'Solstice. Isn't that perfect?'

'It couldn't be more perfect,' Heather said quietly.

'Please say you'll come,' Pippa said. 'Sheila is quietly spreading the word amongst her friends. It turns out that Rosemary has helped a lot more people out than anyone else realised.'

'Sounds like Rosemary,' Heather said. 'I'll think about it.'

'That's all I'm asking,' Pippa said. 'Now go on. Have a cold shower and book some flights – it's the right thing to do. I'm going back out to play with my goats! I finally have goats!'

Heather laughed as her mother hung up the phone. She looked down at her feet again, then lifted them from the basin. As she dried them, she heard a knock at the door. Tutting and hoping it wasn't Sally looking for a chat, she opened it.

Simon stood there. His jacket was slung over his arm. 'Sally texted me that you're back . . .'

Heather gripped the door handle tightly. There was a solid sensation in the pit of her stomach, one that she hadn't expected to feel on seeing him after all this time. Her heart wasn't doing somersaults for him like it used to. It was time they had a talk.

'Do you want to come in?' She held back the door and stood back to let him in.

'Thanks.' Simon's warm brown eyes never left hers as he walked by her. Heather clenched her toes, her bare feet damp on the parquet floor. She padded after him into the kitchen.

'I can offer you a beer, if you'd like?' She leaned down to look in the fridge.

'Water is fine.' Simon stood still.

'You can sit down, you know.' Heather handed him a glass of water. 'You look like you want to run out of here.'

'Ha,' Simon laughed. 'I kind of do.'

'Oh.' Heather sat down in her chair and grasped the hem of her T-shirt. She watched him slowly hang his jacket over the back of the other chair and sit down. 'This is it, isn't it?'

He looked sadly at her. 'I think so. Look, Heddie, It's not that I don't love you. I do. But you're not in the same place as I am.'

'I know,' Heather said. 'And it sucks.'

'It does.' He looked at her with such love that she started to cry.

'Things are different now,' she said. 'I'm different.'

'I don't want you to change,' he said. 'I've never wanted you to change.'

'But I have,' Heather said. 'It just happened. Si, I'm not sure what's happening. I want to go home – back to Wicklow. But I want you too.'

Simon ran his hand over his black hair. 'That's definitely a change.'

'It is, and it gets worse.'

'How can it get worse?' He tilted his head.

'I want to run a goat farm with my mother and make beauty balms and lotions with her in a shed at the bottom of her garden.'

Simon stared at her. 'Are you serious?'

'Yes, except the beauty things are made in the kitchen, not the shed. That's for the goats.'

'Bloody hell,' Simon said. 'You have changed.'

'Yep. And I don't know where we go from here.' Heather wiped her face.

'Me either. Heddie, if this makes you happy, you should go for it,' he said gently.

'But you made me happy,' Heather said quietly.

'I did, for a while,' he said. He frowned. 'We have to be real here, Hed. We have one life and love shouldn't be this . . . I don't know what I'm trying to say, but I want you to be happy. And it's a total cliché, but I want us to be friends. Who knows what might happen . . .'

'Friends, that's a lot to ask, Si. Six months ago you wanted to marry me.' Heather grimaced.

'I did, didn't I?' Simon smiled sheepishly. 'You were right. I got carried away with Paris and everyone was asking when I was going to propose. It was stupid of me to give in to them. I keep thinking if I hadn't proposed we'd still be together.'

'Maybe we would. And by now you'd have met my mother,' Heather said. 'It's kind of sad.' Heather looked down at the basin of cold water beneath the table and wished he'd never proposed, but it had happened, and they were where they were now. Her heart sank when she thought of him not in her life, but he was right. They weren't moving forward together anymore. She needed to let him go.

'So, this is it – you're going home to Wicklow . . .' Simon broke the silence.

'Looks that way,' Heather said.

'I wish I knew what brought this on.'

'A million and one different things,' Heather said. 'Not in the least you – you really helped me, Si. All the talks we had about my childhood . . . my father . . . my mother – you don't know how close to the bone you were about things. Then actually going home and finding Pippa on her own, and this part makes me so sad: she's so *nice*, so *lovely*, Si. I never saw it because she was afraid to show it. And I love being around her now. It feels like . . .' She stopped talking, unable to continue as tears flowed down her face. Her shoulders shook as she cried.

Simon shoved his chair back. He knelt down in front of her and pulled her into a hug. It was just what Heather needed. She sobbed onto his shoulder, soaking his shirt, until she couldn't cry anymore.

Sitting back in her chair she looked at him kneeling in front of her. He laughed.

'Don't worry, I'm not proposing this time.' He stood up.

Heather looked up at him through damp lashes. Was it fair to him to stay friends? He still had feelings for her, she could tell – because she still had feelings for him. Was it wrong to want him in her life? Was there a possibility that they might be ready to love each other more romantically in the future? Her head said it wasn't fair, but her heart told her head to be quiet – friends was better than not having him at all, and to give them time.

Taking a deep breath she stood up and took his hand. 'Friends – on one condition.'

'What's the condition?' He squinted at her.

'Come home and meet my mother, and her goats, and . . . swim in the lake with me. It's not called Lough Caragh for nothing.'

Simon scratched his chin. 'Meet your goat-herding mother?'

'She will *love* that you called her that.' Heather beamed.

'Swim in a lake?'

'Don't question it – it's the right thing to do,' Heather beseeched him. 'Just say yes?'

'As friends?' He searched her face.

She nodded.

'Okay, this is crazy but . . . yes.' He burst out laughing. 'You said you have a sister?'

'She's not available!' Heather swatted his arm, then flung her arms around him. 'Let's go swim in a lake!'

29

21st June 2024

Heather peeped in at the goats. They sleepily bleated at her from the upper level of their straw-strewn bunk beds. Gertie trotted down immediately and nibbled at the hem of Heather's dress, one of Pippa's cast-offs. The smallest one, Baa-bara, was as usual, the most tricksy. She liked to be coaxed down from the high straw bunk bed that she preferred to sleep in, bleating until she was lifted down, and then scoot back up the ramp only to bleat for a lift down again. Heather stood in front of the ramp the fifth time Baa-bara tried her trick, much to the little goat's consternation.

'I didn't mean to wake you,' she said, scratching Gertie's head as Gertie followed her around, nudging her hand looking for goodies. 'I was only making sure you were okay. Go on back to bed.'

Gertie looked at her inquisitively then gave a little hop.

'No, young lady, I will not bring you with me.' Heather opened the shed door. 'But you can go out into the top field.' She watched as the five goats tripped outside into the brightening morning. It was just after three thirty and the night sky grew lighter with each passing minute. Heather looked in the direction of the lake. Lauren would be there now, she was sure, and Shane. She wondered if they'd moved back to Lough Caragh permanently. Pippa refused to tell her anything, saying that she should go and talk to Lauren and give over this nonsense. They were all grown-ups and should be capable of moving past teenage grievances, she'd said last night when Heather had mulled over the idea of not going to the lake this morning.

Now, watching Baa-bara follow Jolene, the second-smallest goat around, she played with the notion that her mother was right. It was still hard to move past Niamh's sharp words, still hard to forget the pain she'd felt when Lauren had looked at her so scathingly that night. She'd thought they were unbreakable, that they were her real family. It had taken her years to move past that. She pinched the hem of her cardigan between her fingers. Maybe she hadn't quite achieved the peace that she needed. If she had, then she wouldn't be prodding her memories again as if it was a mouth ulcer she couldn't leave alone.

Coming back from London she'd fully planned on going to the lake this morning, but now fear crept into her heart. What if Lauren didn't want her there? What if it caused another row?

'Penny for your thoughts?' Simon's deep voice made her jump.

Heather smiled to see him standing by the gate in a pair of old jeans and a paint-stained check shirt. His sleeves were rolled up showing his strong arms, and he wore an old black pair of wellies too. Her heart skipped a beat at how good he looked. She'd only ever seen him dressed in the best of clothes, but these worn and fitted clothes suited him far better than anything she'd seen him wear. Pippa had taken one long look at him when he'd arrived two days ago, and had all but interrogated him over tea and brack in the kitchen. It had given Heather a warm feeling seeing her mother so concerned for her welfare.

After dinner and a game of cards she'd finally nodded her approval of him and that was that. He'd won her over by being himself, Heather knew, and that was huge. It was how he'd made himself at home by clearing up after dinner, and a hundred other little things that showed Pippa, and Heather, that he wasn't expecting to be treated special. It was a million miles away from how Cash had behaved, and Heather could see how much Pippa had liked it.

'Summer solstice. Thinking of Rosemary and the lake . . .' she answered him.

'If Rosemary means as much to you as you've told me last night, then you should be there.' He nodded towards the lake. 'Don't make this a moment you'll regret.'

Heather swallowed. 'What if . . .'

Simon shook his head. 'No what-ifs – deal with it afterwards.'

'I . . . will you come with me?'

'Of course.' He pointed to the bag he'd dropped just out of sight. 'Towels, coffee, brandy and scones.'

'I'm coming too,' Pippa called. She ambled down the

back garden, a towel slung over her shoulder, her long hair tied up in a messy topknot. 'So, you're not alone.'

Heather felt the fizz of tears in the back of her nose, sniffed them away and blinked back any rogue tears that threatened to fall. She plucked at her shoulder, revealing the strap of her swimsuit. 'Let's go then, it's almost time.'

*

'Joseph, Mary and sweet Baby Jesus, will you get a move on?' Niamh frowned at Evan, who was sitting bleary-eyed at the kitchen table. 'Pull your socks up.'

'He's not wearing any socks.' Katie giggled from within her hoodie that she was pulling on over her bedraggled head.

Niamh opened her mouth, then closed it. It was far too early for these shenanigans. Stifling a yawn, she tugged the hoodie down over Katie's head and kissed her quickly. 'Well, at least you're ready.'

'We're ready too,' Ava said.

Niamh looked up to see Ava and Sophie standing in the hallway, towels in their arms and a bag stuffed with blankets between them.

'Thank goodness,' she said. 'Now if one of you could inject your father with rocket fuel . . .' She looked at Evan, who was stirring his coffee. 'Ev, for crying out loud. Come on!'

'Come on, Daddy, upsie-bupsie!' Katie took hold of her father's arm and hoisted him to his feet. She grinned. 'See, it wasn't that difficult, was it?'

Evan took one last slug of his coffee. 'Right, let's get this show on the road.'

Niamh followed her family out of the back door to where Maura and her daughters and granddaughters were just coming out of their rooms. Evan was fully awake now and behaving as if he was captain of the ship. Maura raised an eyebrow at her, and Niamh walked over to her.

'Don't ask me, I'm just glad he's up and moving.'

'That's all we need,' Maura said with a knowing smile. 'I'm depending on you to lead the way; it's been a while since I've been here.'

'Follow me.' Katie took Maura's hand and looked up at her. 'I'll mind you.'

'You're a pet,' Maura said, looking down at Katie. 'Thank you.'

Niamh hung back on the pretence of locking the back door, knowing full well that no one locked their back doors in Lough Caragh. She watched her family walk alongside Maura's family. They made a merry bunch; Rosemary would be very happy. Ava looked back and waved. Then she stopped and skipped back to Niamh.

'I'll walk with you, Mam.' She slipped her hand into Niamh's and a prickle of joy ran through Niamh. Not for the first time she sent up a prayer of thanks that her relationship with her teenage daughter was getting better, and then sent up another one that it would continue to do so. Glancing over at her eldest, Niamh's heart constricted. Ava was very quiet.

'Are you worried about being at the lake?' Niamh kept her voice low.

'A little,' Ava said quietly. 'I know it's silly. Everyone is there – it's just that after what happened the last time . . .'

'Me too,' Niamh said. 'We have to try and trust that

it'll be okay, and Ava, I've got you, I promise that. I won't let anything happen to you.'

Ava gave a small smile. 'You *really* are the best mammy.'

*

Lauren woke up at four in the morning. She slipped from the bed and looked out the window. It was already bright, and she wondered if it had gotten dark at all.

Today was the day. Birdsong rose all around her. Today she'd bring Rosemary back to her beloved lake, just as she'd wanted to be, and everything would begin to feel a little better.

Maura had called up last night with Rosemary – Lauren still couldn't bring herself to say *ashes* – and had stayed for drinks in the garden. Sheila had joined them, then Pippa, then Old Moll and Shirley, and even Mucker. Sheila had insisted that they bring Rosemary out to join them and the urn had stood in the centre of the old outdoor table as they all sat out until just after midnight, chatting and sharing memories, tears and laughter. It was as close to an Irish wake as they could get. As the church chimed midnight, they'd raised a glass to Rosemary, although Lauren had abstained.

She'd been using wine as a way to numb her emotions and as a crutch. She leaned out of the window and breathed in the cool early morning air. It had been the only thing that helped her to fall asleep, until Shane had moved in. Since he'd come home her sleep problems had all but disappeared. She sighed. It seemed that they lived at Mill House now, with Shane suggesting that they stay for the summer, even though summertime was known to be the best time to sell property.

Shane stirred in the bed behind her, and she turned around to see him pulling on his swimming shorts. He looked up at her, his gorgeous eyes carefully watching her.

'Morning,' he said gently. 'Are you ready?'

'Ready as I'll ever be.' Lauren shrugged. 'It's just so sad, but you know, I'm glad she's home. I'm glad I can do this for her.'

'I know,' Shane said.

'I wish I'd gone to see her.' Lauren sat down on the bed. 'I promised her, and I feel as if I've let her down.'

'You didn't let her down.' Shane sat beside her. 'She knew what we were going through. Rosemary wouldn't have been happy if she'd thought she had added any extra stress to you.'

'You're right,' Lauren said. 'I know you mean well but right now it's not helping.'

Shane hugged her, pulling her into his still sleep-warm arms.

'Shut up, Lauren,' he said gently. She could hear the smile in his voice. 'This isn't about you. Rosemary wouldn't want you all maudlin, as she always said – get down to the lake – you'll feel better.'

'Feck off, you.' She laughed softly. 'Gah, I hate it when you're right.'

'It's not often it happens.' He grinned. 'I'm taking this victory.'

Lauren watched him head downstairs. He was right. Rosemary would've kicked her out the door and told her to go for a walk. She got up, suddenly wishing she'd arranged more of a celebration for the moment, that she'd planned a ceremony or something. It didn't seem right to be going down to the lake and scattering Rosemary all over the place and then carrying on as if nothing had happened. Well, it was too late now. It was almost sunrise and she'd better get a wriggle on if she didn't want to miss solstice.

She pulled her shorts on and tugged her T-shirt down over her stomach. A bubble of excitement stirred in her. The memory of the three blank heart pebbles came back to her and she flew up to the third floor and into the bedroom where Rosemary's boxes still stood. They'd migrated back up from the hallway as Lauren couldn't bear to do anything else with them. Now, kneeling in front of the box marked 'Sitting Room Shelves' she rooted inside it until she found the jam jar. Discarding its lid on the floor, she tipped the jar out and searched for the three heart pebbles with their names on them and slipped them in her pocket. It felt like the right thing to do, to have the girls there somehow. She left the room and hurried downstairs, the pebbles bouncing in her pocket as she went.

'Coffee?' Shane called from the kitchen.

Lauren followed the sound of his voice. 'No, thanks. I just want to get down there now, but first I'm going to pick some flowers from the garden for her.'

Shane nodded. 'I'll help.'

The garden was in full bloom, so it only took a few minutes to gather a colourful and fragrant bouquet of Rosemary's favourite flowers from the garden she'd loved so much. Lauren carried them carefully as she followed

Shane down the pathway to the lake. Her heart felt as if it had slipped down into her belly; every beat seemed to make her stomach flip over.

Yvonne had said she'd come, and Lauren had told her mother a number of times about what was happening and why, but her mother hadn't made any promises. She was still grieving. Debbie had mentioned that on bad days she imagined her mother on a beach in Australia, smiling and searching for seashells. Scattering her ashes would make it very real. Lauren climbed over the stile. She hoped Debbie would come; it would help her heal her loss. And losing Rosemary had broken so many people's hearts. They'd all been so sure they'd see her again, and now this was it. All that was left of Rosemary and her huge heart, her gregarious laughter and her gentle encouragement was in the urn that Shane so carefully carried. Once again, Lauren wished she'd made more of a celebration of Rosemary's life. She'd have to settle on the bouquet she'd pulled together and swimming out to cast her intentions into the lake.

Looking up as she rounded the last curve in the path, she caught a flash of something apricot-coloured. Sheila, in a billowing kaftan, stood on the small beach. Then Lauren saw Old Moll waving, and Mucker. Stella stood beside Enda from the bookshop. Meg was shaking out a picnic blanket, a box with the label *Bake Me Home* at her feet. Hal and Shirley Goodman were gathering dry sticks for the crackling campfire they were all gathered around. Lauren looked around. There were more people she hadn't seen in ages filling the tiny sandy shoreline.

Stumbling onto the pebbles Lauren began to cry. The

little beach was filled with Rosemary's friends, and they were eagerly awaiting her arrival. Lauren reached for Shane's hand as she made it to the gathering. He ushered her into the middle of the group. Lauren laughed. Mucker was wearing swimming shorts. His white legs were the skinniest she'd ever seen. He copped her looking and pointed his finger at her with a laugh.

'I see you looking, young Lauren,' he said with a grin. 'Less of that now.'

Lauren scrunched her nose up and pulled a face at Mucker.

'We couldn't send Rose off alone,' Sheila said, slipping an arm around Lauren's shoulders.

'Not on your nelly,' Old Moll said. 'If it wasn't for Rosemary, I'd never have gotten that job in Billy's. She convinced Old Billy, God rest his soul, that I was well able for it, and it was the making of me. I'll miss her forever.'

Shirley Goodman thrust a bouquet of peonies into Lauren's hands. 'There'll never be the likes of her again.'

'She was some woman; I'll tell you that. That stamina!' Mucker shifted and puffed out his chest. 'How she managed to refuse me year after year is a testament to her firm resolve and stubbornness. But that was what I loved most about her.'

'Didn't we all?' Debbie came forward. Lauren gasped to see her mother in a swimsuit, a towel grasped tightly around her shoulders. She began to cry as she spoke. 'My mother was an amazing woman. I miss her so much.'

Lauren hurried to her mother and hugged her tightly. 'I love you, Mam.'

'I love you too,' Debbie whispered.

Over her mother's shoulder, Lauren spotted Yvonne and her family, and her brother Thomas.

Lauren ran to him. 'Tom? You came back for Rosemary?'

He nodded. 'What kind of a person would I be if I hadn't?' He stood aside. 'This is my partner, Joe.'

Lauren hugged them both close. 'Rosemary would've loved to have met you.'

'Oh, she did,' Joe said. 'Via the wonders of the internet. It was Rosemary who got us together.'

Lauren turned to Tom with raised eyebrows.

'Long story,' he said. 'I'll fill you in later.'

'Where's Dad?' Lauren looked around.

'He's on his way,' Tom said. 'He's bringing a few people.'

'More people?' Lauren gasped.

Sheila nodded. 'It's the echo of small kindnesses,' she said. 'When word got out that Rosemary was coming back to Lough Caragh everyone wanted to come to send her off. I don't think there's one person, young or old, in the village who hasn't been touched by her small kindnesses. Everyone I met had a story.'

'This is wonderful,' Lauren gasped as a steady stream of people began to arrive. 'Look at them all. This is magical.'

Lauren's father directed family and friend groups over to the campfire. People were joking, talking and laughing at their madness but loving it all the same. There were picnic blankets and baskets everywhere. So many had flowers too. It looked like there were enough flowers to fill the lake. Lauren felt a huge lump in her throat. Stella was walking down the lane towards the lake; she blew a kiss. Lauren looked at the people who were with her: two women, one walked with a slight limp, and a young red-haired boy. She didn't know them, but they looked happy to be here. Not far behind her she spied Maura and her family. Then she saw Niamh.

Lauren's heart lurched into her throat. Niamh was holding her daughter's hand. Her face was taut as her eyes met Lauren's. Lauren smiled gently, hoping that Niamh knew she was happy to see her. *It wouldn't be right if she wasn't here.* Lauren crossed her fingers that Heather would also come. She wasn't holding out any hope though. Old Moll had said that Heather had gone back to London a few weeks ago.

Letting go of Shane's hand, Lauren walked towards Niamh, wondering how to say thank you when Ava shrieked. She threw her hands up in the air and galloped away. Niamh and Lauren turned to watch her run. Ava flew across the shingles and flung herself at Heather, who staggered back in fright. Lauren looked at Niamh, who was taking it all in quietly. Niamh's face was still. Her hands were loose by her sides. Lauren walked towards her and stood beside her as Ava dragged Heather over to where the two women stood.

'Mammy, look! It's her – your friend – the woman who saved me.' Ava was giddy and holding tightly on to Heather's arm as if she was still being saved. Heather stood in front of Lauren and Niamh and shrugged. Ava slipped away, running towards her best friend who had just arrived.

Then the three women started to speak, all talking over each other.

'I'm so sorry . . .'

'Thank you for . . .'

'I didn't mean anything I said that night.' Niamh's words carried over the others. She reddened. 'I was so wrong. Jealous and scared. I was probably that way for years.'

Lauren reached for her. 'It's okay, Niamh. We all said stupid things that night.'

'Some were more stupid than others.' Heather stepped back.

Niamh turned to Heather. 'Heather, I didn't get a chance to tell you in the hospital that I am sorry for what happened all those years ago. You'd left the village before I'd calmed down. I was so hurt, but I deserved every word that night, and I thought that you'd send me a text, you know, but you didn't.'

Lauren gasped. It wasn't like Niamh to straight-up apologise, for anything, ever.

'You didn't text me either,' Heather said. 'After a while it became easier to not even think about you.'

Niamh's face crumpled. 'I understand.'

Lauren squeezed Niamh's arm. She took a deep breath, at a loss for words, and, for the millionth time, wished that Rosemary was here to help them fix this mess. Rosemary would've known just how to manage this ridiculous teenage row that had driven them apart for years. She'd have straightened her shoulders and told her *that when in doubt come to the lake*. That was it. That was exactly what she'd have said, and it was exactly where they were – *at the lake*, together. The circumstance of why they were there was undeniably sad, but it was also serendipitous.

'You know what Rosemary would've said to me if I'd told her about that night,' she said, looking from Niamh's pink face to Heather's stony one.

'*Get down to the lake.*' Heather's face softened. 'Whenever I was upset or didn't know what to do, she'd tell me that.'

'Me too,' Niamh whispered.

'Yes,' Lauren said. 'She'd also tell me to cop on to myself. To pull my socks up and say sorry. Our friendship was special, and she knew that. Why didn't we?'

'I don't know.' Heather's eyes filled with tears.

'Pride, shame, embarrassment,' Niamh volunteered. 'Well, that's how I felt.'

'Yeah, me too.' Lauren nodded. 'Life is hard, isn't it?'

'Harder without you two.' Heather's voice broke. 'I'm really sorry. I can't tell you how many times I've wished I could go back in time and change that night.'

'Do you think we might be able to fix this?' Lauren asked. Her stomach tightened. It was a big ask of all of them, but it had to be said.

Niamh was the first to answer. 'I'd like to try.'

Heather smiled tentatively. 'We should try.'

Lauren nodded; then, remembering the heart pebbles, reached into her pocket and took them out. She held them in her palm before her friends.

'I found these in Rosemary's things.'

Heather's hand flew to her mouth.

Niamh touched the one with her name on it. Tears rolled down her face. 'She was always thinking of others.'

'Take it,' Lauren said. 'It was meant to be yours.'

Niamh gently took the pebble.

361

Lauren turned to Heather. 'And you.'

Heather shook her head. 'I don't deserve it. She was so good to me, and I upped and left without saying goodbye to her, and not once in all my travels did I go see her.'

'You're here now.' Niamh picked up Heather's heart pebble and pressed it into Heather's hand.

Ava, who was standing at the water's edge, shouted and pointed to the sky. 'Mammy, look!'

The entire crowd, which was made up of almost the entire village, turned as one. A cheer went up as the sun rose and the lake sparkled.

'It's time,' Lauren said softly, nervous now the moment was upon them. 'Come on.'

Heather looked at Niamh. 'Well, it is why we're here.'

They followed Lauren to the water. Some ran in; some took their time. She chuckled at the squeals of either shock at the cool water, or delight that it wasn't as cold as they'd expected. She swam out a bit, then stopped and looked at the sun. Sounds of laughter and joy drifted all around her, it seemed that everyone was having fun, and she lay back to float. Closing her eyes, she felt a huge sense of peace envelop her. Then she set her intention, crossing her fingers as she did.

Memories of time spent with Rosemary washed around her. Picnics on the shore, sleepovers at the house, laughing in the garden. It was as if Rosemary was with her as she thought of the day she'd gone with Heather and Lauren to the lake, the day they'd started teaching her how to swim. Rosemary had loved them all, she realised. There was no room for anything but love in her life and

362

everywhere she'd gone she'd made sure everyone felt loved and special. It was a gift, and it felt as if Rosemary was passing that gift on to her right in that moment. Feeling more at peace than she had in a long time, Lauren swam back to the shore where she waved at Shane to join her.

*

Niamh stayed in the shallows near her family, although the two younger girls were bravely going out deeper as they watched their friends swimming and splashing about. The sun was warming the day already, and it looked like it was going to be a scorcher. Evan waded up to her and touched her shoulder.

'Why don't you go out and do your thing?' he said softly. 'I'll stay with Ava.'

Ava had waded out up to her waist but was coming back towards her parents with a pale face. 'Thanks,' Niamh said. She kissed his cheek and felt a weight lift from her shoulders as he smiled into her face, his eyes warm and bright. It hadn't felt wrong, but it still felt a little strange. They were agreed on taking it slow, and that was fine with her. With a gentle smile she waded out into the water and swam out until she was almost alone. Sheila and Maura bobbed close by. Stella and her friends weren't too far away either. Stella was holding the little red-haired boy and teaching him how to kick his legs out behind him while the younger woman looked on anxiously.

Niamh swam on, stopping when she was truly alone. Then, treading water, holding her heart pebble tightly in her hand, she raised her face to the sun and sent her intention up to Rosemary.

*

Heather watched as Simon and Pippa swam strongly out to where Sheila and Maura were. Old Moll had made a brave attempt but was now happy to wade in the shallows, holding her great-grandchild's hand as the toddler tried to pick up every sparkling granite stone she could see. It was lovely having Simon here, but something had changed between them. She knew he'd felt it too. The heat that had once melded them together had changed. These days they were gentler with each other, less passionate. She wasn't sure if this meant they were drifting into friendship or was this a more nuanced understanding between them.

Either way, she was glad he was still a part of her life. Her thumb rubbed the heart pebble in her hand. Feeling a little lonely, she swam over to Pippa and Simon and the women. In the midst of the chat, she sent out her intention and dipped herself under the water completely.

30

Lauren sat by the campfire; Rosemary's urn nestled between her feet. Her stomach grumbled and she looked down. She was starving the whole time these days – for all the right reasons. She couldn't wait to tell Shane she was twenty-four weeks pregnant; it was the longest she'd ever carried a baby, and her doctor was sure that this one would go to full term. Nevertheless, she was taking all the precautions, and ignoring her cravings for shellfish and cream cheese, not together though – her cravings weren't that bad. She hadn't even realised she was pregnant until two days ago when she'd gone in for a scheduled cervical check and had almost fainted when her doctor had broken into a huge smile and told her the good news.

On her way home she'd called the clinic where she'd had scan after scan over the years and they'd been ecstatic for her, telling her to come in immediately. They'd scanned her and confirmed everything her doctor had said, and now the scan photos were in her bag, and she couldn't wait to hand them to Shane. She couldn't wait to see his reaction, but first she had to thank everyone for coming.

The lake was almost empty now, except for two swans striking out towards the far shore, and Sheila and Maura who were just coming out of the water, laughing and dripping. Everyone else had gathered in their little groups of family and friends, some still in towels, others dressed and drinking hot tea to warm up. Lauren got up and picked up Rosemary. Hoisting the urn into her arms she called everyone to attention.

'Good morning!' she called out. 'Happy solstice!'

Cheers and clapping rose around her, and she smiled although her stomach was in a knot and she was unsure as to how to go on. 'Well, I'd, eh . . .'

She searched the crowd and saw her parents standing close to her. Her mother's face was blotchy, a twisted and crumpled piece of tissue was held under her nose. As Lauren watched she saw her father take her mother's hand and squeeze it. He pulled her in and kissed her forehead. Her father's tenderness caught her off guard, and for a moment, Lauren felt that she didn't have it in her to go on. Then she felt it; Rosemary's strength was in her bones, and the love she'd always found in Shane filled her as he slipped his arm around her shoulders. His warm energy surrounded her, and after clearing her throat, she started again.

'I want to thank you all for rising from your beds at an ungodly hour to celebrate my grandmother, Rosemary Dwyer, who, as you all know, was an absolute legend.' Lauren looked around at everyone. Many were smiling; some were crying. Holding back her own tears Lauren carried on. 'To see so many friends here, in her honour, is unbelievably uplifting. You have no idea how much seeing you here this morning eases my sore heart. *Go raibh míle maith agaibh* – a million thank yous to you all. Rosemary has been a huge part of Lough Caragh, and I think always will be. She won't be easily forgotten, by any of us. I don't know how to say goodbye to her, but I do know how much she loved this lake, *Lough Caragh*, the lake of beloved friendship, so it's with love and privilege that I, *we*, get to give her her final wish and bring her home to Paddy.'

Opening the urn, Lauren looked down and shook her head. This was the hardest part. Stepping to the water's edge she took a handful of Rosemary's ashes and held them tightly in her hand, then with a cry she opened her hand. The warm breeze took hold of the ashes and carried them up into the air and out across the lake before they drifted to the water.

'Goodbye,' Lauren called out. Her voice cracked and she started to cry. Maura hurried to her side and took the urn from her. Sheila, Stella, Shirley and Old Moll surrounded her too, gently steering her back to her family. Lauren looked around at her grandmother's oldest friends. Their tear-stained faces were bravely smiling at her. Stella and Maura were holding hands tightly; Old Moll was patting Sheila on the shoulder.

Their gentle kindness towards each other made her turn and look at Heather and Niamh, who were standing close to each other. Heather reached for Niamh's hand and Niamh's face crumpled. Lauren bit her top lip. This was what it was all about. Mucker shuffled across the sandy part of the pebble beach, a champagne flute in his hand. Lauren shook her head in wonderment as he handed her the glass. The man was an enigma.

'To friends,' Mucker said gruffly as he pressed her hand gently. He nodded his head and stood aside.

'Yes,' Lauren raised the glass to the crowd, her eyes finding Heather and Niamh again. 'To friends.' The two women smiled at her, softly at first, then beaming as the crowd called out 'To friends.' Whatever the future held for their friendship was unknown, but at least they were talking to each other now. They could only go from there.

'That was lovely.' Shane appeared by her side.

'It wasn't easy,' Lauren said.

'I know.' He nudged her. 'Aren't you going to drink that?'

Lauren handed the champagne to Shane. 'Two things – one it's five o'clock in the morning . . .'

'Hasn't stopped some.' Shane laughed and gestured around the small beach where people were topping up their drinks and clinking glasses. Lauren noticed her father wasn't drinking. He was pouring tea, and her heart swelled with happiness.

'As I was saying.' Lauren could hardly stand still. '*Two things* . . . the second one is . . .'

'It's just one glass – for Rosemary,' Shane said.

'Shane! Shut up!' Lauren spluttered. 'I'm trying to tell you that I'm pregnant.'

Shane's face stilled. His eyes searched her face, and she felt his hands on her hips. She placed her hands on his and moved them to her stomach and nodded into his questioning face.

'And it's twins.' She looked at him. 'Say something.'

His reply was to take her in his arms and lift her off the ground in a bear hug. She could feel him shaking, and with all her heart she wished she could make him understand how good she felt, how she felt that this time it would all be okay.

*

Niamh looked over and caught the exchange. Her heart softened as Debbie and Yvonne were told, smiling as they shrieked with happiness. She turned away and looked at her own family. Watching Evan dry Katie's toes even though she was now ten, Niamh felt a surge of love. She really was incredibly lucky and maybe they would be okay. Time would tell.

*

Heather caught Pippa wiping away a tear as she watched Shane and Lauren share their news with their family. Her nose was red and there was a sprinkling of grey in her hair. Heather felt a pang of longing for the years she'd missed out on with her mother. Even though she knew she was looking back with rose-tinted glasses, she could remember times when her mother *had* put her and Willow first. Times before the house had become filled with other people and her mother had lost herself. Pippa turned to make her way back to their house, and Heather took a step, then she ran after her.

'*Mam*, wait up!' she called.

Pippa stopped and looked back, a huge smile on her face. 'You called me Mam.'

'I did.' Heather took her mother's hand. 'It's about time, don't you think?'

Pippa squeezed her hand and started singing 'Wild Mountain Thyme'. Heather joined in. Nearby, under the sun-kissed tree canopy, a young stag bowed his head and slipped into the woods.

Acknowledgements

I'm in the most delicious place of having to write acknowledgements for my second book and it's giving me heartburn! The anxiety! The joy! The tears of happiness as I remember the people who've backed me all these years as I struggled to get published . . . it's wonderful! I love it.

Writing this book was a complete and utter joy. I cried, a lot. I laughed too. I was reminded of my teenage years and how filled with angst and fear that time was. I even swam in Annaghmakerrig Lough while staying at the Tyrone Gutherie Centre – for research purposes – and it was as beautiful as anything! I'd already written part about the heart shaped pebbles and then I found one there too, which made me feel that I was on the right track. It is with a lot of love that I wish to thank everyone who has helped me in any way at all – there are so many – forgive me if I appear to miss you, believe me, your support has not gone unnoticed. Here I go!

While my pen name is on the cover, there are a lot of names that should be there too. I'll always be grateful to my editors and the whole team at Avon. Rachel Hart, Amy Mae Baxter, Raphaella Demetris, Ella Young, Elisha Lundin, Helen Huthwaite, Sarah Bauer, Gabby Drinkald, Maddie Dunne Kirby and Samantha Luton. Once again it's been an absolute pleasure to work with such a hardworking, warm and dedicated team. I highly recommend each and every one of them for making this story better than I ever could have on my own. I also want to thank the Dublin division of HarperCollins, especially Courtney Fitzmaurice.

To the librarians, booksellers and promoters – you have my admiration and gratitude. To the wonderful Dawn, Paula and Saoirse at Woodbine Books who are the most supportive bookworms you'll ever meet – you are amazing and I love ye.

And all the readers, reviewers, and bloggers who've been so supportive, thank you.

Huge love to my darling Twitter friends, Shiv, Meg, the Taywimmen . . . and more xxx.

To everyone who I'm wanting to thank but can't list – I see you! I thank you too xxx.

In the writing arena I have been blessed by the Goddesses! Bláithín O'Reilly Murphy , Annie Syed, Lisa Timoney, Lauren McKenzie – what would I do without your wonderful messages? The Dooligan gang and the Christmas Collective Penguins too. Your constant support and willingness to natter over all things book related gives me life.

It would be remiss of me to not mention Hazel Gaynor,

Patricia Scanlan, Marian Keyes, Vanessa O'Loughlin, Sarah Moore Fitzgerald, Liz Nugent, Liz Fenwick and many more authors who've reached out to support me and guide me. I get such inspiration and strength from all of them. More than I'm able to express.

I have two particularly amazing friends, Caro and Gill, who've known me a looooong time. We have the kind of friendship that memes are made about, and that makes me very happy. Without their constant support, encouragement I'd never leave my desk. I'd be a decrepit and creaky hermit who overdoses on coffee and lacks Vitamin D. I love their humour, their patience, their kindnesses to all in their lives (me included!), their knowledge of great places to eat and our sometimes podcast length WhatsApp voice notes.

My family – and there's a lot of family! I'm unbelievably blessed. This is the hardest part of writing acknowledgements because every member of my family has supported and encouraged me in some way my whole life. I wish I was able to list each one, I wish I could tell them how much I appreciate them and all they do for me. My family-in-law too. Like I said, I am unbelievably blessed to be surrounded by people with the kindest hearts.

David, the love of my life, for everything, always and forever.

New friends. New beginnings. Old secrets…

Fall head over heels for this emotional story about secrets, fresh starts and the power of friendship, set in enchanting Ireland.